James Eugene Munson

The Complete Phonographer and Reporter's Guide

an inductive exposition of phonography, with its application to all branches of

reporting

James Eugene Munson

The Complete Phonographer and Reporter's Guide
an inductive exposition of phonography, with its application to all branches of reporting

ISBN/EAN: 9783337399948

Printed in Europe, USA, Canada, Australia, Japan

Cover: Foto ©Andreas Hilbeck / pixelio.de

More available books at **www.hansebooks.com**

THE

COMPLETE PHONOGRAPHER,

AND REPORTER'S GUIDE:

AN INDUCTIVE EXPOSITION OF

PHONOGRAPHY,

WITH ITS APPLICATION TO ALL BRANCHES OF REPORTING, AND
AFFORDING THE FULLEST INSTRUCTION TO THOSE WHO
HAVE NOT THE ASSISTANCE OF AN ORAL TEACHER;
ALSO INTENDED AS A SCHOOL-BOOK.

REVISED EDITION.

By JAMES E. MUNSON,

OFFICIAL STENOGRAPHER, N. Y. SUPERIOR COURT; LAW AND GENERAL VERBATIM REPORT-
ER SINCE 1857; AUTHOR OF THE "DICTIONARY OF PRACTICAL PHONOGRA-
PHY," ETC., AND EDITOR OF "MUNSON'S PHONOGRAPHIC NEWS."

NEW YORK:
HARPER & BROTHERS, PUBLISHERS,
FRANKLIN SQUARE.
1877.

PREFACE TO THE REVISED EDITION.

The first edition of the Complete Phonographer was published in December, 1866. During the ten years that it has been before the public many old phonographers have been converted to the new system of Practical Phonography, attracted by the simplicity of its fundamental principles and the completeness of its practical adaptation to the requirements of the verbatim reporter. And the number of new phonographers who have acquired their first and only knowledge of shorthand from this source is legion. In fact, the system has advanced so rapidly in public favor that it is now the most popular in America.

As was naturally to be expected, however, further experience, including the preparation of a Phonographic Dictionary, has added to the author's knowledge of the application of phonography to the writing of the language; and from time to time changes of a minor character have been made in the details of the system, until the old edition ceased to be a perfect exponent of it. To remove this defect in the text-book, and to render it a much more efficient instructor than ever before, a thorough revision has been made, so that it corresponds in every respect with the system as it is now best written.

The chief changes that have been made, and to which special attention is invited, are the following:

1. The order of the Alphabet of Consonant Signs, on page 18, is restored to that originally used in the early editions of Phonography, namely, *pee, bee, tee, dee, chay, jay, kay, gay, ef, vee, ith, dhee* (pronounced *the*), *ess, zee, ish, zhee, lee, er, ree, em, en, ing, way, yay, hay.* Several changes in the text have been made, that were necessitated by this change in the order of the consonant arrangement.

2. The list of Word-signs has been perfected, and the arrangement made to correspond with the changed order of the Alphabet of Consonants.

3. The chapter on Prefixes and Suffixes has been entirely rewritten, and some new and important features added.

4. Two lists of Word-signs and Contractions are given, one ar-

1

ranged in the order of the A, B, C Alphabet, and the other in the order of the Alphabet of Phonographic Consonant Signs—the first as used while *writing* phonography, and the other while *reading* it. These lists have been kept within small compass by confining them to the abbreviated outlines of *primitive* words only ; and they are to be thoroughly memorized so that they can be written and read without any hesitation. When this has been done, the outlines of the words derived from them will be readily formed by general rules. But for the sake of ready reference, and to prevent possible error, a third list, comprising the outlines of derivatives, has been also added. This mode of presenting the Word-signs and Contractions will render their acquisition much easier than ever before.

5. The chapter on Phrase-writing has been rewritten, new matter added, and the List of Phrases considerably extended.

6. The chapter on Reporting has been enlarged, and a great number of forms for the use of the reporter introduced. In this department will be found a fund of information as to the details of reporting that is to be obtained in no other work on shorthand writing.

7. The Reading Exercises are entirely new, and consist of forty instead of thirty-two pages, as in the former editions. They are given in a plain, bold style of phonographic outlines, that are much more legible than those in the old exercises, or than are usually given in phonographic books.

8. The " Lessons" are also new, and greatly improved. These, together with the Reading Exercises, have been compiled and arranged with special reference to their efficiency in school instruction.

9. The book closes with extended Writing Exercises for the use of the teacher and the advanced learner, and a complete set of Questions on the entire course.

The author wishes to acknowledge his great indebtedness to Mr. C. A. Walworth for suggestions and assistance during the preparation of these revisions. Mr. Walworth's experience as a teacher of phonography for many years, and especially during the past six years in the College of the City of New York, and at the New York Institute of Phonography, have given him a commanding position as an instructor in the Art of Shorthand. The new Reading Exercises and " Lessons " are the result of his individual labor.

The drafting of the forty pages of Reading Exercises was done by Mrs. Amalia Berrian, a lady whose enthusiasm for the " beautiful art " is only equalled by the wonderful speed and skill that she has been able to attain in writing it.

J. E. M.

PREFACE TO THE FIRST EDITION.

THE use of Phonography by shorthand writers has become so general, and the superiority of the system over all other kinds of stenography so universally acknowledged, that it is now unnecessary to say anything of its comparative merits, or to press its claims upon the public, for no one about to commence the study of shorthand would think for a moment of taking up any other. The principles, too, of the Science of Phonetics, upon which Phonography is based, are, in a sort of general way, so commonly understood, that an extended explanation of them seems to be no longer necessary. It is, however, highly proper, on presenting this new phonographic instruction-book to the public, that I should state my reasons for so doing, and more especially as it introduces several important modifications of the system.

The leading features of Phonography are the result of the labors of Mr. Isaac Pitman of England, who for nearly thirty years has devoted much of his time to its development and propagation; but the high degree of perfection to which it has been brought, is owing in great measure to the suggestions of thousands of practical phonographers, both in England and the United States. This mode of development has its merits and demerits. Coming as it has from the brains of such a vast number and variety of people, Phonography possesses a richness of material which could hardly have been obtained in any other way; but, on the other hand, this kind of growth has had a tendency to render the system less uniform and consistent in matters of detail than it would have been had it emanated from a single mind.

Now, my first aim has been to restore, as far as possible, simplicity and harmony, by adhering to general principles and discarding all unnecessary expedients; and my second, to more completely adapt the system to the requirements of the reporter. Mr. Pitman, in his very laudable desire and efforts to bring the benefits of Phonography within reach of the masses of England, has seriously, and as I think unnecessarily, impaired it as a mere system of stenography. This work, however, has been prepared expressly in the interest of reporting, and hence everything that would tend to hinder the learner in acquiring a knowledge of the art for that purpose, has been omitted.

With this end in view, what is termed the "Corresponding Style" of Phonography has been entirely discarded, because its tendency was to foster a disconnected and lengthy style of writing wholly incompatible with reporting habits; for, as it is a principle of the human mind that first impressions are the most lasting, it often takes years of practice to fully acquire the "Reporting Style" when the writer has once indulged himself for any considerable time in the use of the "Corresponding." In fact, I have often heard many of the oldest reporters say (and I will add that it also accords with my own experience) that in very rapid reporting they were still troubled with a tendency to use long and disconnected forms; or, in other words, to return to the forms and style of writing that they used while learning. Therefore, instead of dividing Phonography into two distinct styles, one to be used as a stepping-stone to the other, I have treated it as one unbroken system, and have endeavored to furnish a series of lessons that will conduct the learner as rapidly as possible, and without any intermediate halting, directly to a knowledge of the principles and practice of the art in its highest development.

The other most important changes that I have made are those of simplification; and in this respect I have merely adhered or returned to established rules and principles where other authors have departed from them. And this has been done at an occasional sacrifice of *apparent* brevity, though not of *real* or *practical* brevity; for it must be borne in mind that swift writing is quite as much a mental as a manual process, and consequently any attempt to shorten the outlines of words by exceptional expedients, or by deviations from general rules, is only transferring the labor from the fingers to the brain, and should never be done unless the gain in brevity is very marked, as the hesitation caused by the anomalous form is apt to more than consume the time saved by the relief to the hand. These seemingly obvious principles have heretofore been but little understood by writers on the subject of Phonography, and the system has in consequence become so complicated by exceptional forms and expedients that it has as yet failed to exhibit its full powers. In one of the earliest American phonographic books* this tendency to complication is noticed and deprecated. The writer says, "Who does not know that a few hundred words subject to exceptional or particular rules throw doubt and uncertainty over every word in the language." This remark must not, however, be construed as condemning the use of contractions, or, to use the words of the same writer, "imperfect skeletons create no confusion, inasmuch as if the contraction happens to be unknown

---

* The Phonographic Word-Book No. 1, by Andrews & Boyle. 1849.

to the writer, he merely writes the word in full, and no breach of any rule is committed ; while, when known, they contribute to brevity, and seldom, in any case, cause any difficulty in reading. They ought, therefore, to be provided for, and are not to be considered as falling under the condemnation of exceptional and particular rules."

The chief material phonographic change introduced in this work, because it is the one upon which most of the other modifications do pend, is the adoption of the vowel-scale of Isaac Pitman's Tenth Edition. This scale differs from the old one in the inversion of the order of the dot-vowels (the dash-vowels remaining the same as before), as shown in the following arrangements :

OLD SCALE.	NEW SCALE.
ē, ĭ — aw, ŏ	ah, ă — aw, ŏ
ā, ĕ — ō, ŭ	ā, ĕ — ō, ŭ
ah, ă — oo, ŏŏ	ē, ĭ — oo, ŏŏ

So radical a change as this would not be adopted by me except for what I consider to be good, and, indeed, imperative reasons ; in fact, nothing would justify it unless it can be shown that the new scale offers some very considerable advantages over the old. This, however, I think I shall have no difficulty in fully demonstrating. But, as no gains can ever be secured in Phonography by introducing changes, without some corresponding losses, and as such losses are always sure to present themselves to the casual observer a great deal sooner, and with much more force, than the gains, it will be necessary for me to state this matter somewhat in detail.

The most important fundamental principle of Phonetics is what is termed the "Second Law" of Dr. Latham, which requires "that sounds within a determined degree of likeness be represented by signs within a determined degree of likeness ; while sounds beyond a certain degree of likeness be represented by distinct and different signs, and that uniformly." The observance of this law in the arrangement of the various details of the phonographic system has made it the most perfect and scientific method of shorthand writing ever devised. In the representation of the consonant-sounds the rule has been strictly carried out, and, although a few exceptions occur, they are only such as could not possibly be avoided. Thus, we see the four Gutturals kay, gay, ing, and hay represented by four of the horizontal signs ; the six Palatals chay, jay, ish, zhee, ree, and yay by signs inclined to the right ; the six Dentals tee, dee, ees, zee, ith, and dhee by perpendicular signs ; and the five Labials pee, bee, ef, vee, and way by signs inclined to the left. Again, the distinction between the breath-consonants and the subvocals is very appropriately marked by a mere difference in

the shading. But when we come to the vowels, a very material deviation is seen, for in the old vowel-scale this important law seems
to have been in a measure ignored or violated, and that without the
excuse of a real or even apparent necessity. By examining into the
nature of the vowel-sounds it will be found that they are susceptible
of three different and distinct classifications; namely, into long and
short vowels, palatals and labials, and into open and close vowels.
Now, in the old vowel-scale the first two of these classifications are
very appropriately and fully shown; the first by employing heavy
signs for long, and light signs for short vowels; and the second, by
writing the palatals with dot-signs, and the labials with dashes. But
the third, and the most important classification practically, and the
one that should have been indicated by the marked distinction of difference of position, is entirely overlooked. In the new vowel-scale
this glaring defect is removed, and the consistency and harmony of the
system completely restored. Still, if the innovation had not carried
along with it great practical benefit, as well as the mere mental satisfaction of being right in principle, I should probably never have felt
justified in making it. Indeed, it was the practical gain to be derived
from the change which first attracted my attention. But I have found
in this instance, as on many other occasions while preparing this work,
that it was impossible to separate principle from practice, and that the
more implicitly I obeyed general and fundamental rules, and the more
closely I adhered to correct principles, rejecting as much as possible
all expedients and compromises, the less difficulty I had with my
practice.

In the early part of my experience as a shorthand reporter, some
eight or nine years ago, I found, and I had also heard it remarked .
by others, that in swift writing a great deal of uncertainty was
oftentimes caused by the indistinctness of the tick or dash word-signs,
arising from the liability, on the one hand, of mistaking them for half-
length signs, and on the other, of confounding them with the dot word-
signs. This difficulty I conceived the idea of remedying, by substi-
tuting for these ticks, full-length stem signs, which would not only
offer the great advantage of being always distinct, but, as a compensation for loss of brevity owing to the increased length, and sometimes
the curvature of the new signs, would furnish much greater facility in
phrase writing, from the application to them of the various principles
of abbreviation and consonant modification, which was not possible
with the tick-signs. But at the very outset of my attempt I encoun-
tered a serious obstacle, and one which for a time seemed insurmount
able. I found that as the vowels were then arranged it would be
impossible to effect anything but a partial reform in this respect, ex

cept by throwing a great many words out of their proper positions, and thus, while removing one defect, introduce or augment another perhaps equally undesirable. However, after a long series of experiments, in which Mr. Charles E. Wilbour gave me very valuable assistance, I discovered that by reversing the order of the dot-vowels of the old scale, the difficulty of position would also disappear; and I immediately adopted the new scale, introduced the proposed change in regard to the word-signs, and have continued to use these improvements ever since.

There are also other advantages that have arisen from the use of the new scale, one of the most important and practical of which is the increased legibility it gives to Phonography. Formerly, when broad, open vowels were paired with close ones, if by accident, in writing vocalized Phonography, a first-place vowel was a sort of "neutral," that is, neither a proper dot nor a proper dash, we had to choose between the dissimilar sounds ē and aw,—the one not being at all suggestive of the other. In the new scale we have to choose between ah and aw, two sounds so similar that the one would, in all probability, immediately suggest the other. Thus, an occasional stumbling in the reading of phonographic writing, owing to uncertainty as to the intended character or length of a vowel-sign, is rendered much less likely to occur in the new scale than in the old. It is also properly claimed by the advocates of the new scale that it is an improvement upon the old one, because in practice it renders the process of writing the vowel-signs much briefer and more simple than it was before. For instance, as the short vowel ă (the sound of a in mad) is much oftener used than the vowel ĭ (the sound of i in pin) as the initial sound of words, and as it is the common practice of phonographers, although in deviation from the general rule, to write the signs of initial vowels before commencing to write the consonant outline, it follows that ă is more conveniently, as well as most appropriately, written in the first position. Again, the sound ĭ is best written in the third position, because that vowel (which is often represented in the common spelling by the letter y) occurs much more frequently than any other at the end of words, and immediately preceding the last consonant or syllable of a word. By writing first according to the old scale, and then according to the new, such words as pity, city, Atlantic, ability, aptly, fossil, many, etc., the gain will be very apparent. Then, too, the third position for final ĭ comes more easily to the writer's hand than does the first, because there is an analogy between the position which it now occupies in a phonographic outline, and its position in the common spelling of the word,—being in both cases at the end.

The greatest practical benefit, however, that comes from the use of the new arrangement of the vowels, is the increased legibility it gives to unvocalized Phonography, by more generally throwing words that contain the same or similar consonants into different positions The reason of this is, that as in the case of such words the consonants cease to be a means of distinction, there is a natural tendency to make it by a marked difference between the sounds of the vowels, and especially those upon which the accent falls; and, hence, as in the new scale those vowels that differ most in sound are represented by signs that differ most in position, and as words are written in the position of their accented vowels, it follows that words of similar outlines will be more likely to take positions distinct from each other, than if the old scale were used. It was this very peculiarity of the new scale that so readily and completely solved the problem—of which mention has already been made—of replacing the tick-signs by simple stems, without detriment to the system.

It has been a common fault with writers of stenographic books, from the beginning of shorthand down to the present day, to plagiarize to an unlimited extent from other authors, trusting no doubt to the almost universal ignorance of the public in regard to the art, or to its mystery, to screen their wholesale piracies from detection. To the honor of authors of phonographic works, however, it should be said, that they have very generally been exceptions to this rule. In emulation of the more honorable of these writers, and also by way of a personal acknowledgment on my part to those who have so kindly and freely assisted me in preparing this work, I propose, as briefly as possible, to give the credit of the more important changes now introduced, to whom it rightfully belongs.

There is probably no one phonographer who has contributed more to the later improvements of Phonography than Mr. Wilbour. It was he, I believe, who first suggested the plan of distinguishing on all curves the *l*-hook from the *r*-hook by making the former large and the latter small; thus removing the necessity for the inconsistency of changing the forms of *f, v, th, dh, m,* and *n,* when the *r*-hook was attached, and of making exceptions to the *r* and *l*-hook principle, of the letters *s, z, l, ng, n, m, h, w, y,* and downward and upward *r.* We are also indebted to him for the *ter*-hook; and to his experiments and practice is due in great measure the high degree of perfection to which the art of phrase-writing has now been brought. To Mr. J. A. MacLauchlan, whose investigations respecting the vowels, and the best modes of representing them, have been very extensive, belongs the credit of having first suggested the idea of arranging and representing the group-vowels substantially as I have done in my double-vowel schemes. The nomenclature that I have adopted is the same as that given by Mr. Pitman in the Seventh Edition of his Manual, with a few slight changes adapting it to the recent alterations of the system. The *yay* and *way* hooks were first suggested by myself. I take this opportunity, too, of expressing my obligations to the reporters of New York generally for the interest they have manifested in this work, and for the encouragement they have so constantly extended to me during its preparation; and especially should I thank Mr. Andrew Devine, whom I have often consulted on doubtful points, and whose reliable judgment has been of very great service to me. The engraving of the illustrations in the text and of the Reading Exercises was done by the skillful hand of Mr. Chauncey B. Thorne, of Skaneateles, N. Y.; and for neatness, clearness, and beauty, I confidently assert that this work has never been equaled by any other phonographic engraver. And when we consider that the whole of it was done over three hundred miles away from the author, its entire freedom from errors and mistakes is almost marvelous. To the carefulness and attention of the reader of the proofs of this work, Mr. Stephen Jenkins, is due in great measure the high degree of accuracy of the letter-press matter.

While preparing this work, I have consulted all the phonographic instruction books, and most of the phonographic periodicals, that have been published from time to time in this country and in England, as well as quite a number of works on other systems of stenography; also many phonetic works, including those of Mr. A. J. Ellis, and Dr. Latham's "Hand-Book of the English Language." I have, however, derived by far the most assistance from the old, but very philosophic, works of Andrews and Boyle.

1*

TABLE OF CONTENTS.

SIMPLE CONSONANT-SIGNS.

OF THE MANNER OF WRITING THE CONSONANT-SIGNS.

SIMPLE VOWELS.

DIPHTHONGS.

CONSONANT POSITIONS.

JOINING THE CONSONANT-STEMS.

METHOD OF WRITING VOWELS BETWEEN CONSONANT-SIGNS.

POSITION OF WORDS.

PHONOGRAPHIC ANALYSIS.

ESS AND ZEE CIRCLE.

THE LARGE CIRCLE.

RULES FOR THE USE OF ISH, SHEE, EL, LEE, ER, AND REE.

GROUP CONSONANTS AND THEIR SIGNS—INITIAL HOOKS.

FINAL HOOK AND OTHER MODIFICATIONS.

PHRASEOGRAPHY.

PUNCTUATION AND OTHER MARKS.

ON PREPARING COPY AND READING PROOF.

REPORTING.

EXPLANATION OF TERMS.

Pho-net'ics, Pho-nol'o-gy, or Phon'ics (from φωνή, a *sound*, *tone*). The science which treats of the different sounds of the human voice and their modifications. The style of spelling in accordance with this science is called Phonetic; the common style, such as is used in this book, being called Romanic, because the alphabet employed was derived from that which was used by the Romans.

Pho-not'y-py (from φωνή, and τύπος, a type). The art of representing sounds by distinct characters or types; also, the style of printing in accordance with this art.

Pho'no-type. A type or character indicating a sound or modification of sound, used in phonotypic printing.

Pho-nog'ra-phy (from φωνή, and γράφειν, *to write*). A method of writing in which each sound has a distinct letter or character; also, a system of shorthand invented by Isaac Pitman.

Pho'no-graph. A type or character for representing a sound; a character used in Phonography.

Pho-no-graph'ic. Relating to Phonography.

Ste-nog'ra-phy (from στενός, *narrow*, *close*, and γράφειν). The art of writing by means of brief signs which represent single sounds, groups of sounds, whole words, or groups of words.

Note.—*Stenography* is a generic term, embracing all systems of shorthand or brief writing, Phonography included; while *Phonography* is a specific name for a single system.

In the arrangement and classification of the consonants at § 10, only the names of the sounds are given. The following table is the same, except that the phonographic signs are shown instead.

Front-Mouth.	Middle-Mouth.	Back-Mouth.

TABLE OF CONSONANTS.

Phonographs.	Name.	Sound represented by the Phonograph.
Abrupts.	pee	*pp* in co*pp*er, and *p* in *p*ay.
	bee	*bb* " e*bb*, " *b* " *b*ay.
	tee	*ed* " look*ed*, " *t* " *t*ame.
	dee	*ed* " lov*ed*, " *d* " *d*ame.
	chay	*tch* " ma*tch*, " *ch* " *ch*est.
	jay	*g* " *g*em, " *j* " *j*est.
	kay	*c* " *c*an, " *k* " *k*ilt.
	gay	*gue* " lea*gue*, " *g* " *g*ilt.
Continuants.	ef	*ph* " *ph*ase, " *f* " *f*an.
	vee	*f* " o*f*, " *v* " *v*an.
	ith	* " * " *th* " *th*igh.
	dhee	*the* " brea*the*, " *th* " *th*y.
	ess	*c* " i*c*y, " *s* " *s*eal.
	zee	*s* " wa*s*, " *z* " *z*eal.
	ish, shee	*s* " *s*ure, " *sh* " *sh*un.
	zhee	*z* " a*z*ure, " *s* " vi*s*ion.
Nasals.	em	*mb* " la*mb*, " *m* " ha*m*.
	en	*kn* " *kn*ow, " *n* " *n*o.
	ing	*n* " fi*n*ger, " *ng* " si*ng*er.
Liquids.	el, lee	*ln* " ki*ln*, " *l* " *l*ay.
	er	*rr* " bu*rr*, " *r* " fu*r*.
	ree	*wr* " *wr*ite, " *r* " *r*ight.
Coalescents.	way	*u* " pers*u*ade, " *w* " *w*ade.
	yay	*e* " *e*uchre, " *y* " *y*ou.
Aspirate.	hay	*wh* " *wh*ole, " *h* " *h*ole.

THE

COMPLETE PHONOGRAPHER

GENERAL REMARKS.—PHONOGRAPHY DEFINED.

§ 1. PHONOGRAPHY, in the widest sense of the word, is the art of expressing the *sounds of a language* by characters or symbols, one character being appropriated exclusively to each sound. As usually understood, however, the term is applied to the system of Phonetic Short-hand, invented by Isaac Pitman, of Bath, England.

CONSONANTS PRESENTED FIRST.

§ 2. In writing according to the common long-hand method, all the letters of a word, both consonants and vowels, are written one after another, in the order in which they are pronounced. In writing phonographically this is not the case, but, as will be more fully explained hereafter, the consonant-signs and vowel-signs are written separately, the consonant-signs being first written, and the vowel-signs afterward placed to them. Hence the more natural order of presentation, and the one adopted in this book, is to treat of the consonants first, and afterward of the vowels.

SIMPLE CONSONANT SIGNS.

CONSONANT DEFINED.

§ 3. A consonant is a sound made by either a complete or a partial contact of the organs of speech obstructing the sounding breath, in some degree varying from an entire break or stoppage of it, as *p* in *rap*, *b* in *rob*, etc., to a simple roughness or aspiration impressed upon a vowel sound, as *h* in *heat*, *hate*.

NUMBER OF CONSONANTS.

§ 4. In the English language there are twenty-two simple consonant sounds. This number does not include *ch* and *j*, which are considered compounds, as they are susceptible of being analyzed into simpler elements; *ch* seeming to be composed of *t* and *sh*, and *j* of *d* and *zh*.

REMARKS ON THE TABLE OF CONSONANTS.

§ 5. The table on page 18 exhibits all the characters used in Phonography to represent each and every simple consonant sound in our language, as well as the double sounds of *ch* and *j*. The first column contains the phonographic signs or letters, called *phonographs*; the second, their *names*; and the third column furnishes examples of the *power* of each phonograph in the common spelling. In every case but one, two words are given; the first in an *unphonetic* or *forced* orthography, tending more to conceal than to indicate the true consonant sound, which must always be determined before it can be expressed by its proper phonographic sign; while in the second the orthography is more natural, and the consonant sound less difficult to be ascertained.

§ 6. The object in thus presenting the irregular example first is to impress on the learner's mind at the very outset, the fact that the *common* spelling of words is no reliable guide to the *phonographic*; for the sooner he learns not to associate the phonographic signs with the letters of the common alphabet, the more rapid will be his progress.

§ 7. If the attention be again directed to the column of phonographs in the table, it will be observed that the first sixteen are arranged in pairs, one of each pair being a *thin* or *light* line, and the other a corresponding *thick* or *heavy* line. The reason of this arrangement is important, and should be thoroughly understood. By comparing the sounds of any two signs thus classed together, it will be found that one is but a slight modification of the other; that they are produced at the same point and by the same contact of the organs of speech in almost precisely the same manner, the only difference being that, in one case, the action of the organs is accompanied by a slight sound— a sound of the breath simply, and in the other, the same action is accompanied by a partially suppressed vocal sound. This undertone or sub-vocal constitutes the only difference between the words *pay* and *bee*, *tame* and *dame*, *chest* and *jest*, *kilt* and *gilt*, *fan* and *van*, *thigh* and *thy*, *seal* and *zeal*, and *shun* and *-sion* in *vision*, given in the last column of examples.

§ 8. To follow nature, therefore, and preserve a correspondence between signs and sounds, and to show their resemblance as well as difference, the *light* or *breath* consonants are represented by *light* or *thin* lines, and their corresponding *heavy* sounds by the same lines shaded. Thus, written in Phonography, *bay* would differ from *pay*, or *dame* from *tame*, etc., only in the heavier shading of their initial signs *bee dee*, etc.

§ 9. None of the remaining consonants in the table have any proper mates in the English language, therefore they are not arranged in pairs; and although the heavy signs *ing*, *way*, *yay*, and *hay* correspond with the light signs *en*, *er*, *el*, and *em*, the likeness is accidental, and does not, as in the case of the others, indicate similarity of sound.

CLASSIFICATION OF THE CONSONANTS.

§ 10. The following arrangement of the consonants classifies them according to their nature or quality and their mode of formation. To make the view complete, the two compound consonants are inserted.

		Labials.	Labio-dentals.	Linguo-dentals.			Palatals.	Gutturals.
Abrupts....	Breathed*	pee			tee	chay		kay
	Sonant....bee				dee	jay		gay
Continuants.	Breathed..		ef	ith	ess		ish	
	Sonant....		vee	dhee	zee		zhee	
Nasals........Sonant....em				en				ing
Liquids ......Sonant....				el			er	
Coalescents....Sonant....way						yay		
Aspirate......Breathed..								hay

QUALITY OF CONSONANTS.

§ 11. The consonants are arranged in six divisions, called *Abrupts*, *Continuants*, *Nasals*, *Liquids*, *Coalescents*, and *The Aspirate*.

I. The *Abrupts* are so called because of their abrupt or explosive nature, being made by a complete contact of the organs of speech, interrupting or entirely stopping the breath or voice. They are the most perfect of the consonants. Sometimes they are termed *Explodents*.

II. The *Continuants* permit a freer escape of the breath or voice, and begin to approximate toward the character of vowels. They admit of indefinite prolongation, and hence their name.

III. The *Nasals* combine in their formation the character of the ab rupts and liquids. They are made by complete contact of the parts of the mouth, while at the same time the sounding breath or voice is permitted freely to escape through the nose

IV. The *Liquids* permit a still freer escape of the breath or voice than the continuants, approaching more nearly than they to the nature of vowels. They have in fact so much of the vowel character that

---

* The word *breathed* has been used here in preference to *whispered*, which is the one generally, but improperly, employed to designate the nature of the light consonant-sounds. That the term *whispered* does not indicate the true character of the sounds, is clearly demonstrated by the fact that the *sonants* are as easily uttered in *whisper* as the *breath* consonants

they readily unite with the other consonants, forming double consonants, and sometimes syllables, without the aid of any vowels.

V. The *Coalescents* and the *Aspirate* are the feeblest of all the consonants, seeming to be mere modifications of vowels, by which the breath
or voice is very slightly obstructed.

FORMATION OF CONSONANT-SOUNDS.

§ 12. In the arrangement of the consonant-sounds according to their
mode of formation, we begin with those formed at the lips alone, as *pee*,
bee, etc. ; and then go back to the teeth and lips, as *ef*, *vee;* then to the
region of the tip of the tongue and the teeth, as *tee*, *dee*, etc. ; then to the
hard palate or roof of the mouth, as *ish*, *zhee*, etc. ; and finally to the
root of the tongue, near the throat, as *kay*, *gay*, etc. Hence these several classes are called, I. *Labials;* II. *Labio-dentals;* III. *Linguo-dentals;* IV. *Palatals;* and, V. *Gutturals.*

§ 13. In sounding these consonants, the different parts of the mouth
are brought into action as follows : With the Labials, the lips are quite
or partially closed ; with the Labio-dentals, the upper teeth are placed
upon the lower lip ; with the Linguo-dentals, the end of the tongue is
placed against, or nearly against, the base of the upper teeth ; with the
Palatals, the tongue just back of the tip is pressed against the roof of
the mouth at a little distance from the teeth ; and with the Gutturals, the root or body of the tongue is pressed against the roof of the
mouth.

ORIGIN OF THE CONSONANT-SIGNS.

§ 14. The remarkable brevity that distinguishes Phonography from
all other systems of Short-hand, is chiefly owing to the extreme *simplicity* of the consonant-signs it employs ; each being a simple straight
or curved line, which requires but a single motion of the pen in its
formation. The source from which these signs are derived is shown
in the following geometric diagrams :

Experience has shown that the straight line can not be placed in
more than four positions, with a sufficient difference to be readily distinguished, and to prevent mistaking one sign for another. These
positions are illustrated by the four diameters in the above circles.
This gives us four distinct straight signs ; but by making use of light

and heavy lines the number is doubled. Again, if the circle is divided into quarters in the two ways shown in the diagrams, eight distinct curved signs are obtained. .Then by making them light and heavy, we have eight more, making sixteen in all, which, added to the eight straight signs, make twenty-four—the greatest number of lines, straight and curved, that can be used without confusion, and corresponding exactly with the number of consonant-sounds (including *ch* and *j*) that there are in our language.

ANALOGY IN THE APPROPRIATION OF THE SIGNS.

§ 15. In the appropriation of these signs to the consonants, the requirements of analogy are strictly observed, the eight inflexible and explosive sounds called *abrupts* being represented by unyielding straight lines, while the more flowing and pliable sounds, as the *continuants*, *nasals*, etc., are represented by curved and flowing lines.

§ 16. The signs of the compound consonants, *chay* and *jay*, take the form of their first elements *tee* and *dee*, and the direction of the second, *ish* and *zhee*.

MNEMONIC ASSISTANCE IN LEARNING THE PHONOGRAPHS.

§ 17. The memory is often greatly aided by local association, and the learner will derive assistance in memorizing the phonographs and their names by studying the table in connection with the following diagrams, in the first of which is shown the position and direction of each *straight* consonant-sign, and in the second, the location, in the circumference of the circle, of each *curved* consonant-sign. The names of the heavy or shaded signs are in **full face** type.

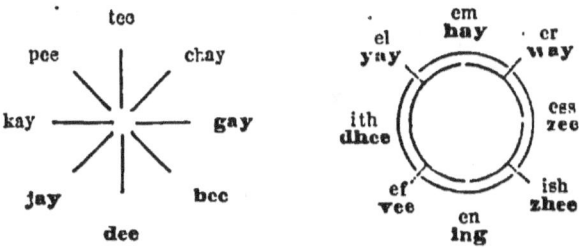

§ 18. Single consonant-signs are sometimes called *stems*, as well as *phonographs*

OF THE MANNER OF WRITING THE CONSO
NANT SIGNS.

§ 19. With one exception (*ree*), every consonant-sign employed in Phonography is written in the direction of the focus of one of the lines of the following diagram :

§ 20. *Horizontal* letters are written from left to right.

§ 21. Perpendicular and inclined letters are written downward

EXCEPTIONS.

§ 22. (*a*) When not joined to another stem, ⌐ʲ (*sh*) is written downward, and ⌐ (*l*) upward ; but when either is so joined it is sometimes written upward and sometimes downward. (*b*) The straight sign for *r*, ╱ *ree*, is always written upward.

§ 23. When written *downward*, ⌐ʲ and ⌐ are called respectively *ish* and *el* ; when *upward*, *shee* and *lee*. Rules by which the learner may determine whether to use *ish* or *shee*, *el* or *lee*, *er* or *ree*, will be given hereafter.

CHAY AND REE DISTINGUISHED.

§ 24. As the stems *chay* and *ree* are inclined in the same direction, they are distinguished, when not joined to other stems, by difference in inclination ; *chay* being written at an angle of *sixty* degrees from the line, and *ree* at an angle of *thirty* degrees : thus, ╱ *chay*, ╱ *ree*. When joined to other stems, they are distinguished by the direction of the stroke, which is apparent : thus, ╲╱ *pee-ree*, ╲ *pee-chay*, ╱ *chay-ree*, ╱ *ree-chay*.

HINTS TO THE BEGINNER.

§ 25. Phonography is best written on ruled paper ; and some recommend double lines, but the ordinary single-line ruling is generally preferred by practical phonographers. The learner should accustom himself to write with either pen or pencil, holding it the same as in writing long-hand. The pen should have a smooth and tolerably fine point, and may be either gold, steel, or quill. Very fine hair lines are found in practice not to be the most legible, especially when read-

ing or transcribing notes at night. If a pencil is used, Faber's No. 3
is of about the right hardness.

§ 26. No effort should be made by the learner at the outset to write
with rapidity. Accuracy alone should be aimed at ; and when his
hand has become accustomed to trace the phonographic characters with
correctness and elegance, he will find no difficulty in writing them
quickly. But if he let his anxiety to write fast overcome his resolu-
tion to write well, he will not only be longer in attaining real swiftness, but will always have to lament the illegibility of his writing.
Each phonograph should be *drawn* slowly, great care being taken to
give it its proper *direction, shading,* and *length.* Beginners are apt to give
the curved signs a little *twist* or *flourish* at the end, and also to incline
the perpendicular stems a little to the right,—defects that should be
carefully avoided. The reading and writing exercises near the end of
the book will afford ample practice upon every principle of Phonography, and, as far as practicable, in the exact order, section by section, of their presentation in the following pages. Those exercises
have been carefully selected, so that no word will be found which in-
volves principles not previously explained. They should be carefully
and repeatedly read and written, in connection with the sections which
relate to them. The learner should also scrupulously avoid writing any
words except those that he finds in the exercises, or even writing words
that are there given, but which are in advance of his regular lesson.
By so doing he will save himself much unnecessary discouragement, and
escape the annoyance of having afterward to unlearn, or forget, improper word-forms.

LENGTH OF PHONOGRAPHS.

§ 27. The usual length of phonographs prevailing among practical
reporters is about one sixth of an inch, or, for example, about like | *tee,*
___ *kay,* ⌇ *ef,*) *zee,* ⌣ *ing.* Some phonographers write a little
smaller, and some larger. Learners should at first write quite large; but
after considerable proficiency is attained the stems may, with advantage,
be reduced to the size of the above illustrations.

SHADING OF THE HEAVY SIGNS, ETC.

§ 28. In making the heavy curved signs, care should be taken not
to shade them at or near the end ; they should be shaded in the middle
only, and taper off toward each extremity, otherwise they will present
a clumsy appearance. And both straight and curved heavy signs
should only be shaded sufficiently to distinguish them from the corresponding light signs. If there be too great a contrast between the
heavy and light lines, the writing will appear stiff and ungrace-
ful The distance from point to point of any curved sign should be

about equal to the length of a straight sign written in the same direction.

PHONOGRAPHIC SPEED.

§ 29. The rapidity of phonographic writing, like that of the common script, must vary with the organism of the writer. Expert phonographers generally write about six times as fast in Phonography as in long-hand.

EXERCISES TO BE READ AS WELL AS WRITTEN.

§ 30. It will greatly facilitate the acquirement of Phonography if the exercises written by the learner are carefully read and re-read by him until they can be deciphered without hesitation. The consequences of omission in this respect are admirably stated by Mr. Dickens in the 38th chapter of "David Copperfield," which may be read with both instruction and amusement.

SIMPLE VOWELS.

DEFINITION.

§ 31. A vowel may be defined to be the smooth or harmonious emission of sounding breath, modulated but not obstructed by the organs of speech ; as the sounds of *a* in *arm*, *a* in *ale*, *ea* in *eat*.

NUMBER OF VOWEL-SOUNDS.

§ 32. In the English language there are twelve distinct vowel-sounds, six of which are long and six short. They are denoted by the *italic* letters in the following words :

LONG VOWELS—*a*rm, *a*le, *ea*t, *a*ll, n*o*te, f*oo*d.
SHORT VOWELS—*a*t, *e*ll, *i*t, *o*n, *u*p, f*oo*t.

§ 33. In producing each of these short vowel-sounds, the position of the vocal organs is nearly the same as in uttering the long vowel-sound of the corresponding word in the line above.

§ 34. For these twelve sounds the common alphabet furnishes but the five letters *a*, *e*, *i*, *o* and *u* (*w* and *y* having no vowel-sounds of their own), while Phonography gives a distinct representation to each.

METHOD OF VOCALIZATION.

§ 35. In writing phonographically, the consonant-sign is made first, and the vowel-sign afterward placed to it. Of the six long vowels, three are indicated by a *heavy dot*, written to the consonant in three positions, viz., at the *beginning*, *middle*, and *end*; and the other three, by a *heavy dash*, written to the consonant in the same positions. Of the six corresponding short vowels, three are indicated by a *light dot*, and three by a *light dash*, written to the consonant in the same manner.

§ 36. A vowel is said to be *first*, *second*, or *third place*, according as it is written at the *beginning*, *middle*, or *end* of a consonant-stem.

§ 37. The six vowel-sounds indicated by the *dot* are lingual in their nature, and the six dash-vowels, labial.

VOWEL-SCALE.

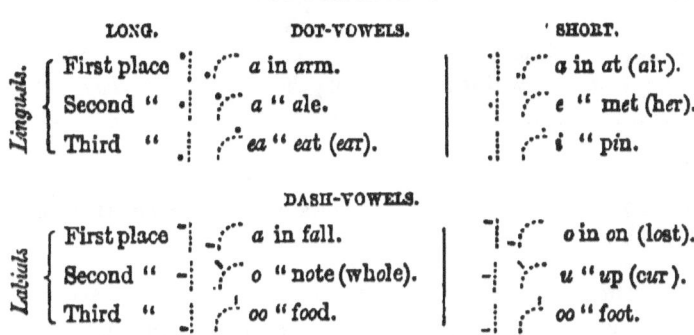

	LONG.	DOT-VOWELS.		SHORT.
Linguals	First place	.⌐ *a* in *arm*.		.⌐ *a* in *at* (air).
	Second "	⌐ *a* " *ale*.		⌐ *e* " *met* (her).
	Third "	⌐ *ea* " *eat* (ear).		⌐ *i* " *pin*.

DASH-VOWELS.

Labials	First place	_⌐ *a* in *fall*.		_⌐ *o* in *on* (lost).
	Second "	)⌐ *o* " *note* (whole).		)⌐ *u* " *up* (cur).
	Third "	⌐ *oo* " *food*.		⌐ *oo* " *foot*.

NAMES OF THE VOWELS.

§ 38. The long vowels may be named by their respective sounds *ah, a, e, awe, o, oo* (not *double o*) ; and the short vowels by pronouncing them with the consonant *tee* subjoined to each; thus, *at, et, it, ot, ut, ŏŏt*. The short vowels may also be named by their sounds, without the consonant *tee*, as soon as the learner is sufficiently advanced to be able to pronounce them correctly without the aid of a consonant. Their common letter representatives would then be *ă, ĕ, ĭ, ŏ, ŭ, ŏŏ*.

RECKONING OF VOWEL-POSITIONS.

§ 39. It has been already remarked that the first vowel-place is at the beginning of the consonant; the second at the middle, and the third at the end. From this it follows that with horizontal consonant-signs the vowel-positions number from left to right; with down strokes, from top to bottom; with up-strokes, from bottom to top; and with signs that are sometimes written upward and sometimes downward, the numbering of the vowel-positions is from the bottom or top, according as the consonant is struck upward or downward; thus, with *shee, lee,* or *ree,* the first position is at the bottom, while with *ish, el,* or *er,* it is at the top.

§ 40. In the above scale, the dots and dashes are written near a dotted *tee,* to show the three vowel-positions in connection with a down-stroke stem; and near a dotted *lee*, to show the positions in connection with an up-stroke stem. The dotted lines of course form no part of the vowel-sign.

VOCALIZATION OF SINGLE CONSONANT-STEMS.

§ 41. When a vowel occurs before a consonant, the vowel-sign is written to the *left* of the consonant-sign, if it is upright or slanting; and *above* if it is horizontal; thus, ·| *aid*, ··|·· *eat*, \ *ebb*, / *etch*, \ *up*, (*ail*, ‿ *ache*, ‿ *oak*. When a vowel comes after a consonant, the vowel-sign is written to the *right* of the consonant-sign, if it is upright or slanting; and *below* if it is horizontal; thus, ··|· *two*, \ *bay*, / *ray*, \ *show*, — *gay*, ⌢ *hay*.

CONSONANT ALWAYS WRITTEN FIRST.

§ 42. In either case, whether the vowel precedes or follows the consonant, the consonant is always written first.

METHOD OF READING SINGLE VOCALIZED CONSONANT-STEMS.

§ 43. When a vowel-sign is placed to the left of an upright or slanting consonant-stem, or above a horizontal, the vowel is read first; thus, ·| *ode*, | *at*, ‿ *aim*. When a vowel-sign is placed to the right of an upright or slanting consonant-stem, or below a horizontal, the consonant is read first; thus, |· *day*, \ *pay*, \ *bah*, ··)· *she*, ⌐ *caw*, ⌢ *may*, ······ *me*.

MANNER OF WRITING THE VOWEL-SIGNS.

§ 44. The dash vowel-signs should be written at right-angles to the consonant-stem, and both *dot* and *dash vowels* should be written at a little distance from the stem, for if allowed to touch, mistakes would be occasioned.

THE VOWEL-SCALE NOT PERFECTLY PHONETIC. TWO SOUNDS SOMETIMES REPRESENTED BY ONE SIGN.

§ 45. If we make a close analysis, we will find that the number of vowel-sounds in the English language is somewhat greater than is indicated by the above vowel-scale. What the exact number is it is difficult to determine, phoneticians not being able to agree in regard to it among themselves. This is owing partly to difference of pronunciation among speakers, and partly to the fact that the shades of distinction between several of the vowel-sounds are so very slight, that, to some ears, they are quite imperceptible. As Phonography is not intended to represent a.l the nice shades of sound, but to be a *practical* rather than a *critically exact* means of writing the language, the twelve-vowel scale is found to be entirely sufficient. From this it follows that in some instances several vowel-sounds, which are recognized as being distinct elements by all accurate orthoepists, are confounded with each other, and represented by a single sign.

§ 46. The attention of the learner is called to the following examples of inexact phonetic representation, which are the only ones of importance, or that will be likely to cause him any embarrassment.

I. The third heavy dot-vowel sign, representing primarily the sound of *ea* in *eat*, is also used to represent the more open sound of *ea* in *ear*. Beginners sometimes fall into the error of employing the light dot-sign of the same position for this sound.

II. The first light dot-vowel sign, representing primarily the sound of *a* in *at*, is also used to represent the sounds of *a* in *ask* and *ai* in *air*. To many ears the vowel-sounds in *at* and *ask* are identical; and, as frequently spoken, there is really no difference; but when correctly uttered, the sound of *a* in *ask* approaches more nearly the sound of *a* in *arm*. The sound of *ai* in *air* has commonly been treated as long *a*, somewhat modified by the following *r*. Although this description corresponds with English pronunciation, in this country prevailing usage gives this vowel the sound of *a* in *at*, but prolonged in quantity.

III. The second light dot-vowel sign, representing primarily the sound of *é* in *met*, *ell*, is also used to represent the sounds of *e* in *her*, and *i* in *bird*, *fir*. As commonly pronounced, the sounds of *e* and *i*, before *r*, very closely resemble the sound of *u* in *fur*; but, as pronounced by our most careful public speakers, they approach nearer the short sound of *e*, as heard in *met*.

IV. The second heavy dash-vowel sign, representing primarily the sound of *o* in *note*, is also used to represent the shorter sound of *o* in *wholly*. This sound of *o* is said to be peculiar to American pronunciation. It is frequently heard here in the words *stone, home, coat, whole,* etc.

V. The first light dash-vowel sign, representing primarily the sound of *o* in *on*, is also used to represent the sound of *o* in *lost, moth, cloth,* etc. This latter sound is less broad than the sound of *aw* in *law*, and yet broader than the sound of *o* in *on, not,* etc.

VI. The second light dash-vowel sign, representing primarily the sound of *u* in *up*, is also used to represent the longer sound of *u* in *cur*.

§ 47. For the use of the critical student, a complete vowel-scale, in which a distinct representation is provided for each and every vowel sound of the language, is given in the Appendix.

DIPHTHONGS.

DEFINITION.

§ 48. A diphthong is a coalition or union of two simple vowel sounds, pronounced in one syllable; as *oi* in *oil*.

NUMBER OF DIPHTHONGS.

§ 49. There are but four proper or perfect diphthongs in the English language. They are illustrated by the *italics* in the words

by,   boy,   bough,   few.

ANALYSIS OF THE DIPHTHONGS.

§ 50. A proper diphthong is a compound or transition vowel-sound, the organs of speech being in the position to utter one simple vowel-sound at the beginning of it, and in a position to utter a different simple vowel-sound at the conclusion of it, so that the two simple sounds are both heard in full or in part, but often so blended together as to seem to the ear but one sound.

1. I—In uttering the sound of *i* in *ice*, or *y* in *by*, or *ai* in *aisle*, the organs at the commencement of the sound are in position to pronounce the vowel *a* in *ask*, and, at the end, they are in position to produce the sound of *i* in *it*.

2. OI—The sound of *oi* in *oil*, or *oy* in *boy*, is composed of the sounds of *o* in *lost*, and *i* in *it*.

3. OW—The sound of *ow* in *now*, or *ough* in *bough*, or *ou* in *our*, is composed of the sounds of *o* in *on*, and *oo* in *foot*.

4. EW—To produce the sound of *ew* in *few*, or *eu* in *feud*, or *u* in *nature*, the organs at the commencement are in position to pronounce the sound of *e* in *be*, and at the end to pronounce *oo* in *food* or *foot*.

REMARKS ON THE DIPHTHONG EW.

§ 51. This last sound has probably perplexed lexicographers and phoneticians more than any other in the language. This has been owing partly to difference of pronunciation among speakers, and partly to the obscure and changeable character of the two close vowels of which the diphthong is composed. When properly pronounced, its first element is very short, the organs merely taking the position to sound the close vowel *e*, and then, the instant the sound commences, passing to the position of the final element *oo*, upon which the voice rests a much longer space of time. In England, this is its uniform pronunciation; but in this country, it is sometimes spoken as if its first element were the more open sound of *i* in *it*. This change occasions the difference in the sound of the syllable *tune* heard in the word *opportune*, as usually pronounced in this country, and in the word *misfortune*, of which our pronunciation does not vary from the English. The close quality and almost imperceptible quantity of the *e* sound of the diphthong, as heard in the last example, and in the final syllables of the words *nature, feature, virtue,* etc., has led may to suppose that the real sound was that of the consonant *y*, which is a sound so nearly allied to it that it has some times been called the "squeezed sound of *e*." And even now thi is the pronunciation given in most dictionaries, and also the one adopted by the American phoneticians. But the phoneticians of England, in their later publications, invariably treat this double sound as a diphthong, — that is, as composed of two vowels, instead of a consonant and a vowel. On the other hand, however, they err in giving the sound of *i* in *u* as its first element, that vowel seldom, if ever, entering into the composition of this diphthong, especially as heard in their own pronunciation.

§ 52. The final element of this diphthong is also subject, under certain circumstances, to a slight change. In accented syllables, it is clearly the long sound of *oo;* as in the words *duty, beauty, review,* etc. ; but in unaccented syllables, it seems to be the short sound of *oo*, as in the words *value, virtue,* etc.

§ 53. From the above observations it appears that, according to the American pronunciation, as a general rule, when the diphthong *u* occurs in an accented syllable, its components are the sounds of *i* in *u* and *oo* in *food*, and that in unaccented syllables, it is composed of the vowel-sounds of *ea* in *eat* and *oo* in *boot*.

§ 54. The four proper diphthongs are represented by four angular characters, written, like the simple vowel-signs, to the consonant, three occupying the first, and one the third position, as shown in the following table.

TABLE OF DIPHTHONGS.

I	v:	v:	Sound of *ai*	in *aisle* and *i*	in *fine*.
OI	<:	<:	"	" *oy* " *boy* " *oi*	" *boil*.
OW	L:	L:	"	" *ough* " *plough* " *ow*	" *cow*.
EW	>:	f:	"	" *iew* " *view* " *u*	" *tube*.

§ 55. If the writer should wish to distinguish between what we may call the American and English pronunciations of this diphthong, it may be done by making both strokes of the sign light for the former, an by shading the first stroke of the sign for the latter, to indicate that th first element is of the *long e* quality. But in practice, no confusion will result from using uniformly the light sign, as, in the common print, we are accustomed to seeing one letter used for both sounds

DIRECTION OF THE DIPHTHONG-SIGNS NEVER CHANGED.

§ 56. Unlike the dash vowel-signs, the signs for the diphthongs are never inclined to correspond with the direction of the consonant-signs to which they are written; thus, ＼ *by*, ⌄ *nigh*, ＼ *boy*, ⌐ *cow*, ..|;. *due.*

TWO VOWELS CONCURRING.

§ 57. When two vowels occur together, either before or after a consonant, the vowel that is sounded nearest to the consonant should be written a little nearer it than the others; thus, ˙| *iota*, ..✕.. *payee*, ⌣ *Noah.*

DIPHTHONG I JOINED TO CONSONANTS.

§ 58. When convenient, initial diphthong i is joined to the consonant; thus, ..|.. *idea*, ⅂ *eyed*, ⌐ *Iowa.*

CONSONANT POSITIONS.

§ 59. Each of the consonant-signs is written, with respect to the line of writing, in three different positions, corresponding with the three vowel-positions, and, like them, respectively called *first*, *second*, and *third*.

§ 60. In the following illustrations, the *dot-line* running under, over, or through the consonant-stem serves to indicate the line of writing.

POSITIONS OF PERPENDICULAR AND INCLINED STEMS.

§ 61. The positions of perpendicular and inclined stems are as follows :

FIRST POSITION.—Above the line, one half the length of a *tee ;* thus, ＼ *pee*, ⌐ *way*, | *tee*, ⌠ *yay.*

SECOND POSITION.—Resting on the line; thus, ＼ *ef*, ⌐ *dee*, ⁄ *chay.*

THIRD POSITION.—Written through the line, so as to extend one half below; thus, ✕. *pee*, ..|.. *dee.*

POSITIONS OF HORIZONTAL STEMS.

§ 62. The positions of the horizontal stems are as follows :

FIRST POSITION.—Above the line, the highest part of the stem distant from it the length of a *tee ;* thus, ⌒ *em*, ⌣ *ing*, ⎯ *kay.*

SECOND POSITION.—The lower part of the stem resting on the line ; thus, ⌒ *hay*, ⌣ *en*, ⎯ *gay.*

THIRD POSITION.—A little below the line, but not touching it ; thus, ⌒ *em*, ⌣ *ing.*

JOINING THE CONSONANT STEMS.

§ 63. In writing a word phonographically, the first thing for the learner to do is, to analyze it into its elementary sounds. Having done this, the consonant-signs are then all to be written first, without taking off the pen ; the second sign commencing where the first ends, the third at the end of the second, and so on ; thus, the consonants of the words *became* and *knave* are respectively ⟍⌒ *bee-kay-em* and ⌐ *en-vee*. This is called the *outline* or *skeleton* of the word ; and no matter how many consonant-stems it may contain, they must all be written before any of the vowel-signs are inserted. The only exception to this is that when initial diphthong ɪ is joined (§ 58), it must be written first.

CONSONANT-STEMS REPEATED.

§ 64. A straight consonant-stem is repeated by doubling its length ; thus, ⎯⎯ *gay-gay,* | *dee-dee,* ⟍ *bee-bee.*

§ 65. Curved consonant-stems are repeated thus : ⌒ *em-em,* ⌐ *vee-vee.*

MODE OF JOINING CERTAIN STEMS.

§ 66. There should always be an angle between the stems of the following combinations : ⌣ *ef-en,* ⌣ *vee-en,* ⌣ *vee-ing,* ⌐ *lee-em,* ⌐ *hay-ess.*

§ 67. When two stems are joined that do not form a distinct angle, if one or both be heavy, they should be so blended that the precise point of junction shall not be discernible, as in the following examples : ⟍ *pee-bee,* | *dee-tee,* ⌞ *ef-gay,* ⌞ *vee-kay,* ⌞ *dee-vee,* ⌞ *vee-gay,* ⟍ *bee-ing,* ⌞ *dhee-ing,* ⌒ *hay-zee.*

§ 68. There should be no angle between the stems of the combinations ⟍ *pee-en,* ⌞ *ef-kay,* ⌞ *ith en,* ⌞ *dee-ef,* ⌒ *lee-er,* ⌒ *lee-ess,* ⌒ *lee-shee,* ⌒ *lee-ish,* ⌒ *em-ess.*

ORDER OF READING CONSONANT-STEMS.

§ 69. The consonant-signs are read in the same order that they are written. It will sometimes happen that a sign which is further along than another in the line of writing, must be read first ; thus, ⌐ is read *ish-dee,* and not *dee-shee ;* for, by the rule, *dee* is written downward, and as the signs must be made without taking off the pen, it is obvious that the ⌐ was written first, and downward, and the | written last.

METHOD OF WRITING VOWELS BETWEEN CONSONANT SIGNS.

§ 70. Vowels and diphthongs occurring between two consonants, are written according to the following

RULE.

1. All first-place, and all *long* second-place vowels are written to the stem which precedes them ; thus, ⎯ *balm,* ⎯ *back,* ⎯ *file,* ⎯ *bake.*

2. All *short* second-place, and all third-place vowels are written to the stem which follows them ; thus, ⎯ *beck,* ⎯ *dumb,* ⎯ *tomb,* ⎯ *pull,* ⎯ *rick.*

EXCEPTIONS.

(*a*) The rule as to first and third place vowel-signs may be violated where its observance would throw a vowel into an angle, and thus occasion ambiguity. The vocalization in ⎯ is better than in ⎯ for *nick-nack.*

(*b*) When two simple vowel-sounds, or a simple vowel and a diphthong, occur between two consonant-stems, and both, according to the rule, would be written to the same consonant, write one to each stem if convenient ; thus, ⎯ *cooing,* ⎯ *duel.* Sometimes it is preferable to write both to the same stem ; thus, ⎯ *puerile.*

POSITION OF WORDS.

§ 71. There are three positions, with respect to the line of writing, in which the consonant outlines of words may be written. These positions correspond with the three vowel-positions, and, like them, are called *first, second,* and *third* respectively. A word is assigned to one of these positions according as it has in its accented syllable a vowel which would be represented by a *first, second,* or *third place* vowel-sign. If a word be a monosyllable, the position to which it should be assigned, is determined by the *place* of its only vowel.

WHEN A WORD IS WRITTEN IN POSITION.

§ 72. A word is said to occupy a particular position when its first *perpendicular* or *inclined* consonant-stem is written in it, in accordance with §§ 59, 61, and 62. If, however, the consonant outline consists entirely of horizontal stems, the position of the first determines the position of the word, as all of the stems must necessarily fall in the same line. Throughout this work, the line of writing is indicated, in connection with words of the *first* and *third* positions, by the *dot-line*. All words that occur without the line of writing being so represented are to be regarded as belonging to the *second* position.

EXAMPLES.

FIRST POSITION : `⌐\` *cap,* `⌐` *fowl,* `⌐` *foil,* `⌐⌐` *calm,* `⌐` *caw* `⌐` *alike.*

SECOND POSITION : `>` *pail, pale,* `∧` *rope,* `⌐` *gale,* `⌐` *Kelly,* `⌐` *make.*

THIRD POSITION : `⌐` *fool,* `⌐` *feel,* `⌐` *coop,* `⌐` *king,* `⌐` *me,* `⌐` *bushy.*

MENTAL AND MANUAL PROCESS IN WRITING PHONOGRAPHY.

§ 73. Before commencing to write a word phonographically, the writer must determine what are its consonant-sounds, and also its accented vowel. Then its consonant outline is written in the proper word-position, as directed at §§ 71 and 72 ; and lastly, the vowel-signs are written to the consonant-stems in accordance with §§ 41 and 70. But, as the beginner will find it difficult to carry the consonant outline of a long word in his memory while his attention is directed to ascertaining the accented vowel and its position, it will be well for him, in his early practice, first to write the outline without regard to position, and then, when he has determined what is its accented vowel, to rewrite it in its proper position.

PHONOGRAPHIC ANALYSIS.

GENERAL RULE.

§ 74. It may be stated, as a general rule, that before the learner is prepared to write a word with its proper phonographic signs, he must first analyze it into its elementary sounds, observing to carefully distinguish the consonants from the vowels.

§ 75. If the common orthography of our language were phonetic,— that is, if each sound had a letter of its own, which always represented it wherever it occurred, the student of Phonography would need no other instruction in analysis than the general rule given in the last section. But unfortunately this is not the case. An alphabet of twenty-six letters, three of which (*c, q,* and *z*) have no sounds of their

own, thus practically reducing the number to twenty-three, is compelled to attempt the service of representing some *forty* different and
distinct sounds. This disparity between the number of sounds and the
number of signs to represent them, is the source of so many defects in
our written language, and has caused the adoption of such an irregular
and whimsical orthography, that the analysis of words into their true
elements, to one who is unaccustomed to it, is rendered exceedingly
difficult. It therefore becomes necessary to furnish assistance to the
earner in overcoming these difficulties which beset him at the very
ommencement of his course.

THE EAR MISLED BY THE EYE.

§ 76. The principal cause of embarrassment is the liability of the
ear, in the comparison of sounds, to be misled by the eye, which is
itself deceived from seeing frequently the same sound, in different
words, represented by different letters, or different sounds represented
by the same letter. Thus, the sounds of *ph* and of *f* in *Philip* and
fillip, differ in their representation to the eye, but to the ear they are
identical. The sounds of *th* in *thigh*, and of *th* in *thy*, differ to the ear,
but to the eye seem the same. In Phonography, the sign *ef* would be
used to represent the sound of both *ph* and *f*, while the two sounds
of *th* would be represented by the two signs *ith* and *thee*.

WORDS SPELLED ALIKE BUT PRONOUNCED DIFFERENTLY.

§ 77. Sometimes words that are written alike in the common spelling, are pronounced differently; as *bow*, an instrument for shooting
arrows, and *bow*, an act of respect ; *job*, a piece of work, and *Job*, a
man's name ; *row*, a number ranged in line, and *row*, a tumult. In all
such cases the phonographic spelling changes to correspond with the
change of sound or pronunciation.

WORDS PRONOUNCED ALIKE BUT SPELLED DIFFERENTLY.

§ 78. In some cases where a sound is used for the expression of several ideas, a difference is made in the common spelling corresponding
to a difference in signification ; thus, *ale, ail ; ark, arc ; aught, ought*, etc.
As such words are alike in sound, they are written alike in Phonography.

CAUTION RESPECTING CH, SH, TH, AND NG.

§ 79. The sounds of *ch* in *chest*, *sh* in *she*, *th* in *thigh* or *thy*, and *ng* in
ing, are not the natural sounds of the combinations *c* and *h*, *s* and *h*,
and *h*, and *n* and *g*, but they are simple single sounds, for which the
combinations *ch*, *sh*, *th*, and *ng* are conventional modes of expression.
The learner must be careful to represent them respectively with the

signs *chay*, *ish*, *ith* or *thee*, and *ing*, and not to write *ess-hay* for *ch* or *sh*, *tee-hay* for *th*, or *en-gay* for *ng*. It should also be noted, that the combination *ng* has two sounds, — that of *ing*, as heard in *sing*, *singer*, *hanger*, and that of *ing-gay*, in the words *linger*, *hunger*, etc.

W AND Y AT THE END OF SYLLABLES.

§ 80. *W* and *y*, at the end of syllables, are never sounded as consonants. One of the most common errors of beginners is to write the strokes *yxy* and *way* at the end of such words as *gay*, *day*, *pay*, *they*, *may*, *way*, *boy*, *xy*, *buy*, *cow*, *dew*, *caw*, etc. In each of these words there is but one consonant-sound, and that is initial. In *gay*, *day*, *they*, etc., the compounds *ay* and *cy*, which are pronounced alike, have a pure simple vowel-sound, represented by the second-place heavy dot vowel-sign. In *boy*, the sound of *oy* is that of the diphthong oɪ. In *buy*, the sound of *uy* is that of the diphthong ɪ. In *cow*, *ow* has the sound of the diphthong ow. In *dew*, the sound of *ew* is that of the diphthong ɛw. In *caw*, *aw* has a pure simple vowel-sound which is represented by the first-place heavy dash vowel-sign.

DOUBLE CONSONANT-SOUNDS RARE.

§ 81. It can not be too clearly understood that in words like *pitted*, *stabbing*, *massy*, etc., there is no real reduplication of the sounds *t*, *b*, and *s*, respectively. The reduplication of the consonant is a conventional mode of expressing in the common orthography the shortness of the vowel preceding, an expedient which would be entirely unnecessary if each sound had a letter of its own, as is the case in Phonography.

§ 82. Real reduplications of consonant-sounds are extremely rare. In English they occur only in compound and derived words, where the original root either begins with the same consonant-sound as the final one of the prefix, or ends with the same that commences the suffix.

§ 83. In the following words we have true specimens of doubled consonant-sounds. *Kay* is doubled in *book-case*; *en* in *unnatural*, *unnecessary*, etc.; *em* in *immortal*, *immaterial*, etc.

§ 84. A consonant-sound can never be reduplicated in the same syllable; hence, in Phonography, a single sign should be used to represent all such double letters as are found in the words *fagged*, *whipped*, *ebb*, *fuss*, *whizz*, *off*, *planned*, *programme*, *call*, *burr*, etc.

DISPARITY IN NUMBER BETWEEN LETTERS AND SOUNDS.

§ 85. Another source of confusion is the frequent use of a larger number of letters than there are sounds in a word. Thus, the word *though* has six letters and but two sounds; *through*, seven letters and but three sounds; *scene*, five letters and three sounds; *day, dey*, and a large number of similar words, three letters and two sounds.

C, Q, AND X.

§ 86. The letters *c, q*, and *x* of the old alphabet, have no sounds of their own. *C* sounds like *k* in *can*, like *s* in *cell*, like *z* in *suffice*, and like *sh* in *commercial*. *Q* always has the sound of *k;* and *x* sounds like *ts* in *exercise*, like *gz* in *exert*, and like *z* in *Xenophon*. These letters, of course, have nothing corresponding to them in Phonography, except that each of their different sounds has its appropriate sign, — *c*, in its different uses, being represented by either *kay, ess, zee*, or *ish; q* by *kay*, and *x* by *kay-ess, gay-zee*, or *zee*.

N BEFORE THE SOUNDS OF KAY AND GAY.

§ 87. Before the sounds of *kay* and *gay, n* has generally the sound of *ing* instead of *en ;* as in *ink, zinc, distinct, distinguish, anguish*, etc. Its proper sign in such cases is *ing*.

SILENT LETTERS OMITTED.

§ 88. All silent letters, such as *b* in *debt, c* in *scene, ch* in *drachm, h* in *hour, k* in *know*, etc., are, of course, omitted in Phonography, as signs are provided only for the sounds actually heard.

§ 89. It is not unfrequently the case that a letter is sounded in certain words, while in others of similar orthography it is silent ; thus, *l* is sounded in *bulk, bilk, elk*, etc., but silent in *balk, talk, chalk*, etc.

FINAL E GENERALLY SILENT.

§ 90. At the end of a large class of words the letter *e* is silent, being placed there simply as a conventional mode of indicating that the preceding vowel has its long sound ; as in the words *fate, mete, ripe, tone, tune*. The final *e* in these words represents no vowel-sound, its only office being to inform the reader that the preceding vowel is long, for by dropping this final letter, we have the words *fat, met, rip, ton, tun*.

'EW' NOT USED AFTER R.

§ 91. The diphthong EW is never heard after the consonant *r*. In the early editions of Webster's Dictionary the vowel *u* in such words as *rude, rule* is marked as if it were pronounced like *u* in *tube ;* but in later editions this sound is considered as that of *oo* in *food*. Worcester also says, "When *u* is preceded by *r* in the same syllable, it has the sound of *oo* in *fool*." Dr. Russell, the elocutionist, says, "The vowel *u*, immediately preceded by the letter *r*, takes properly the sound of *oo* in *rood*, or of *oo* in *root*," giving as examples the words *rule, rude, fruit, true*, etc.

Walker also gives the same pronunciation. It therefore follows that the proper sign for the sound of *u* after *r* is the third-place heavy dash, and not the diphthong sign EW; thus, write -⟋⌐--, and not --⟋⌐--, for the word *rude*.

UNACCENTED VOWELS. GENERAL RULE.

§ 92. It is often difficult to determine satisfactorily the quality and quantity of vowel-sounds in unaccented syllables. That the learner may not be without some guide in this respect, it may be stated that in a majority of cases, when the precise *quality* can not be readily determined, the vowel should be regarded as the short sound of the letter used to represent it in the common spelling; thus, ăgain, tenăble, mentăl, metăl, travĕl, rĕfer, prĕfer, pĕruse, rĕceipt, rĕform, perĭl, idŏl. And, generally, when the quality is clear, but the quantity is in doubt, the short vowel is preferred to the long; thus, ĕ represents better than ā, the sound of *ai* in *certain*, *captain*.

EXCEPTIONS.

§ 93. Sometimes, however, unaccented vowels retain their proper long sound, and should be so written; as ā in the final syllable -ate, in *carbonate*, *sulphate*, *vacate*, *mandate*, etc.; ō in *obey*; ē in rē-seat, rē-form (to form again), etc. And some writers always regard these obscure sounds as long in quantity and quality, except in cases where they clearly appear to be short; thus, they would write āgain, tenāble, rēfer, etc.; but mentăl, metăl, etc.

PHONOGRAPHIC SPELLING.

§ 94. Although in Phonography there is, strictly speaking, no such thing as *spelling*, in the usual sense of the term, yet there is a process of analyzing words into their elements, and pronouncing the names of those elements, very analogous to spelling, and which the learner will find to be an excellent practice for the purpose of training his ear and judgment to habits of accuracy and quickness in the discernment of sounds. In this phonographic spelling, the consonants should first be analyzed and named, afterward the vowels, then the consonants and vowels in the order that they are spoken, and lastly, the complete word should be pronounced. An illustration of this process may be had by pronouncing the following words and syllables : ought, tee, aw, aw-tee, ought ; own, ĕn, ō, ō-en, own ; me, em, ē, em-ē, me ; take, tee, kay, ā, tee-ā-kay, take ; orb, er, bee, aw, aw-er-bee, orb ; elbow, lee, bee, ĕ, ō, ĕ-lee-bee-ō elbow The words and syllables separated by commas should be spoken deliberately, with considerable pause between, while those connected by hyphens are to be pronounced in rapid succession, with little or no pause.

ESS AND ZEE CIRCLE.

§ 95. The *s* and *z* are consonant elements of such frequent recurrence, that it has been found convenient to furnish them with an additional and briefer means of representation. The *full* or *stem* forms are given in the Table of Consonants; the other form is a small circle; thus, ₀ *ess, zee.*

§ 96. The circle is extremely useful because it affords great facility for joining the consonant-stems, and also because it compresses the writing into smaller space, thus tending to preserve its lineality.

NAME OF THE S-CIRCLE.

§ 97. The *s*-circle, when not named in conjunction with a stroke-consonant, is called *circle-ess.* In this way a distinction is secured between its name and that of the stem or alphabetic sign. When joined to a stem, the circle is named with it. [See § 99.]

METHOD OF JOINING THE CIRCLE TO CONSONANT-STEMS.

§ 98. The circle is joined to consonant-stems as follows :

I. To single straight stems, by a motion from the right over to the left; thus, ⌒₀ *s-kay-s,* (*s-tee-s,* ⟍ *s-pee-s.*

II. To simple curved stems, by writing it on the inside of the curve · thus, ⌣ *s-ish-s,* (*s-ith-s,*) *s-ess-s,* ⌢ *s-em-s,* ⌣ *s-en-s,* (*s-lee-s.*

NAMES OF THE ESS-CIRCLE COMPOUNDS.

§ 99. These compounds may be named by inserting the short vowel-sound *ĕ* between the sounds represented by the circle and the stem to which the circle is attached; thus, s-pee is called *sep;* pee-s, *pess;* s-pee-s, *seps* or *spess;* s-bee, *seb;* bee-s, *bess;* s-tee, *set;* tee-s, *tess;* s-tee-s, *sets* or *stess;* s-dee, *sed;* dee-s, *dess;* s-dee-s, *seds;* s-chay, *sech;* chay-s, *chess;* s-chay-s, *schess* or *seches;* s-kay, *sek;* kay-s, *kess;* s-kay-s, *seks* or *skess;* s-gay, *seg;* gay-s, *gess;* s-ith, *seth;* ith-s, *thess;* s-ith-s, *sethess;* er-s, *erss;* s-em, *sem;* em-s, *mess;* s-em-s, *sems* or *smess;* s-en, *sen;* en-s, *ens* or *ness;* s-en-s, *sens* or *sness.*

§ 100. When the circle is joined to stems that are written upward, the names of the compounds should be formed by using the long sound *ē* or *ee* instead of *ĕ;* thus, s-shee, *seesh;* shee-s, *shees;* s-shee-s, *seeshees;* s-lee, *slee;* s-ree, *sree* or *seree;* ree-s, *rees;* s-ree-s, *serees;* lee-s, *lees;* s-lee-s, *slees.* The compound s-way should be represented by *sway;* but way-s by *wess.* When it is difficult or impossible to form syllabic names in the manner just described, the full names of the circle and stems should be given; thus, s-hay, *ess-circle-hay;* s-yay, *ess-circle-*

yay. The compounds s-el and s-er are named *ess-circle-el* and *ess-circle-er.*

§ 101. Except in rare cases, no confusion results from employing the same sign for both *ess* and *zee*, because we are accustomed in the com· mon print to the frequent use of the single letter *s* for both of those sounds; as in the words, *base, bays, lease, lees, rise* (noun), *rise* (verb) *gus, has,* etc.

§ 102. If, however, it should sometimes be necessary to make a dis· tinction, the circle may be made a little heavier on one side for the sound of *zee;* thus, ₒ *z;* as in the sentence, "I said the $\subset$ *laws* of the state, not the $\subset$ *loss* of the state." But in rapid writing this distinc tion can not easily be made, and therefore should not be attempted

METHOD OF WRITING THE CIRCLE BETWEEN TWO CONSONANT-STEMS.

§ 103. The circle is written between consonant-stems as follows:

I. Between two straight stems, both of which are written in the same direction, — by writing it to the first the same as if it were not followed by another stem; thus, ___ *kess-kay,* | *dess-tee,* \ *pess bee.*

II. Between two straight stems that form an angle at their junc tion, — by writing it on the outer side of the angle; thus, ⌐ *kess-jay,* ⟩ *bess-jay,* | *dess-kay,* ⌐ *ress-kay.*

III. Between a straight and a curved stem, — by writing it on the inner side of the curved stem; thus, ⟩ *pess-vee,* ⌐ *tess-el,* ⌐ *tess-lee,* ⌐ *less-pee.*

IV. Between two curved stems, if both are arcs of circles struck in the same direction, — by writing it on the inner side of both; thus, ⟩ *fess-el,* ⌐ *mess-lee,* ⌐ *mess-em.*

V. Between two curved stems that are arcs of circles struck in oppo· site directions, and that do not form a distinct angle at their junc tion, — by turning it on the inner side of the first stem; thus, ⌐ *mess-en,* ⌐ *fess-er,* ⌐ *ness-em,* ⌐ *mess-vee.*

VI. Between two curved stems that form an angle at their junction, and that are arcs of circles struck in opposite directions, — by turning it on the outer side of the angle; thus, ⌐ *fess-lee,* ⌐ *thess-lee,* ⌐ *ness-lee.*

§ 104. All of the examples given in the last section, of the circle

occurring between stems, except a few under heads III. and IV., are
covered by the following rule : When the circle occurs between two
stems of any kind, if there be no angle at their junction, it is written
to the first stem as if it stood alone ;—if there be an angle between
the stems, the circle is written on the outer side of the angle.

VOCALIZATION OF STEMS WITH CIRCLES ATTACHED.
ORDER OF WRITING.

§ 105. When a vowel immediately precedes a consonant-stem that
has an initial circle, or immediately follows a consonant-stem that has
a final circle, the vowel-sign is written to the stem as if it had no circle
attached; thus, *seat* and *teas* are vocalized the same as *eat*
and *tea.*

ORDER OF READING.

§ 106. In reading words in which circles are used, an initial circle
is read first ; then the vowel-sign, if one precede the stem ; thirdly,
the stem ; then its following vowel-sign, if there be one ; and lastly, a
final circle ; thus, *s-u-pp-o-se.*

CAUTION. — THE CIRCLE JOINED TO UP-STROKE STEMS.

§ 107. With up-stroke stems, an initial circle will, of course, be at
the bottom, and a final circle at the top ; thus, *sale, sail; luce,
lays; race, rays.*

VOCALIZATION WHEN THE CIRCLE OCCURS IN THE MIDDLE OF A WORD.

§ 108. When a circle occurs between two consonant-stems, if a vowel
immediately precede the circle, — write its sign to the first stem; thus,
desk; — but if the vowel immediately follow the circle, — write its
sign to the second stem ; thus, *unsafe.*

§ 109. The rule at § 70 as to vowels-signs between stems, does not
apply to these outlines.

USES OF THE CIRCLE.

§ 110. The circle is generally used at the commencement of words
that begin with the *ess*-sound; at the end of words that terminate
with an *ess* or *zee* sound, and for the sounds *ess* and *zee* when they occur
in the middle of words; thus, *sake, soap, said, case, days,
mouse, vase,* and the words *desk* and *unsafe* in § 108.

EXCEPTIONS.

§ 111. When an *ess* or *zee* sound is immediately preceded, or immediatcly followed, by two concurrent vowels, the stem-sign should be used, as it furnishes more convenient facilities for vocalization; thus, ⟍⟋ *science,* ⌢⟋ *chaos.*

§ 112. When two ess-sounds are the only consonants in a word, one should be written with the circle, and the other with the stem-sign. But, as the circle may be joined to either end of the stem, we have two forms, ⟍ and ⟍, which are equivalent to each other. The first of these forms should be used in words where the sound of *ess* is final, — that is, where no vowel is sounded after both the consonants; thus, ⟍ *cease;* — and the second form, in words that end with a vowel thus, ⟍ *saucy,* ⟍ *sissy.* There is a third form, ⟍, that is generally used in words where the second of the two consonants is a *zee*-sound; thus, ⟍ *size.*

WHEN THE STEM-SIGN SHOULD BE USED INSTEAD OF THE CIRCLE.

§ 113. The stem-sign should be used when the *ess*-sound is the first consonant in a word that commences with a vowel; thus, ⟍ *ask.*

§ 114. The stem-sign for the sound of *zee* is always used when that sound is the first consonant in a word, whether there be an initial vowel or not; thus. ⟍ *oozing,* ⟍ *zero.*

§ 115. The stem-sign is also used when the sound of *ess* or *zee* is the last consonant in a word that ends with a vowel; thus, ⟍ *Racey, racy;* ⟍ *rosy;* — also when either of those sounds is the only consonant in a word; thus, ⟍ *ace,* ⟍ *say,* ⟍ *essay,* ⟍ *ayes.*

THE LARGE CIRCLE.

§ 116. When the sound of *ess* or *zee* occurs twice in a word, with no other consonant between, or when the sounds of *ess* and *zee* occur in like proximity, the two sounds are generally represented by making the circle twice the size of the single *ess*-circle; thus, ○ *ess* or *zee,* ○ *ess-ess,* or *zee-zee,* or *ess-zee,* or *zee-ess.*

NAME AND USE OF THE LARGE CIRCLE.

§ 117. The large circle may be called *sis* or *siz.* It is commonly used to represent any of the combinations *ses, sis, ces, cis, sas, sos, sus,* etc., of the common spelling.

THE LARGE CIRCLE JOINED TO CONSONANT-STEMS.

§ 118. The large circle is joined to consonant-stems precisely in the same manner as the small circle, and such combinations are named in a manner similar to that described in § 90; thus, o̱ *sis-kay*, ꞏo *kesis*, ꞌ⊙ *fessis*, ꞏ⟨ *kessis-ree* ;—and also, like the small circle, may be used either at the beginning, in the middle, or at the end of a word; thus, ...ꞏꞏ *system*, ꞏꞏ *necessity*, ꞏꞏo *cases*.

VOCALIZATION OF STEMS WITH THE LARGE CIRCLE ATTACHED.

§ 119. The rule at §§ 105, 108, in reference to the vocalization of stems that have the small circle attached, also applies in vocalizing stems with the large circle attached.

VOCALIZATION OF THE LARGE CIRCLE.

§ 120. When necessary, a vowel that occurs between the two sounds represented by the large circle, may be expressed by writing its sign inside the circle, and, if convenient, in the *upper*, *middle*, or *lower* part of the circle, according as the vowel is *first*, *second*, or *third* place ; thus. ꞏꞏ *season*, ꞏꞏ *schism*, ...ꞏꞏ *secede*, ⊙ꞏ *Sussex*, ꞏꞏ *decease*, ꞏꞏ *recess*.

ESS AND ZEE SOUNDS DISTINGUISHED.

§ 121. When great exactness is required, the large circle may be shaded a little on one side to indicate that both of its sounds are that of *zee*; thus, ꞏꞏ *raises*, instead of ꞏꞏ *races*.

LOOPS FOR ST OR ZD, AND STR.

SMALL LOOP, — ST OR ZD.

§ 122. When the consonant-sound *tee* immediately follows *ess* (as in the words *most*, *cost*, etc.), or, when *dee* follows *zee* (as in the words *amazed*, *raised*, etc.), the two sounds are represented by lengthening the circle into a small loop, extending about one third the length of the stem; thus, ꞏꞏ *st-kay*, ꞏꞏ *kay-st*, ꞏꞏ *st-kay-st*.

LARGE LOOP, — STR.

§ 123. A large loop, extending about two thirds the length of the stem, may be used to represent the sound of *str*, with any vowel-sound that occurs between the *t* and the *r* (as in the words *master*, *castor*, etc.); thus, ꞏꞏ *kay-str*.

NAMES OF THE LOOPS. — VOCALIZATION OF STEMS WITH LOOPS ATTACHED.

§ 124. When not sounded in conjunction with a stroke-consonant, the small loop may be called *stee;* and the large loop may invariably be called *ster*. When the loops are joined to consonant-stems, the combinations may be named in a manner similar to that given for the *ess*-circle compounds at § 99; thus, st-kay, *stek*; kay-st, *kest*; st-kay-st, *stekest*; kay-str, *kester*; em-str, *mester*, etc.

§ 125. The rule at §§ 105, 108 also applies to the vocalization of stems with loops attached. The small loop, like the circle, may be used both at the beginning, in the middle, and at the end of words; thus, ·ʃ *state*, ⌐̣ *destiny*, ⌐ *taste*, ⌐̈ *east*, ⌐ *lost*. The large loop is not used at the commencement of words, but may be in the middle and at the end; thus, ⌐ *disturb*, ⌐ *castor*, ⌐ *master*.

SMALL LOOP SHADED FOR ZD.

§ 126. If great accuracy be required, the small loop may be shaded when it represents the sounds *zee-dee*; thus, ⌐ *raised*, instead of ⌐ *raced*.

THE SMALL CIRCLE ADDED TO SIS, ST, AND STR.

§ 127. The small circle is added to the large circle and to the loops by turning it on the opposite side of the stem; thus, ⌐ *excesses*, ⌐ *toasts*, ⌐ *coasters*.

RULES FOR THE USE OF ISH, SHEE, EL, LEE, ER, AND REE.

§ 128. In order to secure among phonographers a uniform manner of writing, and to give increased legibility to certain words, the following rules are prescribed regulating the use of those signs that may be written either upward or downward. These rules are general in their application, covering nearly all the words in which those stems occur. They may, however, be violated in a few cases, where their observance would occasion difficult or awkward forms.

USES OF ISH.

§ 129. The consonant-stem ⌐ is written downward (being then called *ish*) in the following cases:

I. When it is the only consonant-stem in a word; thus, ⌐ *she*, ⌐ *sash*.

II. When it is the first consonant-stem of a word that commences with a vowel; thus, ⌐ *Ashby*.

III. When it is the final element of a word; thus, ⌐ *bush*.

USES OF SHEE.

§ 130. The consonant-stem ⌐ is written upward (being then called *shee*) when it is the last stem of a word the final element of which is a vowel; thus, ⟨shorthand⟩ *bushy.*

EITHER ISH OR SHEE.

§ 131. At the commencement and in the middle of words, either *ish* or *shee* may be used; thus, ⟨shorthand⟩ or ⟨shorthand⟩ *shop,* ⟨shorthand⟩ or ⟨shorthand⟩ *shake,* ⟨shorthand⟩ or ⟨shorthand⟩ *bishop; — ish,* however, is generally more convenient in such cases.

USES OF EL.

§ 132. The consonant-stem ⟨shorthand⟩ is written downward (being then called *el*) in the following cases:

I. When it is the first consonant-stem in a word that commences with a vowel, and is next followed by a horizontal stem; thus, ⟨shorthand⟩ *alike,* ⟨shorthand⟩ *alum,* ⟨shorthand⟩ *Olney,* ⟨shorthand⟩ *Elihu.*

II. When it is the final element of a word; thus, ⟨shorthand⟩ *gale,* ⟨shorthand⟩ *pull,* ⟨shorthand⟩ *file.*

USES OF LEE.

§ 133. The consonant-stem ⟨shorthand⟩ is written upward (being then called *lee*) in the following cases:

I. When it is the only consonant-stem in a word; thus, ⟨shorthand⟩ *ale, ail,* ⟨shorthand⟩ *lay,* ⟨shorthand⟩ *allay,* ⟨shorthand⟩ *sail, sale,* ⟨shorthand⟩ *lace.*

II. When it commences a word; thus, ⟨shorthand⟩ *lake,* ⟨shorthand⟩ *lame* When, however, *l* (whether preceded by a vowel or not) is the first consonant-sound in a word, and *em,* followed by *pee* or *bee,* is the second, the down-stroke *el* may be used invariably, as better outlines are thereby secured; thus, ⟨shorthand⟩ *lump.*

III. When it is the last consonant-stem in a word the final element of which is a vowel; thus, ⟨shorthand⟩ *felly,* ⟨shorthand⟩ *Kelley.*

IV. Generally, when it is the first consonant-stem in a word (whether it commences with a vowel or not), and is next followed by a down-stroke stem; thus, ⟨shorthand⟩ *elbow,* ⟨shorthand⟩ *lobe,* ⟨shorthand⟩ *elegy.*

EITHER EL OR LEE.

§ 134. In the middle of words, either *el* or *lee* may be used; but *lee* is generally preferred, because more convenient.

USES OF ER.

§ 135. The down-stroke stem ⟨shorthand⟩ *er* is used in the following cases:

I. When *r* is the first or only consonant-sound in a word that commences with a vowel; thus, ⟨shorthand⟩ *ark, arc,* ⟨shorthand⟩ *array,* ⟨shorthand⟩ *orb.* For exceptions, see § 136, heading III.

II. When *r* is the final element of a word; thus, ⟋ *bore*, ⟍ *fair*, ⟍ *soar, sore,* ⟍ *store.*

III. Always for *r*, before the stems *em* and *hay*, whether an initial vowel precede it or not; thus, ⟍ *arm*, ⟍ *Rome, roam*, ⟍ *rehash.*

USES OF REE.

§ 186. The up-stroke stem ⟋ *ree* is used in the following cases ..

I. When *r* commences a word; thus, ⟋ *road*, ⟋ *rope*, ⟋ *rush.* For exceptions, see § 135, heading III.

II. When *r* is the last consonant-sound of a word the final element of which is a vowel ; thus, ⟍ *berry*, ⟍ *sorrow*, ⟍ *story.*

III Always for *r*, before the stems *ith, dhee, chay*, and *jay*, whether it is preceded by an initial vowel or not ; thus, ⟋ *earth*, ⟋ *wrath*, ⟋ *arch.*

EITHER ER OR REE.

§ 137. In the middle of words, either *er* or *ree* may be used ; but *ree* is generally preferred, being more convenient.

GROUP CONSONANTS AND THEIR SIGNS.

§ 138. If the learner has carefully studied and mastered the principles thus far explained, he has acquired the means of writing phonographically, and with tolerable brevity, any word in the language But there yet remains unemployed much stenographic material, without which no system of short-hand can justly claim to be complete. If we were obliged to write all the consonants with their full stem-signs, there are many words in which they are so grouped together and pronounced with such rapidity that the pen would find it difficult, if not impossible, to keep pace with the tongue. To obviate this difficulty, Phonography adopts the very natural plan of modifying the simple stem of some one of the consonants to provide a sign for the entire group. There are four different ways of modifying or altering simple stems into group-signs, namely : 1. By an initial hook ; 2. By a final hook ; 3. By lengthening ; and 4. By halving.

INITIAL HOOKS.

THE LIQUIDS L AND R.

§ 189. The liquids *l* and *r*, in a large number of words, are found immediately following other consonants, and blending with them so as to form double consonant-sounds somewhat analogous to the double vowel-sounds or diphthongs. Thus, in the words *clay, flay, gray, fray,* the first consonant of each of the combinations *cl, fl, gr, fr,* glides so quickly and imperceptibly into the second, or liquid, that the two seem to become actually one sound. In Phonography, such compounds are represented by the stem of the consonant that precedes the liquid, modified by an initial hook.

THE EL-HOOKS.

§ 140. A small hook at the beginning and on the circle side of any straight stem, and a large hook at the beginning and on the concave side of any curved stem, indicates that such consonant is immediately followed by the liquid *l;* thus,

STRAIGHT STEMS: $\searrow$ *pee-l,* $\searrow$ *bee-l,* $\lceil$ *tee-l,* $\lceil$ *dee-l,* $\diagup$ *chay-l,* $\diagup$ *jay-l,* $\smile$ *kay-l,* $\smile$ *gay-l,* $\diagup$ *ree-l.*

CURVED STEMS: $\mathcal{C}$ *ef-l,* $\mathcal{C}$ *vee-l,* $\mathcal{C}$ *ith-l,* $\mathcal{C}$ *dhee-l,* $\mathcal{)}$ *ess-l,* $\mathcal{)}$ *zee-l,* $\mathcal{J}$ *ish-l,* $\mathcal{J}$ *shee-l,* $\mathcal{J}$ *zhee-l,* $\mathcal{C}$ *lee-l,* $\mathcal{C}$ *el-l,* $\mathcal{N}$ *er-l,* $\mathcal{C}$ *em-l,* $\smile$ *en-l,* $\smile$ *ing-l,* $\mathcal{N}$ *way-l,* $\mathcal{C}$ *yay-l,* $\mathcal{C}$ *hay-l.*

THE ER-HOOKS.

§ 141. A small hook at the beginning, and on the side opposite the *l*-hook, of any straight stem, and a small hook at the beginning and on the concave side of any curved stem, indicates that such consonant is immediately followed by the liquid *r;* thus,

STRAIGHT STEMS: $\searrow$ *pee-r,* $\searrow$ *bee-r,* $\rceil$ *tee-r,* $\rceil$ *dee-r,* $\diagup$ *chay-r,* $\diagup$ *jay-r,* $\smile$ *kay-r,* $\smile$ *gay-r,* $\diagup$ *ree-r.*

CURVED STEMS: $\mathcal{C}$ *ef-r,* $\mathcal{C}$ *vee-r,* $\mathcal{C}$ *ith-r,* $\mathcal{C}$ *dhee-r,* $\mathcal{)}$ *ess-r,* $\mathcal{)}$ *zee-r,* $\mathcal{J}$ *ish-r,* $\mathcal{J}$ *shee-r,* $\mathcal{J}$ *zhee-r,* $\mathcal{C}$ *lee-r,* $\mathcal{C}$ *el-r,* $\mathcal{N}$ *er-r,* $\mathcal{C}$ *em-r,* $\smile$ *en-r,* $\smile$ *ing-r,* $\mathcal{N}$ *way-r,* $\mathcal{C}$ *yay-r,* $\mathcal{C}$ *hay-r.*

§ 142. These hooks for *l* and *r* being initial, will of course, when joined to $\mathcal{C}$ or $\mathcal{J}$, be at the top or bottom, according as the stem is written downward or upward.

§ 143. The signs *shee* and *el,* with the *el* or *er* hook, should never be used except in connection with other stem-signs (see §§ 22, 129, I., and 133, I.).

NAMES OF THE EL AND ER HOOK COMBINATIONS.

§ 144. The double consonant-signs of the *el* and *er* hook series should not be called *pee-el, pee-er, bee-el, bee-er,* etc., but by names formed, like those of the *ess*-circle compounds, by inserting the short vowel *ĕ* between the two consonant-sounds represented by the sign; thus, *pel, per, bel, ber, fel, fer, vel, ver.* The hook-signs formed with the stems *ess, zee, ish, shee, lee, el, er, ree, ing* are named respectively *es'l, es'r, zeel, zeer, ish'l, ish'r, sheel, sheer, leel, leer, el'l, el'r, reel, reer, ing'l, ing'r.*

CAUTION.

§ 145. The *el* and *er* hooks, though made at the *beginning* of the stem signs, are not read *before* but *after* them. The learner, therefore should be very careful not to confound such signs as ⌐ *kel*, ⌐ *ker*, etc., with ⌐ *lee-kay*, ⌐ *ree-kay*, etc.

MNEMONIC ASSISTANCE IN LEARNING THE EL AND ER HOOK-SIGNS.

§ 146. The following diagrams will assist the learner in remembering the sides of the *el* and *er* hooks on the straight stems. If the *left* hand, with the first finger bent, be held up and turned in the directions of *kay, pee, tee,* and *chay*, the outlines of *kel, pel, tel,* and *chel* will be formed; thus,

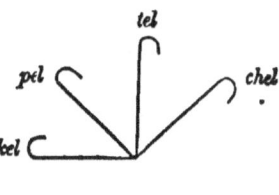

And if the *right* hand be held up and turned in the same way, the outlines of *ker, per, ter,* and *cher* will be formed; thus,

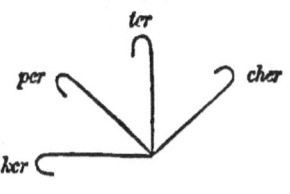

Observe that the *Left hand* (which word commences with *L*) is associated with the *el*-hook, and the *Right hand* (which commences with *R*. with the *er*-hook.

VOCALIZATION OF DOUBLE CONSONANT-SIGNS.

§ 147. The double consonant-signs of the *el* and *er* hook series are vocalized the same as if they were simple stems; thus, -| *ode*, ·| *odor*, ⟍ *pay*, ⟍ *play*.

ORDER OF READING VOCALIZED DOUBLE CONSONANT-SIGNS.

§ 148. If a vowel be placed to the left of a perpendicular or inclined double consonant-sign of the *el* or *er* hook series, or above a horizontal, it is read *before* both elements of the compound ; thus, ⌒ *oval,* ⌒ *eagle ;* if it be placed to the right of a perpendicular or inclined sign, or under a horizontal, it is read *after* both elements ; thus, ⟍ *pray* ⌐ *glow.*

§ 149. A vowel may be placed on each side of a double consonant sign ; thus, ⌣ *only.*

§ 150. If a distinct vowel-sound is heard between the liquid and the preceding consonant, each must be written by its stem-sign ; thus, ⤳ *pail,* ⤳ *feel,* ⤳ *fool,* ⟍ *bore.*

USES OF THE EL AND ER HOOK SIGNS.

§ 151. The double signs of the *el* and *er* hook series are used principally for such close combinations of the liquids with other consonants as occur at the commencement of the words *clay, grow, flow, pry, brow,* etc. ; but·they are also generally used where there is a slight unaccented vowel separating the liquid from the preceding consonant, as in ⟍ *apple,* ⤳ *evil,* ⌒ *every.*

EL OR ER HOOK SIGNS JOINED TO PRECEDING STEMS.

§ 152. An *el* or *er* hook sign may be joined to a preceding stem without raising the pen from the paper ; thus, ⤳ *knuckle,* ⟍ *busily,* ⤳ *caper,* ⤳ *copper,* ⤳ *razor.*

§ 153. But when an *el* or *er* hook comes on the outside of a right or an acute angle, formed by two straight stems, and sometimes when it occurs after the *ess*-circle, the hook can not be perfectly formed without interfering with speed. In such cases, however, a slight offset or shoulder serves instead of a hook ; thus, ⤳ *reply,* ⎸ *tiger,* ⌐ *checker,* ⤳ *gospel,* ⤳ *registry.*

§ 154. The rules for the use of *ish, shee,* etc., commencing on page 45, also apply when those stems are modified by initial hooks ; thus, ⤳ *official,* ⤳ *officially,* ⤳ *fisher,* ⤳ *fishery.*

EXCEPTION—REL.

§ 155. The sign ⁄ *rel,* however, is generally preferred at the end of a consonant outline, whether the word ends with a vowel or not ; thus, ⟍ *pearl,* ⟍ *pearly,* ⤳ *nearly,* ⌣ *furl,* ⤳ *girl.*

SPECIAL VOCALIZATION.

§ 156. For the sake of obtaining briefer and more convenient outlines, double consonant-signs are occasionally used even where there is
a distinct vowel-sound between the two consonants they represent.
When necessary, such intervening vowel may be represented as follows:

I. DOT-VOWELS are indicated by a small circle, written in the three
vowel positions and placed *before* the double sign for the long vowels,
and *after* it for the short vowels; thus, ..].. *dear,* [. *tell,* ..[... *till.* But
when the position of the consonant-signs renders it inconvenient to observe this rule, the circle may be written on either side for a long or a
short vowel; thus, ⁓ː⁓ *engineer.*

II. DASH VOWELS and DIPHTHONGS are struck through the double
consonant-sign; thus, ⌐₊ *coal,* ⌐₊₀ *coarse,* .:⁓].. *endure.* When a
hook would interfere with the striking of a vowel-sign through the stem,
it may be written at the end; thus, ⌐⁓ *call,* ⁓⁓ *empire.*

TWO FORMS FOR SL, SR, ZL, ZR.—THEIR USES AT THE COMMENCEMENT OF WORDS.

§ 157. The signs for *l* and *r* with the *ess*-circle prefixed, and the stems
ess and *zee* with the *el* and *er* hooks, give two modes of representing the
combinations *sl, sr, zl,* and *zr;* thus, ⌐ *slee,* ⁓ *see-er,*) *sel,*) *ser,*
) *zel,*) *zer.* According to the rules laid down at §§ 110, 113, and 114,
the above forms that have the initial circle should be used in words
that begin with the sound of *ess;* thus, ⌐ *sail,* ⁓ *soar;* the forms *sel*
and *ser,* when an *ess*-sound is the first consonant in a word that commences with a vowel; thus, ') *assail,* ·) *acer;* and the forms *zel* and
zer, when a *zee*-sound is the first consonant in a word, whether there be
an initial vowel or not; thus, .).. *easel,* .).. *zeal,*) *Ezra.*

THE ESS-CIRCLE PREFIXED TO THE EL AND ER HOOK SIGNS.

§ 158. The *ess*-circle may be prefixed to all the *el*-hook signs, and
to the *curved er*-hook signs, both at the commencement and in the
middle of words, by turning it on the inside of the hook; thus, ⌐
skel, ⁓ *spel,* ℂ *sfel,* (° *sthel,* ⁓ *serl,* ⌐ *smel,* ⌐ *snel,* ⌐ *sfer,* ⌐
singr, ⌐ *smer.*

§ 159. A loop or large circle is never prefixed to any of the *el*-hook
signs, or to an *er*-hook sign on curves.

THE CIRCLES AND ST LOOP PREFIXED TO THE STRAIGHT ER-HOOK SIGNS.

§ 160. The two circles and the *st* loop are prefixed to the straight *er*-hook signs, both at the commencement and in the middle of words, by merely writing them on the *er*-hook side of the stems, or, in other words, by making the hook into a small circle, a large circle, or a loop, as the case may be ; thus, ＼ *per*, ＼ *sper*, ＼ *sis-per*, ＼ *steper*, ＿ *kay-sker*, ⌊ *tee-sker*, ∠ *chay-sper*, ＼ *pee-sker*, ＼ *pee-sper*, ⊄ *dee-sis-ter*.

§ 161. The classes of signs treated of at §§ 158 and 160 may be called respectively the " *spel* series" and the " *sper* series."

ORDER OF READING VOCALIZED SPEL AND SPER SIGNS.

§ 162. When signs of the *spel* and *sper* series are vocalized, the consonants and vowels are read in the following order: *firstly*, the initial circle or loop ; *secondly*, all vowels written before the stem ; *thirdly*, the stem with its hook, and the intervening vowel, if there be one ; and, *fourthly*, any vowel written after the stem ; thus, ＼ *sable*, ＼ *saber*, ＼ *spray*, ＼ *supply*, ＼ *suspire*, ·ƒ *stager*, ⌊ *disclosed*, ⌊ *disgrace*, ＼ *prosper*, ⊄ *disaster*.

§ 163. Sometimes, in the middle of words, it is more convenient to express both the circle and the *er*-hook distinctly ; thus, ＼ *express*, ⌐ *extreme*.

§ 164. The consonant *r* may generally be omitted from the syllables *scribe* and *scrip*, in such words as *describe, prescribe, proscribe, description*, etc. ; thus, ⌐ *describe*.

THE WAY HOOK.

§ 165. The semi-consonant sound *way*, when preceded by several of the consonants, also coalesces with them in a manner similar to the liquids *l* and *r*, as in the words *twist, request*, etc. To represent these combinations, a large initial hook is used on the *el*-hook side of any straight consonant ; thus, ⊂ *kay-w*, ⊂ *gay-w*, ⌠ *tee-w*.

§ 166. These signs may be named *kwee, gwee, twee*, etc. They are vocalized the same as the *kel* and *ker* series ; and the *ess*-circle is prefixed to them the same as to the *kel* signs.

EXAMPLES : ⌠ *twice*, ⌐ *acquire*, ⌐ *quick*, ⌐ *squaw*, ⌐ *request*

THE YAY HOOK.

§ 167. For stenographic reasons, the consonant *yay* is expressed by a large hook on the *er*-hook side of the straight stems ; thus, ⊂ *kay-y*,

⌐ *lee-y*, ⟍ *bee-y*. The use of this hook will be fully explained hereafter, it being seldom employed, except in phrase writing.

HOOK FOR EN, IN, OR UN.

§ 168. The syllables *en*, *in*, and *un* may be prefixed to the straight
treble signs of the "*sper* series," by turning a small backward hook on
the *el*-hook side of the stem; and to curved stems with initial circles,
by turning a similar hook on the outside of the curve; thus, ⟍ *inscribe*, ⟍ *unstrung*, ⟍ *enslave*.

NAME AND USE OF THE INITIAL EN-HOOK.

§ 169. This hook may be called either the *in*, *en*, or *un* hook, according to which of those syllables it represents. It is used before any
straight stem of the "*sper* series," and before any curved stem that is
the arc of a circle struck in the direction opposite to that of the stem *en*.

FINAL HOOKS.

EF AND VEE HOOKS.

§ 170. *Ef* or *vee* may be added to any straight stem (whether it be
simple, or have an initial *hook*, *circle*, or *loop*) by a small final hook on
the circle side; thus, ⟋ *kay-f* or *v*, ⎮ *tee-f* or *v*, ⟋ *chay-f* or *v*, ⟍ *bee-f* or
v, ⟋ *ger-f* or *v*, ⟋ *sek-f* or *v*, ⟍ *slep-f* or *v*.

NAMES OF THE EF-HOOK COMPOUNDS.

§ 171. These compounds may be named respectively *kef*, *tef*, *chef*,
bef, *gref*, *skef*, *slepef*.

VOCALIZATION.—RULE FOR WRITING.

§ 172. When a vowel occurs between the consonant represented by
the stem-sign and the *ef* or *vee* indicated by the hook, the vowel-sign
is written to the stem as if no hook were affixed; thus, ⟍ *pay*, ⟍ *pave*.

RULE FOR READING.

§ 173. A vowel-sign written to a stem that has an *ef* or *vee* hook, is
always read before the hook; thus, ⎮ *deaf*, ⟋ *cave*.

EF AND VEE DISTINGUISHED.

§ 174 When great exactness is required, the hook may be made
heavy for *vee*; thus, ⟍ *prove*, instead of ⟍ *proof*. But generally
no confusion will result from using the light-hook for both *ef* and *vee*.

§ 175. A long narrow hook may be written to the curved stems for *ef* or *vee*; thus, (*dhef*, *mef*. This hook should, however, be used very sparingly by inexperienced phonographers. It is principally used by reporters in phrase writing.

EN HOOK.

§ 176. The consonant *en* may be joined to any straight stem (whether simple, or compounded with an initial *hook, circle*, or *loop*) by a small final hook on the side opposite the *ef*-hook; and to any curved consonant, by a small final hook on the concave side; thus, *kay-n*, *tee-n*, *ef-n*, *lee-n*.

§ 177. The *en*-hook signs are named in a manner similar to the *ef*-hook signs; thus, the characters in the last section are called respectively *ken, ten, fen, len*. The signs *el-n, ish-n, shee-n, er-n, ree-n* are called *el'n, shen, sheen, ern, ren*.

§ 178. The *en*-hook signs are vocalized the same as those of the *ef* hook; thus, *cane*, *attain*, *shown*, *vain*, *flown*.

§ 179. When *ef, vee*, or *en* is the final consonant-sound in a word that ends with a vowel, the stem-sign must be used, because the hook does not furnish the requisite position for the sign of such final vowel; thus, *cough*, *coffee*, *grave*, *gravy*, *men*, *many*.

SHUN HOOKS.

§ 180. The syllables *shun* or *zhun*, as heard in *nation, fusion*, etc., may be added to any straight stem by a large final hook on the *ef*-hook side; and to any curved stem, by a large final hook on the concave side; thus, *kay-shun*, *ef-shun*.

§ 181. The *shun*-hook signs are named as follows: kay-shun is called *keshun*; ef-shun, *feshun*; el-shun, *elshun*; lee-shun, *leshun*; em-shun, *meshun*, etc.

§ 182. The *shun*-hook signs are vocalized the same as the *ef* and *en* hook signs; thus, *caution*, *occasion*, *motion*, *nation*, *fashion*.

§ 183. If it should be necessary to distinguish between *shun* and *zhun*, the hook may be thickened for the latter; thus, ⟨⟩ *evasion*, in stead of ⟨⟩ *ovation*, which words, in unvocalized phonography, might in rare instances be confounded.

§ 184. In the common orthography, the two sounds represented by this hook are indicated by a variety of spelling, as *tion* in *notion*, *cean* in *ocean*, *ssion* in *mission*, *sion* in *fusion*, *shion* in *fashion*, *cian* in *logician*, *sian* in *Persian*, etc.

§ 185. When *ish* and *en* final are the only consonant-sounds in a word, the sign ⟨⟩ *shen* must be used; thus, ⟨⟩ *ocean*. *Shen* should also be used when the only other consonants in the word are represented by an initial small or large circle; thus, ⟨⟩ *session*, ⟨⟩ *secession*.

§ 186. The word *ocean*, and any similar word, may, however, be represented by the *shun*-hook by joining it to the preceding word; thus, ⟨⟩ *Pacific Ocean*.

§ 187. The syllable *shun* or *zhun* may be added to any stem that has a final circle or loop, by turning a small hook on the back of the stem; thus, ⟨⟩ *kess-shun*, ⟨⟩ *fess-shun*, etc. This may be called the *ishun*-hook. It may be vocalized by writing a first or second place vowel *before* the hook, and a third-place vowel *after* it; thus, ⟨⟩ *accession*, ⟨⟩ *physician*. But *ishun* may generally be left unvocalized without endangering the legibility of the writing; thus, ⟨⟩ *cessation*.

HOOK FOR TR, THR, OR DHR. ⟨⟩

§ 188. The compounds *tr*, *thr*, and *dhr*, with any intervening vowel, may be added to any straight sign by a large final hook on the *en*-hook side; thus, ⟨⟩ *kay-tr*, ⟨⟩ *tee-tr*; and such combinations are vocalized the same as those of the other final hooks; thus, ⟨⟩ *eater*, ⟨⟩ *actor*, ⟨⟩ *clatter*, ⟨⟩ *equator*, ⟨⟩ *gather*, ⟨⟩ *rather*.

§ 189. This hook may be called *ter*, *ther*, or *dher*; and its compounds may be named like those of the *ess*-circle, or those of the *en* and *ef* hooks; thus kay-ter or -dher is called *ketter* or *kedher*; gay-ter or-dher, *getter* or *gedher*; ree-ter or -dher, *retter* or *redher*, etc.

§ 190. This hook is used for *tr* or *dhr*, the combination *dr* being written with the stem ⟨⟩ *der*.

§ 191. Whenever it is necessary to express a vowel or diphthong that occurs between the *tee* and *er* sounds represented by the *ter*-hook, it may be done in accordance with the rule for "special vocalization" at § 156, or, if it belong to the third position, by writing it within the hook; thus, ⹋ *creature.*

CIRCLES AND LOOPS ADDED TO THE FINAL HOOK SIGNS.

ESS-CIRCLE ADDED TO THE EF, SHUN, TER, AND CURVED EN HOOK SIGNS.

§ 192. The *ess*-circle (but not the loops or large circle) may be added to an *ef*, *shun*, or *ter* hook, and to an *en*-hook on a curved sign, by writing it inside the hook; thus, ⹋ *caves,* ⹋ *occasions,* ⹋ *fashions,* ⹋ *actors,* ⹋ *vanes.*

CIRCLES AND LOOPS ADDED TO THE STRAIGHT EN-HOOK SIGNS.

§ 193. All the circles and loops may be added to the straight *en*-hook signs by simply writing them on the *en*-hook side, without attempting to show the form of the hook; thus, ⹋ *pun,* ⹋ *puns,* ⹋ *punster,* ⹋-*dunce,* ⹋- *dunces,* ⹋ *against.*

NAMES OF THE COMBINATIONS OF STEMS, FINAL HOOKS, AND CIRCLES OR LOOPS.

§ 194. These compounds are named by adding the sound of the circle or loop to the name of the sign to which it is affixed; thus, kef-s is called *kefs;* keshun-s, *keshuns;* ketter-s, *ketters;* ven-s, *vens;* ken-s, *kens;* ken-ss, *kensis;* ken-st, *kenst;* ken-str, *kenster.* The circles and loops on the *en*-hook side and end of straight stems are also called the *ens* and *ensis* circles, and the *enst* and *enster* loops.

CAUTION.—EN-HOOK CIRCLES SELDOM USED IN THE MIDDLE OF WORDS.

§ 195. The *en*-hook circles and loops should never be used in the middle of words, except that *ens* may in a few instances be written, when the direction of the stems between which it occurs permits both the circle and hook to be distinctly formed; thus, ⹋ *ransom,* ⹋ *gainsaid.* Therefore, such outlines as ⹋ *dess-kay,* ⹋ *kessis-ree,* ⹋ *pee-sper,* ⹋ *kay-sker,* etc., must not be read respectively *dens-kay,* *kensis-ree, penspee, kens-kay,* etc.

ESS-CIRCLE USED FOR ENS.

§ 196. In the middle of a few words the simple *ess*-circle may be used for *ens* without endangering the legibility of the writing, the *en* being omitted from the word; thus, $\mathcal{L}$ *transpose.* And, in a few instances, the *ess*-circle may be so used in connection with a succeeding straight sign from which an *r*-hook is omitted in accordance with § 164; thus, $\mathcal{L}$ *transgress.* But the *ens*-circle may sometimes be distinctly written when it can be turned on the back of a succeeding curve; thus, $\mathcal{L}$ *dancing.*

THE ESS-CIRCLE AND ISHUN ADDED TO THE EN-HOOK CIRCLES AND LOOPS.

§ 197. The *ess*-circle and *ishun* may be added to the *en*-hook circles and loops by turning them on the opposite side of the stem; thus, $\mathcal{V}$ *punsters,* $\mathcal{L}$ *transition.*

THE ESS-CIRCLE ADDED TO ISHUN.

§ 198. The *ess*-circle may be added to *ishun* by turning it inside the hook; thus, $\mathcal{L}$ *physicians,* $\mathcal{L}$ *transitions.*

FINAL HOOKS USED IN THE MIDDLE OF WORDS.

§ 199. When more convenient, the final hooks may be used in the middle of words instead of the stem-signs; thus, $\mathcal{L}$ *cover,* $\mathcal{L}$ *cunning,* $\mathcal{L}$ *national,* $\mathcal{L}$ *processional,* $\mathcal{L}$ *transitional.*

CIRCLE INSIDE OF HOOKS.

§ 200. When the *ess*-circle is written inside of the hooks, it may be made a little smaller than usual, and it is not essential that it should be a perfect circle, as there is no danger of its being confused with the loops, which are never so used.

LENGTHENING.

DOUBLE-LENGTH CURVED SIGNS.

§ 201. Doubling the length of any curved sign adds either *tr, dr, thr,* or *dhr;* thus, $\mathcal{L}$ *en-tr,* etc.

NAMES OF DOUBLE-LENGTH CURVES.

§ 202. The double-length curved signs, like the *ter*-hook combinations, are named generally by inserting the vowel sound *ĕ* between the sound of the simple stem and the added consonants or syllable; thus, ef-tr is called *fetter;* ef-dr, *fedder;* ef-dhr, *fedher;* em-tr, *metter;* way-dhr, *wedher;* hay-tr, *hetter;* en-dr, *nedder.* But ish-tr, shee-tr, el-tr, lee-tr, er-tr, and ing-tr are named respectively *ishter, sheeter, elter, leeter, erter,* and *ingter.*

POSITIONS OF LENGTHENED STEMS.

§ 203. Some phonographic writers indicate any given position of a

lengthened curve by commencing it at the same point in relation to the
line of writing that the single length of the same stem is commenced
at for the same position. But the following rule is found to give
greater distinctness and increased legibility to these signs.

POSITIONS OF HORIZONTAL STEMS.

§ 204. The positions of horizontal double-length curves are necessarily the same as those of single lengths ; thus,

FIRST POSITION : ⌢ *metler,* ⌣ *netler.*

SECOND POSITION : ⌢ *metler,* ⌣ *ingter.*

THIRD POSITION : .... *hetler,* .... *netler.*

POSITIONS OF DOWNWARD LENGTHENED CURVES.

§ 205. The positions of downward double-length curves are as
follows :

FIRST POSITION.—The lower end resting on the line ; thus, ⌊....
vetler, ⌋ *ishter.*

SECOND POSITION.—Divided by the line into two equal parts ; thus,
·(··· *dhetler.*

THIRD POSITION.—About two thirds of the sign below the line ; thus,
··⌊··· *fetler,* ·(·· *thetter,* ···)·· *ishter.*

POSITIONS OF UPWARD LENGTHENED CURVES.

§ 206. The positions of upward double-length curves are as follows :

FIRST POSITION.—Commencing about one third the length of a *tee*
above the line ; thus, ⌐ *leeter.*

SECOND POSITION.—Commencing at the line ; thus, ⌐ *lecter.*

THIRD POSITION.—Commencing about one third the length of a *tee*
below the line ; thus, ..⌐... *leeter.*

VOCALIZATION OF LENGTHENED CURVES.

§ 207. Any vowel or diphthong sign written to a lengthened curve
is read before the added consonants *tr, dr,* or *dhr ;* thus, ⌣ *under*
⌐ *letler,* ⌢ *mother.*

FINAL HOOKS READ BEFORE THE ADDED CONSONANTS.

§ 208. The power of any final hook on a lengthened curve takes
effect before the added consonants *tr, dr, thr,* or *dhr ;* thus, ⌐ *slender,*
⌐ *tormentor.*

LENGTHENING OF STRAIGHT STEMS WITH FINAL HOOKS.

§ 209. It is allowable also to lengthen any straight stem, *provided it has a final hook*, to add *tr*, *dr*, or *thr*; thus, ⟋ *render*, ⟋ *rafter*. This new principle improves the outlines of a great many words by de- creasing the number of strokes required to write them, and introduces a large number of improved and valuable outlines in phraseography, as will be seen hereafter. The principle can not be applied with safety to other straight stems than those with final hooks; and, indeed, it is not needed by them, as they are already supplied with other means of indicating final *ter*, *ther*, etc.

FINAL CIRCLE OR LOOP TO BE READ AFTER THE ADDED CONSONANTS.

§ 210. A final circle or loop is read after the added consonants *tr*, *dr*, etc.; thus, ⟋ *matters*, ⟋ *mothers*, ⟋ *cylinders*.

SPECIAL VOCALIZATION.

§ 211. A vowel or diphthong occurring immediately before the final *r* of a lengthened curve may be written in accordance with the rule for "special vocalization" at § 156; thus, ⟋ *entire*, ⟋ *adventure*.

HALVING.

HALF-LENGTH STEMS.

§ 212. Either *tee* or *dee* may be added by halving to any consonant- sign, whether simple or compounded with an initial circle or loop, or with any hook, final as well as initial; thus, ⟋ *kay-t*, ⟋ *sek-t*, ⟋ *stek-t*, ⟋ *sis-pee-t*, ⟋ *sker-t*, ⟋ *kel-t*, ⟋ *ker-t*, ⟋ *kwee-t*, ⟋ *pef-t*, ⟋ *pen-t*, ⟋ *peshun-t*, ⟋ *petter-t*, ⟋ *plen-t*, ⟋ *pren-t*, ⟋ *spen-t*.

NAMES OF THE HALF-LENGTH SIGNS.

§ 213. The half-length compounds are named by pronouncing the vowel *ĕ* with the consonants represented by the sign, the vowel being placed where it will make the most easily uttered name; thus, the half lengths at § 212 are respectively called *ket*, *sekt* or *sket*, *stekt*, *sis-pet*, *skret* or *skert*, *klet* or *kelt*, *kert* or *kret*, *kwet*, *peft*, *pent*, *peshunt*, *petterd*, *plent*, *prent*, *spent*. But the stems *ess*, *ish*, *shee*, *el*, *lee*, *er*, and *ree*, when halved are named, respectively, *est*, *isht*, *sheet*, *elt*, *leet*, *ert*, and *reet*.

CAUTION.—HALVING OF STEMS WITH FINAL CIRCLES OR LOOPS ATTACHED.

§ 214. It will be observed that when a stem with any final hook is halved, the added *tee* or *dee* is read after both stem and hook; but when a stem with a final circle or loop is halved, the added *tee* or *dee* must be read immediately before the circle or loop. In other words, final circles and loops are added to the half-length signs in the same manner as to the full-length stems; thus, ___ kay-s (*kess*), ___ kay-t-s (*kets*), ___ der-f-s (*drefs*), ___ der-f-t-s (*drefts*), ___ kay-n-s (*kens*), ___ kay-n-t-s (*kents*), ___ em-st (*mest*), ___ em-t-st (*metst* or *medst*).

POSITIONS OF HALF-LENGTH STEMS.

HORIZONTAL STEMS.

§ 215. The positions of half-length horizontals are, of course, the same as the positions of the full-length horizontals (see § 61); thus,

FIRST POSITION : ⌒ *met*, ⌣ *sent*, ⌐ *kent*.

SECOND POSITION : ⌣ *net*, ⌐ *gent*, ⌣ *ingt*.

THIRD POSITION : .... *ingt*, ... *sent*, ... *get*.

PERPENDICULAR AND INCLINED STEMS.

§ 216. The positions of perpendicular and inclined stems are as follows:

FIRST POSITION.—Above the line, the lower end of the stem distant from it about one half the length of a *tee*; thus, | *tet*, ⟍ *brent*, ⌐ *teft*, ⟋ *reets*, ⟍ *jent*, ⌐ *dent*.

SECOND POSITION.—Resting on the line; thus, ∫ *stent*, ⟍ *jent*, ⌐ *dent*.

THIRD POSITION.—Just below the line; thus, ·⌐· *tlent*, ·⌐· *dent*.

§ 217. Half-lengths in the third position should always be written close to the line, so that they will not conflict with the fourth position, which will be explained hereafter.

VOCALIZED HALF-LENGTH SIGNS.—ORDER OF READING.

§ 218. A vocalized half-length sign is read in the following order: *First*, the stem (with its hooks, initial circle or loop, if there be any) and its vowel-signs, in accordance with rules heretofore given, the same as if it had not been halved; *second*, the *tee* or *dee* added by halving; and, *third*, the final circle or loop, if there be any.

EXAMPLES: ___ *get*, |. *date*, ___ *sect*, ___ *plate*, ___ *prate*, ___ *hurt*, ___ *word*, ___ *settled*, ___ *sobered*, ___ *trained*, ___ *sprained*, ___ *patient*, ___ *blend*, ___ *blends*, ___ *friend*, ___ *ancient*, ___ *brands*, ___ *stand*, ___ *approved*, ___ *efficient*.

DEE AND TEE DISTINGUISHED.

§ 219. When a stem with an *en*-hook is halved, if it be deemed desirable ever to distinguish whether the added sound be *dee* or *tee*, it may

be done by shading the hook for *dee;* thus, ⟍ *pained,* instead of ⟍ *paint.*
This distinction is, however, seldom necessary in practice, the context
being generally a sufficient guide.

§ 220. The half-length signs may be joined with other signs, whether
of the same or different lengths, or whether simple or compound; and
they may be used either at the *beginning,* in the *middle,* or at the *end*
of words.

EXAMPLES: ⌒ *bottom,* ⌒ *fortified,* ⌒ *affidavit,* ⌒ *sentiment,*
/⌒ *reputable,* ⌒ *puzzled,* ⌒ *named,* ⌒ *muzzled.*

SPECIAL REMARKS UPON THE HALF-LENGTHS.

IMPROPER JOININGS.

§ 221. A full-length and a half-length stem must not be joined, if
one or both be straight, or if both be curved, but are arcs of circles
struck in the same direction, except they form an angle at the point
of junction; for instance, *kay* and *ket, lee* and *ket, ef* and *ket,* etc., are not
allowable combinations, because it is difficult to distinguish such signs,
on the one hand, from a full-length stem, and on the other hand, from
two full-length stems. Thus, *kay-ket* joined, might be supposed to be
kay made a little too long, or *kay-kay* made too short. In these cases
the full-length stems should be used; thus, write ⌐ not ⌐ for
correct, ⌐ not ⌐ for *liked,* ⌐ not ⌐ for *effect.*

SHT AFTER EF OR VEE.

§ 222. When the combination *sht* is immediately preceded by *ef* or
vee, it must be represented either by the full-length stems *shee-tee,* or
by the downward half-length *isht;* thus, ⌒ *lavished,* ⌒ *fished.*

STRAIGHT HALF-LENGTHS IN SAME DIRECTION NOT ALLOWED.

§ 223. Two straight half-lengths running in the same direction can
not of course be joined, because they would appear the same as one full-
length stem; thus, | is *dee,* not *ded-ded.* To avoid the inconvenience
of disjoining in such cases, the first compound should be written with
full-length stems, and the other with a half-length, as in the word
⌐ *catgut.*

SYLLABLES -TED AND -DED.

§ 224. The syllables *-ted* and *-ded,* terminating adjectives and the
perfect participle and preterit of regular verbs, are generally written
with the signs *ted* and *ded,* without regard to the manner of writing
the primitive word; thus, write ⌐ *act,* but ⌐ not ⌐ for *acted;* ⌐
goad, but ⌐ not ⌐ for *goaded.*.

HALF-LENGTHS DISJOINED.

§ 225. Sometimes it is necessary to detach a half-length from the preceding stem, or else to write its equivalent full-length stems; thus

|ᵢ. *dated,* ＼ᵢ. *waited,* ¹ᵢ. *dreaded.*

EST STRUCK UPWARD.

§ 226. Occasionally, when it is difficult or inconvenient to join the half-length *est* to a final *shun* or *en* hook, it is allowable to strike it upward; thus, ⌣ *factionist,* ·⟨⟩··· *elocutionist.*

MEDIAL VOWEL AFTER HALF-LENGTH.

§ 227. When a vowel occurs immediately after *tee* or *dee* added by halving, if the next succeeding consonant-sign be a circle or loop, there is no position in which to write the vowel-sign, and it must be omitted; as the first *i* in ⟨⟩ *anticipate.* But if the next consonant after a *tee* or *dee* sound be written with a stem-sign, the vowel may be written to that; thus, ·ᵧ···· *esteem.*

STEM-SIGNS FOR TEE OR DEE BEFORE A FINAL VOWEL.

§ 228. When either *tee* or *dee* is the last consonant-sound in a word, of which the final element is a vowel, it should be written with the stem-sign, because, if the halving principle were used, no vowel-position would be provided for the sign of the final vowel; thus, ·⌐ᵢ·· *into.* The same is also true when a word ends with a circle or loop preceded by *tee* or *dee,* with an intervening vowel; thus, ·⌐ᵢ·· *induce.* This rule gives a distinction by outline between such words as ··⟩·· *pity* and ·ᵧ·· *pit,* ¬⌐. *notice* and ᵧ *notes,* etc.

AMBIGUOUS OUTLINES.—HOW AVOIDED.

§ 229. The use of the halving principle to indicate both *tee* and *dee* will sometimes give the same form for two different words; thus, ⌐ may be either *got* or *God,* ＼ either *bat* or *bad;* but, in the great majority of cases, the context will show which word is intended. If, however, it should ever be deemed desirable to distinguish between such words, the consonant *tee* may be indicated by halving, and *dee* written with the full stem-sign; thus, ＼ *pate,* as distinguished from ＼ *paid;* though, generally, no ambiguity would arise from writing *paid* the same as *pate,* and so with most other words of the same class.

HALF-LENGTH LEE FOR LT.

§ 230. Half-length *lee*, when standing alone, is used for *lt*, and not for *ld*—as in the words *light, late, let*, etc.

THE STEMS LEE-DEE FOR LD.

§ 231. In words containing only the consonants *ld*—as *lad, lady, old*, etc.—the stem signs *lee-dee* are used.

HALF-LENGTH REE FOR RT, ETC.

§ 232. Half-length *ree*, when standing alone, is used for *rt*, and not for *rd*, the latter being written with the stem-signs *ree-dee;* thus, ⟋ *rate*, ⟋ *raid*. But after another consonant-stem, *ree* may be halved to add either a *tee* or *dee* sound; thus, ⌒⟍ *mart* or *marred*, ⌣ *fired*.

TWO VOWELS BEFORE FINAL TEE OR DEE.

§ 233. When the sound of *tee* or *dee* is immediately preceded by two vowels, the stem-sign should be used; thus, ⟍⟍ *poet*. This rule, and the one given at § 232, secures a distinction by outline between such words as ⟋ *right*, ⟋ *ride*, and ⟋ *riot*.

FINAL DEE PRECEDED BY EL, REE, OR EN, ETC.

§ 234. When the sound of *dee* is final, and is preceded by either *lee, ree,* or *en*, which is itself both preceded and followed by a vowel, the *stem*-sign should generally be used; thus, ⌐⌐ *solid*, ⌐⌐ *tarried*, ⌒⌐ *moneyed*.

UPWARD AND DOWNWARD STEMS HALVED.

§ 235. When convenient, the rules for the use of upward and downward stems (see page 45 and onward) should be observed when those stems are halved; thus, ⟍ *pulled*, ⟍ *appellate*.

GROUP VOWELS AND THEIR SIGNS.— IMPROPER DIPHTHONGS.

GENERAL REMARKS.

§ 236. As has been before remarked, there are but four proper diph-thongs recognized in our language. These diphthongs and their signs have been already fully treated of at page 30 and onward. We have, however, many other double vowels that do not come strictly within the definition of proper diphthongs, but which are yet so like them in their nature, and are of such frequent occurrence in words, that it has been found convenient to represent them in a similar manner, and to give them signs that may be made with facility and without taking off the pen.

§ 237. These double sounds differ from the *close* or *proper* diphthongs in having a less intimate connection of their components; they may, therefore, be termed *open* or *improper* diphthongs.

COALESCENCE OF THE DOUBLE VOWELS.

§ 238. The degree of intimacy with which these double sounds co-alesce varies in different words. Sometimes they approach very nearly to the character of close diphthongs, as, for instance, the sounds of *ah-i* in the word *aye* (yes), or *oo-i* in *Louis*, etc. ; while in other words the two concurrent vowels are entirely severed, as *ah-i* in hurra*hi*ng, *oo-i* in co*oi*ng, etc. When, however, the primary accent of the word falls upon the second of the two vowel-sounds, as in *deistic*, the most com-plete separation occurs, and they cease in any degree to resemble proper diphthongs, except in the fact that they are two vowels pronounced in succession, with no consonant intervening.

COMPOSITION OF THE DOUBLE VOWELS.

§ 239. It will also be seen that in nearly all of the double vowels, whether they are close or open diphthongs, the short sound i is one of the elements, being united, either initially or finally, with some one of the other vowel-sounds of the scale, as well as with another i sound.

REMARKS ON THE DOUBLE-VOWEL SIGNS.

§ 240. The *improper diphthongs*, like the *proper diphthongs*, are repre-sented by small angular characters, which are written to the consonant-stem in the position of the distinguishing vowel, or the vowel with which the sound i is joined. The first or second stroke of the sign is made *heavy*, according as the first or second vowel of the combination is *long*. The signs representing the *dot-vowels* in combination with i open *upward* and *downward*, while those representing the *dash-vowels* so combined, open to the *right* and *left*. In the table below, at the right of each sign are placed the letters that represent its two sounds; and under the sign is given a word in which they are heard. We have not been able to find any English word containing the double sounds *ŭ-ĭ*, as represented at No. 17, and some of the others occur very rarely; but they, together with the proper diphthongs, ɪ, oɪ, ow, and ɛw, have been inserted in their appropriate places in order to make a complete exhibit of the scheme of double-vowel signs. The learner will observe that the compound *ĭ-ĭ* has given to it two signs, Nos. 6 and 12. These are so exhibited, because the mode of constructing the scale gives such a result; but, as in practice only one sign would be required for those sounds, the sign No. 12 may be invariably used for them, and No. 6 used for the diphthong ɪ when it will be more convenient than its proper sign, No. 4, of the first position. The diphthong ɛw has also two signs, Nos. 21 and 24, the first representing the sound of the diphthong in accented, and the latter in unaccented syllables; but in ordinary practice, No. 24 is employed in all cases, whether the syllable be accented or not. By bearing in mind that the double-vowel signs are arranged in the precise order of the scale of simple vowels, the learner will be greatly aided in committing them to memory.

TABLE OF DOUBLE-VOWEL SIGNS.

DOT-VOWELS.

1.	2.	8.	4.	5.	6.
ᵛ⦙ *ah-ĭ*,	v⦙ *ā-ĭ*,	⦙ *ē-ĭ*,	ᵛ⦙ *ă-ĭ* (ɪ), v⦙ *ĕ-ĭ*,		v⦙ *ĭ-ĭ*, (ɪ)
hurra*h*ing,	say*i*ng,	see*i*ng,	*I*,	hyg*ei*st,	

7.	8.	9.	10.	11.	12.
ᴧ⦙ *ĭ-ah*,	ᴧ⦙ *ĭ-ā*,	ᴧ⦙ *ĭ-ē*,	ᴧ⦙ *ĭ-ŭ*,	ᴧ⦙ *ĭ-ĕ*,	ᴧ⦙ *ĭ-ĭ*,
*I*ago,	op*i*ate,	hyg*ie*ne,	man*ia*c,	carr*ie*r,	carr*yi*ng

DASH-VOWELS.

18.	14.	15.	16.	17.	18.
ᶜ⦙ *aw-ĭ*,	<⦙ *ŏ-ĭ*,	⦙ *oo-ĭ*,	ᶜ⦙ *ŏ-ĭ* (oɪ),<⦙ *ŭ-ĭ*,		<⦙ *ŏŏ-ĭ*,
saw*i*ng,	go*i*ng,	do*i*ng,	o*i*l,		Bedou*i*ns,

19.	20.	21.	22.	23.	24.
>⦙ *ĭ-aw*,	>⦙ *ĭ-ō*,	>⦙ *ĭ-oo* (ɛw),	>⦙ *ĭ-ŏ*,	>⦙ *ĭ-ŭ*,	>⦙ *ĭ-ŏŏ* (ɛw)
carry-*all*,	ol*i*o,	d*u*ly,	id*i*om,	var*i*ous,	resc*ue*.

EXAMPLES : ⌐⦘ *opiate*, ⸌⸱⸱⸱ *officiate*, ⌒⸍ *maniac*, ⟍ *Arabia* ⌣⟋ *Ontario*, ⸱⸐⸱⸱⸱ *idiom*

§ 241. In a similar manner, another series of double signs might also be provided for double vowels having as their basic component the other short close vowel *ŏŏ* ; but it would be of little practical value in writing English, as we have only one instance of such a combination that does not fall within the series given in the above table, namely, the proper diphthong ⁴| *ŏ-ŏŏ* (ow).

SIMPLE SIGNS INSTEAD OF DOUBLE ALLOWABLE.

§ 242. It is not imperative that the double signs should be used: the double vowels may be correctly represented by the simple signs of their elements, written to the consonants in accordance with the principles laid down at §§ 35 and 57 ; thus, we may write ·······⸲· or ⸱⸱⸱⸱⸱⸱⸱⸱· for *cooing*, ⸝⸜ or ⸝⸜ for *clayey*.

TREBLE VOWEL-SIGNS.

§ 243. When the vowel-sound *ĭ* precedes the proper diphthongs ɪ, oɪ, and ow, it may be represented by an initial tick ; thus,

ᴬ| *ĭ*-ɪ,   ²| *ĭ*-oɪ,   ⁴| *ĭ*-ow.

EXAMPLES : ·⸜⸱⸱⸱· *genii*, ⸝⸜ *Honeoye*.

§ 244. When the vowel-sound *ĭ* follows one of the four proper diphthongs, it may be represented by a final tick ; thus,

ᴬ| ɪ-*ĭ*,   ⁵| oɪ-*ĭ*,   ᵇ| ow-*ĭ*,   ₌| ɛw-*ĭ*.

EXAMPLES : ⸜⸝ *vieing*, ⸝⸜ *annoying*, ⸜⸝ *avowing*, ··⸝⸜⸱

renewing, ··|⸳ *dewy*.

SAME SIGNS USED FOR OTHER DOUBLE OR TREBLE VOWELS.

§ 245. No confusion will result in reading if the above series of signs are also sometimes used to represent such double or treble vowels as are composed of an accented long-vowel or diphthong, and *any* short-vowel, except *ŏŏ*; thus, sign No. 14 may be employed for *ō-ĕ* in ⸝ *Owen*. In like manner, sign No. 8 may be used for *ēā* in *creator*, No. 22 for *ĕŏ* in *theology*, etc.

LICENSE AS TO DIRECTION OF THE GROUP-VOWEL SIGNS.

§ 246. When more convenient, the signs opening to the right and left may be inclined a little from the horizontal ; thus, ⁴| oɪ, ⁷| *ĭŏ*, ⁷| oɪ-*ĭ*, as in the words ⸜ *void*, ⸜ *drawing*, ⸝ *showy*, ⸝⸝ *folio*, ⸝⸝ *boyish*. Care must be taken, however, not to incline them so much that they will be liable to be mistaken for those opening upward and downward

ADDITIONAL CONSONANT-SIGNS.

DOT-SIGN FOR H.

§ 247. The consonant *h* is usually written with the stem *hay;* but before *pee* and *bee*, with simple beginning (that is, without initial hooks, circles, or loops) and in the middle of words, when the outline can be shortened or improved thereby, the *h* is either omitted or else written by a dot placed before the following vowel.

EXAMPLES: *heap*, *hub*, *habit*, *perhaps*, *Alhambra*.

TICK OR DOT SIGN WITH WH.

§ 248. In the compound *wh* generally the *h* need not be written. When, however, it is necessary to distinguish between words or names, such as *White* and *Wight*, the *h* may be indicated by prefixing an upright tick to the stem *way*, or by writing a dot between the stem and the following vowel; thus, *whey (way)*, *White (Wight)*.

BRIEF SIGNS FOR W AND Y.

§ 249. Owing to the difficulty of joining a number of the stems to a preceding *way* or *yay*, in the case of a few words a small semicircle is employed as an additional sign for these letters. For *w* it opens to the right (c), and for *y* upward (ᵕ); thus, *waived*, *wash*. These signs are seldom used before any stems but *tee, dee, chay, jay, ef, vee, ith, dhee, ish*, and *zhee*. See § 333.

THE NOMINAL CONSONANT.

§ 250. When a word contains only vowel-sounds, it may be written by placing the vowel-signs to a cancelled *tee* stem ($\top$ $+$ $\bot$); thus, *Eah*, *Io*. This sign is called the Nominal Consonant, and it is used by some in correspondence in writing initials of names.

STENOTYPY.

§ 251. Phonographic outlines may be indicated by the letters of the ordinary printing alphabet in the following manner: Each consonant-sign is represented by the letter or letters of the common alphabet by which it is most readily and naturally suggested. In the following list the phonographic name of each consonant-stem is placed directly under its stenotype.

CONSONANTS.

P	B	T	D	CH	J	K
pee	bee	tee	dee	chay	jay	kay

G	F	V	TH	DH	S	Z
gay	ef	vee	ith	dhee	ess	zee

SH	*SH*	ZH	L	*L*	R	*R*
ish	shee	zhee	el	lee	er	ree

M	N	NG	W	Y	H
em	en	ing	way	yay	hay

'SHEE,' 'LEE,' 'REE,' AND 'ESS.'

§ 252. The stenotypes of the upstroke stems *shee, lee,* and *ree,* are distinguished from *ish, el,* and *er* respectively, by being printed in italics. The stenotype of *ess,* when struck upward, as in ⸱⸱⸝⸱⸱⸱ *elocutionist,* ⸝ *factionist,* etc., should also be printed in italics.

STENOTYPES OF STEMS AND OF CIRCLES, HOOKS, ETC., DISTINGUISHED.

§ 253. The stenotypes of the stem-signs are distinguished from the stenotypes of consonants represented by the circles, loops, and hook modifications, and the dot and tick signs for *hay,* by printing the former in capitals and the latter in small letters; thus, ― K, | D, ∟ F; (sTs,) sSs; ⟋ ssK; ⟋ Kss, ∟ Fss; ⌐ stK, ⌐ Kstr; ⌐ Kl, ⟋ Jl,) ZHl, ⌒ Hl; ― Kr, ⟋ CHr, (THr, ⟍ Wr; ⟍ sPl, ⟍ sFl, ⟍ sFr, ⟍ sPr, ⟍ ssPr, ⟍ stPr; ⌐ Kw, ⸢ Tw; ⟋ Ky, ⟍ By; ⟍ nsKr; ⟍ Kf, (DHf; ⟍ Kn, ⟍ Fn; ⟍ Kshn, ⟍ Fshn; ⟍ Ktr; ⟍ Kfs; ⟍ Pns, ⟍ Pnstr; ⟍ Ntr, ⟍ Fltr, ⟋ Ltr, | Dt, ⟍ Plnt, ⌐ sKt, ⌐ sKrt, ⟍ Prnt, ⟍ Drfts.

§ 254. When a stem modification may be employed to write more than one consonant, or group of consonants, its stenograph may vary accordingly; thus, ⟍ sPs or sPz, ⟍ sNs or sNz, ⟍ Kss, Kez, or Kzz, ⟋ Rst or Rzd; ⟍ Mf or Mv, ⟍ Grf or Grv, ⟍ sKf or sKv, ⟍ Ttr, Tdr, or Tdhr, ⌒ Mtr, Mdr, or Mdhr; ⟍ sPnt or sPnd.

STENOTYPES OF SHADED CIRCLES, ETC.

§ 255. The phonotype of a consonant written with a shaded circle, loop, or hook, may be printed in full-faced type ; thus, *Lz* (laws) *Rzd* (raised); *Rzz* (raises), Prv (prove), *Rdr* (rider). The stenotype of the *ishun*-hook is printed in italics when it occurs after the *ess*-circle ; thus, Ks*shn*, Fz*shn*.

STENOTYPES OF OUTLINES CONTAINING MORE THAN ONE STEM.

§ 256. A *hyphen* is printed between two stenographs (whether of single or group stems) to indicate that the signs they represent are joined ; an *inverted semicolon*, to indicate that they are disjoined and written near each other ; a *colon*, to indicate that they are disjoined, and the second sign written close to, but a little under the first ; an *inverted period*, to indicate that they are disjoined, and the second sign lapped over the first ; and a *cross* (+), to indicate that they are disjoined, and the second sign written through the first. A simple space marks the ordinary separation between words. A numeral just after and generally near the upper part of a stenotype, whether of a simple or compound sign, indicates the position of its phonograph. When no numeral is given, the second position is understood. A stenotype should be named according to the phonographic nomenclature already given.

EXAMPLES : N-V, B-K-M, G-G, F-N, P-B, V-G, H-Z, L-SH, Ks-K, D₃-K, Ps-V, SH-K, SH-K, L-M, L-M, F-R, P-R, K-Pr, P-Rl, nsKr-B, ns*L*-V, Gr-V, Trs-Ps, Trs-Gs, Dns-NG, Prs*shn*-L, Kltr-J, R-Pt-Bl, P-Zld, K-T-Gt, P-Ld, P-*L*t ; K : Dshn ; D·Td ; Nn+D-Ktr ; M¹, .·|.. D², R¹-T, Pˢ-T.

§ 257. When one of the signs mentioned in the last section is printed before a stenograph standing alone, it indicates how its outline is to be written in relation to any outline that may precede it ; thus, !Pln² denotes the outline of *complain*, and also that it should be written near the next preceding word. See the prefix *com*, § 284.

ESS-CIRCLE BETWEEN STEMS.

§ 258. A circle between two stems may be considered as joined to either ; thus, Ms-M or M-sM, Ms-*L* or M-s*L*. Generally, however, the circle should be represented in connection with the stem that precedes it, except in cases where the phonographic outline would be best suggested by attaching it to the succeeding stem ; thus, Ks-J, Bs·J, Rs-K ; but T-s*L*, F-s*L*, N-s*L*.

VOWELS.

§ 259. The vowel-signs, both single and double, though seldom used in advanced Phonography, may, when necessary, be indicated as follows :

ă,   ā,   ĕ,   ā̆,   ŏ,   o̱,   ä,   ĕ,   ĭ,   ŏ,   ŭ,   o̱,

ɪ or ĭ,   oɪ,   ow,   ɛw or ū,   á̆ɪ,   ā̆ɪ,   ĕ̆ɪ,   ä̆ɪ,   ŏɪ, etc.

§ 260. The stenotypes of the vowels may be written in with the consonant stenotypes in the order of their occurrence in the word. A *hyphen* between the stenotype of a vowel or diphthong commencing or ending a word, and the stenotype of the nearest stem, indicates that they are to be joined in writing. The stenotypes of vowels to be written according to the rule for " special vocalization" at § 156, are in parentheses.

EXAMPLES : ·| ăD, ⌣ ŏN,· — Gŏ, ⌄ Bá̆¹-M, ⌄ Fɪ¹-L, ⌄ B-ĕK, ·|··· T³-o̱M ; ˥ ɪ-D¹ ; ⌐ K(ă)r, ·⌐·· D(ĕ)r³, ∫· T(ĕ)l, ⌐ K(ä)l¹, ·⌐· D(ū)r³, ⌐ ssP(ĭ)r¹.

GENERAL REMARKS ON OUTLINES OF WORDS.

§ 261. One of the peculiarities of Phonography is its variety of consonant forms, it often being possible to represent the consonants of a single word with several different, and sometimes very unlike, outlines. This variety results from the employment of more than one means of representing certain of the consonants, some of them having both an upward and a downward sign, and others being sometimes written with a stem, and sometimes included in a group sign. This is frequently the source of not a little perplexity to the beginner, who is embarrassed at having to select outlines before he has become familiar with the principles that should control such choice. This is a difficulty, however, which a little practice, in both reading and writing, soon overcomes. The general rule in regard to such words is, that they should be written with the briefest outlines that are consistent with legibility and ease of vocalization ; care being taken to observe Analogy of Form, which requires, without regard to their derivation or meaning, that words of similar construction, as regards the consonants and vowels and their arrangement, be written in a similar man ner ; thus, _ℓ_ *suddenly,* _⌒_ *lovingly,* ⋯⋯ *nearly,* ⌐ *goaded,* _⌐_ *likewise,* _⌐_ *slackwater;* their primitives, or components, being written -ƒ· *sudden,* _⌒_ *loving,* ⋯⋯ *near,* ⎯ *goad,* L¹-K *like* and Wz¹ *wise,* sL¹-K *slack* and Wtr¹ *water.*

§ 262. There are occasional exceptions to the rule given in the last section, as where uncommon, rarely used, or peculiarly formed words, for the sake of increased legibility, are written according to what may be called Analogy of Derivation or Composition, which requires that the derivative be written like its primitive, the signs for the additional sounds being simply joined on, or that a compound word should be written by merely joining together the ordinary outlines of its components, even in violation of the requirements of Form Analogy. But when both analogies agree in requiring a word to be written with a particular outline, but which can not easily be made without taking off the pen, it is better to disjoin than to change the outline ; thus, write F²-Kshn:T, instead of F²-K-SH-Nt, for *affectionate.*

SPECIAL DIRECTIONS AS TO CERTAIN OUTLINES.

§ 263. Speed in writing Phonography depends chiefly upon the ability of the writer to make the various outlines of words without hesitation. This facility can be more readily attained by becoming thoroughly familiar with the best modes of writing those syllables, or small groups of consonants, that are common to classes of words, than by attempting to learn the outline of each word of the language separately. The following tables and rules will be found useful in this connection.

INITIAL LETTERS.

Prefix.		Sign.		Examples.
ant,	by	Nt	in	antagonist, antedate, antidote
cal,	"	Kl	"	caligraphy, calumny, calvinistic
car,	"	Kr	"	carbon, caricature, carpet
cat,	"	Kt	"	catalogue, category, catenation
cent,	"	sNt	"	centage, centennial, centiped, centage
chir,	"	Kr	"	chirography, chironomy, chirurgeon
chr,	"	"	"	Christmas, chromatic, chronic
cir,	"	sR	"	circuit, circus, Circassian
"	"	sR	"	circle, circulate
col,	"	Kl	"	collateral, collect, colloquy
cor,	"	Kr	"	cork, correct, coroner
counter,	"	Kntr	"	counterfeit, countersign
cut,	"	Kt	"	cuticle, cutlet, cutting
del,	"	Dl	"	delicate, deliver ⌒

Prefix.		Sign.		Examples.
enter,	by	Ntr	in	entertain, enterprise
fer,	"	Fr	"	ferment, fervid, fervor
fur,	"	"	"	furniture, furtive, further
hydra,	"	H-Dr	"	hydrant, hydraulic
hydro,	"	Hdr	"	hydrogen, hydrometer, hydropathist
hyp,	"	P	"	hypocrite, hypothesis
iut,	"	Nt	"	intent, intense, intention
inter,	"	Ntr	"	intercede, interdict, interline
jur,	"	Jr	"	jurisdiction, jurisprudence
met,	"	Mt	"	metal, metaphor, meteoric
oct,	"	Kt	"	octave, October
par,	"	Pr	"	paragraph, parchment, parliament
per,	"	.."	"	percolate, perfect, person
phil,	"	Fl	"	philology, Philadelphia
qua,	"	Kw	"	quadrant, quadruped, quadruple
rel,	"	Rl	"	relation, relevant, relief
retro,	"	Rtr	"	retroaction, retrograde, retrospect
sept,	"	sPt	"	September, Septuagint
super,	"	sPr	"	superb, supercargo, superfine
supr,	"	"	"	supramundane, supreme
sis, sys, sus,	"	ss	"	sister, system, sustain
under,	"	Ndr	"	underdone, undersign
val,	"	Vl	"	value, valve
ver,	"	Vr	"	verbal, verge, version
vol,	"	Vl	"	volcano, volume, voluptuous
vul,	"	"	"	vulgar, vulnerable, vulture

FINAL SYLLABLES.

§ 274. The following are some of the principal final syllables that are liable to trouble the learner:

Suffix.		Sign.		Examples.
cise,	by	ss	in	precise, criticise, exercise
cism,	"	ssM	"	ostracism, criticism, solecism
hood,	"	Hd	"	childhood, sisterhood, boyhood
ive,	"	V	"	relative, native, active
cal,	"	Kl	"	radical, periodical, ethical
tial,	"	SHl	"	solstitial, nuptial, martial
holder,	"	Hldr	"	stockholder, upholder
ometer,	"	Mtr	"	thermometer, barometer, hydrometer
ster,	"	str	"	register, cloister, minister
sis, sus,	"	ss	"	basis, thesis, crisis, colossus
tude,	"	Td	"	quietude, solicitude, latitude

'-LY.'

§ 265. When the final syllable -*ly* is preceded by a consonant written with a stem-sign, and there is no distinct vowel intervening, it is generally expressed by the *el*-hook on such preceding stem ; thus ＼⁄· *pearly,* ⁘⁘· *officially,* ⌐‿· *calmly.* In all other cases it should be written, if possible, with the upstroke *lee;* thus, ＿ſ· *Kelly,* Grs-*L grossly,* Mt-*L² mutely,* Fthr¹-*L fatherly.* But when *lee* can not conveniently be written, *el* may be used instead, or else a disjoined *lee ;* thus, Jnt˄-L, or ⸲*L jointly,* J-sNt-L, or ⸲*L adjacently.*

'-RY.'

§ 266. The final syllable -*ry* is sometimes expressed by the *er*-hook and sometimes by the stems *ree* and *er,* being governed by the same rule as -*ly;* thus, ↖⁘· *fishery,* ⟩ *drudgery ;* but ＼⁄· *berry,* ⤜· *story,* Ms-*R² misery,* Rt¹-*R artery.*

'-TY.'

§ 267. The final syllable *ty* may sometimes be expressed by halving the preceding consonant-stem; thus, ⸝· *utility,* ≍· *activity.* This exception is only allowed for the purpose of improving or shortening certain outlines.

'IN' AND 'ON.'

§ 268. *In* and *on* are never written with the *n*-hook except in the words ...(·· *therein,* ⟨ *thereon.* ⟨ ⸗⸲⸗⸲·⸲

'-TURE.'

§ 269. The final syllable -*ture* (as well as -*ter* and -*tor*) may sometimes be indicated by the *ter*-hook on straight stems, by the lengthening of curves and straight stems with final hooks, and by changing an *ess*-circle into the *ster*-loop; thus, ⸗⸒ *creature,* ⎰⸜⸝ *adventure,* N-Dntr² *indenture,* ⎿⸒ *texture.*

THE PAST TENSE

§ 270. The past tense of regular verbs is written as follows :

1. When the present tense ends with a full-length stem, whether simple or compounded with anything but a final circle or loop—by halving such final stem ; thus, Bl-M *blame,* Bl-Md *blamed,* Pln *plane,* Plnd *planed,* Brv *brave,* Brvd *braved,* Kshn¹ *caution,* Kshnd¹ *cautioned.*

2. When the present tense ends with a half-length stem—by making its final stem full length, and then adding *tet, ted,* or *ded;* thus, Prt²-Kt *protect,* Prt²-K-Td *protected,* R²-P-Rt *report,* R²-P-R-Td *reported,* D²-Grd *degrade,* D²-Gr-Dd *degraded,* R²-Fnd *refund,* R²-F-N-Dd *refunded.*

3. When the present tense ends with the *ess*-circle, not written inside of a final hook,—by changing the circle to an *st*-loop; thus, Ks³ *accuse*, Ksd³ *accused*, Glns¹ *glance*, Glnst¹ *glanced*. But when the circle is written inside of a final hook, the consonant represented by such hook should be written with its stem-sign, and the circle changed to a loop; thus, Fns *fence*, F-Nst *fenced*, Vns³ *evince*, V²-Nst *evinced*.

4. When the present tense ends with the *st*-loop,—by changing the 'oop to the *ess*-circle, and adding *ted;* thus Kst¹ *accost*, Ks-Td¹ *accosted.*

ABBREVIATION.

§ 271. Although Phonography provides an exceedingly perfect means of representing all the sounds used in the English language, so that it meets the requirements of a very exact phonetic analysis, yet it is by no means essential to legibility that in actual practice the signs of all those sounds should be written. The advanced phonographer from choice, and the practical reporter from necessity, omit almost entirely the signs of the vowels and diphthongs, and also abbreviate many of the consonant outlines.

OMISSION OF VOWELS.

§ 272. To the casual observer it might seem that the omission of the vowel-signs would occasion great uncertainty, if not absolute illegibility, in reading Phonography. This, however, is so far from being the case that all experienced writers prefer unvocalized to vocalized outlines, and consider that an extensive insertion of the vowels is an actual detriment in reading. The principal causes of this legibility are these : (1.) As the vowel-signs form no part of the outline, the general appearance of a word is not changed by their omission. (2.) The great majority of words are distinct from others in their consonant sounds, and consequently have different and distinct outlines. (3.) As the outlines of words are placed, in respect to the line of writing, in three positions, according as their accented vowels are of the first, second, or third place, even if two or more words bould happen to be written with the same outline, they may generally be distinguished by this difference of position. (4.) In the few cases of words that contain the same consonant-sounds, and that belong to the same position, when necessary, distinctions are obtained by some arbitrary difference of position or outline, or else by vocalizing, partially or in full, one, and generally the more uncommon, of the conflicting words

§ 273 When the learner has mastered the principles of Phonography thus far explained, and has become somewhat familiar with the outlines of words, he should begin to leave out the signs of the vowels, or, in other words, to write what is called "Unvocalized Phonography." But, in order that his writing may not become illegible to him by a too sudden transition, it will be found the safer plan to commence by omitting the vowel-signs only in the following cases :

I. When the existence of the vowel is indicated by some peculiar method of writing the consonant outlines, as is the case with the ital·icized vowels in the words ask [§ 113] ; racy [§ 115] ; bushy [§ 130] ; alike [§ 132] ; folly [§ 133] ; ark [§ 135] ; berry [§ 136] ; coffee, gravy, many [§ 179] ; into, induce [§ 228] ; poet [§ 233] ; solid [§ 234] ; appel late [§ 235].

. II. From short words of frequent occurrence, as in by, be, at, it, up, say, they, on, in, etc.

III. Unaccented vowels, as in votary, capital, possible, enemy, prom inence, etc.

IV. In long words, medial vowels, whether accented or not, as in unostentatious, incidental, statesmanship, etc.

§ 274. The vowel-signs most essential to legibility, and which the learner should still continue for a while to insert, are the following :

I. An accented in preference to an unaccented vowel ; thus, _⌵ occasion.

II. A diphthong, whether accented or not, in preference to a simple vowel.

III. An initial or final vowel, unless it is indicated by some peculiarity of the consonant outline ; thus, '⌞ attic, ⌐ ergo.

IV. The sign of the diphthong ı generally at the end of a word, and usually at the commencement when it can be joined to the first

consonant-stem ; thus, ⌊ᵧ᷍ defy, ·⌐· idea. Initial ı, when joined, may generally be abbreviated, its last stroke only being written, which may be struck either upward or downward, as is most convenient; thus, ⌐ island. The stenotype of this sign is 1—the direction of the accent mark showing the inclination of the sign.

V. In words having a vowel before and after a single consonant-stem, both should be written, if possible ; but if only one can be inserted, the accented one will generally afford the best clue to the word ; thus, ⤬ or ⤬ obey.

WORDS DISTINGUISHED BY DIFFERENCE CF OUTLINE, POSITION, ETC.

§ 275. The general omission of the vowel-signs, as we have seen, renders it necessary to make distinctions between certain words by ar bitrary differences of outline, position, or vocalization.

WORDS COMMENCING WITH 'IL,' 'IM,' 'IN,' 'IR,' 'UN,' 'EN.'

§ 276. When negatives are formed by prefixing the particle *in* to positive words that begin with *l*, *m*, or *r*, for the sake of euphony, the particle is changed respectively to *il*, *im*, or *ir*, so that the first consonant of the negative becomes doubled, as in the words *illegal*, *immaterial*, *irregular*, etc. This doubling of the first consonant also occurs, of course, in negatives made by prefixing *in* or *un* to positive words beginning with *n*, as in *innoxious*, *unnerve*, etc. Now, in ordinary speech, we frequently hear but one of these consonants spoken, the negative being distinguished from its corresponding positive word only by the sound of its initial vowel. In unvocalized Phonography, however, this distinction would not appear, and therefore both consonants should be written, even in those cases where only one is heard; thus, write ·· *legal*, ·· *illegal*, ∼ *moderate*, ∼ *immoderate*, ∫ *resolute*, ∫ *irresolute*, ⌣⌐ *noxious*, ⌣⌐ *innoxious*, ⌣∕ *necessary*, ⌣∕ *unnecessary*. But if a negative so formed have no corresponding positive in use, only one of the consonants should be written, unless both are actually heard; thus, ⌣ *innocence*. The preceding remarks are also applicable to those similarly formed, though not negative, words that begin with the prepositional, or intensive particle *in* or *en*; thus, N-Nt innate, N-Nr-V innerve, N-N-Bl annoble, M-Mnt-*L*¹ emmantle.

§ 277. LIST OF WORDS DISTINGUISHED BY DIFFERENCE OF OUTLINE, POSITION, OR VOCALIZATION.

Kst¹, cost—Kz-D¹, caused
. K-Jl², cudgel—K-J²-L, cajole
Kzshn¹, causation—Ksshn², accession—Kzshn³, accusation
Ks-T²-N-SHn, extenuation—Ks-T²-Nshn, extension
Klzhn¹, collision—K-*L*shn³, coalition—K-*L*ūzhn³, collusion
K-s*R*sz, exercise—K-s*R*-Sz, exorcise
Kr-Pr¹-L, corporal—Kr-P²-*R*l, corporeal
Gd¹, God—G-D¹, guide
Grd¹-N, garden—Gr-Dn¹, guardian
T¹-*R*tr, tartar—Trtr², traitor—Tr²-Dr, trader

Trn², train—T²-*R*n, turn
Tr², truth—Tr³, true
Tn²-B(-L), attainable—T²-N-Bl, tenable
Dtr¹, daughter, doubter—Dt¹-R, auditor—Dt¹-*R*, auditory
Dtr², debtor—Dt²-R, editor
D²-*L*t-*R*, adultery—ī-D¹-*L*-Tr, idolatry—ī-D¹-*L*tr, idolater
Dss³, decease—D³-sZ, disease
Dss³-T, deceased, desist—D³-sZd, diseased
ī-D¹-L-Ns, idleness—D²-L-Ns, dullness
D²-M-Ns-Tshn, administration—D²-Mns-Tshn, demonstration
D¹-M-Nshn, damnation—D²-M-Nshn, dimension—!D²-M-Nshn, condemnation—Dŏ²-M-Nshn, domination
D²-*R*shn, adoration—Drshn², duration
Jnt¹, gentleman—J¹-Nt, giant
Jnt², gentlemen—J²-Nt, agent
Jnt¹¹*L*, gentlemanly—Jnt²-L, gentle—Jnt³-L, genteel
P³-R, poor—P³-*R*, pure
Pt¹-*R*n, pattern—P²-Trn, patron
Pshnt², patient—Pshn¹-T, passionate
P²-*R*-Ps, purpose—Pr²-Ps, propose
Pr¹-P-*R*-T, property—Pr¹-Pr-T, propriety
Pr²-Prshn, appropriation—Pr²-Pshn, proportion—Pr²-P-*R*shn, preparation
Pr²-Pshn-D, proportioned—Pr²-Pshn-äT, proportionate
Pr¹-Bshn, approbation—Pr²-Bshn, probation—Pr³-Bshn, prohibition
Prt²-Kshn, protection—Pr²-D-Kshn, production, predication
Pr²-Tn, pertain—P²-*R*-Tn, appertain
Pr³-sKshn, prosecution—P³-*R*s-Kshn, persecution
Pr¹-sK-B, proscribe—Pr³-sK-B, prescribe
Pr²-sR, oppressor—P³-*R*-S-R, pursuer—P³-*R*-Zr, peruser
Pr²-*SH*, Prussia—P²-*R*-SH, Persia
Prshn², Prussian—P²-*R*shn, Persian—P³-*R*shn, Parisian
P¹-*R*shn, apportion—P²-*R*shn, portion
Pr¹-Fr, proffer—Prf²-R, prefer
Pr¹-Ms, promise—Pr¹-Mīs, premise
Pr²-Mn-Nt, permanent—Pr³-Mn-Nt, preëminent — *Pr'-Mn-Nt, prominent*
Prt¹-Nr, partner—P¹-Nr, part-owner
B¹-s*L*ēt, obsolete—B¹-s*L*t, absolute
B²-*R*-TH, birth—Br²-TH, breath
Brt¹, bright—Br¹-D, broad
Bf², before—B²-V, above
Bn¹-Dnd, abandoned—Bnd²-Nt, abundant
stD², steady—sTd², staid

stJ², stage—ŠT²-J, stowage
sl²-*Rt*, support—slʳt², separate—sPr²-D, spread
sCHshn², situation—sTshn², station
āTHst², atheist—THst², theist
āTHs²-T-K, atheistic—THs²-T-K, theistic
āTH²-Z-M, atheism—TH²-zM, theism
F²-Vrd, favored—F²-Vr-T, favorite
F¹-Ml, formal-ly—F¹-Mr-*L*, formerly
F²-Nr-L, funeral—F²-N-*Rl*, funereal
F²-Rs, fierce—F²-*Rs*, furious
F¹-Wrd, forward—Fr²-Wrd, froward
F²-R-M, af-firm—F¹, form
Vl¹-Bl, valuable—V²-L-Bl, available—V¹-*L*-Bl, voluble
Vlshn², valuation—V²-*Lshn*, violation
Vī¹-*Lnt*, violent—V¹-*Lnt*, valiant
V¹-Kshn, avocation—V²-Kshn, vocation
N²-Bd, nobody—N²-Bd, anybody
Nd²-Kshn, indication—N-D²-Kshn, induction
N-V²-*SHn*, innovation—N-Vzhn², invasion
N-Vt²-Bl, inevitable—N-V¹-D-Bl, unavoidable
N-Df²-Nt, indefinite—N-Df¹-*iNd*, undefined
Nd²-*Ls*, endless—Nd²-*Ls*, needless
N-J²-Ns, ingenious—N-J²-N-S, ingenuous
Ntrs-Td², interested—Ndrs-D², understood
M-Pshn¹-D, impassioned — M-Pshn¹-āT, impassionate — M-Pshnt², impatient
M-Bl², amiable—H-M-Bl², or M-Bl², humble
Mn²-Nt, eminent—Mn²-Nt, imminent
Ms-S², Mrs.—Mss², Misses
M-N-TH², month—Mn-T², minute
M¹-Grt, migrate—M²-Grt, emigrate—M²-Grt, immigrate
M¹-Grshn, migration — M²-Grshn, emigration — M²-Grshn, immigration
Mshn², mission—M-SHn², machine
Mshn-*R²*, missionary—M-SH²-Nr, machinery
R²-Nd, ruined—*R²*-Nd [tick for *ew* joined], renewed
R²-Prshn, repression—*R²*-P-*Rshn*, reparation
R¹-Fr-Kshn, refraction—*Rf²*-*L*-Kshn, reflection
Rz²-M, resume—*R²*-S-M, reassume
Ls², less—ð*Ls²*, else
Lt¹-Td, latitude—*L¹*-T·Td, altitude
ï-*Lnd¹*, island—*Lnd¹*, land
W²-Mn, woman—W²-Mn, women

OMISSION OF CONSONANTS.

§ 278. The omission of consonant-signs from the outline of words will be treated of under the general heads of "Word-Signs" and "Contractions."

WORD-SIGNS.

§ 279. It has been ascertained by calculation that about a hundred different words constitute more than one half of all the English that is spoken or written ; that is, in a sermon, newspaper, speech, or debate, in which say ten thousand words occur, full five thousand will be made up by the repetition of certain common words, not exceeding a hundred in number. Now one of the prime necessities of a practicable system of shorthand, is a simple and brief means of writing these frequent words. Many of them are short words of but one consonant, which, being written by a single stroke of the pen, do not, of course, require abbreviation. But a considerable number contain several consonants, which, if written in full, would make outlines of inconvenient length ; therefore, as far as possible, they are contracted, and one, two, or three consonants, as the case may be, used to represent the entire word. Strictly speaking, all such abbreviations would come under the general designation of "Contractions;" but, for the sake of convenience, such of them as are written with only one stem-sign, either simple or compound, are called "Word-Signs," and the use of the word "Contractions" restricted to those that contain two or more stems. The term Word-Sign is also applied to uncontracted outlines containing single stems, simple or compound, that are written out of the position to which their accented vowels would entitle them, as well as to the signs of a few words that are written with vowel or diphthong signs not in connection with any consonant-stem. A word that is represented by a word-sign is called a "Sign-Word."

§ 280. The following is a list of the word-signs arranged in the order of the tables of consonants and vowels. Each consonant word-sign is represented by its phonotype, and opposite it are its sign-words, printed in three lines and united by a brace   The words in the upper line are written with the word-sign placed in the first position ; those in the second line with it in the second position ; and those in the third line with it in the third position. When several words of the same position are represented by the same sign, they are such words as from practical experience are found not to conflict when so written, the context always showing which is intended : and the word for which the sign is most frequently employed is given first. When a word-sign outline is used for sign-words of only one or two positions, the vacant positions are filled by words that are fully and properly expressed by the outline and position. As such words, however, do not come within the definition of Sign-Words, they are distinguished by being printed in italics. In case no word at all can be found to fill a place, a blank is left in the brace. A few signs have opposite them words printed with more than one termination; thus, *here-ar*, *differ-ence-ent*, *give-n*, to intimate that the corresponding signs represent *here* and *hear*, *differ*, *difference* and *different*, *give* and *given*.

§ 281. LIST OF WORD SIGNS.

P

\	{ part | - ذ
	{ plaintiff
	{ opportunity

◟	{ *spy*
	{ spoke, special-ly
	{ *speak*

◡	{ possible-y
	{ opportunities

◟	{ *apply*
	{ *play*
	{ people

◝	{ practice
	{ *pray, upper*
	{ principal-le

◞	{ practiced
	{ *oppressed*

◞	{ surprise
	{ *suppress*
	{ spruce

◞	{ *sprains*
	{ experience

P (right column)

◞	{ *pine*
	{ *open*
	{ opinion

◟	{ *span*
	{ spoken
	{ *spin*

◝	{ *pride*
	{ *prate*
	{ particular

B

\	{ óbject, *by*
	{ but, objéct
	{ be

◟	{ *sob*
	{ subject

◟	{ belong
	{ *able*
	{ belief-ve

◝	{ *brow*
	{ number
	{ *brew*

\	{ before
	{ *beef*

Ꮜ	{ objection	Ꮷ	{ deliverance
Ꮥ	᠂{ subjection	᠂	{ Dr. (Doctor) *dray* during

T

ǀ	{ *at, out, ought* what *it, to*	᠋	{ dwell
ꝑ	{ society system	ᢁ	{ differ-ence-ent

᠋	{ *try* truth *true*	**CH**
᠌	{ *town* *attain* between	/ { charge which, change *each*
ʃ	{ circumstantial-ly citizen	⌒ { children

ʃ	{ *satins* circumstance citizens	**J**

D

ǀ	{ had, dollar do, defendant did	/ { large advantage
ᒥ	{ advertise *does* *dues*	/ { largely angel
ᒧ	{ advertised *dust* distinct	⁊ { larger Jr. (Junior)
᠋	{ deliver-y	/ { join general-ly *June*
		᠂ { gentleman gentlemen

K

- can
- come
- could, kingdom

- because
- comes
- *accuse*

- *crown*
- *crane*
- Christian

- describe
- *succor*
- *screw*

- [:] *consecration*
- description

- question

- quarter
- *equator*

- called
- *cold*
- difficult-y

- according
- *court*
- *accrued*

- county
- *Kent*

G

- go
- gave, together
- give-n

- *sag*
- signify

- significance

- signification

- significant

- *augur*
- *grow*
- degree

- language

- govern

- began
- begun
- begin

- altogether

F

- form, half
- for
- *if*

- *fast*
- first
- *feast*

- phonography
- *fun*
- *fin*

- *fashion*
- formation
- [:] *confusion*

{ fact
{ fate
{ feet

{ frowned
{ friend
{ frequent

V

{ have, halve
{ ever
{ view

{ salve
{ several
{ sieve

{ over
{ every

{ vine
{ heaven
{ even

TH

{ thank, hath
{ worth
{ think, youth

DH

{ that
{ them
{ with, *thee*

{ other, *either* [īdhr]
{ there, their
{ either [ĕdhr]

{ than
{ then
{ within

S

{ astonish-ed
{ east

Z

{ was
{ these

SH

{ shall
{ show
{ should

ZH

{ usual-ly

L

{ all
{ well
{ will

{ already

R

{ or, *are* [middle or end
{ her   [of phrases]
{ here-ar

{ swear
{ swore
{ seer

R

[mencing phrases]
{ our, are [alone or com-
{ were, where, recollect
{ rue

{ *arrive*
{ refer-ence
{ roof

4*

{ recollection

{ world
{ *ruled*

M

{ from, time, *my*
{ member, home
{ *me*

{ similarity
{ *same*
{ similar

{ almost
{ *most*
{ amused

{ *smite*
{ somewhat
{ *seemed*

{ *more*
{ Mr. (Mister)

{ *mind*
{ *mend*
{ movement

N

{ own
{ *know, no*
{ any

{ *noise*
{ *knows*
{ insurance

{ *honest*
{ next

{ another, entire
{ *under*
{ *neither*

NG

{ long
{ among
{ thing

{ song
{ sung
{ singular

{ amongst

{ longer

W

{ why
{ when
{ would, *we*

{ while
{ wealth-y
{ *weal*

{ *water*
{ whether
{ whither

Y

{ beyond
{ yet, young
{ you-r, year

{ younger

H

{ how
{ he, him
{ who-m

° as, has	.... the [emphatic]
is, his	I
an, and	awe
. a	, O, oh, owe
.... the	owing
ah	owes
• aye [meaning 'ever']	aye [meaning 'yes']

'NOW' AND 'NEW.'

§ 282. *En* is the only consonant-sound of so large a number of words that it becomes necessary to increase their legibility by making a some-what arbitrary distinction in the case of the two words *now* and *new*; the first being written with the first stroke of the sign ow joined finally to the stem, and the other with the last stroke of EW joined also at the end; thus, ⌐ *now*, ... *new*.

CONTRACTIONS.

PREFIXES AND SUFFIXES.

§ 283. One of the most convenient modes of abbreviation is the use of contractions for certain initial or terminal syllables that are of fre-quent occurrence, called PREFIXES and SUFFIXES. By this means a large number of words may sometimes be abbreviated without burdening the memory with more than a single sign.

PREFIXES.

§ 284. The prefixes are written as follows:

1. COM, CON, CUM, COG.—The syllables *com*, *con*, *cum*, whether at the commencement or in the middle of words, and *cog* in the middle of words, are generally not written, but indicated by proximity, that is, by writing the part of the outline that comes after the omitted syllable near the part that precedes it; thus, ⟨ *they complained*, ⟨ *in complete*, ∕ *rec-ommend*, |⟨ *decompose*, |⟨ *discompose*, ⟨ *unrecompensed*, ⟨ *in-constant*, ∕⟨ *irreconciliation*, ⟨ *incumbent*, ⟨ *encumbered*, ⟨ *disencumber*, ⟨- *incognito*.

When, however, proximity can not be used, as at the beginning of a paragraph, sentence, or line, or when any indistinctness would be occasioned by it, either of those syllables, except *cog*, may be written with a light dot, placed near the beginning of the succeeding part of the outline; thus, ⟍ *complain*, j. *content*, ⟍ *cumbersome.*

The dot should also be inserted in words commencing with *self-con-* [see prefix for *self*]. .

Initial *cog-* is always written K-G.

Sometimes it is allowable to join the latter part of the word to the first, without taking off the pen; thus, ⌐ instead of ⌐ ; for *accommoda-* *tion*, ⌣ *inconsistent*, ⌐ *inconsiderable*, ∿ *circumference*, ⌐ *circumflex.* But this should be done only in the case of a few words of frequent occurrence, and when the outline so formed is unlike that of any other word with which it might conflict.

2. FOR—sometimes by F joined to the remainder of the word; thus, ⌣ *forward*, ⌣ *forever.*

3. MAGNA, MAGNE, MAGNI—by the stem M written partially over the remainder of the word; thus, ⌣ *magnanimous*, ⌐ *magnetic*, ⌐ *magnify.*

4. SELF—by the *ess*-circle placed invariably on the line.

This prefix may be joined to the remainder of the outline if it commences with a down stroke, and if it does not need to be written in its proper position for the sake of legibility; thus, ⌣ *selfish*, ⌣ *self-evident.*

If the remainder of the outline commences with an up-stroke, a horizontal stem, a circle or loop, or an initial hook, the prefix should not be joined, but placed at the left and close to it; thus, ⌐ *self-love*, ⌣ *self-interest.*

In words commencing with *self-con-* the *con-*dot should be inserted; thus, ⌣ *self-conceit.*

Un is prefixed to *self* thus : ⌣ *unselfish.*

5. WITH—by the stem DH joined to the remainder of the word; thus, ⌣ *withdraw.*

SUFFIXES.

§ 285. The suffixes are written as follows :

1. BLE or BLY—by the stem B joined, when it can not conveniently be written by Bl; thus, ⌣ *sensible-y*, ⌣ *profitable-y.*

2. BLENESS, FULNESS, IVENESS, and LESSNESS—by detached Bs, Fs, Vs, and Ls respectively; thus, ⌣ *profitableness*, ⌣ *doubtfulness*, Tnt²:Vs *attentiveness*, ⌣ *thoughtlessness.*

3. EVER—by the *v*-hook; thus, / *whichever*, ⌐ *whenever*, Hv¹ *however.*

4. FORM—by F joined; thus, ⌣ *uniform*, ⌐ *reform.*

5. ING—by a light dot at the end of the preceding part of the word, when it can not conveniently be expressed by the stem NG; thus, ⸜ *petting,* ⸝ *meeting.* '

The plural INGS, in such words, may be expressed by a circle in place of the dot; thus, ⸺ *meetings.*

The suffix-signs for *ing* and *ings* are used generally after contractions, after stems with final loops, and always after half-length P, B, M, and H; thus, P(·)¹ *parting,* Bl(·)¹ *belonging,* Rst(·)² *resting,* Mstr(·)¹ *master-ing,* Bt(·)² *betting,* ⸺° *mattings,* Hd(·)¹ *hiding.*

6. MENTAL or MENTALITY—by Mnt written near the end of the preceding part of the word; thus, ⸜ *instrumental-ity,* ⸝ *fundamental-ity.*

7. OLOGY—by J joined to, or disjoined and written partially under, the preceding part of the word, when it can not as conveniently be written in full; thus, ⸝ *physiology,* ⸝ *astrology.*

8. SELF—by the *ess*-circle joined to the preceding part of the word; thus, ⸝ *myself.* .

9. SELVES—by the large circle joined to the preceding part of the word; thus, ⸝ *themselves.*

10. SHIP—by the stem SH written near, or joined to, the preceding part of the word; thus, ⸝ *lordship,* ⸝ *partnership.*

11. SOEVER—by sV joined to the preceding part of the word; thus, ⸝ *whatsoever.*

12. WORTHY—by DH, usually joined, but detached when it does not make a good junction with the preceding stem; thus, ⸝ *praiseworthy,* S³:DH *seaworthy.*

OMISSION OF CERTAIN CONSONANTS.

§ 286. Consonants may be omitted from the outlines of words, without impairing their legibility, in the following cases:

1. K or G—generally after *ing,* unless the K or G is final; thus, ⸝ *sanction,* ⸝ *sanctify,* ⸝ *anxiety,* ⸝ *angle,* ⸝ *banker.*

2. A T sound—at the end of a syllable immediately after the *ess*-circle, when the next syllable begins with a stem-sign; thus, ⸝ *postpone.*

3. P—after the sound of M and before another consonant, if no vowel-sound follows the P; thus, ⸝ *tempt,* ⸝ *assumption,* ⸝ *pumpkin,* ⸝ *glimpse.* When it is necessary to distinguish *md* from *mpt,* it should be written with the full stem-signs; thus, ⸝ *thumped,* ⸝ *thumbed.*

4. N—frequently before Jr; thus, ⸝ *passenger.*

5. M—frequently before Pr or Br; thus, ⸝ *temper,* ⸝ *chamber.*

WORDS ENDING IN '-NTIAL-LY.'

§ 287. Most words ending in *-ntial* or *-ntially* may be abbreviated by leaving off the final syllables *-tial* or *-tially*; thus, ⌐ *prudential-ly*, ⌐... *substantial-ly*. *If terminate with an n-hook.*

OMISSION OF HOOKS.

§ 288. When in the middle of a word we would naturally be disposed to write a consonant with a final hook, but find it impracticable, such consonant should be written with its stem-sign. But if the stem-sign also makes a bad or awkward joining, the consonant may be omitted. And if the outline is not then sufficiently legible, the sign of the vowel which occurs immediately before the omitted consonant may be inserted.

EXAMPLES: ⌐ *attain*, ⌐ *attainment*, ⌐ *assign*, ⌐ *assignment*, ⌐ *trans*, ⌐ *transpose*, ⌐ *lord*, ⌐ *landlord*.

LIST OF WORD-SIGNS AND CONTRACTIONS.

§ 289. The following are complete lists of the word-signs and contractions. In the first they are arranged in the order of the *a, b, c* alphabet, and in the second, in the order of the phonographic alphabet. Learners should consult the first while *writing* and the second while *reading* phonography.

WORD-SIGNS AND CONTRACTIONS—A, B, C ORDER.

A

according, Krd[1]
advantage, J[2]
advertise, Dz[1]
almost, Mst[1]
already, Lr[2]
altogether, Gthr[1]
among, NG[2]
an-d,
angel, Jl[2]
another, Nthr[1]
any, N[3]
archangel, R[2]-Jl
archbishop, *R*[2]-CH-B
architect-ure-al, R[1]-K-T
are, *R*[1]
aristocracy-atic, Rs[1]-T-K
as,
astonish-ed, St[1]
awe,

B

bankruptcy, B[1]-NGr-S
baptism, Bt[1]-zM
because, Kz[1]
become, B[2]-K
before, Bf[2]
began, Gn[1]
begin, Gn[3]
begun, Gn[2]
belief-ve, Bl[3]
belong, Bl[1]
between, Tn[3]
beyond, Y[1]
bishopric, B[3]-SH-K
brethren, Brn[2]
brother-in-law, Br[2]-Nl
but, B[2]

C

cabinet, K-B[1]
can, K[1]

capable, K-Bl²
captain, K-Pn¹
catholic, K-TH¹
certificate, sRt³-F
change, CH²
characteristic, Kr²-Ks-K
charge, CH¹
children, CHl³
Christian, Kr
circumstance, sTns²
citizen, sT'n³
collect, Kl²-K
come, K²
correct, Kr²-K
could, K³
county, Knt¹
cross-examine, Kr¹-sMn

D

December, D²-sM
defendant, D²
degree, Gr³
deliver-y, Dl³
democracy-tic, D¹-M
democrat, D²-M
describe, sKr¹
description, sKrshn²
develop, Dv²-P
did, D³
differ-ence-ent, Df³
difficult-y, Klt³
discriminate, Ds²-Kr-M
distinct, Dst³
do, D²
Dr. (Doctor), Dr¹
doctrine, D¹-Trn
dollar, D¹
domestic, D²-Ms-K
during, Dr²
dwell, Dw²

E

effect, F²-K
endeavor, N-Dv²
especial-ly, S²-P
establish, St¹-B
ever, V²
experience, sPrns³
extraordinary, sTr¹-R

F

fact, Ft¹
familiar, F²-M
familiarity, F¹-M
February, F²-B
first, Fst²
for, F²
form, F¹
frequent, Frnt²
from, M¹
found

G

gave, G²
general-ly, Jn²
gentleman, Jnt¹
gentlemen, Jnt²
give-n, G³
go, G²
govern, Gv²
governor, G-V²
Great Britain, Grt²-Brt

H

had, D¹
half, F¹
halve, V¹
has, °
hath, TH¹
have, V¹
he, H²
health-y, L²-TH
hear-re, R³
heaven, Vn²
help, L²-P
her, R²
him, H²
his, °
home, M²
held

I

I,
immediate, M²-Md
importance-t, M-Prt¹
indispensable-y, Nds-Pns²
influence, N-Fs³
insurance, Ns³
intelligence, Nt-Jns²
is, °

J

January, J¹-N
Jr. (Junior), Jr³

K

kingdom, K²
knew (same as *new*)
knowledge, N-J¹

L

language, Gw¹
large, J¹
legislature, L²-J
length-y, NG-TH²
long, NG¹

M

manufacture, M-N-F¹
Massachusetts, Ms-CH³
member, M²
memoranda, M-M-D¹
memorandum, M¹-M
mistake, Ms²-K
Mr. (Mister), Mr³
movement, Mnt³

N

neglect, N²-G
never, N-V²
new, ...
New York, N-Y¹
next, Nst²
no, sir, Ns²
November, N-V³
now, ...
number, Br³

O

O, oh, owe,
ob'ject, B¹
object', B²
observation, B²-zRshn
opinion, Pn³
opportunity, P³
other, DHr¹
our, R¹

over, Vr¹
own, N¹

P

part, P¹
particular, Prt³
peculiar, P³-K
peculiarity, P¹-K
people, Pi³
performance, Pr¹-Fs
perpendicular-ity, Pr³ or ¹-Pn-D
phonography, Fn¹
plaintiff, P²
plenipotentiary, Plu²-P
popular-ity, P¹-P
possible-y, Ps¹
practice, Pr¹
preliminary, Pr²-L-M
principal-le, Pr²
privilege, Prv³-J
probable-y, Pr¹-B
probability, Pr³-B
proportion, Pr²-Pshn
public-sh, P²-B

Q

qualify, Kw-F¹
quarter, Kwtr¹
question, Kw³

R

recollect, R²
refer-ence, Rf³
regular, R³-G
regularity, R¹-G
religion, Rl³-J
remark, R¹-M
remember, R²-M
represent·ative, R³-P
republic-sh, R²-P-B
responsible-y, Rs¹-Pns
responsibility, Rs³-Pns
Rev. (Reverend), R²-V
Roman Catholic, R²-K-TH

S

San Francisco, sNss³-K
satisfactory, sT¹-sR
September, sPt²-M

Saviour C

several, sV²

shall, SH¹

should, SH³

signify, sG³

similar, sM³

similarity, sM¹

singular, sNG³

somewhat, sMt²

southern, sDHn²

speak, sP³

special-ly, sP²

subject, sB³

suggestion, sJn²

surprise, sPrz¹

swear, sR¹

swift, sFt³

system, ssT³

T

thank, TH¹

that, DH¹

the, ...

them, DH²

their, there, DHr²

these, Z³

thing, NG³

think, TH³

time, M¹

together, G²

transubstantiation, Tr⁻-sB

truth, Tr²

U

understood, Ndrs-D³

United States, Ys²

usual-ly, ZH³

W

was, Z¹

wealth-y, Wl²

well, L²

were, R²

what, T²

when, W²

where, R²

which, CH²

whom, H³

will, L³

with, DH³

without, wDH¹

world, Rld²

worth, TH²

would, W³

Y

year, Y³

yes, sir, Yss²

yet, Y²

young, Y²

your, Y³

youth, TH³

§ 290. WORD-SIGNS AND CONTRACTIONS—PHONOGRAPHIC ORDER.

P

P¹, part

P², plaintiff

P³, opportunity

P¹-P, popular-ity

P²-B, public-sh

P¹-K, peculiarity

P³-K, peculiar

Ps¹, possible-y

Pl², people

Pln²-P, plenipotentiary

Pr¹, practice

Pr², principal-le

Pr¹-B, probable

Pr³-B, probability

Pr¹-Fs, performance

Pr³-L-M, preliminary

Pr³ or ¹-Pn-D, perpendicular-ity

Pr²-Pshn, proportion

Prt³, particular

Prv³-J, privilege

Pn³, opinion

sP², special-ly, spoke

sP³, speak

sPrz¹, surprise

sPrns³, experience

sPt³-M, September

B

B¹, ob'ject

B², but, object'

B²-K, become

B²-SH-K, bishopric
B¹-NGr-S, bankruptcy
B²-zRshn, observation
Bl¹, belong
Bl², belief-ve
Br², number
Brn², brethren
Br²-Nl, brother-in-law
Bf², before
Bt¹-zM, baptism
sB², subject

T

T², what
Tr², truth
Tr²-sB, transubstantiation
Tn², between
sT¹-sR, satisfactory
sTr¹-R, extraordinary
sTn², citizen
sTns², circumstance
ssT³, system

D

D¹, had, dollar
D², do, defendant
D³, did
D¹-M, democracy-tic
D²-M, democrat
Dz¹, advertise
D²-sM, December
D²-Ms-K, domestic
Dst², distinct
D¹-Trn, doctrine
Dl², deliver-y
Dr¹, Dr. (Doctor)
Dr², during
Dw², dwell
D³-sKr-M, discriminate
Df³, differ-ence-ent
Dv²-P, develop

CH

CH¹, charge
CH², which, change
CHl², children

J

J¹, large
J², advantage

J¹-N, January
Jl², angel
Jr³, junior
Jn², general-ly
Jnt¹, gentleman
Jnt², gentlemen
sJn², suggestion

K

K¹, can
K², come
K³, could, kingdom
K-B¹, cabinet
K-TH¹, catholic
Kz¹, because
K-Bl², capable
K-Pn¹, captain
Kl²-K, collect
Klt³, difficult-y
Krm³, Christian
Kr²-K, correct
Kr²-Ks-K, characteristic
Kr¹-sMn, cross-examine
Krd¹, according
Kw², question
Kw-F¹, qualify
Kwtr¹, quarter
Knt¹, county
sKr¹, describe
sKrshn², description

G

G¹, go
G², gave, together
G³, give-n
G-V², governor
Gr³, degree
Grt²-Brt, Great Britain
Gw¹, language
Gv², govern
Gn¹, began
Gn², begun
Gn³, begin
Gthr¹, altogether
sG³, signify

F

F¹, form, half
F², for
F²-B, February

F^2-K, effect,
F^1-M, familiarity
F^2-M, familiar
Fst^2, first
Frnt^3, frequent
Fn^1, phonography
Ft^1, fact
sFt^3, swift

V

V^1, have, halve
V^2, ever
Vr^1, over
Vn^2, heaven
sV^2, several

TH

TH^1, thank, hath
TH^2, worth
TH^3, think, youth

DH

DH^1, that
DH^2, them
DH^3, with
DHr^1, other
DHr^2, their, there
sDHn^2, southern
wDH^1, without

S

S^2-P, especial-ly
St^1, astonish-ed·
St^1-B, establish

Z

Z^1, was
Z^3, these

SH

SH^1, shall
SH^3, should

ZH

ZH^3, usual-ly

L

L^2, well
L^3, will

L^2-P, help
L^2-J, legislature
L^2-TH, health-y
Lr^2, already

R

R^2, her
R^3, hear-re
R^1-K-T, architect-ure-al
R^1-M, remark
R^2-M, remember
Rs^1-T-K, aristocracy-atic
R^2-Jl, archangel
sR^1, swear

R

R^1, are, our
R^2, were, where, recollect
R^2-P, represent-ative
R^2-P-B, republic-sh
R^2-CH-B, archbishop
R^2-K-TH, Roman Catholic
R^1-G, regularity
R^2-G, regular
R^2-V, Rev. (Reverend)
Rs^1-Pns, responsible-y
Rs^3-Pns, responsibility
Rl^2-J, religion
Rld^2, world
Rf^2, refer-ence
Rshn^2, recollection
sRt^3-F, certificate

M

M^1, from, time
M^2, home, member
M^1-M, memorandum
M-M-D^1, memoranda
M-N-F^1, manufacture
Ms-CH^2, Massachusetts
Ms^2-K, mistake
Mst^1, almost
M-Prt^1, importance-t
M^2-Md, immediate
Mr^3, Mr. (Mister)
Mnt^3, movement
sM^1, similarity
sM^2, similar
sM^2-NG, something
sMt^2, somewhat

N

N¹, own
N², any
N¹ (with final perpendicular tick), now
N² (with tick inclined like CH), new, knew
N-J¹, knowledge
N²-G, neglect
N-V², never, November
N-Y¹, New York
N-Dv², endeavor
Ns², no, sir
Ns³, insurance
N-Fs³, influence
Nst², next
Ndhr¹, another
Ndrs-D³, understood
Nt-Jns², intelligence
Nds-Pns², indispensable-y
sNss³-K, San Francisco

NG

NG¹, long
NG², among
NG³, thing
NG-TH³, length-y
sNG³, singular

W

W², when
W³, would
Wl², wealth-y

Y

Y¹, beyond
Y², yet, young
Y³, your, year
Ys², United States
Yss³, yes, sir

H

Hl², he, him
Hl³, whom

CIRCLE AND VOWEL SIGNS.

as, has

is, his

an, and

the

I, of

awe

O, oh, owe

who, whom

§ 201. In the foregoing lists of contractions only the forms of primitive words are given; in the following list the forms of the derivatives will be found. Sometimes a word that in one of its parts is contracted, in others is best written in full.

A

according—accordingly, Krd¹ !L
advantage—advantageous, J³-S
advertise — advertised, Dzd¹; advertising, Dz(·)¹; advertisement, D¹-zMnt
among—amongst, NGst³
angel—angelic, Jl³-K
astonish — astonishing, St(·)¹; astonishingly, St¹ !L; astonishment, St¹-Mnt
awe — awed, äD¹; awing, same as awe with ing-dot; awe-struck, 'awe':str²-K; awful-ly, Fl¹

B

bankruptcy—bankrupt, B¹-NGr-Pt, etc.
become—becoming, B²-K(·); became, B²-K-M

begin—beginning, Gn(·)²; beginner, B²-G-Nr
believe — believed, Bld²; believing, Bl(·)²; believable, Bl²-Bl; believer, Bl²-Vr; unbelief, N-Blf²; unbeliever, N-Bl²-Vr
belong—belonged, Bld¹; belonging, Bl(·)¹

C

capable — capability, K-Bl²-T; capableness, K-Bl²-Ns; incapable, N-K-Bl²
change — changed, CHd²; changing, CH(·)²; changeable, CH²-Bl; changer, CH²-Jr; interchange, Ntr-CH²; unchanged, N-CHd²
charge—charged, CHd¹; charging, CH(·)¹; chargeable-y, CH¹-Bl
Christian—Christianity, Krs-CHnt¹; Christianize, Krs-CH²-Nz; anti-Christian, Nt²-Krn
circumstance—circumstanced, sTnst²; circumstantial-ly, sTn¹; circumstantiate, sTn¹-SHt
collect—collected, Kl-K-Td²; collecting, Kl²-K(·)
correct — corrected, Kr-K-Td²; correcting, Kr²-K(·); correctly, Kr-K-L²; correctness, Kr²-K-Ns

D

deliver—delivered, Dld²; delivering, Dl(·)²; deliverance, Dlns²; deliverer, Dl²-R
describe—described, sKrd¹; describing, sKr(·)¹
develop — developed, Dv²-Pt; developing, Dv²-P(·); development, Dv²-P-Mnt
differ — differed, Dfd²; differing, Df(·)²; differs, Dfz²; indifferent, N-Df²
discriminate—indiscriminate, N-D²-sKr-M
distinct—distinction, Dst²-NGshn; distinctive, Dst²-NGt-V; distinctness, Dst²-Ns
domestic—domesticate, D²-Ms-Kt; domestication, D²-Ms-Kshn
dwell—dwelt, Dw²-Lt; dwelling, Dw(·)²

E

effect—effected, F²-K-Td; effecting, F²-K(·); effective, F²-K-Tv
experience—experienced, sPrnst²; experiencing, sPrns²-NG
extraordinary—extraordinarily, sTr¹-R-L

F

familiar—familiarize, F²-Mz; unfamiliar, N-F²-M
form—formed, Fd¹; forming, F(·)¹; formal, F¹-Ml; formation, Fshn²; perform, Pr¹-F; performer, Pr¹-F-Mr; inform, N-F¹; information, N-Fshn²; reform, R¹-F; reformation, R²-Fshn
frequent—frequence, Fr²-Kwns

G

general — generality, J¹-N-Rlt; generalize, J²-N-Rlz; outgeneral, T¹-Jn
gentleman—gentlemanly, Jnt¹!L; ungentlemanly, N-Jnt¹!L
govern—governed, Gvd²; governing, Gv(·)²; government, Gv²-Mnt

I

important—unimportant, N-M-Prt[1]
influence — influenced, N-Fst[3]; influencing, N-Fs[3]-NG ; influential, N-Fn[2]
intelligence—intelligent, Nt-Jnt[2]; intelligible-y, Nt-J[2]-Bl; unintelligible-y, N-Nt-J[2]-Bl

K

knowledge—acknowledge, K-N-J[1]

L

large—larger, Jr[1]; largest, Jst[1]; largely, Jl[1]
long—longer, NGr[1]; longest, NGst[1]; long-hand, L[1]-NG-Hnd

M

manufacture — manufactured, M-N-F[1]-K-CHrd ; manufacturing, M-N-F(·)[1]; manufactory, M-N-F[1]-R; manufacturer, M-N-F[1]-R
mistake — mistaken, Ms[2]-Kn ; mistook, Ms[3]-K ; unmistakable-y, N-Ms-K-Bl[2]
movement—move, M-V[3]

N

never—nevertheless, N-Vt[2]-Ls
New York—New-Yorker, N-Y[1]-Kr
number—numbered, Brd[2] ; numbering, Br(·)[2] ; outnumber, T[1]-Br ; unnumbered, N-Brd[2]

O

object—objected, B[2]:D ; objecting, B(·)[2] ; objection, Bshn[2]
opinion—opinionated, Pn[3]-N-Td ; opinioned, Pn[3]-Nd
owe—owed, ōD[2] ; owing, same as *owe* with *ing*-dot.

P

part—parted, P[1]:D ; parting, P(·)[1] ; partly, Prt[1]-L
particular—particularly, Prt[3]:L ; particularity, Prt[1]-Kl-Rt ; particularize, Prt[3]-Kl-Rz
people—peopled, P[3]-Pld
phonography—phonographer, Fn[1]-R ; phonographic, Fn[1]-K
popular — popularize, P[1]-P-L-Rz ; popularly, P[1]-P-L ; unpopular, N-P[1]-P
practice—practiced, Prst[1] ; practicing, Pr(·)[1] ; practicable-y, Pr[1]-K-Bl ; practicability, Pr[3]-K-Blt ; practices, Prs[1] ; impracticable, M-Pr[1]-K-Bl
principle—principled, Pr[3]-Ns-P-Ld ; unprincipled, N-Pr[3]-Ns-P-Ld
probable—improbable, M-Pr[1]-B
proportion—disproportion, Ds[2]-Pr-Pshn
public-sh — published, P[3]-B:T ; publishing, P[3]-B(·) ; publication, P[2]-Bshn ; publicly, P[3]-B:L ; republic-sh, R[2]-P-B ; republication, R[2]-P-Bshn ; republican, R[2]-P-Bn ; republicanism, R[2]-P-B-zM

Q

quarter—quartered, Kwtrd[1] ; headquarters, Hd[2]-Kwtrs
question—questioned, Kws-CHnd[2] ; questioning, Kw(·)[2] ; questionable, Kw-Bl[3] ; unquestionable-y, N-Kw-Bl[2]

R

recollect—recollected, R^2'D; recollecting, $R(\cdot)^2$; recollection, Rshn²
refer—referred, Rfd²; referring, Rf$(\cdot)^2$
regular—regularly, R^2-G-L; irregular, Rr²-G; irregularity, Rr¹-G
remark — remarked, R^1-Mt; remarking, R^1-M$(\cdot)$; remarkable-y, R^1-M-Bl
remember—remembered, R^2-Md; remembering, R^2-M$(\cdot)$; remembrance, R^2-Ms
represent—represented, R^2-P'D; representing, R^2-P$(\cdot)$; representation, R^2-Pshn; misrepresent, Ms-R^2-P; misrepresentation, Ms-R^2-Pshn

S

satisfactory—satisfactorily, sT^1-sR-L
signify—signified, sGd³; signifying, s$G(\cdot)^3$; significance, sGns³; significancy, sGn-S³; significant, sGnt³; signification, sGshn²
similar—similarly, sM^2'L; dissimilar, D^2-ss$M$
singular—singularity, sNG-Lrt¹; singularly, sNG³'L
southern—southerner, sDH²-Nr
speak — spoke, sP^2; spoken, sPn²; speaking, s$P(\cdot)^3$; speakable, sP^3-Bl; outspoken, T^1-sPn
special—specialty, sP^2-$S$$R$-T
subject—subjected, sB^2'D; subjecting, s$B(\cdot)^2$; subjection, sBshn²
surprise—surprised, sPrzd¹; surprising, sPrz¹-NG
swear—swore, sR^2; swearing, sR^1-NG; sworn, sRn²
swift—swifter, sFtr³; swiftest, sF^3-Tst; swiftly, sFt³-L; swiftness, sFt²-Ns

T

thank — thanked, THt¹; thanking, T$H(\cdot)^1$; thankful-ly, TH^1-Fl; thanksgiving-day, THs¹-G-D
thing—something, sM^2-NG
think—thinking, T$H(\cdot)^2$; thinker, TH^3-Kr; unthinking, N-T$H(\cdot)^3$
time—timely, T^1-M-L
truth—truthful-ly, Tr²-Fl; untruth, N-Tr²; untruthful-ly, N-Tr²-Fl

U

usual—unusual-ly, N-ZH^3

W

well—welled, Ld²; welling, L^2-NG
what—whatever, T^2-Vr
where—somewhere, sM-R^2
will—willed, Ld³; willing, L^3-NG; willful-ly, L^3-Fl
world—worldly, Rld²-L

Y

young—younger, Yr²; youngest, Yst²
your—yours, Yz³
youth—youthful-ly, TH^3-Fl

REMARKS ON THE WORD-SIGNS AND CONTRACTIONS.

§ 292. The foregoing list of contractions is designed mainly for the use of the reporter; therefore the non-professional writer may adopt only so many and such of these signs as suit his taste or convenience. It is recommended, however, that all who can spare the time should familiarize themselves with the entire list, because it is always easier to write long forms after committing to memory shorter ones, than to adopt abbreviated forms, having first formed the habit of using full outlines.

SAME SIGN FOR PRESENT AND PAST TENSES.

§ 293. When a word-sign or contraction represents a verb in the present tense, the past tense, if formed regularly by the addition of *d* or *ed*, may be expressed by the same sign; thus, ⁄ *recollect-ed*, ∧ *represent-ed*. In such cases the context may generally be relied upon to determine the time of the action; if necessary, however, the additional sound of the past tense may be expressed either by halving, or by a disjoined *tee* or *dee*; thus, Bld² *believed*, P²-B!T *published*, ＼| *subjected*. This rule may also be extended to a few words that are written with uncontracted outlines, but whose past-tense signs present unusual difficulties; thus, Pr²-sWd *persuaded*, Dt¹ *date-d*.

THE PLURAL OF NOUNS.

§ 294. When a noun is written with a word-sign or contraction, the plural is formed, as in the ordinary way, by merely adding the *ess*-circle to the contracted outline; thus, ∧ *representative*, ∧₀ *represent atives*, | *defendant*, | *defendants*.

THE POSSESSIVE CASE OF NOUNS.

§ 295. The possessive case of nouns, whether written with full or contracted outlines, is formed by adding the *ess*-circle; or, if the nominative ends with the *ess*-circle, by enlarging it to *sis*; thus, ℯ⸱ *son's*, ⸰ *Case's*.

THIRD PERSON SINGULAR OF VERBS.

§ 296. The third person singular of regular verbs in the indicative mood, present tense, that are written with word-signs or contractions, is also formed by adding the *ess*-circle; thus, ___ *come*, ___₀ *comes*.

SAME SIGN FOR ADJECTIVE AND ADVERB.

§ 297. The same sign may be used for the adjective and adverb when the latter is derived from the former by affixing *ly*; thus, ⁄ *general-ly*. When the *ly* is written, it should be disjoined; thus, Jnt¹!L *gentlemanly*.

PHRASEOGRAPHY.

§ 298. The learner has now had presented to him all the steno-graphic material used in Phonography. He has also been made acquainted with the fact, that in practice the signs of the vowels are seldom expressed; so that, in great measure, they may hereafter be excluded from consideration, and his attention directed to the consonants alone. Thus far, however, the consonant-signs have been used to represent the consonant-sounds, both singly and in groups, as they are found in separate words only; and it yet remains, therefore, to extend their use to the representation of groups of consonants as they occur in phrases, or collections of words. This mode of writing, by which the consonants of several words are joined or grouped in one character, is called Phraseography.

TWO KINDS OF PHRASES.

§ 299. There are two ways of forming phrase-signs; the simplest is to merely join the phonographic outlines of two or more words together without altering the form that each would have if written by itself, and is exactly like joining words in writing ordinary long-hand; thus, $\mathcal{V}$ which were, $\mathcal{S}$ may as well, ... in any case, etc. The other mode of phrase-writing, and the only one which requires extended explanation, is to group together, by means of the stem-signs and their various modifications, the consonants of several words, without regard to the form of each individually—a portion, and sometimes all of the words, as it were, losing their identity of outline; thus, $\mathcal{S}$ by all their.

§ 300. The following is a statement of the power of the different consonant modifications, or attachments, when used in phrase-writing, and in the precise order of their introduction on the preceding pages of this work.

CIRCLES AND LOOPS.

'AS,' 'HAS,' 'IS,' 'HIS,' OR 'US' ADDED BY THE ESS-CIRCLE.

§ 301. As, has, is, or his may be added both initially and finally, and us finally, by the ess-circle; thus, $\mathcal{)}$ as so, $\int$ has done, ... is in, ... who has or is, $\mathcal{/}$ where is, $\mathcal{)}$ so h-as, $\mathcal{L}$ for us, $\cdot\mathcal{)}\cdot$ see us.

§ 302. An ess-circle word-sign is prefixed to a word commencing with the circle, or suffixed to one ending with it, by enlarging the circle into ss; thus, $\int$ has said, ... is seen, $\mathcal{C}$ has some, $\mathcal{P}$ raise us, ... gives us, $\mathcal{O}$ knows us, $\mathcal{O}$ as his, or as is, ... is as, or his is.

CAUTION IN REGARD TO 'US.'

§ 303. *Us*, when added by the circle to verbs, will sometimes conflict with another form of the verb, as *give-us* with *gives*, *put-us* with *puts*, etc., and should therefore be used cautiously in such cases; and when in doubt as to its safety, the writer should employ the stem S.

'TO,' 'IT,' OR 'THE' ADDED BY CHANGING THE CIRCLE TO A SMALL LOOP.

§ 304. *To*, *it*, or *the* may be added to any of the *ess*-circle word-signs, either at the commencement or end of a phrase, or when standing alone, and also at the end of most words ending with the circle, by changing it to the small loop; thus, ∫ *as to what*, ⌐ *as to her*, ⌒ *as the man*, ⟋ *as it were*, ∤ *what is the*, ⌐ *because the*, ⟋ *raise the*, ⌐ *face the*, ⊘ *h-as the* or *to*, ⋅⋅⊘ *is the* or *to*, ⊘ *as it is*, ⋅⊘ *is it as.*

'THERE,' 'THEIR,' OR 'THEY ARE' ADDED BY CHANGING THE CIRCLE TO A LARGE LOOP.

§ 305. *There*, *their*, or *they are* may be added, in the cases stated in the last section, by changing the circle to a large loop; thus, ⌐ *has there been*, ⌐ *is there any*, ⌐ *takes their*, ⌐ *because they are*, ⌐ *because there is*, ⌐ *unless they are*, ⊘ *as there*, ⋅⊘ *is there.*

§ 306. When it is impossible or inconvenient to join a loop to another outline in the ordinary way, it may be written with the detached form, and then joined; thus, ⊘⌐ *has there not been*, ⋅⊘⋅ *is there soon*, ⊘ *as there is.* Some writers find more difficulty than others in joining loops initially; for such the detached loops are generally the best.

THE HOOKS.

'ALL' OR 'WILL' ADDED BY THE EL-HOOK.

§ 307. *All* or *will* may be added by the *el*-hook; thus, ⟍ *by all*, ∫ *what will*, ⋅∫⋅ *it will*, ⟋ *which will*, ⌐ *can all*, ⌐ *they will*, ⌐ *for all*, ⋅⌐⋅ *if all*, ⌐ *among all.*

'ARE,' 'OUR,' OR 'OR' ADDED BY THE ER-HOOK.

§ 308. *Are*, *our*, or *or* may be added by the *er*-hook; thus, ⌐ *what are*, ⟍ *by our*, ⟋ *which are*, ⟋ *where are*, ⌐ *on or* or *our*, ⌐ *they are*, ⌐ *among our.*

'WE' ADDED BY THE WAY-HOOK.

§ 309. *We* may be added to straight stems by the *way*-hook; thus, ∫ *what we*, ∫ *ought we*, ∫ *do we*, ⌐ *can we*, ⟋ *where we.*

'YOU' OR 'YOUR' ADDED BY THE YAY-HOOK.

§ 310. *You* or *your* may be added to straight stems by the *yay*-hook; thus, ╲ *by you-r*, ╲ *but you-r*, ⌐ *what you-r*, ⌐ *can you-r*.

'IN' ADDED BY THE IN-HOOK.

§ 311. The preposition *in* may be written by the *in*-hook; thus, ↶ *in some*. The outline of the word to which *in* is thus prefixed should always be written in its proper position, instead of following that of *in*.

'HAVE' OR 'OF' ADDED BY THE EF-HOOK.

§ 312. *Have* or *of* may be added by the *ef*-hook; thus, ╲ *part of*, (*out of*, (*what have*, ⌐ *can have*, (*they have*, ⌐ *may have*. The *ef*-hook on curves should be made larger than on straight stems.

'AND,' 'AN,' 'OWN,' 'BEEN,' OR 'THAN' ADDED BY THE EN-HOOK.

§ 313. *And, an, own, been,* or *than* may be added by the *en*-hook; thus, ⸤ *you and*, ⸤ *if an*, ↳ *for an*,) *or an*, ⟩ *her own*, ↳ *have been*, (*other than*, ⌐ *more than*. It is allowable to turn a small hook for *n* on the inside of the *ter*-hook, or of the *vee*-hook on curves; thus, ⟋ *rather than*, (*they have been*. The phrase *my own* is written M¹-N to distinguish it from Mn¹ *mine*.

'THERE,' 'THEIR,' 'THEY ARE,' OR 'OTHER' ADDED BY THE TER-HOOK, AND BY LENGTHENING.

§ 314. *There, their, they are,* or *other* may be added by the *ter*-hook, and by lengthening, thus, (*what there*, ⌐ *can there*, (*of their*,) *shall there*, ⌐ *should there*, -(*though there* or *though they are*, ⸤ *if their* or *if they are*, ⸤ *will there*, ⌐ *from their*, ⌐ *on their*, ↳ *no other*, ⸱⸱⸱ *in there*, ↳ *among their*, ⌐ *may other*, ⸍ *loan their*, ⟋ *run there*, ⸱⸱⸱ *could have their*.

§ 315. As the words *other* and *their* would sometimes conflict if written alike, a distinction is made when necessary by putting the short second-place dash-vowel *ŭ* after stems to which *other* is added as in the preceding section. Full information on this point is given under the word *other* in the Dictionary of Practical Phonography.

'THE,' 'IT,' 'HAD,' OR 'TO' ADDED BY HALVING.

§ 316. *The, it, had,* or *to* may be added by halving; thus, ╲ *by the*, | *at the*, ⌐ *from the*, ⌣ *among the*, ↳ *out of the*, ↳ *of it*, ⌐ *may it*, ⟩ *why the*, ⌐ *yet the*, ⸱⸱⸱ *it had*, ╲ *able to*, | *ought to*.

'AFTER' ADDED BY THE EF-HOOK AND LENGTHENING PRINCIPLE.

§ 317. *After* may be added by the *ef*-hook and lengthening principle combined; thus, Dftr²-D *day after day*, Bf²-*Rftr before or after*, M-N-Dftr²-Nn *Monday afternoon*, Yftr³-Y *year after year*.

'ANOTHER' ADDED BY THE EN-HOOK AND LENGTHENING PRINCIPLE.

§ 318. *Another* may be added by the *en*-hook and lengthening principle combined; thus, ⟍ *but another*, ⟋ *where another*, ⌒ *from another*.

'ITS' ADDED BY THE HALVING PRINCIPLE AND ESS-CIRCLE.

§ 319. *Its* may be added by the halving principle and *ess*-circle combined; thus, Vts¹ *of its*, Tts¹ *at its*, Nts¹ *on its*.

'NOT' ADDED BY THE EN-HOOK AND HALVING PRINCIPLE.

§ 320. *Not* may be added by the *en*-hook and halving principle combined; thus, ⌡ *had not*, ⌡ *do not*, ·ȷ· *did not*, ⌐ *can not*, ⌒ *may not*, ·ȷ· *it will not*.

COMBINATION OF FOREGOING PRINCIPLES.

§ 321. The foregoing principles of phrase-writing may be used in combination with each other, as well as separately; thus, ⌒ *can all of*, ⌣ *can all of the*, ⌐ *can all their*, ⌐ *can all their own*, ⌇ *do you mean to say*.

WORDS WRITTEN BY AN INITIAL AND FINAL MODIFICATION OF THE PRECEDING STEM.

§ 322. In phrases, sometimes a word is best written by an initial hook and a final modification, on the stem of the preceding word; thus, ⟨ *what was*, ∫ *at one*.

POSITION OF PHRASE-SIGNS, ETC.

§ 323. As a general rule, the first word of a phrase-sign should be written in the position it would occupy if written by itself, and the other words then joined, one after another, without regard to position; thus, ⌒ *as mine*, ⌣ *has not*, ⁝ *is not*.

EXCEPTIONS.

§ 324. When the first word of the phrase belongs to the first position, and is represented by a circle, loop, horizontal stem, or any half-length stem, if necessary to secure greater legibility, the first word may be raised or lowered so as to allow the second word of the phrase to be written in the position it would occupy if standing alone, providing the first word is not thereby brought through or below the line; thus, ⌐ *has had*, ⌡ *as shall*, ℯ... *as if*, ⌐° *as well as*, (*as to that*, ⌐... *as it would*, ⌐ *on those*, ⌐... *on this*, ⌐ *about those*, ..⌐. *about this*.

CERTAIN WORDS DISTINGUISHED.

§ 325. It will be observed that sometimes two or three words are written with the same sign, being distinguished, one from the other, only by difference of position. Now, it is obvious that, in phrase-writing, this mode of distinction can be preserved with such words only when they commence phrases. Therefore, when the context can not be relied upon to show which word was intended, in case the sign is thrown out of its proper position, the writer must make a distinction in some special manner; as by vocalizing, or changing the form, of one of the conflicting words. For instance, K and Knt may always be used for *can* and *can not*, even when, in phrases, they are removed from the first position; thus, T^3-K-B *it can be*, T^3-Knt *it can not*. But K and Knt must not be used for *could* and *could not* unless they stand alone or commence a phrase—*it could be* is written T^3 K^3-B; and *it could not*, T^3 Knt^3 or T^3-Kd-Nt. When it is more convenient to join *could*, *did*, *should*, or *that* to a preceding word than to disjoin, they should be written respectively Kd, Dd, SHd, DHt; thus, DH^2-Dd *they did*, T^3-*SH*d-B *it should be*, N^1-DHt *on that*, F^2-DHt *if that*. Generally, however, it is best to disjoin *could*, *did*, and *should*, and to join *that* to the preceding word. DH for *them* may be joined freely in any part of a phrase. *Had* and *do* may generally with safety be written D in any part of a phrase; but if there should arise any conflict, *do* should be disjoined, leaving the field to *had*. When the words *no*, *go*, *own*, *else*, *least*, *see*, *ill*, are joined to a preceding word that is written with a stem-sign, they should always be vocalized, to distinguish them respectively from *any*, *come*, *know*, *less*, *last*, *say*, *well*. Write T^1-Lst *at least* to distinguish from T^1-Lst *at last*. *Ree* is never used for *are* except alone or commencing a phrase. When *are* is joined to a preceding word, the stem R or the r-hook is used; thus, DHr^2-R *there are*, DHr^2 *they are*. R for *were* may be used in any part of a phrase. If *charge* is thrown out of position, as by *to* in the phrase *to charge*, write it CHr-J; but write CH^4 for *to change*. *Part* is joined freely in phrases; when more convenient, it is occasionally changed to Prt; thus, N^1-M-Prt *on my part*. *Opportunity* should always be written P^3 and alone. Certain words are written out of the position of their accented vowels in order to avoid collision with other words—in the following list the conflicting words are put in parentheses: J^2 *advantage* (joy), $Ndhr^1$ *another* (no other), $Gdhr^1$ *altogether*

(again), N² *any* (no), D² *do* (did), F² *for* (of, form), Jnt¹ *gentleman*,
(gentlemen), G¹ *go* (come), H² *he* (me), H² *him* (whom), DHr¹ *other*
(their), Vr¹ *over* (very), N¹ *own* (know), Tr² *truth* (true), T² *what* (at,
out), CII² *which* (each), Ys² *yourself* (use). *Society* is written in any
part of a phrase, but *system*, except when standing alone or commencing a phrase, is written ssT-M. *Inner* should always be vocalized, to
distinguish it from *near*. Always carefully vocalize *leave*, to distinguish
it from *live*.

'EVER' AND 'HAVE' DISTINGUISHED.

§ 326. *Ever* as a word-sign, whether standing alone or used in phrases,
should always be written with the stem V, to distinguish it from *have*,
which, in phrases (except at the commencement), is written with the *vee*-
hook; thus, ⎰ *do you ever,* ⎱ *do you have.* But *ever* as a suffix may be
written with the *vee*-hook. See § 285.

TICKS FOR 'I,' 'A,' 'AN,' AND 'AND.'

§ 327. The words *I, a, an,* or *and* may be joined by a light tick, the
position of which is governed by that of the word to which it is so attached—as follows:

1. *I,* at the commencement of phrases—by a light tick struck in the
direction of either *ree* or *chay*, according to which gives the best joining;
thus, ⟍ *I hope,* ⟍ *I believe,* ⟍ *I suppose,* ⎰ *I sought,* ⌣ *I know,*
⌢ *I am.* Before the signs for *can, can not, could, could not,* the upward tick is used, so as to avoid collisions with several other outlines.

2. *A, an,* or *and,* at the commencement of phrases—by a light tick
written invariably in the direction of *pee;* thus, ⎰ *and then,* ⌢ *and
my,* ⌣ *and we,* ⟍ *and as for.* This hook is not used unless it makes
an easy angle with the following stem, the dot being preferred in other
cases.

3. In the middle or at the end of phrases, a tick inclined in either
direction may be used for either *I* or *a*—and for *an* or *and* when they
can not be written with the *n*-hook; thus, ⎯ *if I may,* ⎯ *in
a moment,* ⟋⟍ *worse and worse,* ⎯ *in a,* Ftr¹- (tick in direction of
chay) *after a or an,* Wdhr²- (tick in direction of *ree*) *whether a or an,*
SIItr¹- (tick in direction of *pee*) *shatter a or an,* Nt¹- (tick in direction of
pee) *not a,* Fdhrz²- (tick in direction of *chay*) *if there is a.*

HOOKS ON TICKS.

§ 328. The following tick-signs with hooks are used, ⌣ *I will,* ⎰ *I
have,* ⌢ *I will not.*

'I,' 'A,' OR 'AND' FOLLOWED BY 'COM' OR 'CON.'

§ 329. When *I* is followed by *com* or *con*, the tick is written close to or over the beginning of the following stem (*com* or *con* being omitted); thus, ⌐ *I contend*. *A, and*, and *the*, before *com* or *con*, should be written with their dot-signs, and then the *com* or *con* indicated by proximity or by the dot for that syllable.

TICK FOR 'THE' AND 'HE.'

§ 330. *The* is generally indicated by halving or by looping; but when it can not be so written (as, for instance, after a lengthened or halved stem), it may be expressed by a light horizontal or perpendicular tick; thus, ‿ *under the*. The same tick may be used initially for *he* when the stem *hay* makes a bad junction.

JOINING OF TICKS WITH CIRCLES, LOOPS, ETC.

§ 331. The tick-signs may also be joined to the circle word-signs, to the detached loops, and to each other; thus, ℃ *as a* or *an*, ⌐ *is a* or *an*, ℃ or ℃ *as I*, ⌐ *and a* or *an*, ⌐ *and the*.

'-ING THE' AND '-ING A-N.'

§ 332. In all cases where the final syllable *-ing* would be expressed by the dot, *the* may be added by changing the dot to a perpendicular or horizontal tick, and *a* or *an* by changing it to an inclined tick written in the direction of *pee* or *chay*; thus, ⌐ *putting the*, ⌐ *separating a-n*, ⌐ *hoping the*, ⌐ *hoping a-n*.

BRIEF SIGNS FOR 'WE,' 'WOULD,' AND 'YOU,' *your, know—*

§ 333. Where the stems W and Y do not join well, the words *we*, *would*, and *you* may be joined by a small half-circle—the left or right form (⌐ ⌐) for *w*, and the upper or lower half (⌐ ⌐) for *y*.

'OF' OMITTED.

§ 334. When *of* between words can not be conveniently written with the *ef*-hook, it may be omitted, and then intimated by writing the adjacent words in proximity; thus, ⌐ *loss of money;* and sometimes by joining them; thus, ⌐ *words of my text.*

'OF' FOLLOWED BY 'COM' OR 'CON.'

§ 335. When *of* precedes a word commencing with *com* or *con*, the *of* may be indicated by proximity and the dot used for the prefix. In practice, however, the dot may generally be omitted with safety.   ·

'TO' OR 'TOO' OMITTED AND INDICATED BY A FOURTH POSITION.

§ 336. At the commencement of a phrase, either *to* or *too* may generally be indicated by dropping the form of the succeeding word one half the length of a *tee*-stem below the third position of the same form; thus, ⌐ *to do*, ⌐ *to be seen*, ⌐ *to receive*, ⌐ *to trade*, ⌐ *too good.* If a word so written in the fourth position begins with *com* or *con*, the prefix may be indicated by proximity; thus, D⁴:P'ln⁴ *had to complain.*

§ 337. It is not well to begin a sentence with a horizontal or a half-length in the fourth position. In such cases, the stem *tee* should be used; thus, ·⌐··· *To me*, etc.

'FROM—TO' OMITTED.

§ 338. From such phrases as 'from hour to hour,' 'from week to week,' etc., *from—to* may be omitted, and intimated by writing the signs of the repeated word near each other, or, when more convenient, by joining them; thus, || *from day to day*, ⌒⌒ *from time to time*, R'-R *from hour to hour.*

'AND' OMITTED.

§ 339. *And* may occasionally be omitted from the middle of a phrase, and the adjacent words joined, especially when they are the same word repeated; thus, Gn-Gn *again and again.*

RULES FOR PHRASE-WRITING.

GENERAL RULES.

§ 340. Words that are naturally collected into a phrase or clause in speaking may generally be joined in a phrase-sign in writing; thus, 'as-well-as,' 'in-the-first-place,' 'on-the-part-of-the,' 'on-the-other-hand,' etc. But there should be no straining after phrase-writing at the expense of introducing indistinct or difficult joinings, awkward outlines, or phrase-signs that are of inconvenient length, or that extend too far away from the line. And words should seldom be joined that are separated in speaking by a distinct pause, either rhetorical or grammatical.

§ 341. Phrases may be composed entirely of contracted words, or of words that are not contracted, or of contracted and uncontracted words mingled. So that for the purpose of making phrases, it is unnecessary for the writer to think whether the words entering into the construction of any phrase are contractions or not.

SPECIAL RULES.

§ 342. A noun or pronoun in the objective case may be joined to the preceding verb or preposition by which it is governed; thus, 'take-this,' 'save-them,' 'by-them,' 'for-him.' If any qualifying word or words intervene, they may also be included in the phrase; thus, 'at-the-time,' 'on-the-part,' 'for-my-sake.'

§ 343. A verb may be joined to its nominative, especially if it is a pronoun; thus, 'I-see,' 'he-lives,' 'they-make,' 'we-look.' If the verb has any auxiliaries, they, together with any intervening adverb or adverbs, may be joined to it, and the whole joined to the nominative; thus, 'I-may-be,' 'I-may-not-be,' 'it-can-not-be,' 'James-will-not-go,' 'I-may-again-return.'

§ 344. A qualifying word may be joined to the word it qualifies; thus, 'good-man,' 'a-great-many,' 'very-certain,' 'quite-likely,' 'a-man,' 'much-esteemed,' 'as-good-as,' 'absolutely-necessary.'

§ 345. Two nouns, or a pronoun and a noun, coming together, the first in the possessive case, and the other denoting the thing possessed, may be joined, and the whole joined to a preceding governing or qualifying word; thus, 'James's-book,' 'on-the-father's-side,' 'on-his-part,' 'on-their-side.'

§ 346. A verb in the infinitive mood, with or without *to*, may be joined to its governing verb, noun, or adjective; thus, 'ought-to-go,' 'I-desire-to-leave,' 'I-dare-say' (í-D-R-S), 'I-need-do.'

§ 347. A copulative conjunction may be joined to the word that follows it, and also to the preceding word, if there is one in the same clause; thus, 'and-then,' 'you-and-I' (Yn²-f), 'worse-and-worse.'

§ 348. When the idiom of the language requires that one word follow another, if in the same clause, they may be joined; thus, 'other-than,' 'more-than,' 'such-as.'

LIST OF PHRASES.

§ 349. The following is a list of phrases that will be found useful to the reporter. Most of them are formed regularly, according to the usual rules for phrasing; but several are contracted outlines, that do not contain all the elements of the words as they are written when standing alone. The list should be thoroughly studied.

A.

about that, Bt¹-DIIt	after a-an, Ftr¹-('a' tick)
about this, Bt¹-DIIs	after all, Ftr¹-L
about which, Bt¹-CII	again and again, Gn²-Gn
absolutely necessary, B¹-sLt-Nss-R	all such, Ls¹-CII
according to, Krd¹	all that, L¹-DIIt
act of Congress, Kt¹-Grs	all the, Lt¹
act of Parliament, Kt¹-Pr-L	all their, $Ldhr$¹
acts of Congress, Kt¹-sGrs	along their, L¹-NGdhr
acts of Parliament, Kt¹-sPr-L	alongside of, L¹-NGs-Dv
	although there is, L²-DIIdhrz
	among the, NGt²

among their, NGdhr²
and so forth, Nds¹-F-TH
any body, N²-Bd
any more than, N³-Mrn
any one else, N³-Wn-Ls
any thing else, N²-NG-Ls
any thing less, N³-NG-*Ls*
are the, *R*t¹
are there, *R*dhr¹
are you, *R*y¹
are you aware, *R*y¹-Wr
are you sure, *R*y¹-SHr
as early as, z*R*²-*Lz*
as far as, zF¹-Rz
as far as possible, zF¹-Rz-Ps
as good as, zGdz⌐ ⌐
as great as, zGrtz²
as it were, st*R*²
as large as, zJz¹
as long as, zNGz¹
as soon as possible, zsNz¹-Ps
at all events, Tlv¹-Nts
at any rate, T¹-Nrt
at last, T¹-*L*st
at least, T¹-Lst
at once, Twns¹
at one, Twn¹
at or about that time, Tr¹-Bt-DHt-
    T-M
at present, T¹-Prz-Nt
at that, T¹-DHt
at the, Tt¹

B.

bank account, B¹-NG-K-K-Nt
Baptist Church, Bts¹-Ch-CH
be able to, B³-Blt
before and after, Bf²-('and'-tick)-Ftr
before or after, Bf²-*R*ftr
before their, Bfdhr²
best of my knowledge, Bst³-M-N-J
between the, Tnt⁷
between their, Tndhr³
book account, B³-K-K-Nt
British America, Brt³-M-*R*-K
but it is not, Bts²-Nt
by and by, Bn¹-B
by the by, Bt¹ B¹

C.

can be, K-B³

can you state, Kys¹-Tt
Catholic Bishop, K-TH¹-B
Catholic Church, K-TH¹-CHr-CH
Catholic Priest, K-TH¹-Prst
Constitution of the U. S., 'stTshn³-
    Ys
could you state, Kys³-Tt
Court of Chancery, Krt²-CH-s*R*
Court of Common Pleas, Krt²-N-Pls
Court of Justice, Krt²-J-sTs
Courts of Justice, Krts²-J-sTs
Court of Sessions, Krts*shns*²
Court of General Sessions, Krt²-
    Jns*shns*
Court of Special Sessions, Krts²-
    Pss*hns*

D.

Dear sir, Dr³-s*R*
defendant's counsel, D²-sKs-L
deputy sheriff, D²-Pt-SHr-F
did you have, Dyv³
did you have any thing, Dyv³-N-NG
do you recollect, Dy²-*R*
do you remember, Dy²-M
during the, Drt³
during the latter part of the, Drt³-
    Ltr-Pvt

E.

Eastern States, Strs³-Tts
eight or nine, T²-*R*-Nn
eight or ten, T²-*R*-Tn
Episcopal Church, P³-sK-CHr-CH
et cetera, T²-sTr
ever since, Vs²-Ns
everlasting life, V²-*Ls*-*L*-F
every where, Vr³-*R*

F.

Fellow citizens, Fls²-Tns
first place, Fs²-Pls
five or seven, Fv¹-*R*s-Vn
five or six, Fv¹-*R*s-Ks
five or six years, Fv¹-*R*s-Ks-Yz
for ever and ever, F²-V-V
for instance, Fs²-Tns
for my part, F²-M-Prt
for several, Fs²-V
for the purpose, Ft²-P
for the purposes, Ft²-Pz

for the sake of the, Fts²-Kvt
four or five, F²-R-F-V

G.

Gentlemen of the Jury, Jnt²-J-R
Great Britain, Grt²-Brt
Great Britain and Ireland, Grt²-Brt-Rlnd
great while, Grt²-Wl
great deal, Grt²-Dl

H.

had another, Dndhr¹
had there been, Ddhr¹-Bn
had you, Dy¹
had we, Dw¹
have been there, Vndhr¹
here and there, Rndhr²
he was, H²-Z
he was not, H²-Z-Nt
he was there, H²-Zdhr
Holy Ghost, H²-Gst
Hon. gentleman, Nr-Jnt¹
Hon. gentlemen, Nr-Jnt²
Hon. member, Nr¹-M
Hon. Senator, Nrs¹-Ntr
House of Commons, Hs¹-K
House of God, Hs¹-Gd
House of Lords, Hs¹-Ldz
House of Parliament, Hs¹-Pr-L
House of Representatives, Hs¹-R-Ps
Houses of Parliament, Hzz¹-Pr-L
how do you do, H¹-Dy-D
how far, H¹-Fr
how long have you been there, H¹-NG-V-Yndhr
how much money, H¹-M-CH-M-N

I.

in consequence, Ns²-Kns
in consideration, nsDrshn²
in effect, N²-F-K
in fact, N²-Ft
in full, N²-F-L
in order, Nrdr²
in point of fact, N²-Pnt-Ft
in reference, N²-Rf
in regard, N²-R-Grd

in relation, N²-Rlshn
in respect, N²-Rs-Pt
in response, N²-Rs-Pns
in that, N²-DHt
in the first place, Nt²-Fs-Pls
in the next place, Nt²-Ns-Pls
in the world, Nt²-Rld
in your direct examination, N²-Y-Drt-sM-Nshn
it is said, Tzs²-D
it is the, Tst²
it is well known, Tz²-L-Nn
it may be said, T²-M-Bs-D
it was not, Twz²-Nt
it will not be, Tlnt²-B

J.

Jesus Christ, J²-sK
just after, Jst²-Ftr
just now, Jst²-N-[upright tick]

K.

Kingdom of Christ, K²-Krst
Kingdom of glory, K²-Gl
Kingdom of Heaven, K²-Vn

L.

Ladies and gentlemen, L²-Dz-Jnt
last will and testament, Ls¹-L-T-sMnt
learned counsel, Lrnd²-Ks-L
learned friend, Lrnd²-Fnd
learned gentleman, Lrnd²-Jnt
learned judge, Lrnd²-J-J

M.

Member of Congress, M²-Grs
Member of the Bar, M²-Br
Member of the Legislature, M²-L-J
Member of Parliament, M²-Pr-L
Members of Congress, Mz²-Grs
Members of the Bar, Mz²-Br
Methodist Church, M-THds²-CH-CH
Methodist Episcopal Church, M-THds²-Ps-CH-CH
more and more, Mr²-Mr
more or less, Mr²-Ls
Mr. Chairman, Mr-CHr¹-Mn

Mr. President, Mr-Prz'-Dnt
Mr. Speaker, Mrs-P²-Kr
My dear brethren, M-Dr²-Brn
My dear friends, M-Dr²-Frndz
My dear madam, M-Dr²-Md-M
My dear sir, M-Dr²-sR

N.

New York, N-Y¹
New York City, N-Ys¹-T
nine or ten, Nn¹-*R*-Tn
No, sir, Ns²
North Carolina, Nr¹-Kr-*L*-N
Northern States, Nrdhrs'-Tts
nothing else, N-TH²-NG-Ls
nothing less, N-TH²-NG-*L*s

O.

objected to, B²-T
objection sustained, Bss²-Tnd
of another, Vndhr'
on his part, Nz¹-P
on my part, N'-M-Prt
on one or two occasions, N¹-W-Nr-
    T-Kzhns
on or after, Nr¹-Ftr
on or before, Nr¹-Bf
on the other, N¹-DHdhr
on these occasions, N¹-Z-Kzhnz
once or twice, Ws²-R-Tws
once in a while, Ws²-N-Wl
one or both, W²-Nr-B-TH
one or two, W²-Nr-T
our own, *R*n¹

P.

part of their, Pvdhr¹
peculiar circumstances of the case,
    P²-Ks-Tnsz-Ks
per annum, P²-*R*-N-M
per cent., P²-*R*s-Nt
per minute, Pr²-Mn-T
personal estate, Prs²-Nls-Tt
phonographic society, Fn¹-Kss-T
plaintiff's counsel, P²-sKs-L or Plt²-
    sKs-L
point of view, Pnt¹-V
Presbyterian Church, Prz²-CH-CH
President of the U. S., Prz²-Dnt-Ys

R.

real estate, *R*ls²-Tt
re-cross-examination, *R*²-Kr-sM-
    Nshn
re-direct-examination, *R*²-Drt-sM-
    Nshn
Roman Catholic, *R*²-K-TH
Roman Catholic Church, *R*²-K-TH-
    CHr-CH

S.

Saviour of the world, sV²-*R*ld
Sec'y of State, sKrts²-Tt
Sec'y of the Treasury, sKrt²-Tr
Sec'y of War, sKrt²-Wr
Senate of the U. S., sNt²-Ys
six or eight, sK³-s*R*-T
six or seven, sK²-s*R*s-Vn
so far as you know, S²-Frz-Y-N
so to speak, Sts²-P
Southern States, sDHs²-Tts
state of facts, stTv²-Fts
Sunday-school, sN-Ds²-Kl

T.

the other, DHdhr²
then there was, DHndhr²-Z
three or four, Thr²-*R*-F-R
two or three, Tr²-THr

U.

under all the circumstances, Ndr²-
    Lds-Tnsz
under the circumstances, Ndrs²-Tnsz
under the circumstances of the case, ·
    Ndrs²-Tnsz-Ks
United States, Ys²
U. S. of America, Ys²-M-*R*-K
U. S. Senate, Yss²-Nt
U. S. Senator, Yss²-Ntr

V.

very likely, Vr²-*L*-Kl
very seldom, Vr²-sLd-M
Vice-President, Vs¹-Pz-Dnt
vice versa, Vs¹-V-S
viva voce, V²-V-S

W.

was he not, Z'-Hnt
Ways and Means, Wz²-Mnz
well, sir, Ls^2-R
we have, Wv³
what was, Twz²
what was done, Twz²-Dn
what was said and done, Twzs²-Dn-Dn
what was said and done there, Twzs²-Dn-Dndhr
what took place, T²-T-Pls
where do you reside, R^2-Dy-Rz-D
where was, Rwz²
where was that, Rwz²-DHt
where was your place of business, Rwz²-Y-Pls-Bz-Nz
which was, CHwz²
with reference, DH²-Rf

with regard, DH²-R-Grd
with relation, DH²-Rlshn
with respect, DH²-Rs-Pt
Word of God, Wrd²-Gd
Words of God, Wrdz²-Gd
words of my text, Wrdz²-Mt-Kst
words of our text, Wrdz²-R-T-Kst

Y.

year and a half, Yn³-F
year or two, Y³-R-T
years ago, Yz²-G
years before, Yz²-Bf
years of age, Yz³-J
years old, Yz³-Ld
yes or no, Ys²-R-N
yes, sir, Yss²
you are sure, Yr³-SHr
Your Honor, Y³-Nr

SPECIAL PHRASE AND WORD CONTRACTIONS.

§ 350. When a phrase or word, whose outline is of inconvenient length, occurs frequently in a particular case or subject matter, the reporter, after writing it once or twice in full, may oftentimes save himself considerable labor by extemporizing an abbreviation for it. Such contractions are generally best formed by omitting from the outline all but the leading and most suggestive signs; attention also being given, in the selection, to ease and convenience of junction. Thus, for instance, in reporting legal proceedings, such outlines as the following may be used: D²-Bs 'defendant objects,' Bss²-Tnd 'objection sustained,' Ls^1-L-T-sMnt 'last will and testament;' in legislative or congressional reporting, Nr¹-Jnt 'Honorable gentleman,' Nr¹-M 'Honorable member,' Nrs¹-Ntr 'Honorable senator,' Nr¹-Jnt-N-Y 'Honorable gentleman from New York;' in sermon reporting, L^1-J-sK 'Lord Jesus Christ,' Tr²-Nl-F 'eternal life,' H-Gst 'Holy Ghost,' N-T²-sMnt 'New Testament,' etc.; in reporting a lecture on Chemistry, Ntr¹-sD 'nitrous acid,' Kr¹-Bs-D 'carbonic acid,' Ks-D¹-Hdr 'oxide of hydrogen;' in a lecture on Anatomy, sP¹-Kl 'spinal column,' G¹-NG-P-TH 'ganglion ophthalmicum,' etc. Names of corporations and companies may also be abbreviated in the same way; thus, L^1-Trs-K 'Life & Trust Co.,' sN²-M-Ns-K 'Sun Mutual Insurance Co.,' CH-Br-Rs 'Chamber of Commerce,' Ns-Nt-Rl^2-D 'N. Y. Central Railroad.' These special contractions, though they may be perfectly legible in the particular subject for which they are made, should not, of course, be employed in general reporting.

PUNCTUATION AND OTHER MARKS.

§ 351. The following are the punctuation and other marks used in Phonography:

COMMA............	,		APPLAUSE.........	⚕
SEMICOLON.........	;		LAUGHTER.........	⚕
COLON............	:		DASH.............	=
PERIOD...........	×		CARET...........	∧
EXCLAMATION......	/		INDEX...........	☞
INTERROGATION.....	? or /		PARAGRAPH.......	⊄
DOUBT...........	(?)		SECTION..........	§
HYPHEN..........	⫽		ASTERISK.........	✳
PARENTHESIS.......	( )		DAGGER..........	†
BRACKETS........	[ ]		DOUBLE DAGGER....	‡

GENERAL REMARKS ON PUNCTUATION.

THE PERIOD.

§ 352. In rapid reporting the writer has no time to indicate the minor pauses, but he should always mark the full stops. As to the mode of doing this the practice of reporters is varied, some using the small cross, or a modification of it like this ($_\infty$); others the long sign given in our table as the reporter's sign of interrogation; while many use no marks at all, but indicate the pauses by spaces in their notes. If the latter mode be adopted, the space for a period should be about three quarters of an inch, and for a colon or semicolon about a third or half an inch in length. In case, however, the reporter writes rather openly, the spaces should be correspondingly increased.

EXCLAMATION AND INTERROGATION POINTS.

§ 353. The marks of exclamation and interrogation should be written as shown in the table above, with the phonographic point at the bottom; for, if made in the ordinary way, with the simple dot, they might be mistaken for phonographic words. Both of these signs should also be placed at the end of the clause or sentence which they are intended to mark. It is recommended in most phonographic works that the interrogation point be placed at the commencement of the interrogation; but, as it is frequently impossible to tell whether a speaker, when he commences a sentence, is going to ask a question or make a simple affirmation, it is obviously impracticable in reporting to follow this rule. Reporters use the long interrogation mark.

PARENTHESIS AND BRACKETS.

§ 354. As the difference between the marks of parenthesis and the brackets is not commonly understood, it is proper that their use should here be explained. The marks of parenthesis serve to indicate that an expression is inserted in the body of a sentence with which it has no connection in sense or in construction, while brackets are generally used to separate two subjects, or to inclose an explanation, note, or observation standing by itself. Therefore, the marks of parenthesis should be used to indicate a statement given in the words of the speaker, but which has no connection in sense or in construction with the adjoining matter; and the brackets, to inclose any explanation, note, or observation given in the words of the reporter.

DASH.

§ 355. The dash should be made double, to avoid its being mistaken for the stem *kay;* thus =

ACCENT.

§ 356. Accent may be shown by writing a small cross close to the vowel-sign of the accented syllable; thus, ⁀ *arrows,* ⁀ *arose;* but generally this mark is unnecessary, as the position of the word almost always indicates its accented vowel.

EMPHASIS.

§ 357. Emphasis is marked as in longhand, by drawing one, two, or more lines underneath the emphatic word. A single line under a single word should be made wave-like, to distinguish it from *kay.*

CAPITALS.

§ 358. An initial capital may be marked by drawing two short parallel lines under the first part of the word; thus, ⌐ *Times* newspaper. The entire word may be marked for capitals by drawing the parallel lines under the whole of it. But as this mode of capitalizing occupies too much time to be of practical use to the reporter, he may, with advantage, substitute a single line drawn under words to mark both proper names and emphasis; thus, ⌐ *James.* Such line should, however, be made a little longer and heavier than a *kay.*

INITIALS OF PROPER NAMES, ETC.

§ 359. The initials of proper names are best written in longhand. If, however, phonographic letters are used instead, as will sometimes be necessary in rapid reporting, signs should be selected to indicate the *common*, and not the *phonographic*, initials.

CONSONANT INITIALS.

§ 360. The letter *B.*, as an initial, may be indicated by the phonograph *bee*, *D.* by *dee*, *F.* by *ef*, *H.* by *hay*, *J.* by *jay*, *K.* by *kay*, *L.* by *lee*, *M.* by *em*, *N.* by *en*, *P.* by *pee*, *R.* by *err* or *ree*, *S.* by *ess*, *T.* by *tee*, *V.* by *vee*, *W.* by *way*, *Y.* by *yay*, and *Z.* by *zee*. The letters *C.*, *Q.*, and *X.* should always be indicated in longhand. [See § 86.]

CAUTION.

§ 361. The phonograph *gay*, and not *jay*, should be used for the initial of such names as George, Germany, etc., as well as of Gerrit, Gouverneur, etc., for *gay* indicates the true initial *G.*, while *jay* would indicate *J.* For a like reason *pee*, and not *ef*, should be used for the initial of Philip, Philo, etc.

VOWEL INITIALS.

§ 362. The letter *A.*, as an initial, may be indicated by a heavy dot on the line, *E.* by a heavy dot under the line, *I.* by the sign of the diphthong ɪ written above the line, *O.* by the word-sign for *owe*, and *U.* by the sign of the diphthong ɛw written on or below the line. The vowel initials should be indicated according to the above directions without regard to their sounds; thus, *A.* should be represented by a large dot written on the line, whether it be the initial of Abraham, Arthur, Alfred, or Augustus. The vowel initials may also be indicated by writing the signs of *ā*, *ĕ*, ɪ, *ŏ*, or ɛw to the nominal consonant. This mode, however, is hardly practicable in swift writing.

INITIALS OF TITLES.

§ 363. The initials of titles are best written with the longhand letters; thus, *LL.D.*, *M.D.*, *A.B.*, etc.

NUMBERS, ETC.

§ 364. Numbers should generally be represented by the ordinary Arabic characters. Though in some instances they are not quite so brief as the words phonographically written, they are somewhat more legible, and their distinctive character renders them conspicuous in a page of notes. But *one* and *ten* are written best with Wn and Tn ; but if the figure 1 is used it should be written / *one*, to distinguish it from *chay* or *jay*. When several noughts occur in a number, instead of writing them all, express the number, in part or in whole, in Phonography ; thus, 800,000,000 by 800 M-*Ln*³, 80,000 by 80 THz¹-Nd, 35,082,000 by 35M-*Ln*³ 82THz¹-Nd, 10,000 by Tn²-THz-Nd.

§ 365. When a speaker mentions a number of dollars or pounds, he first utters the number and then the denomination ; therefore, the reporter should write the word 'dollars' (for which Ds¹ is a good abbreviation), or 'pounds' *after* the number, instead of going back and placing before it the sign $ or £ ; thus, 421 Ds¹, instead of $421.

PHONOGRAPHIC FIGURES.

366. Numbers may, however, be expressed much more rapidly than in the ordinary way by using the phonographic consonant-signs with numerical values. The following assignment of them for that purpose is believed to present unusual advantages in point of brevity and legibility.

§ 367. The circles, and the *el*, *er*, *ef*, and *en* hooks may also be generally employed with numerical values. But the loops, and the *way*, *yay*, *shun*, and *ter* hooks, if used at all, should be very carefully written ; and, perhaps for general purposes, it is better to exclude them entirely.

EXAMPLES : ⌐ 5, ⌢ 33, ⌐ 87, / 64, ⌐ 47, ∨ 94, ⌐ 804, ⌐ 407, ⌐ 908, ⌐ 509, ⌐ 7,000, ⌐ 95, ⌐ 91, ⌐ 75, ⌐ 74, ⌐ 12, ⌐ 7,004.

§ 368. Before the phonographic numerals can be used in reporting, they must be thoroughly committed to memory and familiarized, particularly the signs which represent the noughts ; the *ess*-circle standing for one nought ; the large circle for two noughts ; the large circle with a turned small circle for three noughts, and the stem *ess*, with an initial large circle, and a final large circle with a turned small circle, for six noughts ; thus, Ts = 10, Tss = 100, Tsss = 1,000, T-ssSsss = 1,000,000.

FORMS MODIFIED BY MOTION.

§ 369. We have already seen (§ 14) that the basis of the phonographic consonant-signs is the segment of a circle extending ninety degrees, and a straight line of equal length. These two characters—a line of beauty and a line of speed—written in various directions, with light and shaded stroke, and modified by means of circles, loops, hooks, etc., constitute the entire variety of phonographic word-forms. Characters more simple or easily drawn can not be devised. But when traced as accurately as may be with skillful pen, with the rapidity of speech, the original geometrical figures appear modified, and filled with life as well as meaning. Phonography written, or engraved as we generally see it, with an attempt at mathematical precision, in accordance with the original geometrical design, appears dead, stiff, and unwieldy, because it is unmodified by the spirit of motion.

§ 370. The principal movement in writing being forward, all indirect or side movements are more or less subordinated to it. So that all perpendicular or partially backward strokes will be shorter than those written forward horizontally or inclined ; and all words which would naturally extend far above or below the line of writing will be brought more into lineality by encroaching a little on the rules of position, and by making the phonographs smaller.

§ 371. All horizontal curves, instead of being segments of a circle, will be segments of an ellipse cut through its longest diameter ; this form being produced by the rapid forward motion which is of necessity more retarded near the beginning and end of the stroke than through the middle, while the upward and downward movements are equal throughout, or, rather, retarded in the middle of the stroke consequent upon the change of direction, upward or downward.

§ 372. Inclined curves will be more or less irregular, curving most near one end, according to the direction of the curve ; thus, *ef* and *ish* are liable to be curved most near the beginning, and *el* and *er,* near the termination.

§ 373. The modification of perpendicular curves is less apparent, but those convex to the right will be curved most near the beginning, and those convex to the left curved most at the lower end.

§ 374. In the joining of simple signs the angles of junction will be more or less modified as the acceleration of speed demands—obtuse angles being made more acute by changing the inclination of inclined straight lines, or by modifying the curvature of curves ; thus, the stem P, in the outlines K-P will be nearer perpendicular than when standing alone. while in T-P it will be nearer horizontal ; and N before

P will be more curved, especially at its termination, than when it occurs before CH.

§ 375. At points of junction of two characters where a hook or circle occurs, the characters will display a sort of courtesy to each other, bending a little now and then from the original geometrical creed that they may form a graceful and neighborly union; for example, L before Br will be more curved than usual, while F before Br will be considerably straighter.

§ 376. Shaded curves rarely have the heaviest portion of the shade precisely in the middle, but more or less toward one end, as the direction of the pen most favors the execution of a shaded stroke; thus, the stems ZH, Z, NG, and W are shaded heaviest a little before the middle, and DH, V, H, and Y just after the middle.

§ 377. And as, by the law of mechanics, increase of speed must be attended with decrease of force, all strokes will be written as light as is consistent with proper legibility; and, short roads being sooner traveled than long distances, the reporter will naturally adopt as small a scale of penmanship as legibility will sanction.

§ 378. The foregoing statement is not in conflict with the directions contained in § 28, for the modifications caused by motion are solely the effect of speed upon outlines, and they will appear even when simple geometrical accuracy alone is aimed at by the writer.

ON PREPARING COPY AND READING PROOF.

§ 379. Although the superintending of printing does not come within the strict duties of a reporter, yet when his reports are printed, it not unfrequently happens that he is called upon to take charge of and correct the proofs. In such case the following hints on the subject will be of use.

PREPARATION OF COPY.

§ 380. In preparing manuscript for the printer the first requisite is to write it in a plain and legible hand. If proper names and foreign or technical expressions occur, care should be taken that they be correctly spelled and clearly written. The i's should be dotted, and the t's crossed, which in the haste of writing are too liable to be left imperfect. J should be distinguished from I, particularly when they are used as initials, by bringing the former below the line. Words or sentences meant to be printed in CAPITALS should be marked by drawing three lines under them; in SMALL CAPITALS, by two lines; and in *Italics*, by one. Should interlineations be made, or additions in the margin, or on the opposite or a separate leaf, the place of insertion should be marked with a caret, with a line, if possible, leading from it to, and inclosing the matter to be inserted ; and if the additional matter is designed as a note for the foot of the page, that fact should also be stated ; putting such or any other direction within a circle, that it may be readily noticed. No abbreviations of words or phrases hould be used. The punctuation should also be carefully attended to. And, at the commencement of any sentence meant to begin a new paragraph, but not distinctly exhibited as such, the mark (¶) appropriated for that purpose, should be placed ; for on no account ought the paragraphing to be left to the compositor.

PROOF-READING.

'9 381. The following are the principal marks used in correcting proof-sheets. When it is desired to change a word to capital, small capital, or Italic letters, it should be underscored with three, two, or one lines, as directed in the last section, and the words *caps*, *sm. caps*, or *Ital.*, as the case may be, written in the margin directly opposite the line in which the word occurs. If a word printed in Italics is to be changed to Roman letters, or *vice versa*, a line is drawn under it, and the abbreviation *Rom.*, or *Ital.*, as the case may be, written in the margin. Omitted words or letters are marked for insertion by being written in the margin, and a caret placed in the text where the omission occurs. But if the omission be too long for the side margin, it may be written at the top or bottom of the page, or on a sheet of paper attached to the proof, and connected with the caret by a line. Anything may be struck out from the text by drawing a line through it, and writing in the margin the character ℒ, appropriately called a *dele*. If anything is to go in the place of the erased matter, it should be written in the margin instead of the *dele* mark. When anything has been erased, and it is afterward decided to retain it as it was before, dots are written under it, and the word *stet* placed in the margin. When there is not sufficient space between two words or letters, a caret is placed beneath the place where they should be separated, and the sign ⚏ written in the margin. When there is too great a space between the letters of a word, they should be connected by two curved lines, one above and the other below, their concave sides being turned toward the space, and the same signs made in the margin ; if two words are to be brought nearer together, only the lower curve is used. When two lines are too near together, a horizontal caret is placed at the end and between them, and the term *lead* or *leads* written in the margin. If the lines are too much separated, the correction is made in the same way, except that *dele lead* or *leads* is written in the margin, using the peculiar sign already given- for *dele.* Two letters or words are transposed by drawing a curved line above the first and beneath the second, and writing the abbreviation *tr.* or *trs.* in the margin. If a misplaced word belongs to a different line of the print, encircle it and draw a line to the place where it should be inserted ; or if it is desired to transpose two words that are not together, encircle each of them, and join-them by a line. When several words are to be transposed, indicate the order by placing the figures 1, 2, 3, etc., over them, and draw a line under them. In all these modes of transposition the letters *tr.* are, of course, placed in the margin. A paragraph may be made where none appears in the proof, by placing a caret in the text where the new paragraph is to begin, and the sign ¶ in the margin. If an improper break into paragraphs has been made, it may be remedied by drawing a line from the end of the first paragraph to the beginning of the second, and writing *No* ¶, or *No break,* in the margin. When it is desired to indent a line, as the first line of a paragraph, a caret is placed before it, and a small square character made in the margin. The crotchet [is placed before a word, and a corresponding one made in the margin, to indi-cate that it should be brought out to the end of a line. If, however, it is also to commence a new paragraph, the marginal mark should be ¶. A word in the middle of a line is carried farther to the left, by placing the sign ∟ before it, and also in the margin. The sign ⌐ is placed after a word, and also in the margin, to carry the word farther to the right. When a letter, word, or character is depressed below the proper level, it is elevated by placing the sign ⌐ over it, and also in the margin. A letter, word, or character that is raised above the proper level, is brought into line by placing the sign ⌐ under it, and also in the margin. When the ends of the lines of a page do not range properly, a perpendicular line should be drawn near them. Attention is called to defective letters by making a dash under them, and a cross in the margin ; and to crooked letters or words, by means of horizontal lines drawn above and below them, and corresponding parallel lines in the margin. An inverted letter is marked by drawing a dash under it, and placing the sign *Ɔ* in the margin. When a letter is of an improper size, it is indicated by drawing a line under it, and writing the letters *w. f.* (wrong font) in the margin. If a space or quadrat sticks up so that it prints, it should be marked by placing a short perpendicular stroke in the margin, and underscoring both it and the mark to be removed with a line curved like a phonographic *en.* When a line is irregularly spaced,—that is, if some of the words are too close, and others too wide apart, the direction *Space letter* should be written in the margin. The printer's proof-reader calls attention to obscurities of language, words illegible in the " copy" (manuscript), etc., by underscoring them and writing *qu ?* or *qy ?* or (?) in the margin, along with his suggestion. A line like a double-length *chay* should be drawn after each marginal correction ; with the exception of the period, which is placed within a circle, and the apostrophe, reference marks, and superiors, which are written over the sign √.

SPECIMEN OF A CORRECTED PROOF-SHEET.

THE CROWNING OF PETRARCH.   *Caps.*

Nothing can be conceived more affecting or noble than *s. caps.*
that ceremony. The superb palaces and porticos by *Rom.*
which had rolled the ivory chariots of Marius and and
Caesar had long mouldered into dust. The laureled *2y.*
fasces, the golden eagles, the shouting Legions, the cap *l. c.*
[tives, and the pictured cities were indeed wanting to *lead*
his victorious procession. The sceptre had passed away
from Rome. But she still retained the mightier influence
of an empire intellectual; and was now to confer the X
prouder reward of an intellectual triumph. To the man *u*
who had extended the dominion of her ancient language *space bet.*
—who had erected the trophies of philosophy and *tr.*
imagination in the L haunts of ignorance and fervency, *ferocity*
whose captives were the hearts of admiring nations
enchained by the influence of his song — whose spoils
were the *treasures* of ancient genius—the Eternal City *Rom.*
offered the glorious and just tribute of her gratitude. *wf*
Amid the ruined monuments of ancient, and the infant erections of modern art, he who had restored the
broken link between the two ages of human civilization
was crowned with the wreath which he had deserved
from the moderns who owe to him their refinement,—from *tr.*
the ancients who owed to him their fame. Never was a X
coronation so august witnessed by Westminster or Rheims. *Cap.*

        MACAULAY. *Ital.* ?

rescued from obscurity and decay

SPECIMEN ON OPPOSITE PAGE CORRECTED.

§ 382. When the corrections indicated by the marks in the specimen on the opposite page are made by the printer, the result will be as given below. The balance of this page was, in fact, set up from a proof taken from the plate of the specimen.

THE CROWNING OF PETRARCH.

Nothing can be conceived more affecting or noble than that ceremony. The superb palaces and porticos by which had rolled the ivory chariots of Marius and Cæsar had long mouldered into dust. The laureled fasces, the golden eagles, the shouting legions, the captives, and the pictured cities were indeed wanting to his victorious procession. The sceptre had passed away from Rome. But she still retained the mightier influence of an intellectual empire, and was now to confer the prouder reward of an intellectual triumph. To the man who had extended the dominion of her ancient language —who had erected the trophies of philosophy and imagination in the haunts of ignorance and ferocity, whose captives were the hearts of admiring nations, enchained by the influence of his song—whose spoils were the treasures of ancient genius, rescued from obscurity and decay—the "Eternal City" offered the just and glorious tribute of her gratitude. Amidst the ruined monuments of ancient, and the infant erections of modern art, he who had restored the broken link between the two ages of human civilization was crowned with the wreath which he had deserved from the moderns who owed to him their refinement,—from the ancients who owed to him their fame. Never was a coronation so august witnessed by Westminster or Rheims.

Macaulay

REPORTING.

GENERAL REMARKS.

§ 383. The two leading requisites of the short-hand writing of the professional verbatim reporter are *speed*—the ability to follow a rapid speaker and catch and convey to paper every word that he utters—and *legibility*—the ability to write such rapid notes so legibly that they may be deciphered quickly and without mistake.

SPEED OF PHONOGRAPHY.

§ 384. By speed of phonography is meant the rate at which one who is thoroughly familiar with both its theory and practice can write it in such a manner that it may be correctly read without hesitation, and it is usually estimated by the number of words so written in a minute. The ordinary rate of public speaking is from 120 to 130 words a minute; an average of 150 words is quite rapid, and 175 to 190 is very rapid, but few speakers reaching that speed, although even that is occasionally exceeded for short spurts by eloquent or excited speakers.

SPEED REQUIRED OF AMANUENSES AND REPORTERS.

§ 385. A phonographer who can write correctly and legibly from 115 to 125 words a minute is competent to do most amanuensis work; and one who can in like manner write 150 words is prepared, so far as his short-hand is concerned, to begin verbatim reporting. A person who commences reporting with a speed of 150 words a minute, well written, may depend upon future experience and the inspiration of the moment to tide him safely over the passages that are spoken above that rate.

LEGIBILITY OF PHONOGRAPHY.

§ 386. By legibility of phonography is meant the certainty and ease with which it can be read after having been rapidly written with all the little deviations from arithmetical accuracy that usually occur in the writing done by a man of ordinary training and skill. The importance of legibility has been underestimated by many, and it is too apt to be unappreciated by learners in their efforts to get speed. In all cases where phonography is used to record an author's composition, as employed by dictation amanuenses, phonographic secretaries, or, in short, for any phonographic work except reporting public speeches, the writer is frequently called upon to read over what he has just written, and he must be able to do so without error in any word. The exactions from short-hand writers in courts now are very much greater than they were formerly, it being an every-day occurrence for them to be required to read in open court their notes of testimony; and if they do not write a legible short-hand, in a legible manner, they must fail. In many portions of the United States official stenographers are employed to report the proceedings of courts, and generally the accuracy of those reporters is implicitly relied upon by litigants and judges. But instances have been known where material and permanent injury has been done through the inaccuracies of reporters; and so it should be the aim of all learners of phonography to get, first, Accuracy; second, Speed. Legibility in itself is an important contributor to speed, because it gives a feeling of confidence and certainty to the writer in regard to his work.

TIME NECESSARY TO ACQUIRE SPEED.

§ 387. As to the length of time required to attain a speed of 150 words a minute, it is impossible to speak with certainty, as very much will depend, of course, on the natural talent of the learner, and the amount of time he devotes daily to the task. The average amount of time necessary to qualify a tolerably expert writer to follow a speaker at that rate is from eight to twelve months, by practicing an hour a day; or six to eight months, with two hours' daily practice. It will generally be found a comparatively easy task to increase the rate of speed from 100 to 130 or 140 words; but to go beyond this, much persistent practice will be required, and the progress from day to day will be less perceptible. The very highest rates of speed can only be attained by those who have through study and practice become so familiar with the outlines of the great mass of words in common use that they can write them without hesitation the instant they are spoken.

MATERIALS USED IN WRITING PHONOGRAPHY.

§ 388. Phonography should always be written on ruled paper. At one time it was quite customary to use paper with double lines, one running at the top and the other at the bottom of a *tee* stem written in the second position; but now phonographers have very generally discarded double lines, and they write on paper with the ordinary single lines. Care should be taken, however, not to rule the paper too closely, especially if the writer uses rather large forms. The author has for several years written all of his notes on paper with two fifths of an inch space between the lines. He has also found in his experience that the best ink for note-taking is Thaddeus Davids' blue ink, because it makes a sharper line than any other, and is more easily read by artificial light. It also has the advantage that when it becomes too thick it may without injury be reduced by adding a few drops of water. If a black ink is preferred by the writer, Thomas's black ink will be found to give excellent satisfaction. This may also be thinned, when necessary, by adding water.

§ 389. Reporting covers—that is, stiff, leather-covered cases for holding reporting paper, with an elastic band stitched to the back for keeping the paper in place, will be found very useful to the general reporter, especially to those employed upon newspapers. The size of these covers should be about $8\frac{3}{4}$ by $4\frac{1}{2}$ inches. They open lengthwise, and notes should be taken only on the leaf that is toward the writer. When the paper is filled up in one direction, the reporter turns it around, commences at the other end, and follows the same plan, viz., writing only on the leaf nearest him, until the book is filled.

§ 390. Reporters' books similar in shape and size to the covers are quite commonly used by reporters in the city of New York, and they may be obtained at many of the stationers. Sometimes these books are made with stiff covers and sometimes with flexible covers, according to the taste or convenience of the writer. It is well that they should not be made too thick, so as to interfere with the free movement of the hand in writing. One hundred leaves is about the maximum number. The author, in his practice, takes all court notes on single, detached sheets of paper of the following dimensions and description : length, 10 inches ; width, 8 inches ; distance between top and bottom lines, 9 inches ; 22 spaces of about $\frac{2}{5}$ of an inch, and 23 lines in the 9 inches ; space above top line $\frac{7}{16}$, the space below lower line $\frac{2}{3}$ of an inch. The writing lines ruled in dark red, on one side of the paper only. Four lines ruled in dark blue from top to bottom, two of them in the middle, $\frac{7}{20}$ of an inch apart, and one at each side, leaving marginal spaces at left and right of the sheet equal to the middle space. Each sheet is paged by machinery at the upper right-hand corner, within the marginal line, and far enough above the upper line not to interfere with the writing—the paging running on continuously, year after year. The sheet has two columns for writing, each $3\frac{1}{2}$ inches wide. This style of paper is very convenient for reporters who have their notes transcribed by others, as the transcriber is enabled to commence work as soon as a single sheet of notes has been written, which would be impossible if a book were used. The author also takes this occasion to urge upon reporters who use his Practical Phonography, especially those employed in the profession of law short-hand reporting, the advisability as far as possible of having their notes transcribed by others. Transcripts so made should always be compared with the notes ; the reporter holding his notes, and the transcriber reading aloud from the long-hand. Corrections may be made at the time of such comparison, or they may be indicated on the margin in pencil, and then inserted in ink afterwards. Some of the proof-reader's marks at § 381 will be found useful in doing this part of the work.

§ 391. The reporter should always write on a table or desk when one can be obtained, which is usually the case in the courts. The newspaper reporter has, however, oftentimes to take notes while standing or sitting in the audience, and then the stiff covers of a note-book may be all upon which he can depend for the support of his hand while writing.

§ 392. The phonographer should in his practice accustom himself to the occasional use of both pen and pencil. For practical reporting there is nothing so effective as a gold pen, when a suitable one can be obtained. The peculiarities of a gold pen to be used in writing phonography, to which attention should be directed, are the following: the nibs should be both straight and short, so that all of the signs, both light and shaded, straight and curved, may be quickly made with the least possible variation in the spring of the pen. Several of the pen manufacturers make what they call a short-nibbed pen, of medium size, from which the reporter can generally select a satisfactory implement for short-hand writing. As a general rule a pencil should be used when notes have to be taken upon the knee or when standing, but pen and ink when a table or desk is provided. Various kinds of pencils are now in use, and each phonographer should decide for himself which is best suited to his hand; but probably more would be suited with Faber's No. 3 pencil than with any other. A few reporters use fine-pointed steel pens, but they are not recommended for reporting purposes, although they are very good for learners in writing their exercises. In order that a reporter may write with uniform speed and accuracy, his pen must be also in a uniform condition; but steel pens are uneven in quality, and they are liable to corrode and suddenly fail at a time when the writer can not stop to replace them with a fresh one.

LAW REPORTING.

§ 393. It is an erroneous though common belief that the duties of a reporter are simply to take down and furnish a transcript of all, and exactly what he hears, and that the merit of a report consists in its being an exact record of every word uttered by the speaker. The fact is that the exact words of an address are very rarely preserved. Of the great majority of even the better class of our public speakers, whether at the bar, on the rostrum, or in the pulpit, few are able to speak extemporaneously in such a manner that they would be willing to see a verbatim report of their words in print. Their sentences must often be remodeled, and occasionally the wording of entire speeches may be said to be almost exclusively the work of the reporter. For this reason facility of composition is a qualification of the greatest importance to him. Good judgment is also absolutely indispensable—indeed, it often happens that a poor stenographer, with judgment, makes a better reporter than a good stenographer, who lacks in that respect. Now, this is especially the case in law reporting, because in this, as in all other legal matters, so much depends upon mere form. The professional law reporter should be conversant with the ordinary legal forms and expressions, particularly those that are met with in trials; and, if he happens to be himself a well-read lawyer, it will enable him to make all the better reports.

§ 394. The proper reporting of objections, motions, and rulings requires more judgment and experience than any other part of the duties of the law reporter. If counsel would always state in so many words the grounds of their objections, little or no difficulty would be experienced, but oftentimes a long argument is made, from the whole of which the reporter is obliged to eliminate the gist of the objection, and to put it in proper legal phraseology. It will not do to take down and write out just the words of the counsel, for this would frequently render the report very voluminous, and at the same time subject the party who orders it to much unnecessary expense. It would therefore seem that some knowledge of the rules of evidence is an almost indispensable qualification of the law reporter. But in the absence of more extended instruction in this respect, the following hints may be found serviceable.

§ 395. When a witness has been regularly sworn, he is first examined by the party who produces him. This is called the " direct examination," or the " examination in chief." After that the other party is at liberty to cross-examine; and then the party who first called him may re-examine. This is called the "re-direct," and, according to strict rule, it closes the examination of the witness. On the re-examination it is permitted to ask him any questions necessary to explain matters elicited from him in the "cross-examination." But the re-examination is not to extend to any new matter unconnected with the cross-examination, and which might have been inquired into on the examination in chief. The strictness of this rule is, however, in the discretion of the court, frequently relaxed. Further questions are oftentimes allowed to be put by the opposite counsel, especially when, on the re-direct, any new matter has been drawn out. This is called the " re-cross-examination."

§ 396. The obligation of proving any fact lies upon the party who substantially asserts the affirmative of the issue. The affirmative of most cases naturally rests with the plaintiff, or party bringing the action, and therefore it is that he proceeds first and gives evidence to substantiate his claim. When the plaintiff has finished his evidence, he rests, and then sometimes defendant's counsel moves to dismiss the action on the ground that even if all the evidence adduced by the plaintiff were admitted to be true, he would have no legal right to recover. If the motion is denied, which is generally the case when there is no jury, as judges generally prefer to hear the whole of a case before deciding any of its material points, the defendant's counsel excepts, and proceeds to produce his proofs. But if the court grant the motion, plaintiff takes an exception, and the trial ends there. Frequently the motion to dismiss is only made *pro forma*, to preserve, for the purposes of an appeal, any rights that may be covered by it. In such case the motion is denied without argument, an exception taken, and the trial proceeds. Sometimes, before the plaintiff produces any evidence, defendant's counsel moves to dismiss the complaint on the ground that it does not state facts sufficient to constitute a cause of action. This objection, however, is generally taken by demurrer, and not on the trial.

§ 397. The order of proceeding in the trial of a cause is generally the following : (1) The impanneling of the jury ; (2) the opening remarks of plaintiff's counsel in which he states the nature of his case, and in general what he expects to prove ; (3) the examination of plaintiff's witnesses ; each of which defendant's counsel cross-examines, unless he waive the right ; (4) the opening remarks of defendant's counsel ; (5) the examination of defendant's witnesses; each of which is cross-examined by plaintiff's counsel, unless he waive the right ; (6) the rebutting testimony of plaintiff ; (7) ditto of defendant; (8) the summing up or arguments of defendant's counsel ; (9) ditto of plaintiff's counsel ; (10) the charge of the judge to the jury ; (11) the verdict. In some courts trials are had without juries ; and sometimes, even when the parties have a right to trial by jury, they waive it and proceed before the judge alone.

§ 398. In ordinary civil trials the reporter has generally nothing to do with the impanneling of the jury ; but in criminal trials this is a very important matter, and should be carefully reported. It is always well to take notes of the opening remarks of counsel, for, although they are seldom ever required to be written out, they will sometimes throw light on obscure or doubtful portions of the testimony, and enable the writer to ascertain whether he has correctly reported the language of the question or answer. Great care should be taken to report every word on the examination of witnesses ; and in transcribing, their exact language, whether grammatical or ungrammatical, should be preserved : and if any words are mispronounced, that fact should also be indicated if possible. By this means, on an appeal, the judges will be able to form a better judgment of the weight that should be attached to the evidence of the respective witnesses in the court below, than if all were made, by means of corrections, to speak with equal propriety. The language of the questions of counsel, however, may be frequently improved when it can be done without introducing any material alterations. It is not usual to report the summing up of the counsel, unless they expressly order it. The judge's charge, however, should be very carefully taken, as oftentimes great interests may be hazarded by a very slight error or change in its verbiage.

FORM OF LAW-REPORTS.

§ 399. A very important consideration in a report, especially of a legal proceeding, is its form. It should be the aim of the stenographer to furnish the report of a trial in such shape that it may be used, without essential alteration, as the "case" on appeal. It should be written on paper that has a margin at the left of about an inch and a half, usually marked by a red line running from the top to the bottom of the sheet. Paper ruled in this way, and which is commonly called "legal-cap," may be procured at most stationers. It is generally ruled on both sides, and if both are written on, it is done in this wise: After finishing the first side, the sheet is turned over endwise, and the second page is written from the bottom to the top of the sheet. This is called by scriveners "backing" the paper. It is the general practice of reporters to write on one side of the paper only, but sometimes it is preferred that both be used. As to this matter, the counsel may be consulted. The numbering of the pages should be in the margin, at the lower end of each sheet, the figures on the first side being placed at the bottom, and on the opposite side, at the top of the written page. The paging is done in this way so that there will be no danger of the numbers being covered up when the sheets are put together. The fastening together of the manuscript is commonly done with red tape, or with small tin clasps made for the purpose. If tape is used, three small holes, about two inches apart, should first be punched in the top margin of the paper, and the tape then drawn through by means of a long, blunt needle, which should be first put down through the middle hole from the front of the manuscript, then up through one of the side holes, next down through the other side hole, then up through the middle hole again, and the ends tied across the tape that extends from one side hole to the other. These minute directions have been given because so many people have such a very slovenly manner of putting together legal papers. If the trial of a case runs through several days, the paging should be continued on consecutively, instead of commencing anew every day. This will enable counsel to ascertain without trouble whether any part of the manuscript is missing.

§ 400. The proper legal names by which the parties to an action are designated, vary in different courts, and also according to the nature of the proceeding. In ordinary courts for the trial of civil causes the party bringing an action is called the *Plaintiff*, and the party against whom it is brought, the *Defendant*. The appealing party in the New York Court of Appeals is called the *Appellant*, and the other party the *Respondent*. All prosecutions for crime are brought in the name of *The People*. When a proceeding is brought in private interest, but which must nevertheless be brought in the name of The People, as, for instance, in election cases, a mandamus, or certiorari, the moving party is designated *The People on the relation of* (or *ex rel*) *So and So*, giving the name of the party for whose benefit the proceeding is brought; and who is generally called the *Relator*. On a proceeding for the probate of a will, the party offering it is called the *Proponent*, and the party opposing the probate, the *Contestant*.

§ 401. The first page of a report is generally used as a title-page, on which appears the name of the court; the title of the suit; the name of the judge before whom it is tried, stating also that it was before a jury, if such be the fact; the date of the trial; the names of the counsel and for whom they appear, and the index to the witnesses. The title-page is also an appropriate place for the reporter to write or stamp his business card. A new title-page should be made out for each day's report. The back of this sheet may be written on, or not, according to the taste or convenience of the writer. In the city of New York it has become the custom of law stenographers to put up reports of trials in covers, generally made of tinted paper of some kind, with printed blank forms on front and back. If covers are used, after the first day of the trial only an abridged title, with the date, need be put at the head of the report. The Index of Witnesses is written on the first page of the cover.

§ 402. At the commencement of the examination of each witness should be written in a plain and rather larger hand than usual, his full name, commencing it just outside of the margin line, and underscoring the whole with one line. Then should be stated for which party he was called; that the witness was duly sworn or affirmed, and the name of the counsel conducting the direct examination. Each question and answer should be preceded by the initials *Q.* or *A.*, written in the margin near the line. These letters should not encroach too much on the margin, as it is required by counsel for their notes and references. Some reporters commence the answer immediately after the question, and do not place the *A.* in the margin at all. This is called " running in the answers." A line should be left blank above the name of each witness that is called, but not between the direct and cross examination; and the following heading should be written on a line by itself: ' *Cross-examination* by

Deft's (or Plff's) counsel,' or 'by Mr. So and So,' giving the counsel's name.   If, in the course of an examination by one counsel, a single question is interposed by the other counsel, or by the judge, the words *By Plaintiff's Counsel* (or *Defendant's*, as the case may be), or *By Mr. So and So*, or *By the Court* should be written just after the initial ' *Q.*,' without indentation, and in parentheses.   Should it be followed by one or two more questions by the same party, the words *By the same* may bo inclosed in the parentheses.   If, however, a considerable number of such questions occur, the words *By Plff's* (or *Deft's*) *Counsel*, or *By Mr. So and So*, or *By the Court* should be written on a separate line, and the questions then recorded in the ordinary way.   When the original examination is resumed by the counsel who was thus interrupted, a similar formula may be used to indicate it.

§ 403.   Remarks made by the counsel or by the Court, such as objections, rulings, exceptions, motions, etc., should generally be written in the third person, and the entire matter indented an inch or more from the margin line.   If the indented matter does not form a complete sentence of itself, it should be inclosed in brackets.   When the words of counsel are given in the first person, they should be preceded by the counsel's name, and then written in the same manner as a question or answer, that is, without being indented.   The name need not be written in full, but merely *Mr. So and So*, writing the *Mr.* just outside, and near the margin line.   The words *Plaintiff's* (or *Defendant's*) *Counsel* are sometimes used instead.   In either case they should be underscored with a single line.   Remarks by the judge transcribed in the first person are written in the same way, but should be preceded by the words *The Court*, underscored.

FORMS.

§ 404.   The specimen forms on the following pages will serve as guides to the reporter in preparing reports.   In regard to the use of the tenses of the verbs in the indented portions of short-hand reports, the practice of reporters varies; some preferring the present tense, as in the following examples: "Plaintiff's counsel *reads* in evidence," etc., "Mr. Jones *opens* for plaintiff," "defendants' counsel *claims* the right," etc.; while others use the past tense, as follows: "Plaintiff's counsel *read* in evidence," etc., "Mr. Jones *opened* for plaintiff," "defendants' counsel *claimed* the right," etc.   The author prefers generally the present form, because it gives greater freedom and facility in the construction of statements, and also permits of more condensation of expression.   Occasionally, however, the past tense seems to be best; and it is not necessary that the reporter should confine himself exclusively to either.   The perpendicular line at the left of the pages represents the margin line of legal-cap paper.

FIRST PAGE—FORM 1.

N. Y. Superior Court, Part 2.

John Adolph
vs.
The Central Park, N. and E.
River R. R. Co.

    Before Judge Sedgwick and a Jury.
    New York, Nov. 23d, 1876.
    Appearances:
For plaintiff,
    M. L. Townsend, Esq.
For defendants,
    Vanderpoel, Green, & Cuming, Esqs.
    Mr. Townsend opened for plaintiff.

A nton Greubelstein, called for plaintiff, sworn.
Direct examination by Mr. Townsend.

Q. Where do you live? *A.* I live at 334 East 22d Street, etc.

FIRST PAGE—FORM 2.

N. Y. Superior Court, Part 2.

Henry Martin and others.
vs.
Henry F. Angell and anor.

    Before Judge Sedgwick and a Jury.
    New York, April 10th, 1876.
    Appearances:
For plaintiffs,
    Wm. H. Williams, Esq., attorney.
    Orlando L. Stewart, Esq., of counsel.
For defendants,
    James M. Smith, Esq.
    Mr. Williams opened for plaintiff.

M ark Finlay, called for plaintiff, sworn.
Direct examination by Mr. Stewart.

Q. Are you one of the plaintiffs in this action? *A.* Yes, sir, etc.

FIRST PAGE—FORM 3.

N. Y. Superior Court, Part 2.

Louis Heidenheimer
vs.
David Mayer.

    Before Judge Sedgwick, without a Jury.
    New York, Nov. 17th, 1876.
    Appearances:
For plaintiff,
    R. W. Townsend, Esq., attorney,
    A. R. Dyett, Esq., of counsel.
For defendant,
    S. Kaufmann, Esq., attorney,
    Lewis Sanders, Esq., of counsel.

6*

Plaintiff's counsel offers in evidence the written guaranty on which the action is brought. Objected to on the ground that there is no proof of its execution. Objection overruled; exception taken. Paper marked Plaintiff's Exhibit No. 1 of this date.

Also, the two promissory notes in suit; one of which is wholly unpaid and the other only partially paid—with the protests attached—marked Plaintiff's Exhibit Nos. 2 and 3 of this date.

With the exception of computing the interest, plaintiff rests.

Defendant's counsel moves to dismiss the complaint upon the ground that the guaranty is, "I make myself responsible to pay at maturity all of the above notes in case Joseph Bernhard should not pay the same," and therefore notice and demand are necessary. Motion denied; exception taken.

Joseph Bernhard, called for the defense, sworn.

Direct examination by Mr. Dyett.

Q. Are you the maker of the two notes produced in evidence here? *A.* I am, sir, etc.

FIRST PAGE—FORM 4.

N. Y. Superior Court, Part 2.

Emma Heilbreth
vs.
The N. Y. Life Insurance Co.

Before Judge Sedgwick and a Jury.
New York, Jan. 19th, 1876.
Appearances:

For plaintiff,
Beach and Brown, Esqs.

For defendants,
Fullerton, Knox, and Crosby, Esqs.

Defendants' counsel claims the right to open the case, on the ground that the affirmative of the issues is with them. Plaintiff's counsel denies the right, on the ground that upon the face of the pleadings the plaintiff is not entitled to a verdict, stating that he proposes to introduce the widow of the deceased to prove the death, the circumstances connected with the death, and the residence of the deceased. Defendants' counsel states that all those facts are admitted in the answer. Motion granted. Plaintiff's counsel excepts.

Mr. Knox opened for the defense.

Albert Lambert, called for the defense, sworn.

Direct examination by Mr. Knox.

Q. What is your occupation? *A.* Physician, etc.

§ 405. The following forms of introduction of witnesses are in use among reporters:

T|HOMAS R. JONES, called for plaintiff, being duly sworn, testifies as follows:
Direct examination by MR. BRADY.

T|HOMAS R. JONES, a witness on behalf of the plaintiff, being duly sworn, testifies:
BY MR. BRADY:

T|HOMAS R. JONES, called for plaintiff, sworn.
Direct examination by Mr. Brady.

Q.|Where do you reside? *A.* In New York. [etc., to the end of direct; then, on next line:]
C|*ross-examination* by MR. EVARTS. [or]
C|*ross-examination.*
BY MR. EVARTS.

Q.|How long have you known the defendant? *A.* I have known him about 15 years; I first saw him in Albany, in this state.

Q.|(By Mr. Brady.) In what year did you first see him? *A.* In the year 1861, I think.

Q.|(By the Court.) Have you known him ever since? *A.* Most of the time.

Q.|(By the same.) Give us the exact time as near as you can. *A.* I knew him from 1861 to about 1868, and then I did not see him until last year.
BY MR. EVARTS.

Q.|Under what circumstances did you first get acquainted with him? [etc., to the end of cross, and then follows the]
Re-|*direct.*

Q.|State the circumstances a little more minutely. [etc.]

§ 406. When a party to the action is called as a witness, he may be introduced the same as any other witness, or this form may be used:

A|LBERT H. JOHNSON, plaintiff, sworn, etc., or 'plaintiff, called on his own behalf,' or 'one of the plaintiffs,' etc.

§ 407. The following extract from an examination furnishes forms for most of the ordinary objections that are raised on trials:

M|ARTIN WILLIS, called for plaintiffs, sworn.
Direct examination by Mr. West.

Q.|Are you the president of the Harlem Chemical and Mining Company? *A.* Yes, sir.

Q.|What was, in the spring of 1873, and during 1873, the capacity of your works?
Objected to and waived.

Q.|Had you any conversation with Mr. John Morris about the 7th of March, 1873? *A.* Yes, sir; I had.

Q.|What was the subject of that conversation?
Defendants' counsel objects to the question on the ground that if the conversation culminated in a written agreement it is incompetent. Plaintiffs' counsel does not concede that the conversation merged in a written contract. Objection overruled; exception taken.

Q. During the winter of 1873 and 1874, early in January, did you receive a message from Mr. John Morris through your cartman Donahue? *A.* Yes, sir.

Q. What was that message?

> Objected to as being too remote. Plaintiff's counsel agrees to connect the message brought by Donahue with the defendant Morris. Objection overruled; exception taken.

———◆———

Q. Look at that letter, and say whether you received that [hands it to witness]. *A.* Yes, sir.

> Plaintiff's counsel reads in evidence letters from defendant to plaintiff, dated April 1st and 2d, 1874 —marked Plaintiff's Exhibits 4 and 5 of this date. Also plaintiff's reply to same—marked Plaintiff's Exhibit 6 of this date.

———◆———

Q. Were they not in fact the successors to the business of Willis, Green, & Jones?

> Objected to as a conclusion of law.

———◆———

Q. Do you know the fact that the firm of Willis, Green, & Jones had a contract with the defendant in this case to sell and deliver a certain amount of carboys of oil?

> Objected to as immaterial, being *res inter alios acta.* Objection overruled; exception taken.

A. Certainly I do.

Q. Do you recollect the date of that? *A.* I can't remember the date precisely. It was in February or March, 1872; but upon my word I can't remember.

> The witness states that he did not notice the word "defendant" in the next to the last question, and adds that there were two parties instead of one. Plaintiff's counsel moves to strike out both the question and answer as immaterial.

Q. I ask you whether you recognize that document—what it is, and whose signature that is [hands witness a paper].

> Objected to.

Q. Whose signature is that? Do you recognize the signature? *A.* I recognize it undoubtedly.

Q. Whose is it? *A.* It is the signature of the firm of Willis, Green, & Jones.

Q. Whose handwriting is it? *A.* It is the handwriting of Mr. Green, one of the firm.

> Defendants' counsel offers in evidence said paper and the counterpart to it furnished by plaintiff's counsel. Objected to by plaintiff's counsel. Objection overruled; exception taken. The papers are read in evidence, and marked Deft's Exhibits A and A 1 of this date.

Q. I will ask you if that is your signature? [Hands witness a letter.] *A.* Yes, sir.

Q. Is that letter in your handwriting? *A.* Undoubtedly.

Q. This letter is dated February 20th, 1873—you were then acting as a corporation—February 20th, 1873? *A.* I think so.

Letter read in evidence, and marked Deft's Exhibit B of this date.

Q. I go back to the original statement and question—Do you state on the stand that that delivery, after you became a corporation, was not a delivery under the original contract with Willis, Green, & Jones? *A.* I have not said that—I don't say that.

Q. Do you say that it was after you became a corporation?

Objected to as immaterial; objection overruled; exception taken.

Q. (By the Court.) Was that delivery made by the company under the old contract? *A.* It was made by the company, but at the same time it is not the same contract.

Q. (By the same.) You referred to a bill for the purpose of getting a date—was that delivery made under the old contract? *A.* No, it was not under the old contract.

Defendant's counsel offers in evidence the proposition, already handed to witness, dated April 25th. Objected to by plaintiff's counsel as only being the heads of that contract, and not the contract itself.

The Witness:—That was simply a memorandum I sent from my office, simply to close the bargain with Mr. Morris, which had not been elaborated.

Mr. Burton:—I claim that this made a completed contract on that day, and that this other contract comes in as a variation of it.

The Court:—The second contract having been made, if there was a contract prior to that it was annulled by the latter.

Excluded.

Q. Do you recollect seeing this letter, the next after that of June 27th, dated June 28th, 1873? [Reads it to witness.] *A.* Yes, sir.

Defendant's counsel reads in evidence letters from defendant to plaintiffs of June 27th and 28th, 1873 —marked Deft's Exhibits E and F of this date. And also letter from plaintiffs to defendant, dated June 27th, 1873—marked Deft's Exhibit G of this date.

Q. Was the oil of vitriol costing you more than a cent and three quarters to produce it at that time?

Objected to; objection overruled.

Q. Is it true under your statement that, as it cost you then to produce it, you were losing money by selling it at a cent and three quarters ? *A.* During the whole of Morris's contract ?

Q. I am asking you in regard to the summer of 1873. *A.* Un-doubtedly; yes, sir.

Q. Had the material advanced ?

T he Court :—We can not go into that question.

> Defendant's counsel excepts, and offers to prove that the witness presented a written statement, ac-cording to his own evidence on the stand, in the previous January, whereby he showed that he was making a profit of a considerable amount on his sales at 1½ cents per pound, to this defendant. He now stating that he was selling undoubtedly at a loss, counsel for defendant proposes to prove by the witness on the stand that the price of the material had not increased, nor had the price of labor em-ployed in its production.
> Excluded. Exception taken.

Q. You are not positive about it ? *A.* No, sir; but I think so.

> Plaintiff rests.
> Mr. Burton opened for the defense.

Q. When did you first commence your purchases of this article, or to deal with these plaintiffs in this case as a firm ?

> Objected to as assuming the identity of the plain-tiff with a firm. Objection sustained.

Q. Now you, in response to this letter, did what ? *A.* Before I answered the letter Mr. Green came in, and I showed him Mr. Willis's letter.

> Plaintiff's counsel objects to any conversation or transaction between the witness and Mr. Green as immaterial, Green not being a member of the cor-poration. Question waived.

> Plaintiff's counsel moves to strike out all the evi-dence concerning the interview of the 25th of Feb-ruary, on the ground that it was an interview with a member of the firm of Willis, Green, & Jones, and is not binding upon the plaintiff. Motion de-nied ; exception taken.

Q. What was done after you received it ? *A.* Well, I wrote a letter at once, and told him it was not like—

Q. Never mind what you told him in the letter. *A.* I wrote him this letter of April 29th.

Said letter is offered in evidence. Objected to as immaterial. Defendant's counsel said he offered the letter to show the circumstances surrounding the making of the contract, and the parties to it. Objection sustained.

Q. What amount of deficiency in delivery occurred during that month?

Objected to as incompetent; objection sustained until it is shown what was demanded.

Q. What was the fact about that—did he furnish 50 carboys a day thereafter?

Objected to as immaterial unless it is shown that plaintiffs were asked to furnish 50 carboys a day. Objection overruled; exception taken.

Q. Will you state how it was in reference to your being able to procure oil in the market—what efforts you made, and whether you succeeded in procuring all you needed from other sources?

Objected to on the ground that there is no claim for damage by reason of defendant not being supplied prior to April, 1874. Testimony excluded.

The Court:—Mr. Burton, take your exception.

Mr. Burton:—That is my theory of the case, and I prefer not to take an exception.

Q. Please state the amount—can you separate those? A. I can't separate them now; I have them together.

Mr. West:—I have no objection to that being done out of the regular order.

Cross-examination by Mr. WEST.

Q. About how many carboys of acid had you used from March 1st, '72, to March 1st, '73? A. Sold?

Q. No, I mean used or disposed of in the course of your business altogether.

Objected to; objection overruled; exception taken.

A. About 6000 carboys.

Plaintiff's counsel, with the consent of counsel for defendant, put in evidence a statement made by Mr. Haynes, a previous witness, subject to being proved hereafter.

Q. Do you understand that you had a right under this contract, in case you were not furnished with all you needed, to buy from other sources?

Objected to as incompetent.   Question waived for the present.

———•———

Q. If the company assumed and paid for that acid, why was not that a furnishing to you by the company under the contract?
Objected to as a question of law.   Objection sustained.

———•———

Plaintiff's counsel offered in evidence the letter of April 30th, 1874.   Objected to as outside of the limit of time, the contract having closed in April. Objection overruled; exception taken.   Marked Plaintiff's Exhibit 7.

———•———

Q. Were your warehouses pretty well filled?
This evidence is all taken subject to defendant's objection and exception.

A. No, sir.

———•———

Q. Are these letters from you?   [Hands witness two letters.]
A. Yes, sir; they are.
Plaintiff's counsel offers in evidence said letters, dated June 12th and 19th.   Marked Plaintiff's Exhibits 8 and 9 of this date.

M r. West:—I would like to have you tell us to-morrow morning, from your books, how long before you had used up 4086 carboys in addition to the amount furnished you.
Objected to as irrelevant.   Plaintiff's counsel offers to prove the time when defendant had used up 4086 carboys besides what had been furnished by the plaintiff.   Objected to; objection sustained; exception taken.

Re- direct examination.

Q. Was there ever any conversation or talk of any kind between you and Mr. Willis about your only wanting or demanding under this contract 20 or 30 carboys a day?

FIRST PAGE—FORM 5.

The Harlem Chemical and Mining Company } Third Day.
vs.
John Morris.

Before Judge Sedgwick and a Jury.
New York, Nov. 16, 1876.

———•———

J ohn Morris recalled for further cross-examination.
By Mr. West.

Q. Have you ascertained how many carboys of acid you procured from other sources than the Harlem Company which were paid for by them during the year of the last contract? *A.* Sixty-seven is all I can find.

Q. After the 26th of April, and after the making of this second contract, what oil of vitriol was supplied, and in what quantities; and what demand, if any, to your personal knowledge was made upon the company of the plaintiff? *A.* Our sales greatly exceeded the supply, and I demanded acid almost daily through Mr. Jones and other people.

> Plaintiff's counsel moves to strike out the evidence as to witness making a demand through Mr. Jones and others.

The Court:—That must be stricken out unless you call Mr. Jones.

Mr. Burton:—We propose to call Mr. Jones to show that he carried those instructions to the plaintiff direct.

The Court:—Then it may remain in.

The Witness:—I also demanded supplies through their truckman that came over with the acid—through the truckman of the Harlem Chemical Works who came over with acids.

Q. Did it meet your requirements—your demands?

> Plaintiff's counsel objects to the word "demands." Objection sustained, and the word stricken from the question.

A. No, sir; it did not.

Q. Did you find that you could procure the quantity required by you or not? *A.* I could not procure it; no, sir.

Examination suspended.

Junius Gridley, called for the defence, sworn.

Direct examination by Mr. Burton.

Q. Where do you reside? *A.* I reside in Brooklyn.

Q. State whether you were present at a meeting of these manufacturers when a Mr. Jones, one of the officers of the plaintiff, representing that company, was present and made any statement about his contract with the defendant.

> Objected to as incompetent; objection sustained; exception taken.

Cross-examination by Mr. West.

Q. When you say the market price of the oil of vitriol is $2\frac{1}{2}$ cents, you mean such vitriol as you deal in? *A.* Yes, sir.

Further direct.

Q. Do you know what was the arrangement among the manufacturers as to the sales to commissions customers?

> Objected to on the ground that there is no evi-

dence that there was any such arrangement. Question waived.

G|EORGE MORRIS's direct examination resumed.

Q.|Do you know how frequently you made demands for acid of their carman, during the summer of 1873, after the making of the contract?

Objected to that the witness should state what he said.

———————

F|urther direct examination.

Q.|The gentleman has asked you what amount you had on hand during that month of April, and whether you had a surplus at that time, and how much you bought; I will ask you now what investigation you made, or what effort you made and for what purpose, to get additional supplies of oil of vitriol?

Objected to; objection sustained. Defendant's counsel offers to prove that during the month of April this firm of defendants had contracts and orders in large quantities that they were unable to supply.

M|r. West:—I would like to see them prove it, if they can.

T|he Court:—I will take the responsibility of ruling that out.

Plaintiff's counsel offers in evidence the papers that were identified by Mr. Morris as accounts recorded by him of acid purchased by him and paid for by plaintiff, 11 in number. Marked Plaintiff's Exhibit No. 10 of this date.

ON TAKING NOTES IN LAW REPORTING.

§ 408. It should be the aim of the reporter, while taking notes of a legal proceeding, to stenograph the matter in the same form that he wishes it to appear in when transcribed. By so doing, especially in reporting objections, rulings, etc., he will save himself much time and trouble when he comes to the most laborious part of his task, the making of the long-hand transcript. And it is indispensably necessary when the reporter has his minutes transcribed directly from the short-hand notes, without dictation or subsequent revision of the notes.

NAME OF WITNESS, ETC.

§ 409. At the commencement of each case its title should be fully written out in long-hand, and there also should appear, either in long-hand or phonography (according to the length of time the reporter has to write it), the name of the court, the name of the judge, whether or not there is a jury, the date of the trial, and the appearances. At the head of the examination of each witness his name should be written in long-hand in full, and followed by the words in phonography, "Kld'-F P'

(or D), sRn² Drt²-sM-Nshn B¹ Mr³ ——." If the reporter is pressed
for time, he may simply write a phonographic *pee* or *dee*, to indicate
whether he was called by Plaintiff or Defendant.

QUESTION AND ANSWER DISTINGUISHED.

§ 410. In notes of testimony it is the practice of most reporters to
distinguish the question from the answer by commencing each line
of the question at the left of the page, and indenting each line of the
answer about one third the width of the page ; thus,

Where do you reside

    I reside in New York city

Where were you on the night of the 28th of December when this
affair occurred

    I was at my house in 26th Street until about
    8 o'clock, and then I went to the opera

Although this mode of writing questions and answers (especially
when they are short, only occupying a portion of a line) takes up
more paper than any other, yet this is more than counterbalanced
by the increased distinctness that is given to the notes, and the
greater ease and convenience with which the reporter is enabled to
refer to particular portions of the testimony, when, as is often the
case, he is called upon to do so by the counsel or the court.

PASSAGES MARKED FOR CORRECTION.

§ 411. When the reporter takes down a question or answer that he
wishes to read over before commencing to transcribe it, in order to
alter its arrangement or correct an error, he should mark it at the time
by drawing near it a perpendicular line at the left of the page.

CASES CITED.

§ 412. When cases are cited by counsel, and extracts read from
them, the reporter need not attempt to write them at length. After
writing the title of the case, and the name and volume of the Report
where it is to be found, it will be sufficient to give the commencing
and concluding words of each period, with a long dash between. This
will enable the reporter when transcribing to ascertain exactly what
portions of the case were read and what omitted.

HINTS ON TRANSCRIBING.

§ 413. Ordinarily the reporter transcribes his own notes into long-
hand. This is the most wearying part of his duties, as it often takes
seven or eight hours to write out what was taken in short-hand in one

hour. An experienced reporter should be able to render his notes of testimony into legible long-hand at the rate of sixteen to twenty folios (of one hundred words each) an hour, and notes of argument, speeches, etc., at the rate of ten to sixteen folios.

§ 414. When great expedition is required, notes may be transcribed by dictating to two rapid long-hand copyists from different parts of the report at the same time. In this case one of the writers may commence with the beginning of the report, and the other at the middle, deviating, however, a little to one side or the other, when by so doing he is enabled to start with a new witness, or at the beginning of a cross-examination. The reader should sit between the copyists, and dictate a few words, first to one and then to the other, keeping one of the places in his note-book with the index finger of his right hand, and the other place with the index finger of his left hand. By turning the head a little, as each sentence is dictated, toward the writer for whom it is intended, all danger of confusion will be avoided. This also may be done by calling each by name every time he is addressed. A little ingenuity and practice will enable the reader to keep both writers constantly employed. In this manner of transcribing, from thirty to forty folios may be written out per hour ; and, if the copyists are careful, the manuscript need not afterward be read over, or compared with the notes.

§ 415. Another mode of expediting this part of the work is to dictate the matter to other phonographers, who then proceed to transcribe their notes. For this purpose advanced learners of Phonography are generally employed, as they are willing to do the work for the sake of the practice it gives them, for a compensation that reporters can afford to give. Manuscript prepared in this way, however, should always be carefully re-read, as errors will occasionally occur.

§ 416. There is another mode of transcribing, by which a report can be gotten out very nearly, or quite, as fast as the original notes were taken ; but it can not be used except in preparing matter for the printer, and it is perhaps well not to resort to it even for that, except where a great amount of work has to be done in an unusually limited space of time. The plan is as follows : Having secured the services of five or six rapid long-hand writers, they are seated about a round table, each having before him a pile of slips of paper, previously numbered—those before the first copyist being marked 1 A, 2 A, 3 A, etc. ; those before the second, 1 B, 2 B, 3 B, etc., and so on. The reporter then commences by dictating a sentence or line to number one, then a like amount to number two, and so on around the circle, until he comes to number one again, and then continues right on without break. The reader should walk around the table and dictate to each in a low tone of voice, so that the other writers will not be confused. A large round table, with an opening in the middle in which the reader might sit on a revolving stool, would be very convenient for this purpose. As each writer finishes the sentence given him, he sticks the slip face downward on a paper-file standing before him, and then is ready to write the next dictation. When the files are full, a boy replaces them with empty ones, and then proceeds to gum the slips together in the following order: 1 A, 1 B, 1 C, 1 D, 1 E; 2 A, 2 B, 2 C, 2 D, 2 E; 3 A, 3 B, etc. This copy will, of course, be serviceable only for the printer.

NEWSPAPER REPORTING.

§ 417. The qualifications necessary in a reporter on the daily press are varied, and a knowledge of stenography is not absolutely necessary to render him generally successful. His business is mainly to get news and put it in a shape which will be readable and interesting; and to this end he should possess good judgment, a quick, intuitive mind, ready at all times to perceive what would be of interest to the public, and to jot down the salient points, and have the requisite ability to prepare them properly for the press. But, although for this the knowledge of short-hand would be very important, as it would enable him to take down the language of parties from whom he gets statements of facts, instead of being obliged to rely in great measure on his memory, yet it can not be said to be an indispensable requisite to the furnishing of good reports.

§ 418. A newspaper reporter, however, who would be equal to anything that may be required of him, must also be a good stenographer, as verbatim reports of speeches, sermons, debates, conventions, etc., are so often required, especially by our metropolitan press.

§ 419. Political meetings in the city of New York are usually held in the evening, and generally the reports of them must appear in the next morning's paper. For this reason, if a tolerably full report is required, a corps of three or four reporters will be needed to get it out before the paper goes to press. To accomplish this successfully, each reporter should take notes for from twenty to forty-five minutes, according to the probable length of the meeting, and then go directly to the office of the paper and begin to transcribe. Sometimes each one takes first a short turn of five or ten minutes, and then afterward a long turn of fifteen to thirty minutes, so that he may be transcribing while his co-reporters are taking notes of the speeches. If the speaking continues to a late hour, the reporter whose turn comes last is generally required to finish up the meeting with a long-hand sketch, which is best given in the third person. The report of a political meeting will be very much more effective and interesting if it have a proper introduction. In this may be included a description of the decorations of the hall, a statement of the number and character of the persons present, and, if any eminent persons are among them, their names. In newspaper reporting much more latitude is allowed for the judgment of the reporter than in reporting law proceedings. It is his duty to correct grammatical errors, improve the construction, to sometimes omit objectionable passages, and frequently to almost rewrite entire speeches. The form of introduction to a speech used at the present time by the New York journals is similar to the following:

The Chairman then introduced the Hon. Thomas Jefferson, who spoke as follows :   ·

SPEECH OF HON. THOMAS JEFFERSON.

Then follows the speech. If the speaker was received with applause, that fact should, of course, be stated in the introduction. The interruptions by the audience during the delivery of a speech should be carefully noted, and written in brackets in their proper places. The following will serve as illustrations : [Applause.] [Great cheering.] [A voice, "That's so."] The Resolutions, Lists of Vice-Presidents, and sometimes entire speeches, may be obtained in manuscript, and the reporter thus relieved from much labor. With these few hints, the reporter will probably find no difficulty in giving satisfaction in this branch of his profession.

APPENDIX.

§ 420 THE material from which a system of stenography must be constructed, is necessarily so limited that it is hardly practicable to furnish one complete and consistent representation for all the sounds heard in the various languages of the world. Nevertheless, for the use of the student of languages and Phonetics, it is thought advisable to give signs for a few of the more common foreign sounds, both consonant and vowel, as well as for those vowel-sounds in the English language that are not represented with exactness by the ordinary twelve-vowel scale. [See §§ 45–47.]

EXTENDED VOWEL-SCALE.
SIMPLE VOWELS.

	1	2	3	4	5	6	7	8	9
Long									
	ah	air	ale	même	cat	car	all	no	food

	10	11	12	13	14	15	16	17	18	19
Short										
	at	ask	met	it	on	lost	up	whole	cur	foot

COMPOSITE VOWELS.

LONG : Fr. *eû ;* Ger. long *ö*   Fr. l. *ū ;* Ger. l. *ü*
EXAMPLES : q*ueue ;* Göthe   v*û ;*   *ü*bel

SHORT : Fr. *eu ;* Ger. sh. *ö ;* Eng. *e* bef. *r*   Fr. sh. *u ;* Ger. sh. *ü*
EXAMPLES : j*eu*ne ; b*ö*cke ; , h*e*r   h*u*tte ;   l*ü*cke.

COMPOSITE VOWELS FOLLOWED BY ĭ.

LONG : long *ö* and *ĭ*   long *ü* and *ĭ*
EXAMPLES : œil   l*ui*t

SHORT : short *ö* and *ĭ*   short *ü* and *ĭ*
EXAMPLES · ———   l*ui*

§ 421. The nasal vowels heard in the French and one or two other European languages, may be written by placing the nasalized vowel to the stem *en* or *em* canceled with a short tick, written between the ordinary vowel-positions; thus, ⌣ *an, en,* ⌣ *in,* ⌣ *on,* ⌣ *un.* The *en*-hook canceled in a similar manner may be used for the same purpose; thus, ⟍ *bon,* ⌣ *enfant.*

SIGNS FOR FOREIGN CONSONANT-SOUNDS.

BREATHED SOUNDS.

§ 422. We have seen (§ 9) that certain of the sonant consonant-sounds have no breathed mates in English, and, therefore, no signs have been provided for them in the ordinary alphabet. If, however, these sounds should be met with in writing foreign words, the writer may use the signs of the sonants with a small semicircle struck through them; thus ∫ , which represents the Welsh *ll,* as in the word ∫ *Llan.*

ABRUPTS CHANGED TO CONTINUANTS.

§ 423. Several of the sounds of consonants that in English are always abrupts, in certain foreign languages partially lose that character and become continuants. Such sounds may be represented in Phonography by the signs of the abrupts with a short waved line written through them; thus, ⤬ represents the sound of Greek φ, or Latin *ph;* and its mate ⤬, the sound of *b* in Spanish and *w* in German. The sounds of German *ch* and *g,* as in *Dach* and *tag,* are represented by ⤙ *ch,* ⤛ *g.*

PHONOGRAPHIC
READING LESSONS.

LESSON I.

LESSON II.

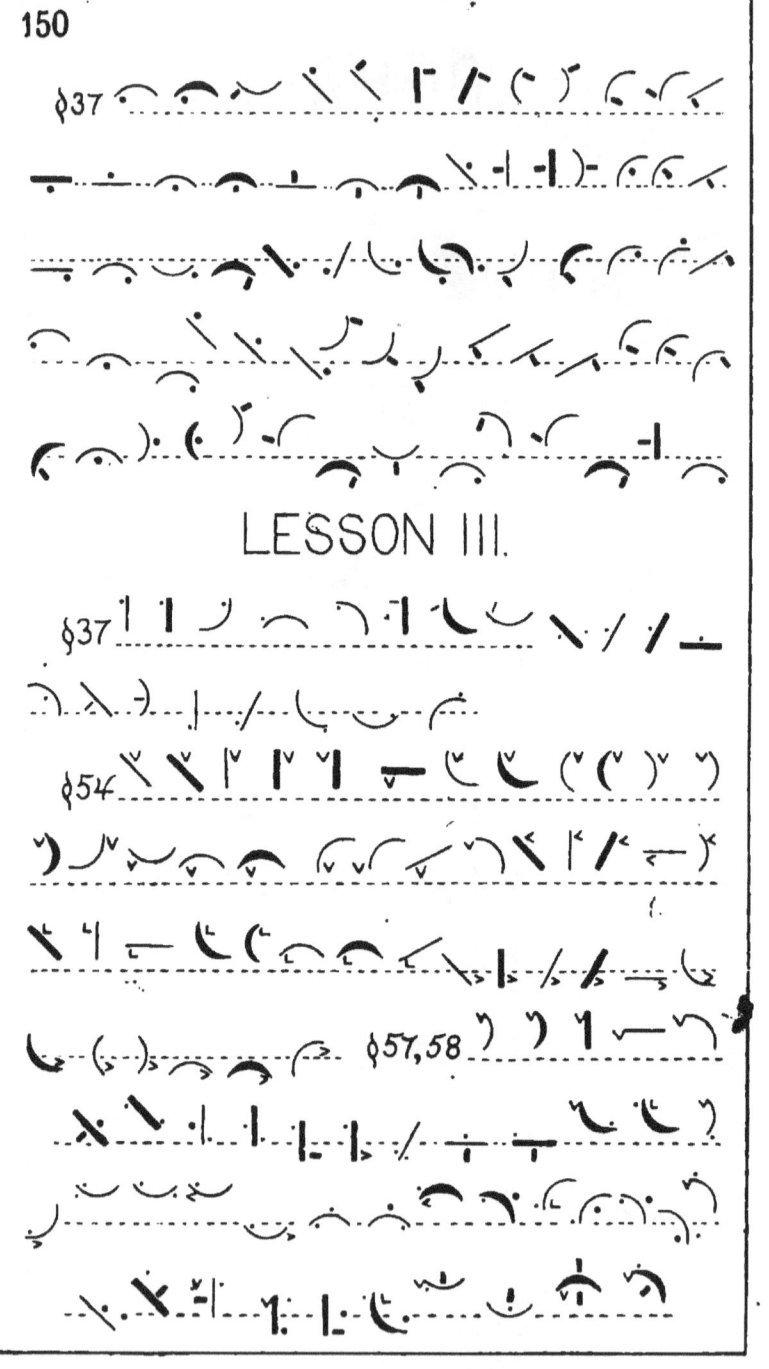

LESSON III.

LESSON IV.

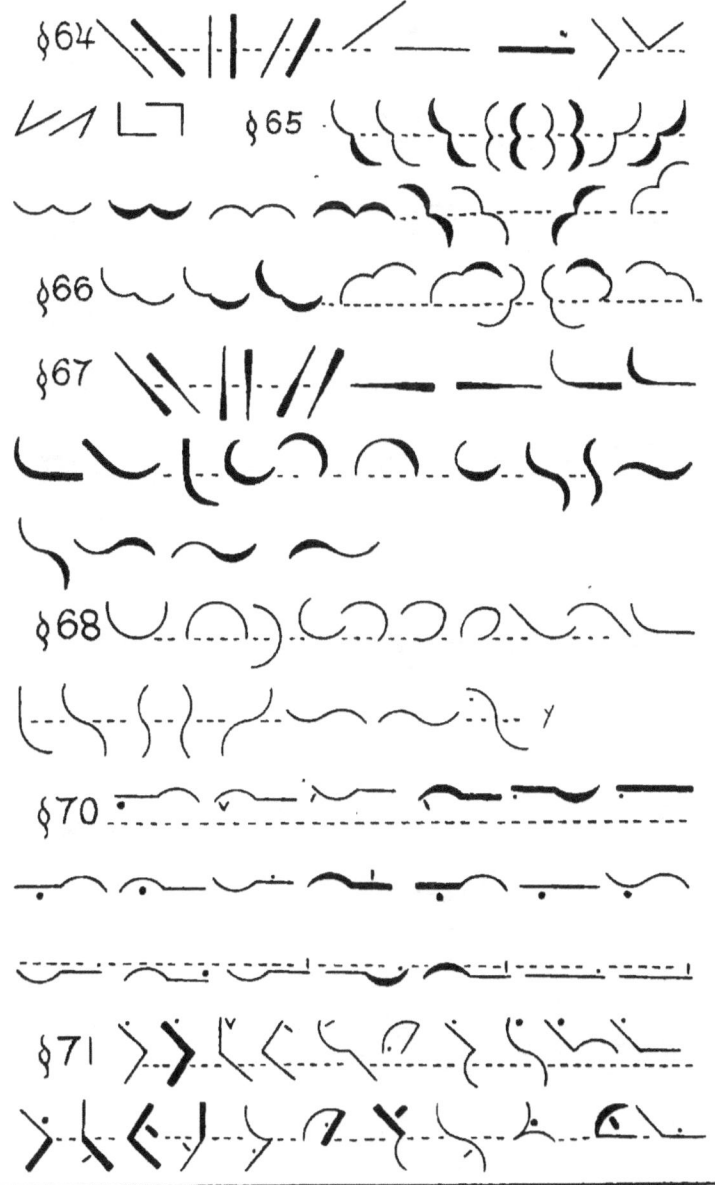

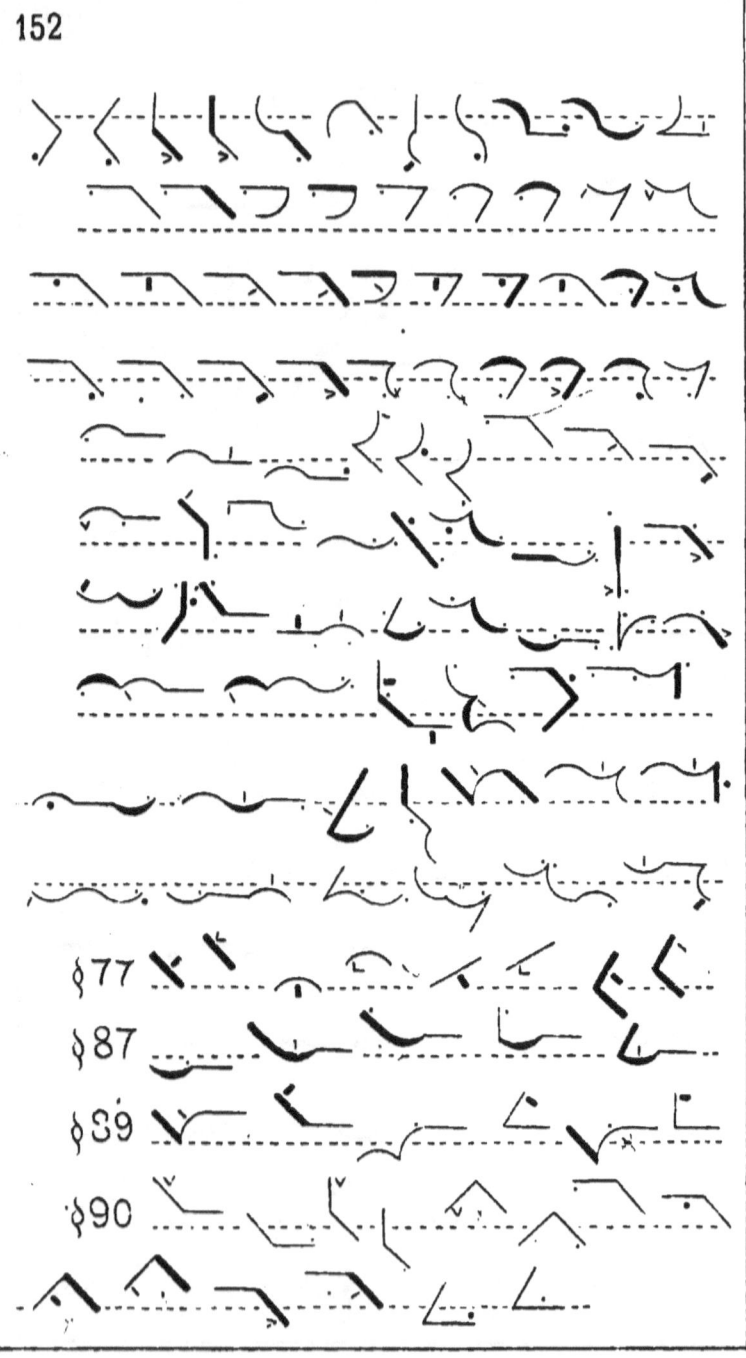

§77

§87

§89

§90

LESSON V.

§106

§103

LESSON VI.

§111 §113 §112 §115 §114 §118 §120 §122 §123 §125 §127

LESSON VII.

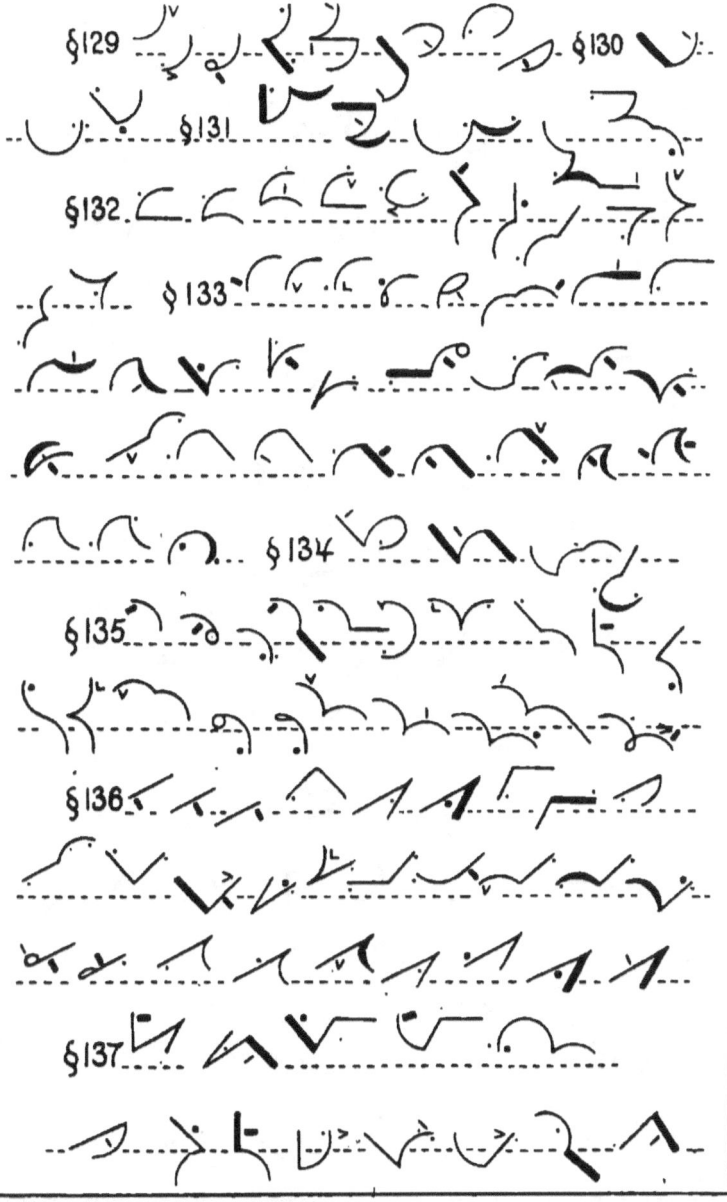

LESSON VIII.

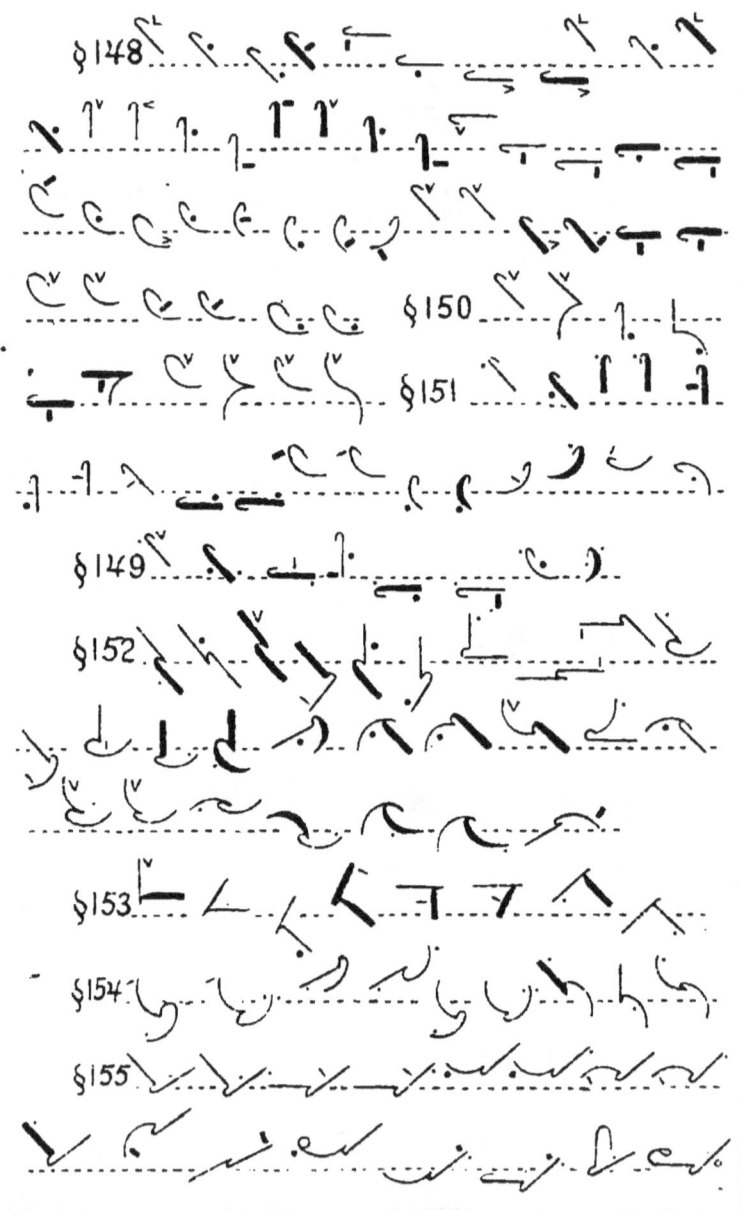

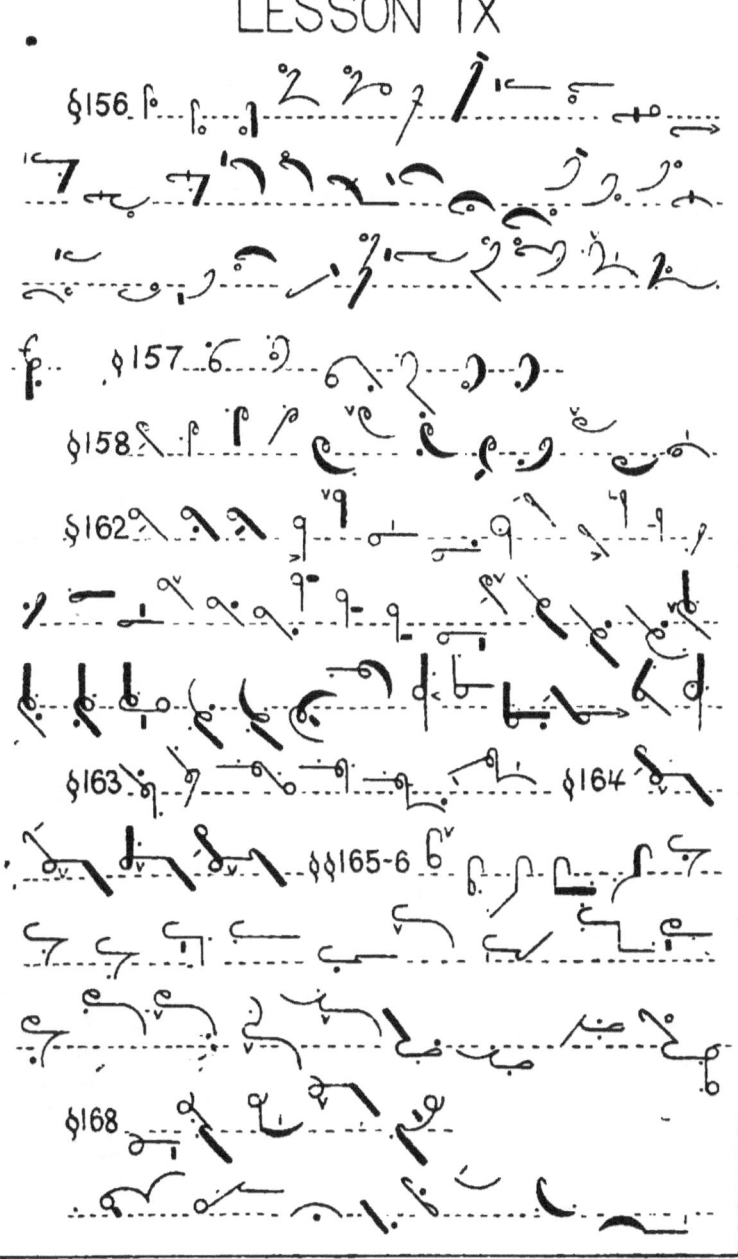

LESSON IX

157

LESSON X.

LESSON XI.

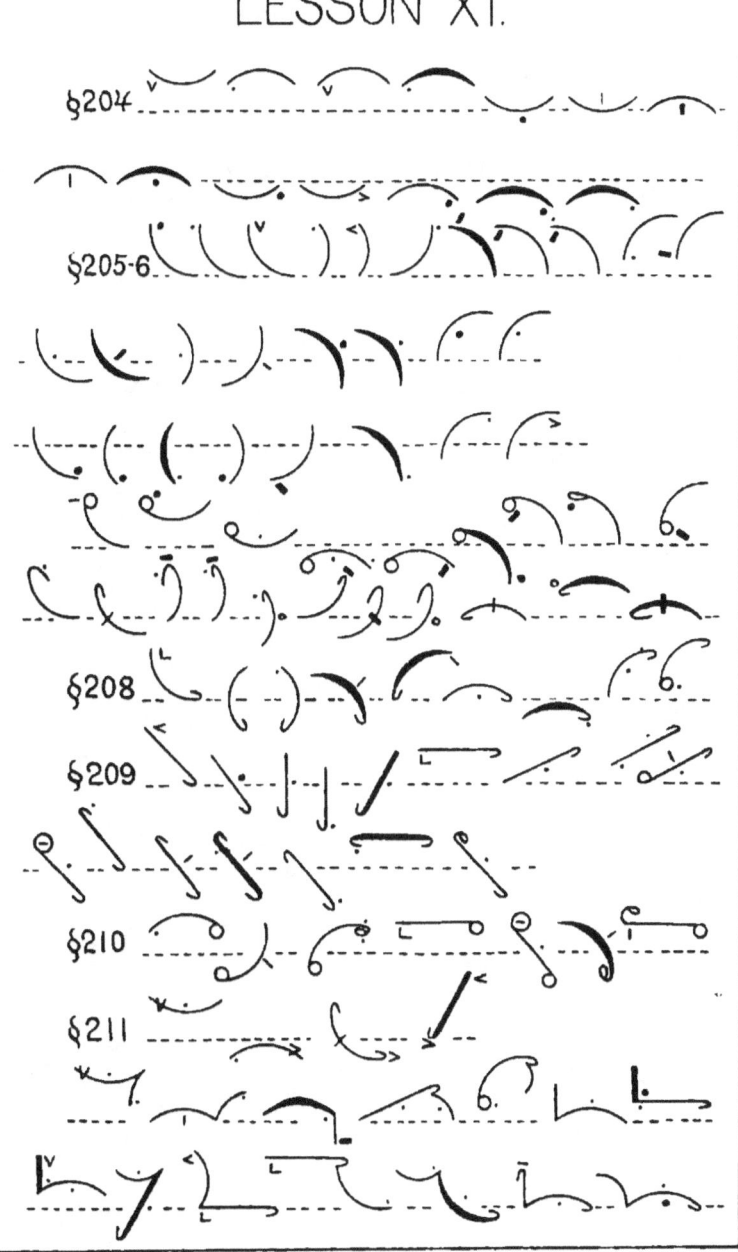

§204

§205-6

§208

§209

§210

§211

LESSON XII.

§§212-18

§214

LESSON XIII.

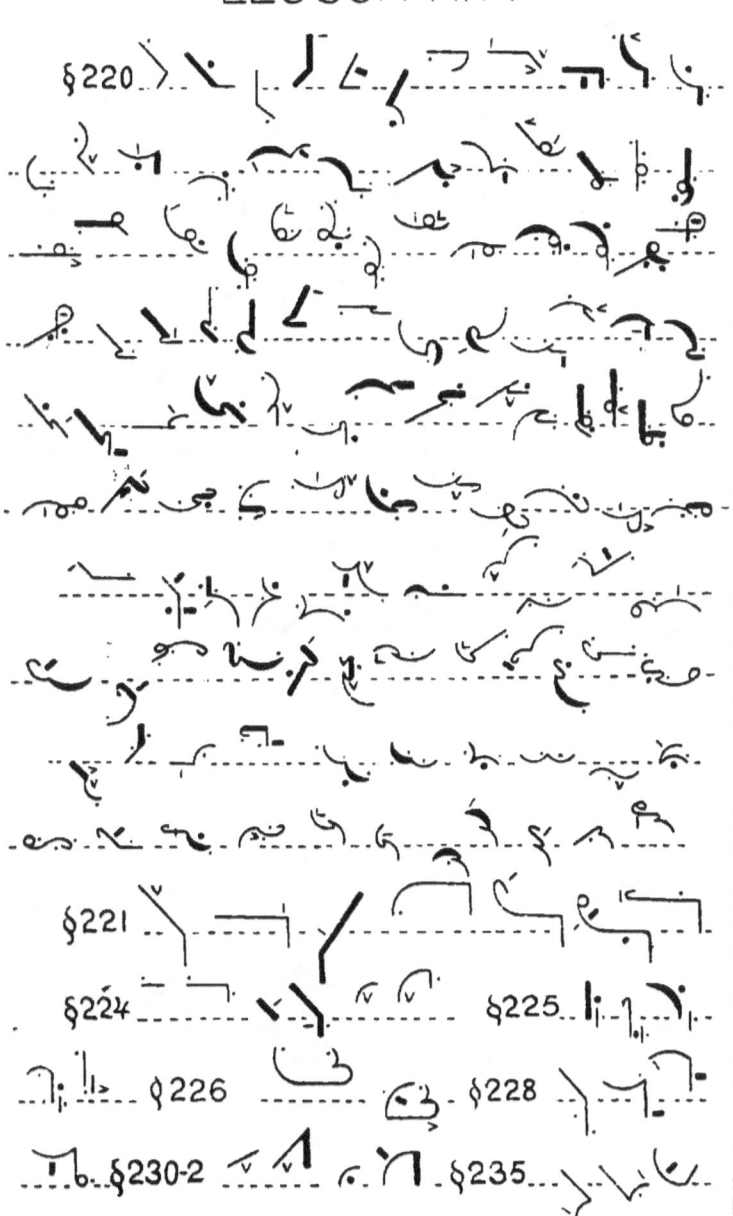

LESSON XIV.

§247

§248

§249

§265

§266

§267

§269

§270

LESSON XV.

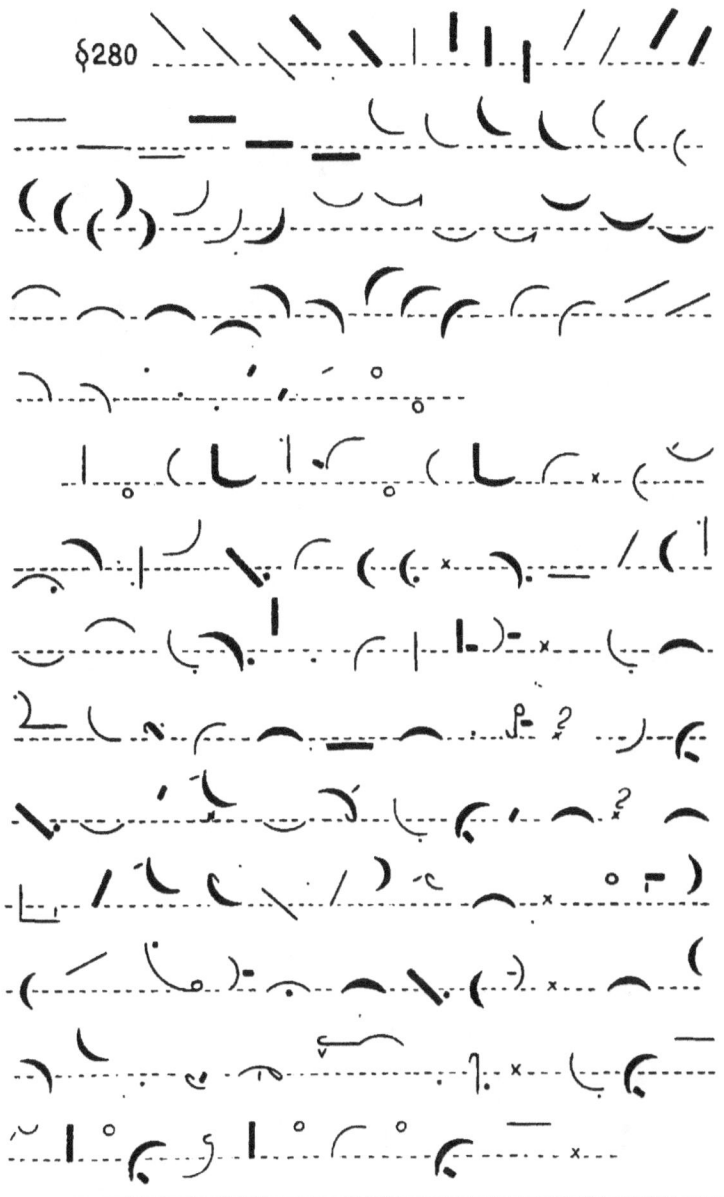

LESSON XVI.

§276.

§284.

LESSON XVII.

§285

§286

§287 §288

LESSON XVIII.

§301

§302

§304

§305

§306

LESSON XIX.

§307

§308

§309

§310

§312

§313

§314

§316

§317

§318

§319

§320

LESSON XX.

§ 327

§ 330

§ 331

§ 332

§ 333

§ 334

§ 336

§ 338

Washington's Birthday.

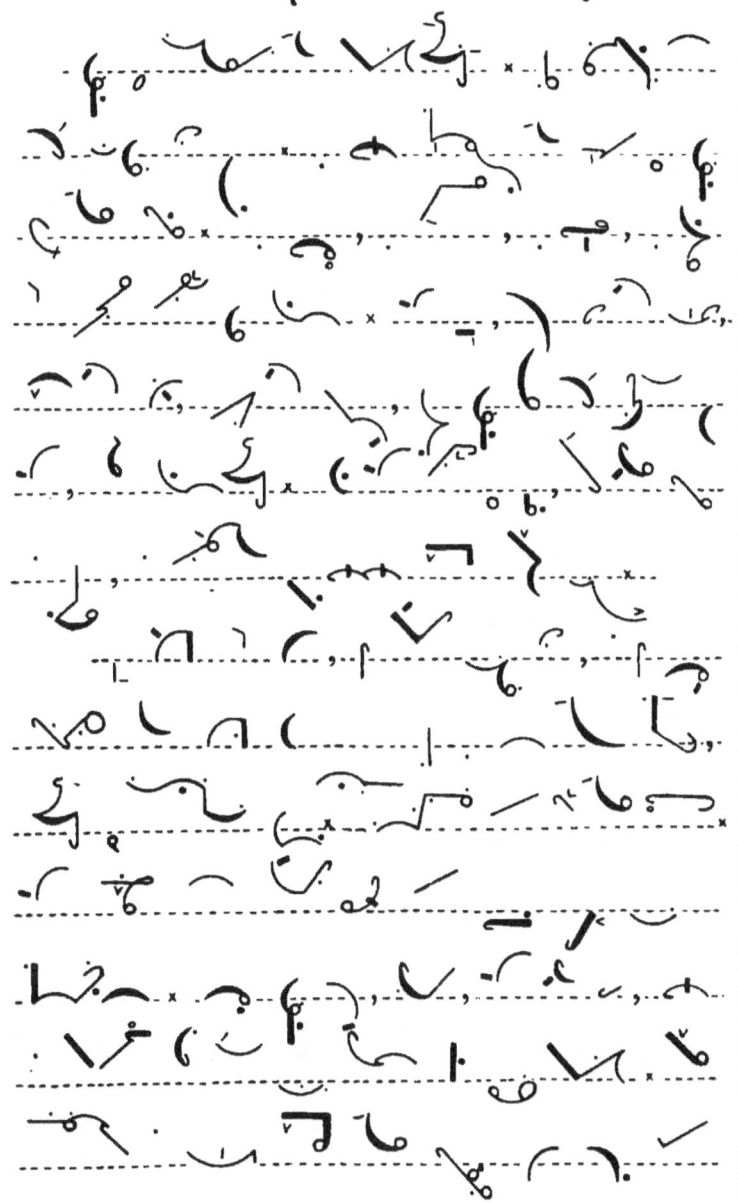

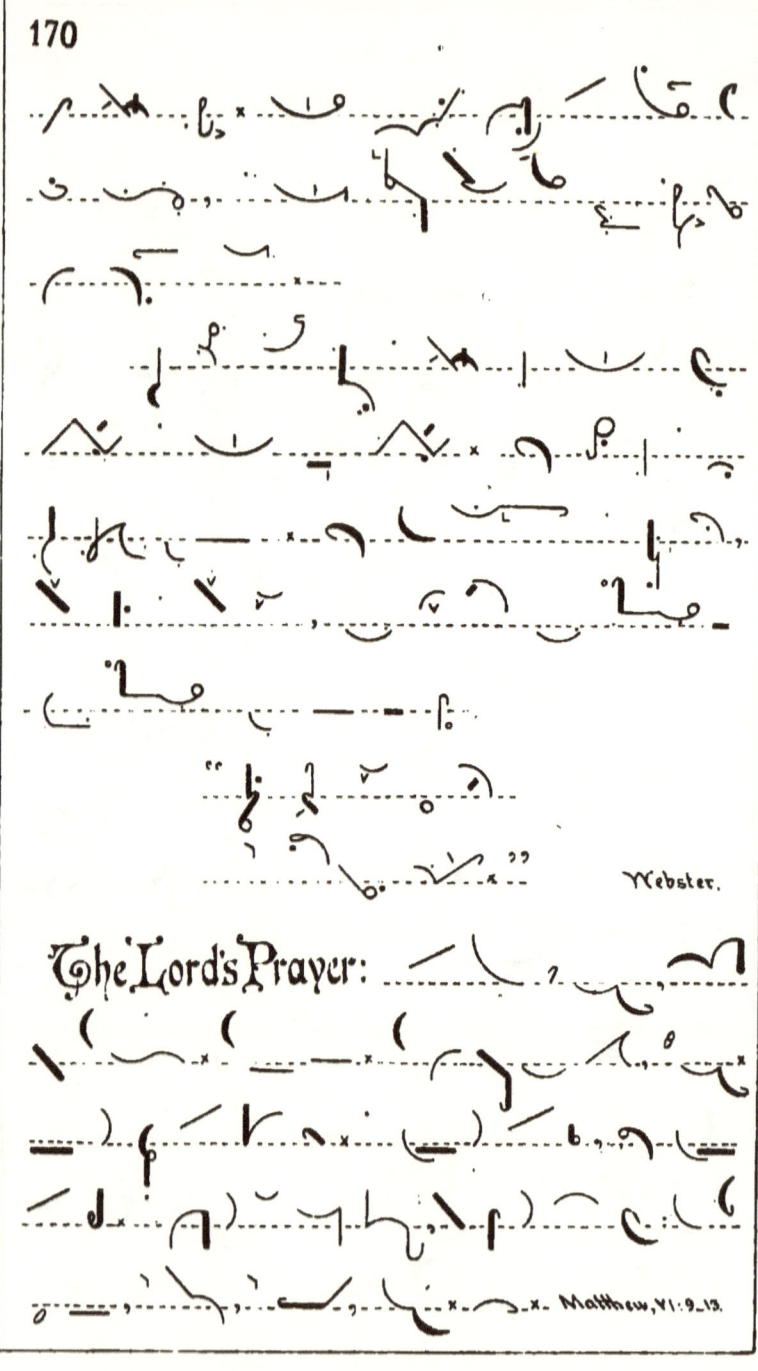

Webster.

The Lord's Prayer:

Matthew, VI: 9-13.

The True Glory of a Nation.

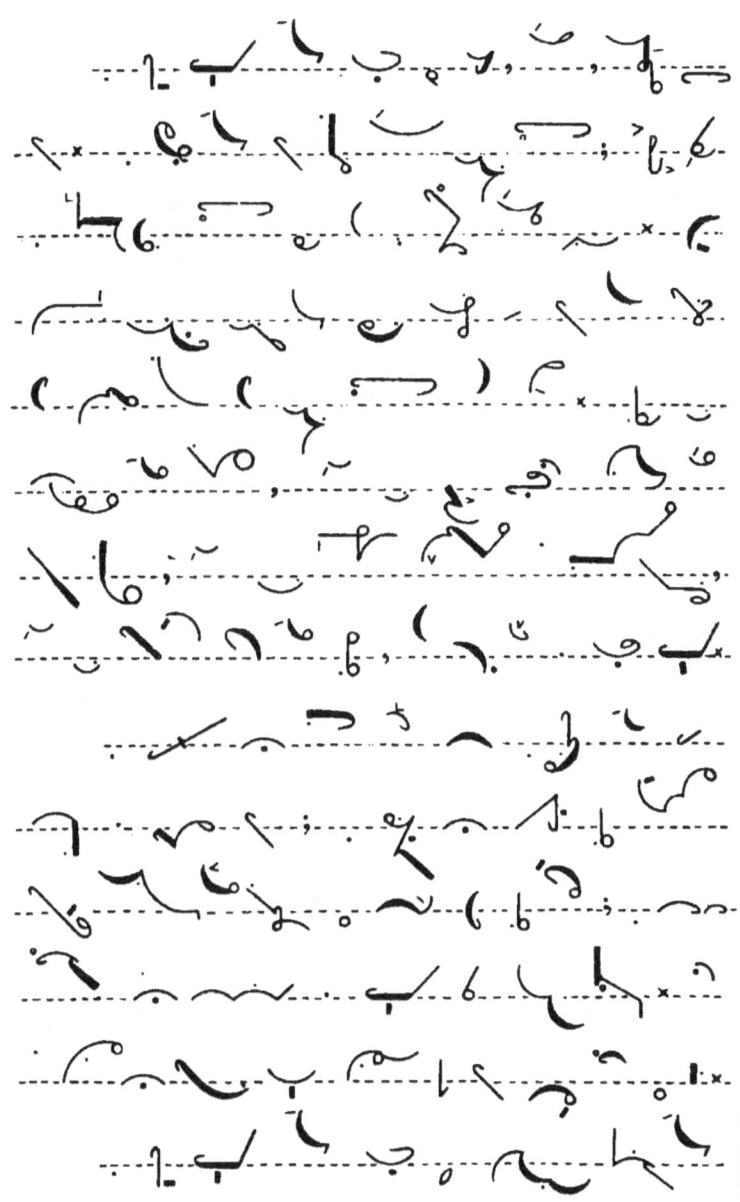

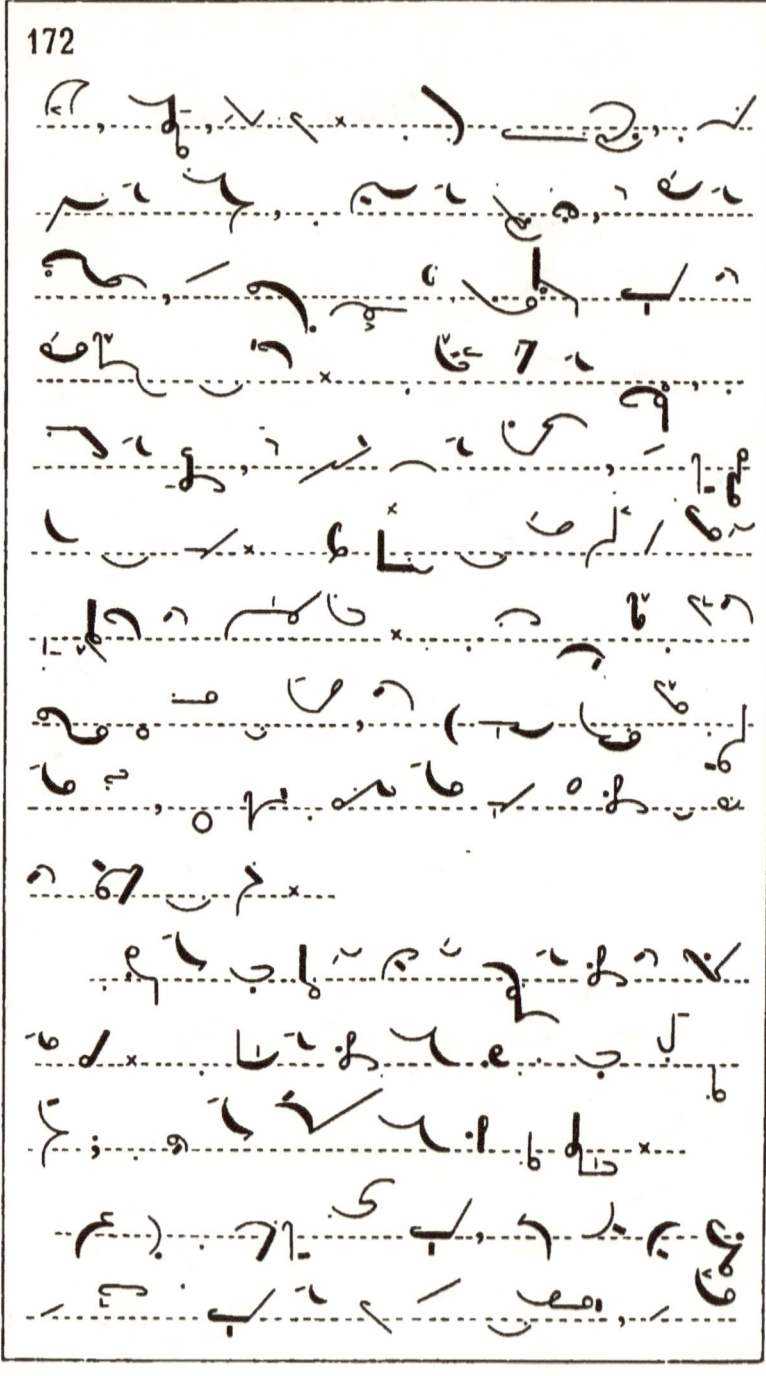

Whipple.

Extract from Hamlet's Soliloquy.

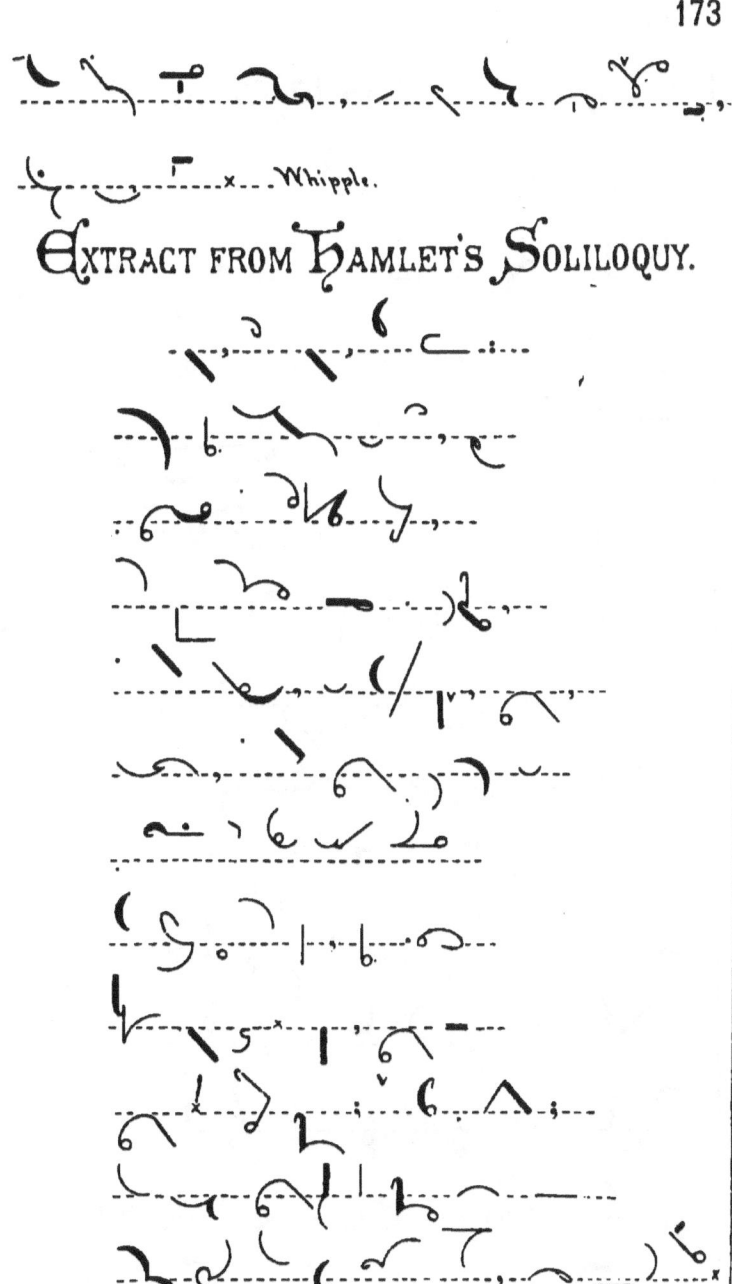

An Address to Students.

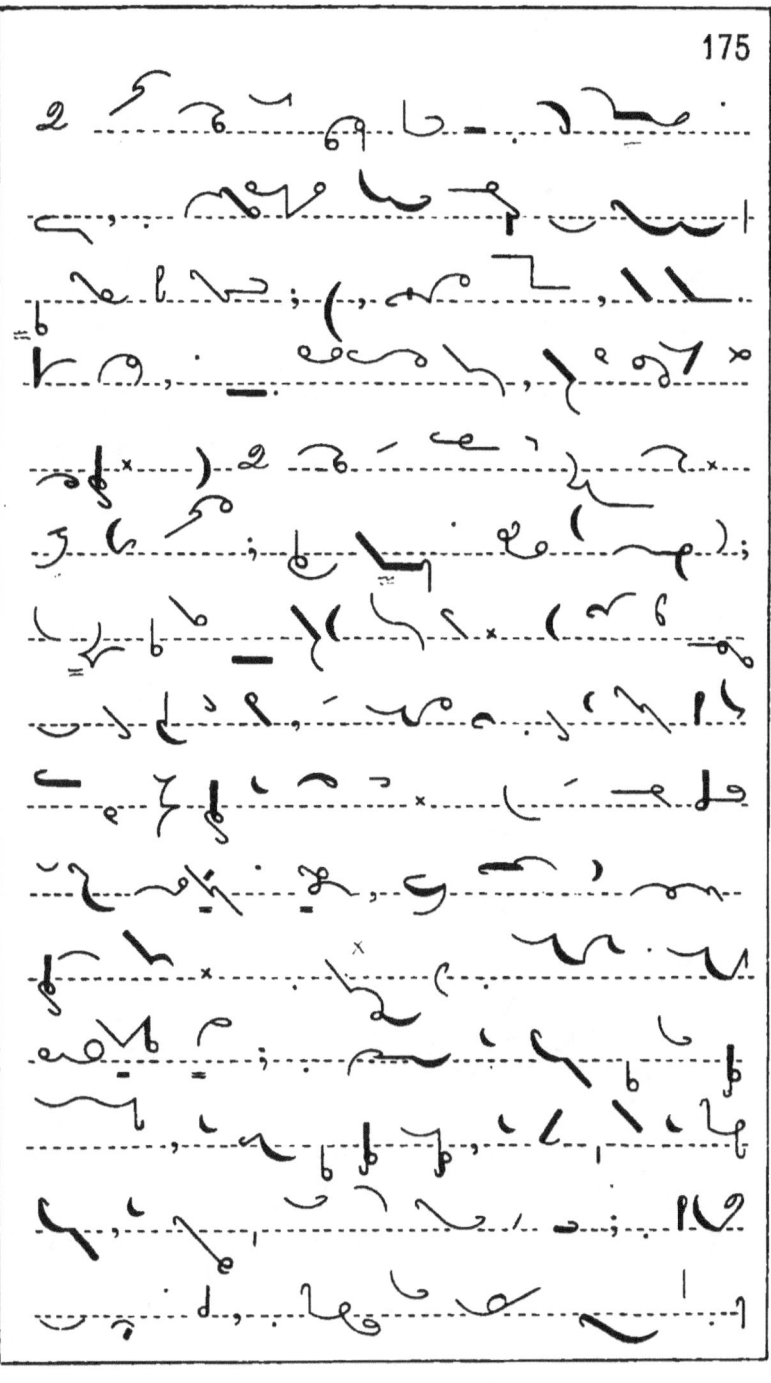

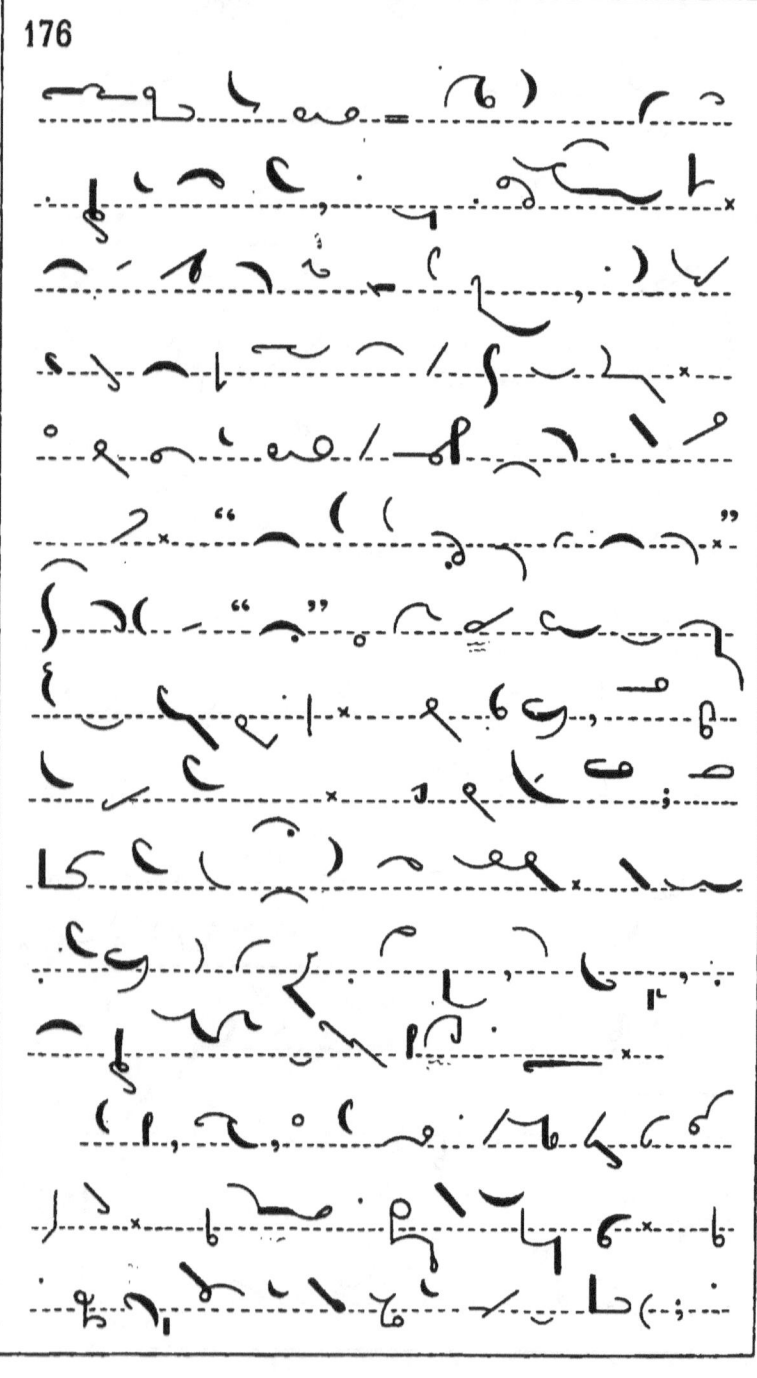

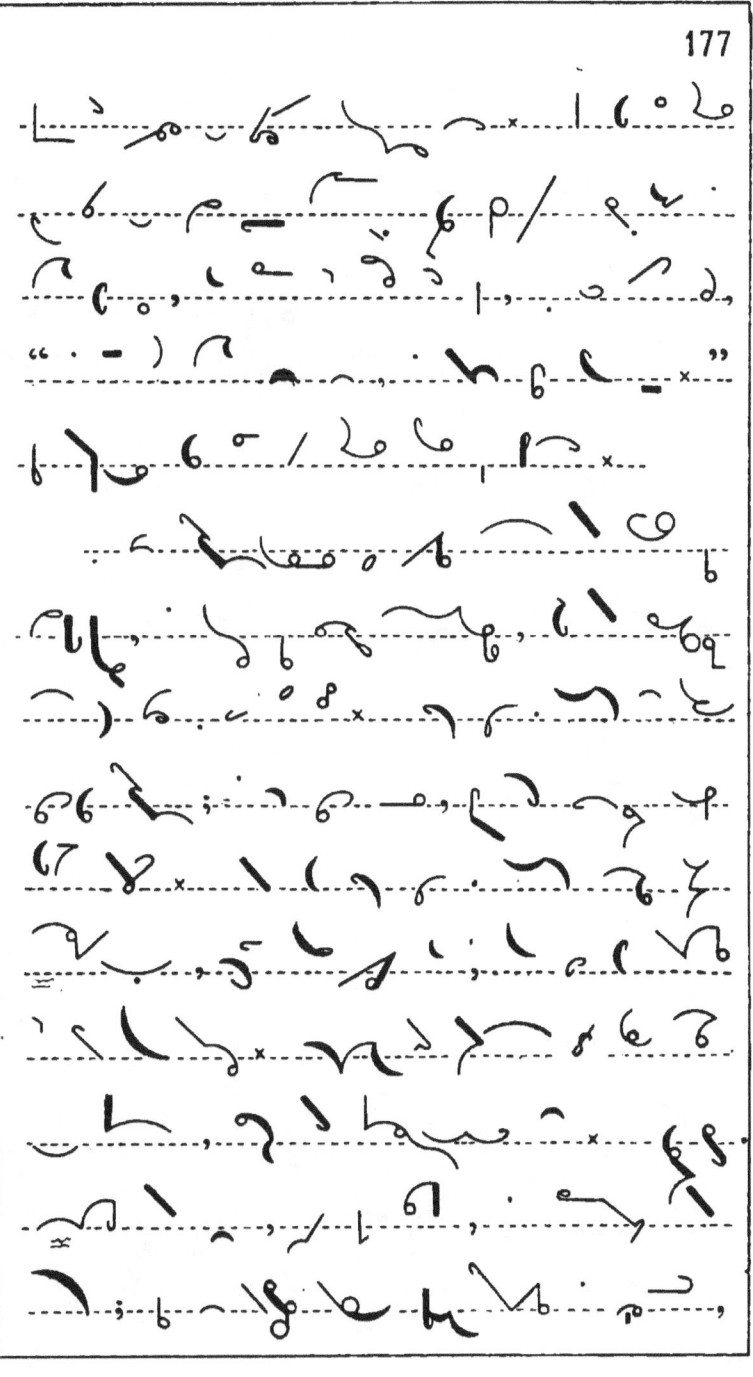

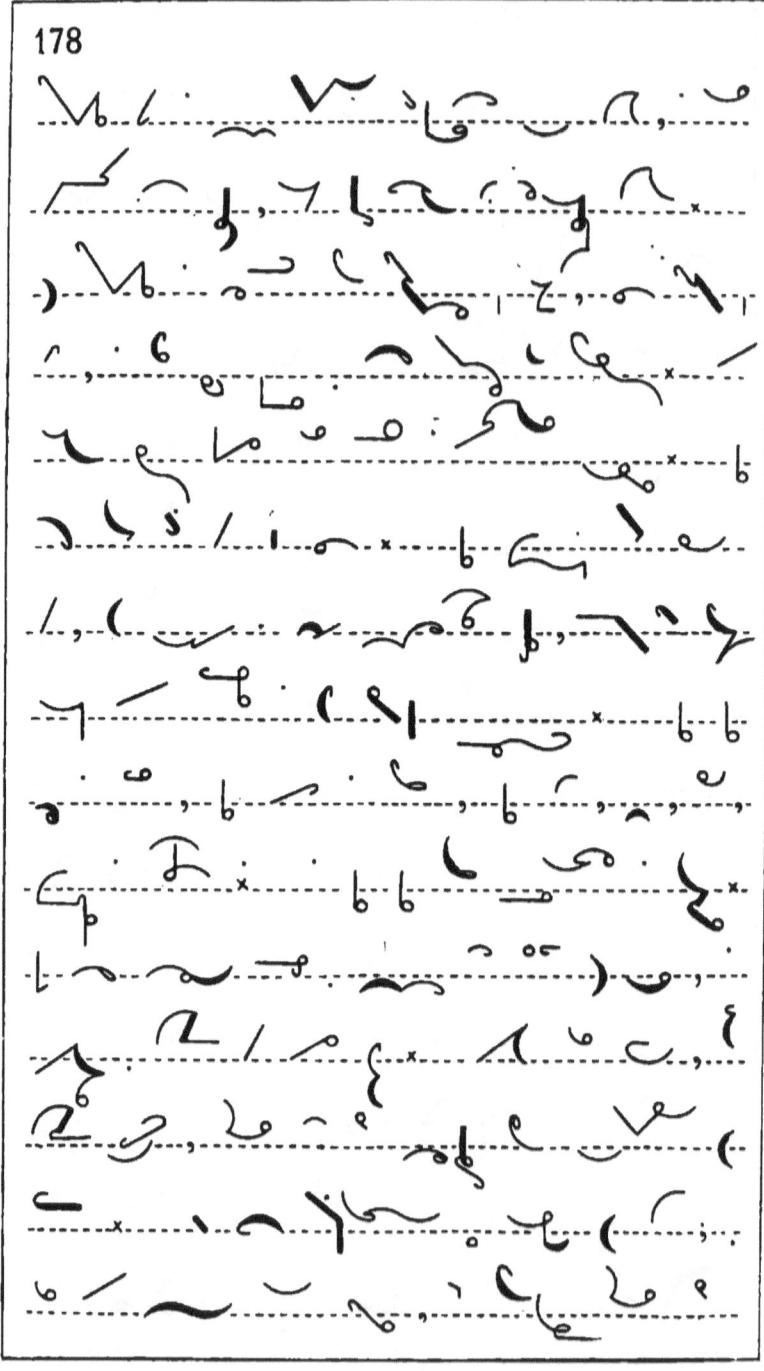

x Tyndall.

Paul Before King Agrippa.

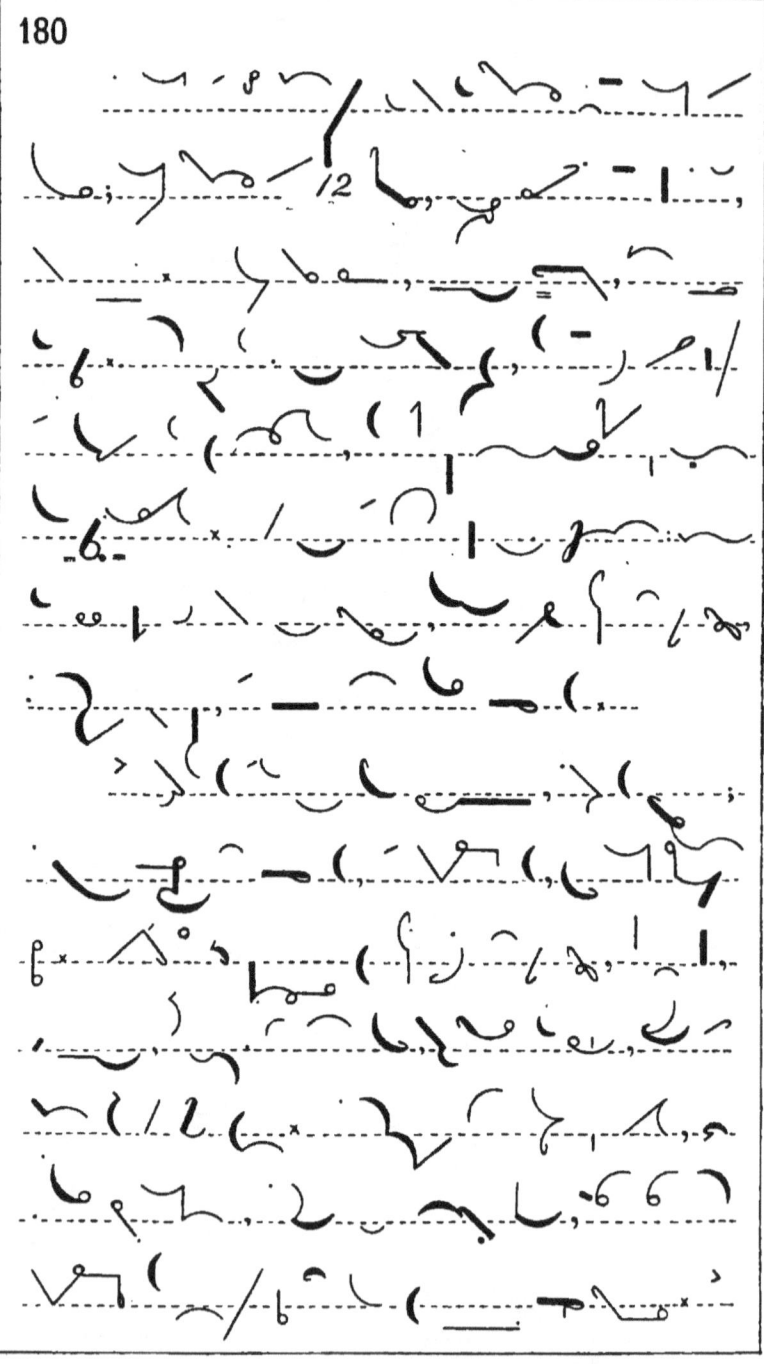

182

Acts, Ch. XXVI.

Business Letter – No. 1.

100 ... *50*

$1000

Business Letter – No. 2.

1 7 29

25

$1500

60

184

Francis W. Brodie

vs.

James O'Brien. 2

18 1876

Francis W. Brodie

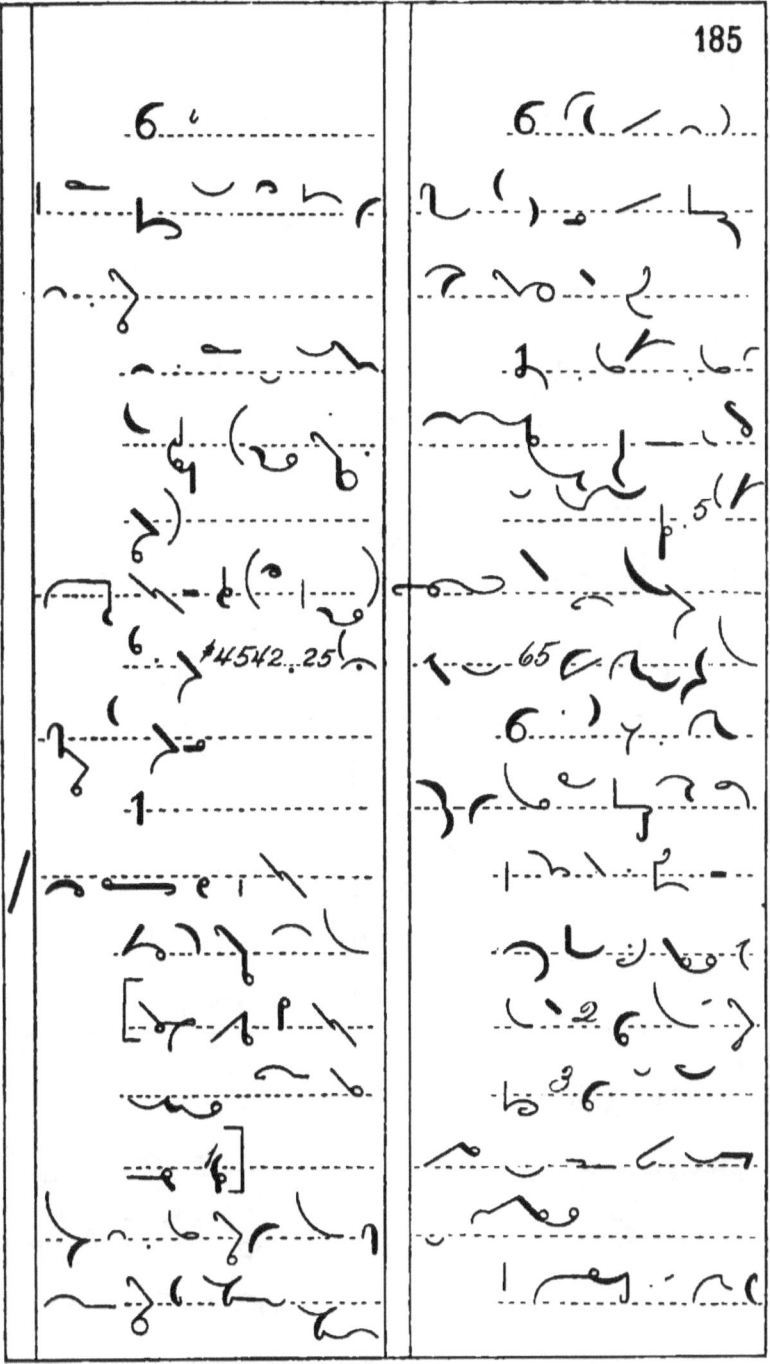

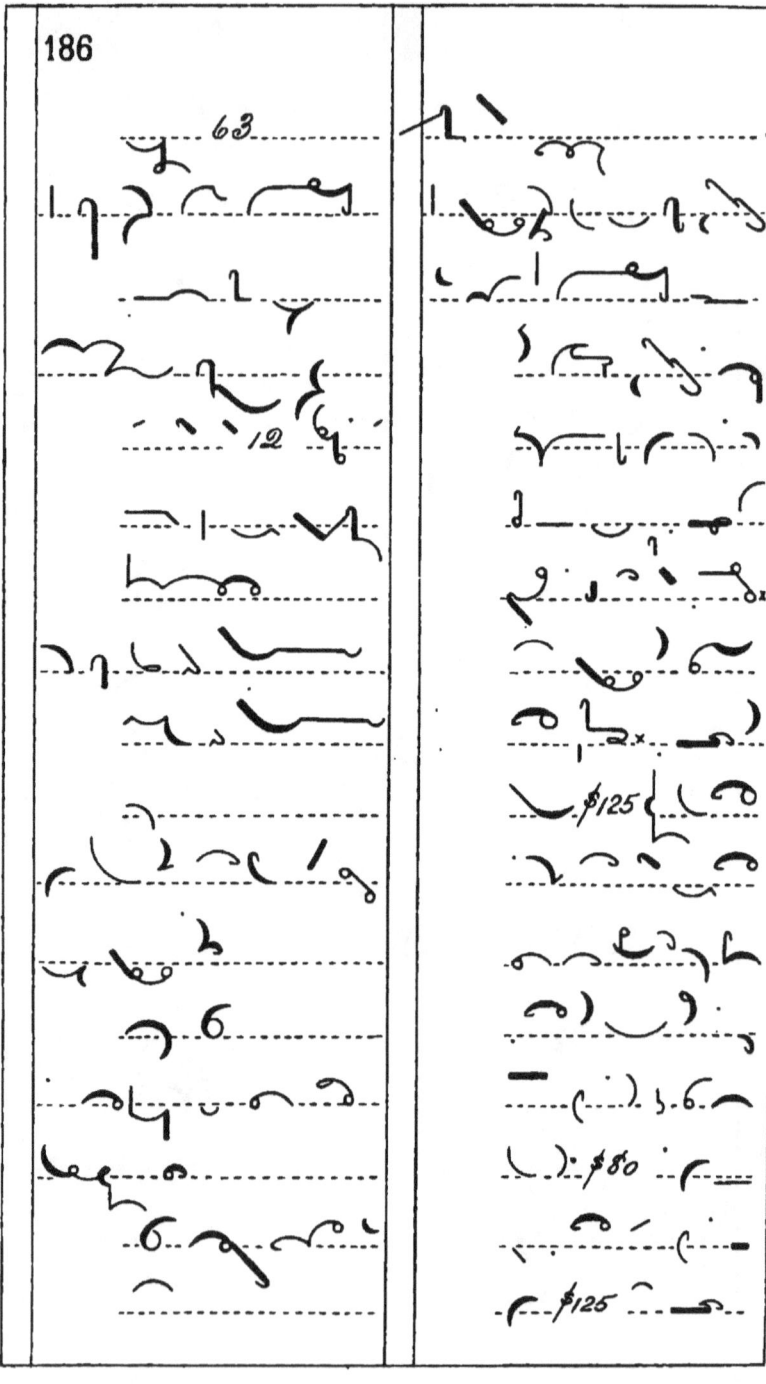

FROM REPORT OF LAW ARGUMENT.

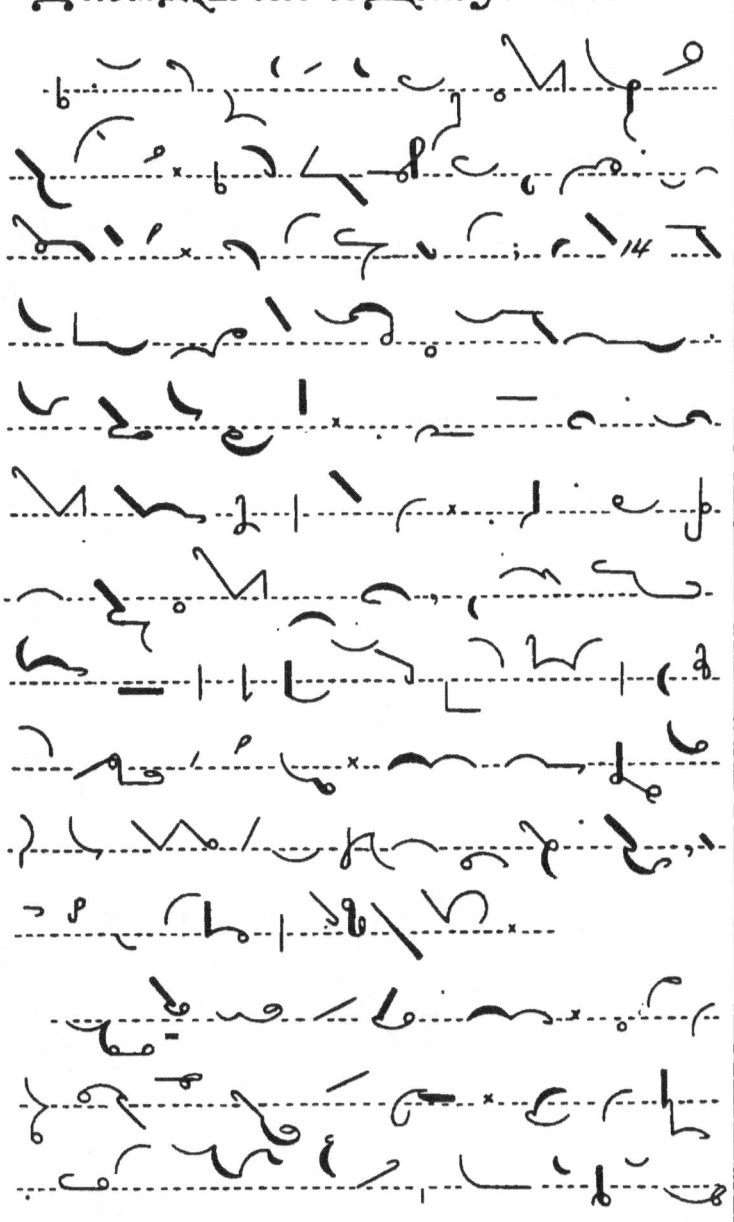

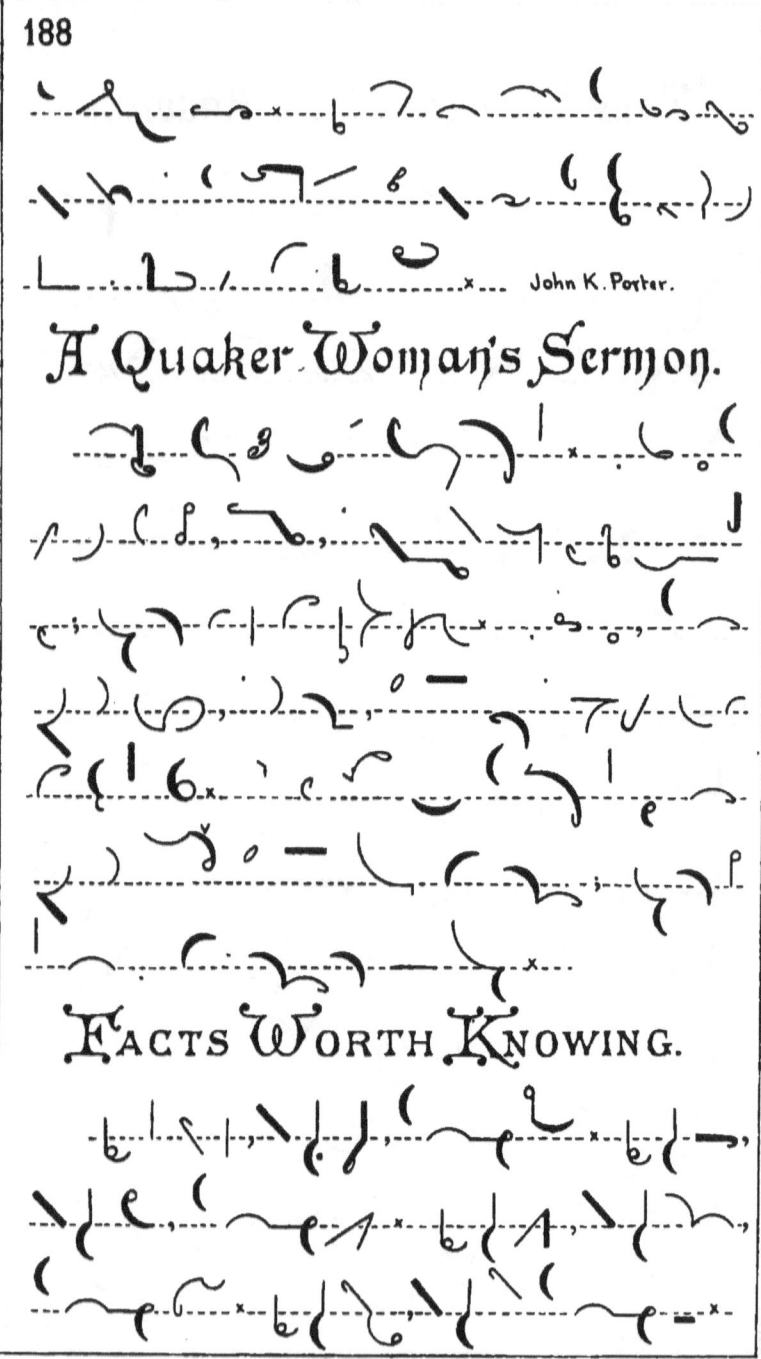

John K. Porter.

A Quaker Woman's Sermon.

Facts Worth Knowing.

A COURSE OF LESSONS

THROUGH

THE COMPLETE PHONOGRAPHER:

FOR THE USE OF CLASSES

AND

FOR SELF-INSTRUCTION.

PREFATORY.

§ 424. THE following Lessons in Phonography are substantially in accordance with the plan adopted by the author in his teaching, and by Mr. C. A. Walworth, teacher of Phonography in the College of the City of New York. They have been prepared and arranged so that if they be faithfully performed *in precisely the order directed* they will surely lead to a thorough and practical knowledge of the art of Phonography.

It will be noticed that each lesson is divided into three parts, which are to be always performed in the same order, namely :

First, certain sections to be learned.

Second, some engraved phonography to be read or translated.

Third, some words in common print to be written in phonography.

Sometimes the learner is directed to *memorize,* or simply to *read* the sections of instruction, instead of to *learn* them ; and by noticing which of these three words is employed, he can tell what degree of mental application to give to each.

The direction "Read or translate" means that the Reading Exercises are either to be read, simply, or, at the same time, to be written in longhand and in the regular English spelling.

All the reference marks in figures, whether in brackets or not, refer, unless otherwise expressed, to the *sections* (not the *pages*) of this book. When two numbers are given with the word "to" between, both the numbers are included.

Should these lessons prove too long for students having insufficient time for their preparation or recitation, they may each or any of them be divided. On the other hand, any student who is learning separately may take more than one lesson at a time without disadvantage, if he *studies*, *translates*, and *writes* systematically and accurately as he proceeds.

LESSON I. .

1. Read §§ 1 to 9, and 14.
2. Memorize first 16 consonant-signs in Table on page 18.
3. Learn §§ 19, 20, and 21.
4. Read first 4 lines in Reading Lesson I., page 149.
5. Read §§ 25 to 30.
6. Learn §§ 31 to 36.
7. Memorize the two second-place long vowel-signs in Table at § 37 —the heavy *dot* for the sound of *a* as in *ale*, and the heavy *dash* for the sound of *o* as in *note* or *whole*.
8. Learn §§ 41 to 44.
9. Read or translate the words of lines 5 and 6 in Reading Lesson I., page 149.
10. Write phonographically the following words :

§ 41, 42, 44. Pay, ape, bay, Abe, day, age, jay, ache, Fay, they, say, ace, bow (*or* beau), toe (*or* tow), ode (*or* owed), Joe, oak, foe, oath, though, so (*or* sew), show.

LESSON II.

1. Memorize remainder (9) of consonant-signs in Table on page 18.
2. Learn §§ 22 to 24.
3. Read first 2 lines in Reading Lesson II., page 149.
4. Read §§ 74 to 94.
5. Read or translate the words of lines 3 and 4 in Reading Lesson II., page 149.
6. Write phonographically the following words :

Nay (*or* neigh), may, aim, hay, way (*or* weigh), lay, ale (*or* ail), no (*or* know), mow, ho (*or* hoe), woe, lo (*or* low).

7. Memorize remainder (4) of the long vowel-signs at § 37.

8. Learn §§ 39 and 40, and 59 to 62, and 71.

9. Write each of the 25 consonant-signs (page 18) in the three consonant positions, as taught at §§ 61 and 62.

10. Read or translate the words of lines 5 to 9 in Reading Lesson II., page 150.

11. Write phonographically the following words, remembering to locate each word in its correct *consonant* position as to the line of writing (see §§ 61, 62, and 71), and to place each vowel in its correct *vowel* position—see §§ 39, 40, and 41.

Pa, pay, pea, jaw, Joe, jew, Shaw, show, shoe, ma, may, me, caw, Coe, coo, law, lo, loo, ought, ate, eat, haw, ho, who, all, ale, eel, daw, thaw, saw, maw, gnaw.

LESSON III.

1. Memorize the short vowels (6) at § 37.

2. Read or translate the words of lines 1 and 2 in Reading Lesson III., page 150.

3. Read §§ 38, 45, 46, and 47.

4. Write phonographically the following words:
At, Ed., it, odd, up, itch, of, us, if, on, Em., in.

5. Read §§ 48 to 50.

6. Learn § 54.

7. Memorize the Diphthongs (4) in Table at § 54.

8. Learn §§ 56 to 58.

9. Read or translate the words of lines 3 to 6 in Reading Lesson III., page 150.

10. Write phonographically the following words:
§ 54. By, boy, bough, pew, tie, toy, Dow, due, thigh, thou, guy, coy, how, mew, Hugh, eyed, ice, eyes, isle, oil, owl, lieu.

11. Read or translate the words of lines 7 to 9 in Reading Lesson III., page 150.

12. Write phonographically the following words:
§ 71. Abbey, eddy, ado, Annie, Emma, anew, avow, away, issue, alloy, allay, Eli.—§ 57. Payee, bayou, Ohio, avowee, Ione.

LESSON IV.

1. Learn §§ 63 to 73.

2. Read the first 9 lines in Reading Lesson IV., page 151.

3. Write the following combinations of consonant-signs or stems:
§ 63–69. P-P, B-B, T-T, J-J, K-K, F-F, DH-DH, N-N, F-N, H-S, P-B, D-T, K-G, M-B, H-Z, M-S, TH-N, M-SH, M-P, P-N.

4. Read or translate the words from line 10 to end of Reading Lesson IV., pages 151, 152.

5. Write phonographically the following words:

§§ 70, 72. Gag, ham, calm, knock, cog, gawk, cake, mum, comb, neck, keg, hung, kick, meek, nook, king, pop, fife, fang, babe, judge, faith, bib, shook, cheap, cap, match, mop, hatch, cup, much, mope, hedge, keep, midge, hitch, myth, comma, honey, inky, body, toady, duty, copy, meadow, ensue, damp, depth, fathom, cabbage, Monday, chimney, Chicago, tobacco, demagogue, antimony, pink, chunk, shank, balk, bulk, type, tip.

LESSON V.

1. Learn §§ 95, 98, 101 to 110.
2. Read or translate Reading Lesson V., page 153.
3. Write the following words:

§§ 105, 110. Sap, soap, sub, sought, set, stay, said, seat, seed, stew, soot, suit, such, sage, sack, soak, seek, sick, sag, safe, sieve, Seth, south, soothe, sash, sign, sang, sun, sin, sing, soda, city, sinew, sallow, sully, silly, pass, pace, pass, ties, toys, dues, choice, jaws, gas, face, foes, thaws, thus, this, shows, shoes, gnaws, nose, knees, mouse, house, ways, yes, use, lace, appease, abyss, ages, accuse, efface, ashes, issues, annoys, amaze, amuse, saps, space, sets, stays, sages, suffice, sashes, sinews, cities.—§ 103. Cask, cossack, decide, desk, gasp, Augusta, accede, excite, visit, chasm, visage, Fisk, mask, deceive, wisp, husk, Joseph, spasms, insane, unsung, evasive, Leslie, mason, missing, hissing, officer, massive, phasma.

LESSON VI.

1. Learn §§ 111 to 127.
2. Read or translate Reading Lesson VI., page 154.
3. Write the following words:

§ 111. Siam, pious, science, Suez.—§ 113. Æsop, espy, aside, eschew.

§ 115. Pussy, Tasso, busy, Jesse, noisy, ensue.—§ 112. Saucy, sauce, seize.—§ 114. Zany, zebu, zenith, zouave, oozing.

§ 118. Pauses, basis, teases, doses, chooses, causes, gazes, fuses, vices, thesis, sauces, nieces, Moses, houses, opposes, accuses.—§ 120. Possess, Jesus, excise, decease, possessed, exist, necessity, exhaust, successive, incisive.

§ 122. Stop, state, stitch, stock, stove, stung, steam, style, study, stagey, stucco, best, chaste, guest, aghast, August, avast, assist, assessed.

§ 123. Poster, jester, castor, master, Worcester, Lester, Rochester, yesterday.—§ 127. Possesses, emphasizes, vests, toasts, dusters, ministers.

LESSON VII.

1. Learn §§ 128 to 137.
2. Read or translate Reading Lesson VII., page 155.

3. Write the following words :

§§ 129 to 131. Show, issue, sash, shoes, issuing, Ashantee, push, cash, gush, gnash, ambush, tissue, Vichy, bushy, dishes, bishop, shop, shake, shame.

§§ 132 to 134. Elm, along, alack, Elihu, pail, bell, toil, towel, dial, jail, fall, Nile, mule, appeal, avail, law, all, sail, stale, less, lest, lustre, lock, leg, lung, limb, Lehigh, lap, allege, laugh, olive, lathe, although, lazy, also, Lizzie, Eliza, lash, pillow, bailey, delay, jolly, coyly, follow, hollow, way-lay, yellow, pulp, bulk, polish, abolish, bellows, gallows, malice, ballast.

§§ 135 to 137. Air, ere, ear, Erie, era, or, oar, ire, Ira, arrows, arose, arrest, arises, arrests, orb, arc, Irish, early, bar, door, jeer, far, Czar, shower, liar, lawyer, appear, affairs, officers, forced, Rome, rheum, arm, army, ripe, rich, rock, wrath, writhe, rash, wrong, rubbish, Sarah, starry, sorrows, hurrah, narrow, weary, zero, thorough, necessary, urge, earth, party, America, exercise.

LESSON VIII.

1. Learn §§ 139 to 155, omitting § 144.
2. Read or translate Reading Lesson VIII., page 156.
3. Write the following words :

§§ 140, 141, 147. Ply, blue, cloy, clay, clue, glue, pry, brew, Troy, tree, dray, crow, gray, claw, craw, glow, grow, play, bray, plough, brow, flay, fray, flee, free, fly, fry, apple, able, addle, adder, eagle, eager, offal, offer, Ethel, author, error, ably, apply, appraise, across, affray.

§ 150. Play, pale, blow, bowl, glow, goal, flaw, fall, fly, follow, prow, power, try, tire, free, fear, freer.

§§ 151 to 153. Bevel, diver, tunnel, dinner, teacher, chapel, juggle, cackle, Orvil, arrival, thinner, shovel, shiner, puzzle, finger, manner, hobble, haggle, heather, hammer, winner, leisure, yoker, baker, tiger, toper, dipper, cudgel, rebel.

§ 155. Curl, curly, pearl, barrel, furl, fairly, marl, Marlowe.

LESSON IX.

1. Learn §§ 156 to 169.
2. Read or translate Reading Lesson IX., page 157.
3. Write the following words :

§ 156. Tell, till, dear, call, care, share, more, mere, nor, near, war, wire, wear, wore, zeal, course, roll, real, rule, hall, hail, hell, hire, hair, their, yell, Yale, very, torpor, charger, Germany, barber, verbal, college, sharper, mark, work, yolk, lurch, railroad, divulge.

§§ 158 to 163. Sable, sabre, settle, setter, saddle, sadder, sickle, seeker, civil, social, saver, seizure, sinner, summer, sister, spry, spray, spree, straw, stray, strew, screw, splice, splash, supply, passable, peaceable, peaceful, disclaim, destroy, disagree, obscure, pasture, pastry, extra, vestry, nostril, subscriber.

§§ 165, 166. Twist, quest, twill, quill, dwell, Dwyer, quake, Quaker, quire (or choir), acquire, require, quibble, quorum, squaw, squall, squab, squabble, squeeze, tweezers.

§§ 168, 169. Unscrew, inscribe, unstrung, insuperable, unsociable.

LESSON X.

1. Learn §§ 170 to 200, omitting §§ 171, 177, 181, 189, and 194.
2. Read or translate Reading Lesson X., page 158.
3. Write the following words :

§ 172. Buff, pave, tough, deaf, chief, Jeff., cough, cave, Gough, rough, reef, skiff, clove, brave, trough, drove, crave, grove, strife, scarf, starve, relief, positive, improve, dwarf.

§ 176. Pain, been, town, dine, chain, gin, coon, gone, fun, thin, thine, assign, ozone, shown, known, man, hen, wine, yawn, loan, rain, arraign, open, often, ocean, alone, spin, stone, scan, Flynn, plan, spleen, brain, warn, strewn, twine, queen.

§ 179. Cough, coffee, chaff, chaffy, fun, funny, men, many.

§ 180. Cushion, fashion, vision, notion, mission, Hessian, lotion, ration, erasion, station, Prussian, collision, Grecian, equation, suppression, education.

§ 187. Possession, sensation, musician, disquisition.

§ 188. Daughter, rather, equator, sceptre, gather.

§§ 192 to 198. Coughs, fines, notions, bitters, chance, chances, chanced, sensations.

§ 199. Define, punish, educational, prepositional.

LESSON XI.

1. Learn §§ 201 to 211, omitting § 202.
2. Read or translate Reading Lesson XI., page 159.
3. Write the following words :

§ 204. Matter, mother, metre, hatter, under, neither.—§ 205. Father, fetter, fitter, aster, Esther, Easter, shouter, shutter, shooter, water, weather, whither.—§ 206. Loiter, leather, Luther, alter, after.

Sifter, senator, smother, Sumter, scimeter, slighter, starter, flutter, further, shrewder, assertor, shorter, martyr, harder, warder, larder.

§§ 208, 209. Fainter, finder, vendor, thunder, asunder, mentor, hunter, wander, cylinder, panther, ponder, banter, tender, dander, gender, counter, candor, gander, ranter, render, rafter, surrender, planter, blunder, printer, grinder, flounder, squander.—§ 210. Feathers, matters, thunders, counters, flinders, glanders.—§ 211. Feature, entire, nature, venture.

Undertake, entertain, enterprise, interposition, remainder, barometer, disorder, legislator, afternoon, entirely, encounter, debenture, juncture, adventure, indenture.

LESSON XII.

1. Learn §§ 212 to 219, omitting § 213.
2. Read or translate Reading Lesson XII., page 160.
3. Write the following words:

§§ 212 to 218. Caught, Kate, cute, dot, date, deed, got, gout, God, bad, bite, end, aimed, etched, edged, writ, root, fat, fade, feud, shot, shut, shoot, east, oozed, hot, wet, lit, yacht, erred, added, aided, emit, spite, salt, sand, stepped, stated, stitched, studied, plate, prate, clad, glad, flight, fried, shrewd, quoit, twit, effort, honored, word, lord, heard, held, split, straight, supplied, sacred, suffered, doffed, Taft, cuffed, roughed, point, caned, thinned, lent, wand, hunt, patient, cushioned, fashioned, ancient, bothered, tattered, scoffed, stand, slant, sufficient, spattered, sustained, cleft, flaunt, clattered, drift, friend, quaffed, quaint, twined, twittered, splint, sprained, squint, puts, hats, midst, spots, skates, slights, flats, throats, shrouds, clouds, crowds, quits, bends, minds, friends, strands, squints, suspends.

LESSON XIII.

1. Learn §§ 220 to 235.
2. Read or translate Reading Lesson XIII., page 161.
3. Write the following words:

§ 220. Packed, snapped, blocked, broached, twilled, flooded, thrashed, shrieked, marked, splashed, striped, squalled, remit, dismayed, breasted, frosted, twisted, necessitate, huddled, loitered, liquid, reward, speckled, bevelled, travelled, mastered, flustered, thefts, biscuits, rebound, declined, engraft, inefficient, vagrants.

Petal, title, cattle, active, native, avidity, chatting, fitting, cottage, dotage, ratify, erratic, emetic, battery, lottery, scuttle, sweetly, validity, brutish, Broadway, acquittal, bundle, blandly, frantic, dwindle, squinting.

Detect, tidbit, deadhead, detached, indicate, latitude, ultimate, gratified, abundant, foundered, ventured, thundered, hindered, wondered, pondered, tendered, floundered, blundered, squandered.

§ 221. Peeped, reared, bribed, flaked, slacked.—§ 224. Vote, voted, hate, hated, rot, rotted.—§ 225. Deed, deeded, trot, trotted.—§§ 230 to 232. Let, led, wrote, rode.

LESSON XIV.

1. Learn §§ 247 to 249.
2. Read §§ 250 to 264.
3. Learn §§ 265 to 270.

4. Read or translate Reading Lesson XIV., page 162.

5. Write the following words:

§ 247. Heap, happy, hubbub, heptagon, habit, inhabit, behave, adhere, prohibit.

§ 248. Why, whip, wheat, whack, whiff, whim, whale.

§ 249. Wide, widow, witty, witch, wedge, waif, waved, wish, unwashed, Washington, Utica, Utah.

§ 265. Lovely, joyfully, bravely, powerfully, meanly, lonely, keenly, hopingly, intuitively.

§ 266. Jeffrey, sundry, archery, machinery, Henry, treachery, roguery.

§ 270. Bake, baked, keep, kept, clothe, clothed, act, acted, include, included, mitigate, mitigated, pass, passed, cross, crossed, dance, danced, wince, winced, possess, possessed, exercise, exercised, rest, rested, twist, twisted, pester, pestered, render, rendered, wonder, wondered, squander, squandered.

LESSON XV.

1. Read §§ 278 to 280.

2. Write the following as word-signs from the list at § 281: Part, opportunity, object, but, what, had, do, did, charge, change, which, large, advantage, can, come, could, go, gave, together, give-n, form, half, for, have, ever, thank-ed, worth, think, youth, that, them, with, was, these, shall, should, usual, own, any, now, new, knew, long, among, thing, from, time, home, member, he, him, whom, when, would, beyond, yet, young, your, year, well, will, her, hear-re, are, our, were, where, recollect, as, has, is, his, an, and, the, I, awe, owe.

3. Learn §§ 292 to 297.

4. Read or translate Reading Lesson XV., page 163.

5. Learn or memorize the word-signs given in this lesson.

6. Write the following sentences, vocalizing the words that are not word-signs:

Do what you ought, come what may. Appoint a time for every thing, and do every thing in time. He that blows in the dust will fill his own eyes. A good word for a bad one is worth much and costs little. When a wolf goes to steal, he goes a long distance from home. None are so deaf as they that will not hear. Pay what you owe, and you will know what you are worth. He who has to deal with a dunce has need of much brains.

LESSON XVI.

1. Read §§ 271 to 275.

2. Learn §§ 276 and 284.

3. Read or translate Reading Lesson XVI., page 164.

4. Write the following words:

§ 276. Limitable, illimitable, licit, illicit, legitimate, illegitimate, refutable, irrefutable, resolute, irresolute, reparable, irreparable, modest, immodest, mutable, immutable, navigable, unnavigable, noxious, innoxious.

§ 284. They contrive, you continue, excellent composition, perfect command, foreign commerce, very cumbrous, encumber, incompatible, unconcerned, decompose, discompose, re-commit, reconsider, recognition, circumvent, circumference, circumnavigate, circumlocution, continuant consonants, comprehensive conditions.

Forward, formal, forbearance, forbid.

Magnify, magnitude, magnanimity, magnetic.

Selfish, self-defense, self-denial, self-evident, self-same, self-reliance, self-interest, self-love.

Withdrew, withheld, withhold, within, withstand, withstood.

LESSON XVII.

1. Learn §§ 285 to 288.
2. Read or translate Reading Lesson XVII., page 165.
3. Write the following words:

§ 285. Reasonably, forcible, sensibly.

Amicableness, suitableness, agreeableness, sociableness.

Joyfulness, carefulness, painfulness, mindfulness.

Destructiveness, apprehensiveness, philoprogenitiveness.

Painlessness, gracelessness, dauntlessness, carelessness.

Whenever, however, whoever, whichever.

Inform, perform, reform, reformed, information.

Resting, arresting, wasting, trusting, roystering, mustering, plastering, ministering, patting, budding, competing, matting, heating, permitting, pleading, breeding.

Bastings, twistings, vestings, beatings, meetings, plottings, holdings.

Fundamental, regimental, sacramental, instrumentality.

Zoology, mythology, astrology.

Thyself, themselves.

Township, courtship, horsemanship, penmanship.

Praiseworthy, trustworthy, blameworthy, seaworthy.

§ 286. Fangle, triangle, shingle, twinkle, finger, stronger, anxious, sanctity, junction, winked, ranked. Pasteboard, breastpin, mistrustful. Pumped, consumption, glimpse, tempter.—§ 287. Essential, substantially.

LESSON XVIII.

1. Learn §§ 298 to 306, and 323 and 324.
2. Read or translate Reading Exercise XVIII., page 166.
3. Write the following phrases:

9*

§ 301. As large, as had, as can, as ever, as that, as them, as long, as he, as usual, as would, as yet, as your, much as, just as, as well, as well as, as large as, as long as.

Has had, has come, has that, has this, has he, has your, has been, has done, has gone, what has, which has, that has, he has, where has, what has been.

Is that, is he, is your, is her, what is, which is, that is, he is, here is, what is your.

For us, with us, among us, from us, beyond us, of us, by us, at us, to us, above us, upon us, through us, about us, around us, after us, under us.

§ 302. As has, as is, as his, has as, has his, is as, is his, his is, as has been, as is usual, as far as his, as much as his is.

§ 304. As the, as it, as to, has the, has it, is the, is it, as to that, as to them, as it were, what is the, which is the, that is the, when is the, where is the, gives the, thinks it, makes the, enters the.

§ 305. As their, has there, is there, what is their, leaves there, unless they are.

§ 306. As it is, is it as, as there is, has it not, is there not.

LESSON XIX.

1. Learn §§ 307 to 326.
2. Read or translate Reading Lesson XIX., page 167.
3. Write the following phrases:

§ 307. But all, what will, had all, do all, did all, which will, can all, that all, they will, with all, among all, from all, he will, are all, when will, to all, you will, of all, on all, among all.

§ 308. They are, we are, on or, by our, of our, to our, among our.

§ 309. Do we, which we, can we, could we, are we, were we.

§ 310. Had you, do you, did you, are you, were you, can you, could you, do your, are your, where do you, how did you.

§ 312. Part of, charge of, which have, can have, could have, that have, they have, shall have, would have, out of, to have, day of.

§ 313. But an, had an, of an, to an, he and, you and, your own, her own, their own, our own, have been, more than, rather than, they have been.

§ 314. By their, up there, are there, were their, can there, to their, of their, for their, on there, fly there, warm their, upon their, plan their, each other, no other, some other, that they are.

§ 316. Of the, of it, to the, from the, ought to, upon the, he had.

§ 317. Day after day, Sunday afternoon.

§ 318. Of another, to another, from another, in another.

§ 319. Of its, on its, in its, by its, upon its.

§ 320. Do not, did not, are not, were not, can not, may not, you are not.

LESSON XX.

1. Learn §§ 327 to 339.
2. Read §§ 340 to 348.
3. Read or translate Reading Lesson XX., page 168.
4. Write the following phrases:

§ 327. I object, I do not, I can, I could, I am, I think, I was, I shall, I know, I would, I suppose, I heard, I wonder. A half, a year, a man, a thought, an oath, an office, and then, and all, and will. Of a, to a, upon a, puts a.

§ 330. Against the, after the, render the, cut the, about the, meet the, quit the, around the ; he ought, he did, he shall, he could.

§ 331. And as, and is, and as a, and as the, and as it, and as their, and is there, and as there is.

As to a, is it an, has there a, is there a, as to the, is it the.

§ 332. Roasting a, blasting the, murdering a, putting a, beating the, meeting a; bidding the.

§ 333. We ought, we had, we do, we did, we do not, we charge, we find, we shall, we should ; we would, you would, he would, she would, it would, it would be, would you, would they ; you had, you do, you did not, you take, you shall.

§ 334. Waste of time, date of payment, hours of study.

§ 336. To be, to run, to move, to date, to me, too far.

§ 338. From day to day, from year to year.

CONCLUDING REMARKS.

The learner has now passed over all the principles of Phonography. He has yet to commit to memory the remainder of the word-signs and contractions at § 289 or § 290, and to familiarize himself with the derivative words at § 291, the list of conflicting words at § 277, and the list of phrases at § 349. Great assistance in learning the word-signs and contractions may be derived by writing and reading the article entitled "A Trip through the Land of Contractions," on page 203. The learner should now continue the reading lessons which consist of miscellaneous articles commencing at page 169, using the key beginning at page 215 as little as possible. After this, if the assistance of a teacher can be had to correct a few exercises, it will be found a valuable aid. For that purpose the learner may cut a slip from a newspaper, write it on alternate lines in Phonography as well as he can, and send it to the teacher. The lessons should not be too long—not over a page of foolscap in length. The teacher's corrections should be on the blank line below the outlines corrected ; and references to the sections of the Complete Phonographer containing the violated rules should also be given. If a teacher can not be had, a good substitute is to be found in the following plan : Write a page of the key, and then compare it with the engraved outlines. Write and rewrite each page until no mistakes are made, and then proceed to the next. No attempt to write fast should be made until the learner can write correctly.

At this time it will be of great advantage to the student to have still further reading-matter in Phonography. Partly to supply this want, "Munson's Phonographic News," a periodical edited by the author, and printed entirely in Phonography, is published. It contains also news, instruction, and other information concerning the art. It is published semi-monthly, and the subscription price is two dollars a year. Persons desiring to subscribe will address, James E. Munson, P. O. Box 5502, New York.

A TRIP THROUGH THE LAND OF CONTRACTIONS,
MADE IN THE YEAR 1877.

By Mrs. AMALIA BERRIAN, New York.

[This ingenious article contains all the word-signs and contractions of the Complete Phonographer, page 88, and is composed almost entirely of those abbreviations. It has been revised by the author from her previous "Trip," which was made from the list published in 1873. It will be found very valuable to the learner as a means of acquiring the list rapidly and pleasantly, by mèrely writing this article in Phonography and reading the written copy until memorized. To acquire still greater familiarity, it may be written from *dictation* until considerable speed is attained. In writing this exercise of course *no phrases* are to be made. The words printed in *italics* are not contractions, but should be written with their full consonant outlines, as usual.]

According *to* the suggestion *of* gentlemen *who* hád the important advantage *of* knowledge, observation, and, I believe, experience *to* help them discriminate, *we* began before September *to* collect lengthy but correct memoranda *of* the parts *of* the United-States beyond which *it* was understood *we* were *not to* go.

Then the first thing *of* importance was *to* deliver *a* dollar *to* advertise *a* description *of,* and *gather* together here *in* Southern New-York, *a* given proportion *of* healthy Christian people, *to* whom *a* doctor, with *a* certificate from his brother-in-law the Governor, was indispensable; as our captain, *being* subject *to* change, and *no* angel, was *a* special responsibility without him, and because any degree *of* neglect would give that large perpendicular gentleman frequent opportunity *to* swear—different from plaintiff *or* defendant, but *in* somewhat *more* general and characteristic language.

To our surprise *a* singular representative *of* the Roman-Catholic religion from Great-Britain *came to* dwell with *us.* His popularity was specially peculiar, difficult *of* insurance, and *not* altogether satisfactory; for, possibly, owing *to a* difference *of* opinion as *to* the probable privilege *of* the archbishop *to* govern the county, *or* the doctrine *of* transubstantiation, *or* what baptism is, ho would remember, cross-examine, describe, and *make* regular reference *to* any remark *of* our generally popular Catholic captain. *This* would astonish another *of* his reverend brethren, the principal junior member *of* the bishopric, *who* was *in* bankruptcy as *to* health, wealth, and his belief *in* the archangels *of* heaven.

Our next movement was *to* go *in* December *to* San-Francisco *to be* there with an architect during January and February—*not* a long time, but where *one* has *a* will and an object he can qualify himself *to* do *or* become *much.*

Several wealthy representatives *who* had *been in* the Massachusetts Legislature over *a* year, and were familiar with the Cabinet and *its* worth, and knew responsibly almost *every* other question *or* circumstance *of* the Democrats, did endeavor *to* establish familiarity between *us;* yet *it* was *not* usually possible *to* practice *or* develop the extraordinary principle *of* Mr. ———, which *in all* probability was preliminary *to* his own youth.

In our memorandum (thanks *to* swift Phonography) I recollect a distinct peculiarity. I refer *to* the fact that *we* were *to* hear *all who* should speak *at* length *in* public, especially *on* architecture *or* architectural manufacture ; what their immediate similarity was did *not* signify. But when *we* are responsible for the charge *of a* number *of* young children, *we* can *not* go *to every* particular quarter *of* the Republic. *In* truth *to* these belong the domestic difficulties which have ever come *up,* when *we* had begun *to* think *all* was well. Oh yes-sir, without mistake, home shall *be* the kingdom *of* her that hath intelligence.

Could *we* form an especial aristocracy, *we* would probably awe the Democracy *by* the similar, capable, and aristocratic performance *of* our plenipotentiary. But no-sir; the Democratic half *of* your astonished citizens, with their usual system *of* regularity and perpendicularity, begin *to* differ, and object *to* represent the influence that here*tofore* gave *it* effect. *They* publish already among them *this* new delivery : November and the world! now *or* never!

ADDITIONAL WRITING EXERCISES.

The following additional Writing Exercises are intended primarily to lighten the work of teachers in preparing black-board illustrations for, or in dictating to, their pupils. They will also be found very useful to learners who wish to perfect their knowledge of particular portions of the system on which they feel that they are weak. The *italicized* words only are to be written in Phonography.

VOCALIZATION OF SINGLE CONSONANT-STEMS.

[§ 41.] The *ape* went *up* the tree with *ease*. *Eve ought* not to *eat* apples. It does not *aid* you to *add* an *oath*. *All* the *ale* will *ooze* from the leaky keg. *Each age* has its pleasures.—The bird laid an *egg in* the *oak*. I *am* going to *aim* at *Amy*.

I *saw* pa *pay* a *fee* to Mr. *Shaw*. Come and take *tea* with *Joe Lee to-day*. They *saw* the snow *thaw*. I could *see* the *foe row* under the *lea* shore.—*Ma* says you *may* come and see *me*. Did you hurt your *knee* on the *key?* *No*. The horse would *gnaw* his stable and *neigh* loudly.

DIPHTHONGS.

[§§ 50, 54, 56.] The *boy* took a *pie* in the *pew*. I heard the cat *mew* on the *mow* of hay. If *thou* should hurt *thy thigh*, rub it well with *oil*. Mr. *Dow* saw him take the *toy out* and *tie* it with a string. *My cow* is very *shy*, and will not allow you to be so *nigh* to her.

[§ 57.] An *avowee* is a person who has a right to present to a benefice. The *payee* is the one to whom money is to be paid. *Noah Owen* has just come through the *bayou* in a canoe.

[§ 58.] *Ida* had no *idea* of going on the *ice*. *Ike, Ira*, and *Isaiah* are constantly *eyeing* me through the *ivy;* but I don't care an *iota* for their *eyes*.

JOINING THE CONSONANT-STEMS.

[§ 64.] *Papa* saw the *Pope* take a *peep* from his window. *Bob* the *booby* took the *baby* with its *bib* to the *Judge*. The *cook* gave the girl a *cake* and the boy a *kick*. The *babe* cries for *pap*, not for a *gewgaw*. Give us liberty and not *gag*-law.

[§ 65.] *Mamma* says *Mamie* is a *ninny* because she keeps so *mum*. *Lulu* loves the *lily* and looks after the *lowly*. *Mike* from *Maumee* tried to *maim* John from *Miami*. *Vive* le roi (French). *Viva* voce (Latin). "For much I dread due payment by the Greeks of yesterday's *arrear*." Away with the "ear-piercing *fife !*"

[§ 66.] *He* saw a *funny* fellow from *Vienna having* a good time with a *lame* man from *Lima*.

[§ 67.] *Beppo* does his *duty* to the *public*. He is *tidy* in his dress, but *gawky* in his manner. He drank a *keg* of beer and then tried to sing a *ditty*. *Vick* says she doesn't care a *fig* for the *fog*. *Davy* buys his own *clothing*. But for its *being* so *hazy* I would go. "The perception of *being* or not *being* belongs no more to these *vague* ideas, signified by the terms 'whatsoever' and 'thing,' than it does to any other ideas." —*Locke*.

[§ 68.] A *lawyer* named *Duffy* called to see *Elisha Massy*. A *puny* man may maim a giant with the *lash*. A *piano* out of tune has a bad *effect* upon the nerves—*also* a melodeon.

VOWELS BETWEEN STEMS.

[§ 70.] (1.) *Both* of us went to the *bath* to *bathe*. "*Bear* the *palm* alone." He left the *path* and went to *poach* on his neighbor's land, but he brought no *game* in his *pouch*. Mr. *Pike*, a miserable old *poke*, brought a huge *pack*. He tried to *bake* a *cake*. He was more than a *match* for the *mob*. Let us *take* a *walk* and have a *long talk* He wrote a *dime novel* about a very. *tame dog*. *Tom Dodge* tried to learn to set *type*.

(2.) You may *pick* a *peck* of *peaches* for me. He *hung* the *pig* on a *peg* in the *beam*. The *boom* may jibe over and *push* Mr. *Booth* into the water. Mr. *Beach* threw a *big bung* and hit *Tim* on the *tooth*. Dr. *Ting* sways people with his *tongue*. *Dick* tried to *tip* the *tub* over. *Cheap Jim* gave his *chum* a *check*. He told a *fib* when he said he didn't care a *fig* for the *fume*. The *ship took* a *tug*, but the captain remained on *deck*.

WORDS IN WHICH THE SECOND STEM IS WRITTEN IN POSITION OF THE VOWEL.

[§§ 71, 72.] I saw the *mob move* on led by a *knave*. A *moth* got in her *muff* and ruined it. He made a *notch* with his *knife*. Messrs. *Cobb* and *Kipp* always *keep* a *coach* to *carry* them home. If you *catch* the bird I will give you a *cage* to *keep* it in. Mr. *Nash* left his *cap* and *cup* out by the *coop*. "'*Neath* yon crimson tree."

WORDS WITH HORIZONTAL STEMS, THE FIRST BEING WRITTEN IN POSITION.

Mike Mack said he would have won the *game* if he had held the *king*. He sounded a *gong* to call the *gang* to dinner. *Mag* sat in a shady *nook* and called the *nag* to her. Her *name* was *Meg*, and she would *mock* at everybody who *came* her way.

WORDS SPELLED ALIKE BUT PRONOUNCED DIFFERENTLY.

[§ 77.] The *bass* singers had a fine *bass* for dinner. *Bow* to the man who has the *bow*. *Does* he know the habits of *does ?* The fish passed a *gill* of water through each *gill*. The breaking of the *hinder* part of the wagon will *hinder* us. He will *lead* you through the *lead* mines. If he *lives* he will spare the *lives* of the prisoners. *Lower* the sails if the sky begins to *lower*. I can not give you a *minute* description in a *minute*. *Mow* the grass and put it on the *mow*. There was a *row* in the lower *row* of buildings last night. The *august* assembly met in *August*. This *gallant* officer is quite a *gallant* among the ladies.

WORDS PRONOUNCED ALIKE BUT SPELLED DIFFERENTLY.

[§ 78.] Nothing would *ail* him if he drank no *ale*. He *ate eight* eggs, and for *aught* I know he *ought* to be sick. A single *awl* is *all* the shoe-maker had left. *I* hurt my *eye*. He *owed* the poet for an *ode*. *O !* that I should *owe* so much to *him* for writing a simple *hymn*. He stuck his *oar* in the sand and raised the bright *ore* o'er our heads. How busy the little *bee* can *be*. I will now *hie* me to yon *high* rock. *You* saw the *ewe* under the *yew*-tree. You must *weigh* the hay on the *way* to market. All last *week* he was quite *weak*. His *sole* aim was to save his *soul*. There is *no* reason why you should *know* it. That it was *new* he well *knew*. Why does *Hugh* raise such a *hue* because he has to *hew* a little wood? Mr. *Reid* can *read* music and play on a *reed* instrument. John *Wright* can *write* a good hand and spell all the words *right*. The swallow *flew* down the chimney *flue*. The carpenter *adds* an *adze* to his tools. Why does the boy *bawl* so about a little *ball ?* The farmer raised a *beet* that can't be *beat*. Have you *been* to our grain *bin ?* Too much *beer* will bring him to his *bier*. He stuck the *sealing*-wax to the *ceiling*. He would stand in his *cell* and *sell* toys. Did he *cite* you to court simply to give you a *sight* of the new City Hall *site ?* He can *climb* trees in any *clime*. Printers oftener use a *quoin* than a *coin*. It is not *fair* to charge so much *fare*. I am *frank* to say I gave him a *franc*. With a limping *gait* he came in the *gate*. A *great* fire glowed in the *grate*. I quickly *guessed* who my *guest* was to be. He hurt his *heel*, but it will quickly *heal*. We can't *hear* over *here*. We *heard* the *herd* run down the hill. He ran *in* the *inn*. He lost his *key* walking on the *quay*. Though a great *liar*, he played the *lyre* well. The pretty *maid made* the slippers with her own hands. The *marshal* put on a very *martial* air. The *miner* was twenty-one, and therefore no longer a *minor*. He was soon *missed* in the thick *mist*. He explained the *mode* in which he *mowed* the grass. I saw him *pare* the *pear* and divide it between the *pair*. One may *raise* a castle for another to *raze* to the ground. I *rode* along the *road* to the landing, and then *rowed* across the river. He tasted, and, making a *wry* face, said it was *rye*. She placed her hand upon her *side* and *sighed* deeply. My *son* is out in the *sun*. Standing on a *stair*, he began to *stare* at me. He said the *tax* on *tacks* was more than he could pay. The boy *threw* a stone *through* the window. The tyrant was *thrown* from his *throne*. Give us *time* and we will gather all the *thyme* you need. They *tracked* the fox across the entire *tract* of land. He tried in *vain* to climb up to the *vane*. I saw a man that *weighed* two hundred pounds *wade* through the muddy stream. Though small in *waist*, she can *waste* much. *Wait* until I ascertain my *weight*. He said he *would* bring a load of *wood*.

ESS-CIRCLE BETWEEN STEMS.

[§ 103.] Mr. *Busby*, a *testy* old *gossip*, full of *deceit*, sat quietly by a *cask* of *whiskey* until he was *passive;* and then he was taken without a *tussle*, or the movement of a *muscle*, by an *officer* named *Mason*. Good-bye to *Busby*, with his *dusty* old *cassock*.

WORDS WITH INITIAL EL.

[§ 132, I.] In the state of *Illinois* there are two brothers *living* at *Elm* Grove named *Elihu* and *Allick Olney*, who look so nearly *alike* that their mother can't tell them apart.

WORDS WITH FINAL EL.

[§ 132, II.] *Paul Buel* and *Neal Doyle* partook of the flowing *bowl until* they began to *feel* like doing things that were *vile;* so going home through the *dale*, *Paul* and his *pal Neil fell afoul* of one *Gill Odel*, and struck him with a *pole* on his bare *poll* and made him *fall* in a *pool*. But *Bill* and *Joel Doll*, who saw them from a *knoll*, seized them and took them to *jail;* and then they turned very *pale* because they couldn't give *bail*.

WORDS WITH INITIAL LEE.

[§ 133, I., II., and IV.] *Elijah Leech*, a *lucky limb* of the *law*, *eloped* with *Olive Lake*. Now *Elijah* was *lame*, and he feared that the *healthy* form of the *lovely Olive's* father would *loom* up before him, and that he would *lay* heavy hands upon him, *lug* him off, *allege* charges against him, and *lodge* him in *Ludlow* Street Jail. But *Elijah* didn't *lack* courage—neither did he *lag* behind nor walk *logy*—the commands of his *love* for his dear *Olive* were all that he would follow. He didn't *look* back until, with the *help* of a parson, their *lives* were united. And now they *live* a *laughing life* in a *leafy* bower on the borders of a *lovely lake* amid *Alpine* scenery.

WORDS WITH FINAL LEE.

[§ 133, III.] *Ophelia Bailey* and *Julia Kelley*, in the month of *July*, went to a *villa* in the *valley*, where they met *Nellie* and *Delia*, and a *fellow* named *Osceola*, who was a great *bully*, and could *outlie* the worst *outlaw* in the country. But *happily* for them, *Polly* and *Emily Paley* and *Philo Bulow*, in strength a perfect *Goliah*, and a *jolly* good *fellow*, went to *follow* them through a *gulley*. Now *Philo* caught the *bully* and made him *bellow loudly*, for he beat him almost to a *jelly*. So much for the *folly* of *Osceola*.

WORDS WRITTEN WITH ER.

[§ 135.] *Ira Aram*, an *airy army* officer from *Erie*, had his *arm* put in a sling by an *Irish* major, whose *ire* had been *aroused* by *Ira* in an *argument* in his *room* at a hotel in *Rome*. It seems this *irate* son of *Erin* was *airing* some verses that he had written to *Arabella*, when *Ira* said they didn't *rhyme* — in fact, that every *thing* about them was *awry*. Then *arose* the hot blood of the major, and with no *care* for law or *eric*, and more like an *Arab* than a Christian, he smote the offender from *Erie*.

WORDS WITH THE EL-HOOK.

[§§ 140, 147.] Some little *children*, in great *glee*, were at *play* about a *plough*, when an *ugly* boy, with an *oval* face all *aglow*, *flew* into an *evil* rage—not at all like an *angel*—and began to *claw* the cheeks of a little girl as if he would *flay* her alive. But her brother, who sat on a *rail*, *flew* to her aid, let *fly* an *apple* that knocked the bad boy down on the *clay*, and then he ran away; but the *blow* made his eye *black* and *blue*. Only the wicked *flee* when no man pursueth. It is *really awful* to think of.

WORDS WITH THE ER-HOOK.

[§§ 141, 147.] *Dr. Gray, Jr.*, *drew* Georgie's tooth, but the boy didn't *cry*. . Men tap the maple-*tree* with an *auger* to get sap. He was *free* to walk to and *fro over every acre* of land of which he was *owner*. *Mr. Frye* was *eager* for the *fray*. He tried to *crow*, but could only *bray*. Men often *pray* loudest when they *prey* on their neighbors most. *Mr. Drew* came from *Troy*, where he was held in great *honor*.

CRUISE OF THE "SPRAY."
EXERCISE ON RULES AT §§ 160, 162.

Mr. Sprague, a *spry sprig* of a fellow, *sprang* upon the deck of the yacht "*Spray*," and, taking a *segar*, immediately *sprawled* himself upon a coil of rope to wait for *supper*. But not being a *sober* man, but rather a *sipper*, he got on a *spree* and soon turned in badly *sprung*. . When

Mr. *Cibber* awoke him he was *sicker* and *sadder* than any other man on board. But Dr. *Segur*, who was in the party, saw the *scrape* that *Sprague* was in and came to his *succor*. The next day the sick man felt *stronger*, and declared that the *supremest* virtue was *sobriety*, and that after that he should only be a *sucker* of *cider* through a *straw*. During all this time the "*Spray*" was *straining* very much, and soon she *sprang* a leak; but the crew were *strong*, and they *strove* hard, and by the *stroke* of their oars and a *streak* of good luck they reached harbor, when *Sprague* was the first to *scramble* up the dock and *strike* his feet on solid land.

WORDS CONTAINING "STR."

Mr. *Astor's oysterman*, a native of *Austria*, but now living at *Astoria*, was a great *stayer*-out-of-nights. Every *Saturday*, when the *starry* evening set in, he would *stray* away from home and *steer straight* for the *store* of one John *Story*. Now the *oysterman's* wife, *Esther*, an *austere* woman, who stood behind the *oyster*-counter, found fault with her husband's going *astray* in this way; but he said he didn't care a *straw* for her *austerity*. But *Esther* had invited the *pastor* of their church to be there on *Easter* Sunday, and, being *strong* in will, she determined to be *master* of the situation; so after supper she took her station by the door, and John *Story* didn't *see there* the *oysterman* of Mr. *Astor* until three days after *Easter*.

WORDS WITH THE EF-HOOK.

[§§ 170, 172.] Mr. *Goff* will *arrive* to-day *before Jeff* does. The *beef* was wrapped in *buff* paper. Mr. *Duff* tried to *pave* the way for a *puff* in the paper, but the editor was *deaf* to all his hints. He even went so far as to *chaff* him about being one of the *riff-raff* that are so hard to *govern*. The sea is rough out by the *reef*. Your *beef* is so *tough* that it makes one *puff* to cut it.

WORDS WITH THE EN-HOOK.

[§§ 176, 178.] *General Dean* went out of *town* to see *Dan Boone*. John *Pyne* had to *pawn* his diamond *pin* and gold *chain* before he could *dine*. Mr. *Dunn* has got my *cane*. *Ben* took his *gun* and drove the lion *down* to his *den*. The *coon run* up a tree. John gave *Jane* a new *gown* in the month of *June*.

It is not *often* that we get a *fine* day for our *fun*. *Aaron* likes to sit under the *vine* with *Ellen* and study *phonography*. Mr. *Allen* came *alone* from *Maine* and arrived between *nine* and *noon*. The night was clear and the *moon shone* bright in the *lane*. Your *urn* is much handsomer *than mine*.

WORDS ILLUSTRATING THE USE AND NON-USE OF THE EF AND EN HOOKS.

[§ 179.] The doctor got a newspaper *puff* because he removed a *puffy* tumor. He contracted to *pave* the streets of *Pavia*. Mr. *Duff* says *Duffy* is a *tough* fellow. *Coffee* is not good for your *cough*. The use of too much *gravy* has sent *many* a man to his *grave*. A *Pawnee* Indian will *pawn* his blanket for a drink. You can buy a good *pen* for a *penny*. The fish was *bony* and *John* got a *bone* in his throat. They caught a *tunny* fish that weighed three quarters of a *ton*. He left his *gun* and *cane* in the *canoe*. *Dan Cooney* shot a *coon*. *Many men* make *money*. *Jane* changed her name to *Jenny*. When *John* was a boy they called him *Johnny*. It is *rainy* to-day, and I think it will *rain* to-morrow. If I am obliged to *assign* I shall make you my *assignee*. He is very *funny*, but never laughs at his own *fun*. *Fanny* lost her *fan*. The *Dane* call upon Mr. *Dana*.

WORDS WITH THE SHUN-HOOK.

[§§ 180, 182.] His *mission* was to effect a *fusion* of the two parties. He always showed *emotion*, and sometimes burst into a *passion*. One must use *caution* in buying at an *auction*. He had a *notion* that he could save the *nation*. You have no *option* about taking the *potion*. The *motion* of the car affects his *vision*. There was a perfect *ovation* the evening he delivered his *oration*.

WORDS WITH THE TR AND DHR HOOK.

[§ 188.] *Peter* is a *better tutor* than James. Mr. *Potter* has a dog that is a good *ratter*. He is a *better writer* than reader [R^2-Dr]. No one likes to *bother* with bad *butter*. The *creditor* feels *bitter* toward the *debtor*. My *daughter* is *rather* inclined to be a *doubter*. The small boys would *chatter* and *titter* and disturb the *tutor*.

THE JEALOUS PUNSTER.
EXERCISE ON RULES AT §§ 193, 195.

Jane *Jones*, who is just out of her *teens*, went last night to a *dance* with John *Gaines*. As will be seen, John *happens* to be no *dancer*, although he does make bad *puns* almost every time he *opens* his mouth. Now it *chanced* that Jane *danced* three *dances* and played two *tunes* with Jack *Ransom*, a smart young man who knows all the moods and *tenses*. But as such conduct does not quite meet with *John's* approval, because already the *bans* have been published, and John *pines* to have Jane working six days each week among his *pans* and *tins* and *cans*, and on Sunday wearing *gowns* and gold *chains* purchased with his *coins*, he takes *pains* to tell *Jane's* brother that if *Jack deigns* to speak to the fair *Jones* again he will *bounce* him the first time he has a *chance*. But *Jane's* head is turned and she *joins* Jack once more; whereupon John says to himself, "I will not be treated so. Although it *rains* and there is a *dense* fog, I will take two *canes*, and before the morning *dawns* I will break Jack's *bones*." Then he *dons* his coat and hat and goes *down stairs* with one hand on the *banister,* and skulks away and hides behind a fence. And when Jack *chances* that way he *pounces* upon him and breaks both his *canes* over Jack's head. Then he *rinses* his hands, and hearing a voice in gentle *tones* saying, "Young man, go West!" he takes his *canes* and a *canister* of powder and *runs* away to *Kansas*, in order to avoid the *consequences* of his rash act. Success to the *dancing Punster*, whether he remains there or goes to *Arkansas*.

WORDS WITH LENGTHENED CURVES.

[§§ 201, 207.] *After father* came there my *future* was brighter. He is too much of a *shouter* to be a good *fighter*. My boy *Luther* likes to *loiter* by the *water*. *Mother* says she saw the *hatter* standing by the *heater*. The *weather* last July was *hotter* than ever before. It seemed as if the whole *order* of *nature* would melt. *Arthur* is a good *orator*. The *theatre* is *lighter* by night than by day. The *entire matter* was disclosed in his *letter*. He is a good friend and a good *hater*.

THE ARTIST AND THE PLANTER.
EXERCISE ON RULES AT §§ 208, 209.

A young *painter* named *Pinder* was sketching *down there* on the place where the *planter Lander* lives in such regal *splendor*. Now it happened that the *planter* had a daughter, one of the loveliest of her *gender*, who stayed there with her father summer and *winter*. One day when he had *been there* about an hour, this artist chanced to spy the fair *enchanter*, and then it had been better for his art had he never *gone there*. Miss *Lander* was *slender* and graceful, and if you had seen her you would not *wonder* that he was compelled to *surrender*. His heart was like *tinder*, and it suddenly was filled with a passion *tender*. Now, though Mr. *Lander* was *kinder* than a mother, yet when he was angry he was *blunter* than an Indian; and when he saw Mr. *Pinder* talking with his daughter, he said in tones of *thunder* to the trembling *offender*, "Why do you come to rob me of my daughter—why will you tear us *asunder?*" But our artist was *blander* than the *planter* was blunt, and with softer words he soon satisfied him that he had not *gone there* for *plunder*.

A year passed by after that *encounter*. Then there was a note received one evening bearing the *signature* of Mr. *Pinder*, asking Mr. *Lander* to *sanction their* marriage. So the kind old *planter,* in order not to *engen-der* hatred and sorrow, but rather to *render* his daughter happy, gave his consent on condition that both should *remain there,* and not *begin their* married life *in another* part of the country. This they agreed to; and on the wedding-day Mr. *Lander* brought out and fired off his old twenty-*pounder.*

WORDS WITH HALF-LENGTH STEMS.

[§§ 212, 218.] You should say he *fought* a battle, not *fit* a battle. It was his *fate* to be *fat.* I *viewed* the *vat.* He *paid* the *debt* on the *date* it fell due. Mr. *Dodd* tried to *oust* Mr. *Tate.* I heard a *shout* and then a *shot,* and the man in the *street* ran like a *cat.* The *maid met* her *mate* at the *gate. Pat* is *apt* to be easily *put* out. Mr. *Choate bought* a *boat.* He *made* a *bet* that the fish would *bite* the *bait* in the *night.*

Mr. *Scott sent* a boy to a *spot* where he could *skate.* He *sided* against me just for *spite.—Cats* and *bats* stay out *nights.* The naughty *goats* push open the *gates.* Mr. *Watts* lost his *wits.—*He *stated the statute* correctly. The vessel *stemmed* the tide and *steamed* out to sea. He *stubbed* his toe as he was about to *start.—*I am *glad* to see you *clad* so as to keep out the *cold.—*Mr. *Pratt tried* to make a *trade.* The coal is a *great* deal too large for the *grate.—*Mr. *Kent* is very *kind.* I *don't want* to *hunt* in such a high *wind.*

EXERCISES ON WORDS DISTINGUISHED.

[§ 277.] It *cost* much money and *caused* great trouble. It is better to *cajole* the policeman than have him *cudgel* you. I make the *accusa-tion* that you are an *accession* to the new theory of *causation.* He might say much in *extension* of his remarks, but nothing in *extenuation* of his conduct. The *coalition* was brought about by the *collusion* of their lead-ers, and thus a *collision* was avoided. *God* is our *guide.* I saw the *train* turn to the right. My *daughter* sat in the *auditory* as an *auditor.* The *editor* is my *debtor.* His *decease* was caused by no *disease.* The ad-*ministration* is making a great *demonstration.* A *giant* may be a *gentle-man.* Our *agent* is one of the finest of *gentlemen.* A *genteel* appearance is out of place unless associated with *gentle* manners and a *gentlemanly* bearing. He was *poor,* but led a *pure* and blameless life. Though ex-ceedingly *passionate,* he could appear to be *patient.* I *purpose* doing just what you *propose.* He believes in *protection* to articles of American *production.* The trial is more like a *persecution* than a *prosecution.* Will you *proscribe* me because I refuse to do what you *prescribe?* Be-ing a *Persian,* he preferred *Prussian* to *Parisian* life. I *prefer* to decline the settlement you *proffer.* He is a *part-owner,* not a *partner.* That which once was *absolute* is now *obsolete.* The *broad* disk was very *bright.* I sat *above* and directly *before* the speaker. *Staid* persons are *steady* in their habits. If we *separate* the boards and *spread* them out they will not *support* the great weight. He has a good *situation* at the railway *station*. The *favorite* was not *favored* by fortune. Death is *enevitable*, bankruptcy may be *unavoidable*. He is *interested* in making himself *understood*. *Mrs.* and the *Misses* Cole were there. He said he would return in a *minute*, and was absent a *month*. They *renewed* the note, and so he was not *ruined*. The angle of *reflection* differs from that of *refraction*. The *island* is not far from the main-*land*. Among all the *women* there was only one *woman* who could write phonography.

NOTE.

Of the preceding Additional Writing Exercises the learner will find the following printed in phonographic characters in "Munson's Phonographic News:" "*Cruise of the Spray*," page 209, in No. 2 of the "News."—"*Words containing 'str,'*" page 210, in No. 13.—"*The Jealous Punster*," page 211, in No. 3.—"*The Artist and the Planter*," page 212, in No. 4.

KEY TO THE MISCELLANEOUS ARTICLES IN THE READING LESSONS.

WASHINGTON'S BIRTHDAY.

This day is the anniversary. of the birth of Washington. It is celebrated from one end of this land to the other. The whole atmosphere of the country is, this day, full of his praise. The hills, the rocks, the groves, the vales, and the rivers resound with his fame. All the good, whether learned or unlearned, high or low, rich or poor, feel this day that there is one treasure common to them all, and that is the fame of Washington. They all recount his deeds, ponder over his principles and teachings, and resolve to be more and more guided by them in the future.

To the old and the young, to all born in this land, and to all whose preferences have led them to make it the home of their adoption, Washington is an animating theme. Americans are proud of his character. All exiles from foreign shores are eager to join in admiration of him. He is this day, here, everywhere, all over the world, more an object of regard than on any former day since his birth. By his example and under the guidance of his precepts will we and our children uphold the Constitution. Under his military leadership our fathers conquered their ancient enemies, and under the outspread banner of his political and constitutional principles will we conquer now.

To that standard we shall adhere, and uphold it under evil report and under good report. We will sustain it, and meet death itself, if it come. We will ever encounter and defeat error, by day and by night, in light or in darkness—thick darkness, if it.come—till

> "Danger's troubled night is o'er
> And the star of peace return." ·WEBSTER.

THE LORD'S PRAYER.

Our Father which art in heaven, hallowed be thy name. Thy kingdom come. Thy will be done in earth, as it is in heaven. Give us this day our daily bread. And forgive us our debts, as we forgive our debtors. And lead us not into temptation, but deliver us from evil: for thine is the kingdom, and the power, and the glory, forever. Amen.

THE TRUE GLORY OF A NATION.

The true glory of a nation is an intelligent, honest, industrious Christian people. The civilization of a people depends on their individual character; and a constitution which is not the outgrowth of this charac-

10

ter is not worth the parchment on which it is written. You look in vain in the past for a single instance where the people have preserved their liberties after their individual character was lost. It is not in the magnificence of its palaces, not in the beautiful creations of art lavished on its public edifices, not in costly libraries and galleries of pictures, not in the number or wealth of its cities, that we find a nation's glory.

The ruler may gather around him the treasures of the world, amid a brutalized people; the Senate Chamber may retain its faultless proportions long after the voice of patriotism is hushed within its walls; the monumental marble may commemorate a glory which has forever departed. Art and letters may bring no lesson to a people whose heart is dead.

The true glory of a nation is the living temple of a loyal, industrious, upright people. The busy click of machinery, the merry ring of the anvil, the lowing of the peaceful herds, and the song of the harvest-home are sweeter music than the pæans of departed glory or the songs of triumph in war. The vine-clad cottage of the hillside, the cabin of the woodsman, and the rural home of the farmer are the true citadels of any country. There is a dignity in honest toil which belongs not to the display of wealth or the luxury of fashion. The man who drives the plough or swings his axe in the forest, or with cunning fingers plies the tools of his craft, is as truly the servant of his country as the statesman in the senate or the soldier in battle.

The safety of a nation depends not alone on the wisdom of the statesman or the bravery of its generals. The tongue of the statesman never saved a nation tottering to its fall; the sword of a warrior never stayed its destruction.

Would you see the image of true national glory, I would show you villages where the crown and glory of the people are in common schools, where the voice of prayer goes heavenward, where the people have that most priceless gift, faith in God.—WHIPPLE.

FROM HAMLET'S SOLILOQUY.

[AFFORDING NUMEROUS ILLUSTRATIONS OF THE USE OF THE FOURTH
POSITION.]

To be, or not to be, that is the question :—
Whether 'tis nobler in the mind, to suffer
The slings and arrows of outrageous fortune ;
Or to take arms against a sea of troubles,
And, by opposing, end them :—To die,—to sleep,—
No more ;—and, by a sleep, to say we end
The heartache, and the thousand natural shocks

That flesh is heir to,—'tis a consummation
Devoutly to be wish'd. To die ;—to sleep ;—
To sleep! perchance to dream ;—ay, there's the rub ;
For in that sleep of death what dreams may come,
When we have shuffled off this mortal coil,
Must give us pause.

AN ADDRESS TO STUDENTS.

The doctrine has been held that the mind of the child is like a sheet of white paper, on which by education we can write what characters we please. This doctrine assuredly needs qualification and correction. In physics, when an external force is applied to a body with a view of affecting its inner texture, if we wish to predict the result, we must know whether the external force conspires with or opposes the internal forces of the body itself; and in bringing the influence of education to bear upon the new-born man his inner powers must be also taken into account. He comes to us as a bundle of inherited capacities and tendencies, labelled "from the indefinite past to the indefinite future;" and he makes his transit from the one to the other through the education of the present time. The object of that education is, or ought to be, to provide wise exercise for his capacities, wise direction for his tendencies, and through this exercise and this direction to furnish his mind with such knowledge as may contribute to the usefulness, the beauty, and the nobleness of his life.

How is this discipline to be secured, this knowledge imparted? Two rival methods now solicit attention—the one organized and equipped, the labors of centuries having been expended in bringing it to its present state of perfection; the other, more or less chaotic, but becoming daily less so, and giving signs of enormous power, both as a source of knowledge and as a means of discipline. These two methods are the classical and the scientific method. I wish they were not rivals; it is only bigotry and short-sightedness that make them so ; for assuredly it is possible to give both of them fair play. Though hardly authorized to express any opinion whatever upon the subject, I nevertheless hold the opinion that the proper study of a language is an intellectual discipline of the highest kind. If I except discussions on the comparative merits of Popery and Protestantism, English Grammar was the most important discipline of my boyhood. The piercing through the involved and inverted sentences of Paradise Lost; the linking of the verb to its often distant nominative, of the relative to its distant antecedent, of the agent to the object of the transitive verb, of the preposition to the noun or pronoun which it governed; the study of variations in mood and tense, the transformations often necessary to bring out the true grammatical structure of a sentence—all this was to my young mind a discipline of the highest value, and, indeed, a source of unflagging delight. How I rejoiced when I found a great author tripping, and was fairly able to pin him to a corner from which there was no escape! As I speak, some of the sentences which exercised me when a boy rise to my recollection. "He that hath ears to hear let him hear." That was one of them, where the "He" is left, as it were, floating in mid-air without any verb to support it. I speak thus of English, because it was of real value to me. I do not speak of other languages; because their educational value for me was almost insensible. But, knowing the value of English so well, I should be the last to deny, or even to doubt, the high discipline involved in the proper study of Latin and Greek.

That study, moreover, has other merits and recommendations which have been already slightly touched upon. It is organized and systematized by long-continued use. It is an instrument wielded by some of the best intellects of the country in the education of youth; and it can point to results in the achievements of our foremost men. What, then, has science to offer which is in the least degree likely to compete with such a system? Speaking of the world and all that therein is, of the sky and the stars around it, the ancient writer says, "And God saw all that he had made, and behold it was very good." It is the body of things thus described which science offers to the study of man.

The ultimate problem of physics is to reduce matter by analysis to its lowest condition of divisibility, and force to its simplest manifestations, and then by synthesis to construct from these elements the world as it stands. We are still a long way from the final solution of this problem; and when the solution comes, it will be one more of spiritual insight than of actual observation. But though we are still a long way from this complete intellectual mastery of Nature, we have conquered vast regions of it, have learned their politics and the play of their powers. We live upon a ball of matter eight thousand miles in diameter, swathed by an atmosphere of unknown height. This ball has been molten by heat, chilled to a solid, and sculptured by water; it is made up of substances possessing distinctive properties and modes of action, properties which have an immediate bearing upon the continuance of man in health, and on his recovery from disease, on which moreover depend all the arts of industrial life. These properties and modes of action offer problems to the intellect, some profitable to the child, and others sufficient to tax the highest powers of the philosopher. Our native sphere turns on its axis and revolves in space. It is one of a band which do the same. It is illuminated by a sun which, though nearly a hundred millions of miles distant, can be brought virtually into our closets and there subjected to examination. It has its winds and clouds, its rain and frost, its light, heat, sound, electricity, and magnetism. And it has its vast kingdoms of animals and vegetables. To a most amazing extent the human mind has conquered these things, and reveals the logic which runs through them. Were they facts only, without logical relationship, science might, as a means of discipline, suffer in comparison with language. But the whole body of phenomena is instinct with law; the facts are hung on principles, and the value of physical science as a means of discipline consists in the motion of the intellect, both inductively and deductively, along the lines of law marked out by phenomena. As regards that discipline to which I have already referred as derivable from the study of languages—that, and more, are involved in the study of physical science. Indeed, I believe it would be possible so to limit and arrange the study of a portion of physics as to render the mental exercise involved in it almost qualitatively the same as that involved in the unravelling of a language.—TYNDALL.

PAUL'S DEFENSE BEFORE KING AGRIPPA.

"I think myself happy, King Agrippa, because I shall answer for myself this day before thee, touching all the things whereof I am accused of the Jews; especially because I know thee to be expert in all customs and questions which are among the Jews: wherefore I beseech thee to hear me patiently. My manner of life from my youth, which was at the first among mine own nation at Jerusalem, know all the Jews, which knew me from the beginning, if they would testify, that after the most straitest sect of our religion I lived a Pharisee.

"And now I stand and am judged for the hope of the promise made of God unto our fathers; unto which promise our twelve tribes, instantly serving God day and night, hope to come. For which hope's sake, King Agrippa, I am accused of the Jews. Why should it be thought a thing incredible with you that God should raise the dead? I verily thought with myself that I ought to do many things contrary to the name of Jesus of Nazareth. Which thing I also did in Jerusalem; and many of the saints did I shut up in prison, having received authority from the chief priests; and when they were put to death, I gave my voice against them.

"And I punished them oft in every synagogue, and compelled them to blaspheme; and being exceedingly mad against them, I persecuted them even unto strange cities. Whereupon as I went to Damascus with authority and commission from the chief priests, at midday, O king, I saw in the way a light from heaven, above the brightness of the sun, shining round about me and them which journeyed with me. And when we were all fallen to the earth, I heard a voice speaking unto me, and saying in the Hebrew tongue, 'Saul, Saul, why persecutest thou me?

It is hard for thee to kick against the pricks.' And I said, 'Who art thou, Lord?' And he said, 'I am Jesus, whom thou persecutest.'

'''But rise, and stand upon thy feet; for I have appeared unto thee for this purpose, to make thee a minister and a witness both of these things which thou hast seen, and of those things in the which I will appear unto thee; delivering thee from the people and from the Gentiles, unto whom now I send thee, to open their eyes and turn them from darkness to light, and from the power of Satan unto God; that they may receive forgiveness of sins and inheritance among them which are sanctified by faith that is in me.'

"Whereupon, O King Agrippa, I was not disobedient unto the heavenly vision; but showed first unto them of Damascus, and at Jerusalem, and throughout all the coasts of Judea, and then to the Gentiles, that they should repent and turn to God, and do works meet for repentance. For these causes the Jews caught me in the temple, and went about to kill me. Having therefore obtained help of God, I continue unto this day, witnessing both to small and great, saying none other things than those which the prophets and Moses did say should come: that Christ should suffer, and that he should be the first that should rise from the dead, and should show light unto the people and to the Gentiles."

And as he thus spake for himself, Festus said with a loud voice, "Paul, thou art beside thyself; much learning doth make thee mad." But he said, "I am not mad, most noble Festus, but speak forth the words of truth and soberness. For the king knoweth of these things, before whom also I speak freely; for I am persuaded that none of these things are hidden from him; for this thing was not done in a corner. King Agrippa, believest thou the prophets? I know that thou believest."

Then Agrippa said unto Paul, "Almost thou persuadest me to be a Christian." And Paul said, "I would to God that not only thou but also all that hear me this day were both almost and altogether such as I am, except these bonds." And when he had thus spoken, the king rose up, and the governor and Bernice, and they that sat with them. And when they were gone aside they talked between themselves, saying, "This man doeth nothing worthy of death or of bonds." Then said Agrippa unto Festus, "This man might have been set at liberty if he had not appealed unto Cæsar."—*Acts* xxvi.

BUSINESS LETTER NO. 1.

Messrs. THURBER & Co., New York.

Your favor of 7th instant is at hand. We enclose you Invoice and Bill of Lading of 100 bbls. Mess Pork and 50 firkins of Butter, shipped this day per Merchant's Line, to be sold for our account as per agreement. We request you not to sell for less than Invoice price, and if you succeed in disposing of this lot satisfactorily, you may be almost sure of receiving further consignments from us. We have drawn on you at ten days' sight, through First National Bank, for One Thousand Dollars. Awaiting your advices, and hoping soon to hear from you, we remain, &c.

BUSINESS LETTER NO. 2.

Mr. LYMAN J. GAGE, 29 Lake St., Chicago.

Yours of the 26th ultimo is received. We are under the necessity of declining to fill your order upon the terms proposed by you. On receipt of Fifteen Hundred Dollars we will ship the goods, with the understanding that the balance will be paid within Thirty Days from the date of shipment. Hoping that these terms will be satisfactory, we remain, &c.

New York Superior Court, Part 2.

Francis W. Brodie ⎫
    vs. ⎬
James O'Brien, Sheriff. ⎭

          Before Judge Sanford and a Jury.
          New York, May 18th, 1876.

    Appearances :

For plaintiff,

    Smith and Cooper, Esqs.

For defendant,

    Vanderpoel, Green, and Cumming, Esqs.

    Mr. Smith opened for plaintiff.

FRANCIS W. BRODIE, plaintiff, sworn.

    Direct examination by Mr. Smith.

    Q. What is your business? *A.* Furrier.

    Q. How long have you been engaged in business as a furrier? *A.* Since 1865.

    Q. Previous to that time in what business were you? I mean previous to 1865? *A.* I was engaged in the lottery business. I was out during the war, and speculated a little in Kentucky.

    Q. What business was your father in in 1865? *A.* The first part of 1865 he was in the fur business—furrier.

    Q. Where was his place of business? *A.* At this time, when I bought him out, it was 58 Maiden Lane.

    Q. (By the Court.) By this time you mean in 1865? *A.* Yes, sir.

    Q. Have you got the bills of the stock that you purchased of him at that time? *A.* Yes, sir; I have.

Q. What stock did he have on hand at the time you made the purchase? *A.* He had a stock in the neighborhood of $10,000.

Witness produces the bills.

Q. Look at that paper—what is that? (Hands it to witness.) *A.* That is a bill of $4542, the 25th of May.

Q. Did you purchase that bill of goods? *A.* I did.

Q. (By the Court.) Whose signature is that to the paper? *A.* James W. Brodie's, my father.

Plaintiff's counsel reads said paper, in evidence, marked "Plaintiff's Exhibit 1 of this date."

Q. After you made the first purchase of your father did you make purchases then on your own account, in your own name? *A.* Yes, sir; all of them were made so.

Q. Do you know that these goods were taken away from your premises by the sheriff? *A.* I do, sir, the 1st of July the first lot.

Q. How many days after that did they come for the balance? *A.* On the following Tuesday, the 5th of July.

Cross-examination by Mr. Vanderpoel.

Q. I believe in 1865 you were living with your father? *A.* Yes, sir; and was until the levy.

Q. When was your father's sign taken down from that store? *A.* It remained up a short time—he was doing a commission business, I think, for about two years after I purchased. It may have been three years, not longer.

Q. Whereabouts in Kentucky were you engaged in the lottery business? *A.* At Lexington. I left there in December, 1863.

Q. What did you do when you left Lexington? *A.* Came direct to New York.

Q. How much money did you bring with you? *A.* I brought about $12,000, and I kept it in a bureau drawer at my mother's house.

Q. When did you first open a bank account? *A.* I never opened a bank account here.

Q. Your father was a man of very large experience in that business, was he not? *A.* He was; yes, sir.

Q. And he has continued in the same stores with you ever since that time, has he not? *A.* Yes, sir; he has been there more or less of the time.

Re-direct by Mr. Smith.

Q. What business arrangement, if any, did you have with the proprietor of the hotel at Lexington, Kentucky? *A.* I was well acquainted with the proprietor, and he said, "I would like to have you here, and, when the trains come in, to treat the guests all sociably; and don't mind about the expense." My business was selling horses to the contractors. The government was paying $125 at that time for horses; and when a man brought in a horse, some men standing around would tell him the horse was under size, and would not go through, and so he would sell him for, say, $80; and you could put the horse right through and get your $125 from the government.

EXTRACT FROM REPORT OF LAW ARGUMENT.

It is a common error to assume that the right of the owner to control his property after his death rises above all other rights. It is one which can be exercised only within the limits and in the mode prescribed by the statute. We are all equal before the law; yet the boy of fourteen, capable of taking millions by inheritance, is incapable of making a valid bequest of a single dollar. The lunatic can hold and inherit property, but he can not transmit it by will. The adult and sane testator may bequeath his property to whom he will, with the important qualification that he can not give it to a donee incompetent to take, or trammel it with trusts or restrictions which the statute forbids. He may make a disposition of his estate for a purpose which in itself may seem praiseworthy and benevolent, but it can not stand if the law condemns it upon considerations of public policy.

In this case Bonard's intentions were generous and humane. His last will fails simply because its provisions are illegal. Your honor will determine the questions of law involved, without reference to the effect of the decision on the interests of the respective claimants. It is much more important that fundamental principles be upheld, and that the integrity of our statutes be maintained, than that this particular estate should take a direction which the law does not sanction.—John K. Porter.

A QUAKER WOMAN'S SERMON.

My dear friends, there are three things I very much wonder at. The first is that children should throw stones, clubs, and brickbats up into fruit-trees to knock down fruit; if they would let it alone it would fall itself. The second is that men should be so foolish as to go to war and kill each other; if let alone they would die themselves. And the third and last thing that I wonder at is that men should be so unwise as to go after the young women; if they would stay at home the young women would come after them.

FACTS WORTH KNOWING.

It is not what people eat, but what they digest, that makes them strong. It is not what they gain, but what they save, that makes them rich. It is not what they read, but what they remember, that makes them learned. It is not what they profess, but what they practice, that makes them good.

10*

QUESTIONS ON THE COMPLETE PHONOGRAPHER.

GENERAL REMARKS.

Note.—The large figures in the margin refer to sections.

1. 1. Define Phonography.
    2. As usually understood, how is the term applied?
2. 1. How does the manner of writing Phonography differ from the writing of long-hand?
    2. As regards consonants and vowels, what is the natural order of presentation?

SIMPLE CONSONANT-SIGNS.

3. What is a consonant?
4. 1. How many simple consonant sounds are there in the English language?
    2. Of what are *ch* and *j* composed?
5. 1. What does the Table of Consonants exhibit?
    2. What do the several columns of that table contain?
6. 1. Why are the irregular examples of orthography in the Table of Consonants presented first?
    2. What should the learner endeavor not to associate together?
7. 1. How many consonants in the table are arranged in pairs?
    2. Give the reason for their being so arranged.
8. Why are one half of the signs in pairs made light, and the other half heavy?
9. Why are not the remaining signs of the table arranged in pairs?
10. How does the arrangement of the consonants in this section classify them?
11. 1. In how many divisions are the consonants arranged?
    2. Name the divisions.
    3. Why are the *abrupts* so called?
    4. Define *continuants*.
    5. Define *nasals*.
    6. Define *liquids*.
    7. What are *coalescents* and the *aspirate?*
12. 1. How are the consonant sounds in § 10 arranged as regards their mode of formation?
    2. Into how many classes are they thus divided, and what are their names?
13. 1. In sounding the labials, what action is given to the mouth?
    2. What in sounding the labio-dentals?

3. What in sounding the linguo-dentals ?
4. What in sounding the palatals ?
5. What in sounding the gutturals ?

14. 1. To what is the brevity of phonographic forms chiefly owing ?
    2. What is the source from which the consonant-signs are derived ?

15. What requirements of analogy are observed in the phonographic alphabet ?

18. What are single consonant-signs called ?

MANNER OF WRITING CONSONANT-SIGNS.

19. In how many directions are the consonants written ?

20. How are horizontal letters written ?

21. How are perpendicular and inclined letters written ?

22. 1. When standing alone, how are *sh* and *l* written ?
    2. When joined to other stems, how are *sh* and *l* written ?
    3. How is *ree*, the straight sign for *r*, written ?

23. How are *sh* and *l* named ?

24. 1. How are *chay* and *ree* distinguished when standing alone ?
    2. How when joined to other stems ?

25. 1. What should Phonography be written on ?
    2. What should the learner accustom himself to write with ?
    3. How should it be held ?
    4. What should the learner aim at in the outset ?

26. What will happen if the learner attempts to write fast before he has acquired accuracy ?

27. What length for the consonants is recommended to the learner ?

28. 1. How should the heavy curved signs be made ?
    2. What should be the length of the curved consonants as compared with the straight ?

SIMPLE VOWELS.

31. What is a vowel ?

32. 1. How many vowels are there in the English language ?
    2. What are they ?

33. In producing each of the short vowel-sounds what is the position of the vocal organs ?

34. 1. For the twelve vowel-sounds how many letters does the common alphabet furnish ?
    2. How many signs does Phonography provide for them ?

35. 1. In what order is a word written phonographically ?
    2. With what signs are the long vowels written, and how are they placed to the consonants ?
    3. The same question as to the short vowels.

36. When is a vowel said to be first, second, or third place?
37. 1. What is the nature of the dot vowels?
    2. What of the dash vowels?
38. How are the vowels named?
39. 1. Where is the first vowel position on *kay, em, en?*
    2. Where is the third position?
    3. Where is the first position on *lee* and *ree?*
    4. Where is the third position?

VOCALIZATION OF SIMPLE CONSONANT-STEMS.

41. 1. When a vowel occurs before an upright or slanting consonant, where is its sign written?
    2. Where when it comes after?
    3. Where when it occurs before a horizontal sign?
    4. Where when it comes after it?
42. In either case, what is always written first?
43. 1. Which side of a consonant-stem must a vowel-sign be placed to be read first?
    2. Which side to be read after the consonant?
44. 1. How should the dash vowels be written to the stems?
    2. How should both dot and dash vowels be written?
46. 1. What vowel sound is used in such words as *ear, fear, dear?*
    2. In such words as *ask, air, bear, care?*
    3. In such words as *her, bird, fir?*
    4. In such words as *lost, moth, cloth?*
    5. In such words as *cur, bur, fur?*

DIPHTHONGS.

48. What is a diphthong?
49. How many diphthongs are there?
50. 1. Analyze the diphthong *i*.
    2. Analyze *oi.*
    3. Analyze *ow.*
    4. Analyze *ew.*
54. 1. How are the four proper diphthongs represented?
    2. How many are written in the first position?
    3. How many in the third?
    4. Are any written in the second?
56. Do the diphthong-signs change their inclination to correspond with the direction of the consonants?
57. When two vowels occur together, how are they written?
58. Which diphthong is sometimes joined to the consonant?

CONSONANT POSITIONS.

59. 1. In how many positions are consonant-signs written?
    2. With what do these positions correspond?
60. 1. What is the first position of perpendicular and inclined stems?
    2. What the second?
    3. What the third?
62. 1. What is the first position of horizontal stems?
    2. What the second?
    3. What the third?

JOINING THE CONSONANT-STEMS.

63. 1. In writing a word phonographically, what is the first thing to do?
    2. What the next?
    3. What are the consonant-signs of a word when so written called?
    4. What is done before any of the vowel-signs are inserted?
    5. State the only exception.
64. How is a straight consonant repeated?
65. How a curved consonant?
66. Between what stems should there be an angle?
67. When two stems, one or both heavy, that do not form a distinct angle are joined, how should they be written?
68. Between what stems should there be no angle?
69. In what order are consonant-signs read?

METHOD OF WRITING VOWELS BETWEEN CONSONANT-SIGNS.

70. 1. When vowels and diphthongs occur between two consonant-stems, which are written to the first stem?
    2. Which to the second stem?
    3. State the exceptions.

POSITION OF WORDS.

71. 1. In how many positions may words be written?
    2. With what do those positions correspond?
    3. What are they called?
    4. When is a word written in the first position?
    5. When in the second?
    6. When in the third?
    7. What determines the position of a word containing only one vowel?
72. 1. When is a word said to occupy the first position?
    2. When the second?

3. When the third?

4. If the word consists entirely of horizontal stems, what determines the position of the word?

73. State the mental and manual process of writing a word phonographically.

PHONOGRAPHIC ANALYSIS.

76. 1. In the comparison of sounds, how is the ear liable to be misled by the eye?

2. How may the eye be deceived?

3. What should be the first consonant-stem of the words *phaeton, phalanx, pharisee, pharmacy?*

4. What of the words *thigh, thank, thatch, theist, thick, thin?*

5. What of the words *thy, than, that, thee, this, then?*

77. When words written alike in the common spelling are pronounced differently, how are they written in Phonography?

79. How is the learner directed to write the signs of *ch, sh, th*, and *ng?*

80. Are *w* and *y* at the end of syllables ever written with consonant stems?

82. When do reduplications of consonants occur in English?

84. Can a consonant sound ever be reduplicated in the same syllable?

86. 1. What sound has *c* in *can, came, cap, coil, cup?*

2. What in *cell, cent, certain?*

3. What in *suffice?*

4. What in *commercial?*

5. What sound does *q* always have?

6. What does *x* sound like in *exercise, exert*, and *Xenophon?*

7. Have the letters *c, q*, and *x* any special corresponding signs in Phonography?

8. How are the sounds of *c, q*, and *x* written in Phonography?

87. Before the sounds of *kay* and *gay*, what sound does *n* generally have?

88. How are silent letters treated in writing Phonography?

90. What is the use of the letter *e* in such words as *fate, mete, ripe, tone, tune?*

91. What is the sound of *u* or *ew* after the consonant *r*.

92. When in unaccented syllables the precise quality of a vowel can not be readily determined, how is it regarded?

93. As exceptions, give some illustrations in which unaccented vowels retain their proper long sound.

94. In phonographic spelling, what is done first, second, third, and lastly?

ESS AND ZEE CIRCLE.

97. What is the name of the *ess*-circle when standing alone?

⟩ 98. 1. How is the circle joined to straight stems?

    2. How to curved stems?

99. How are stems with *ess*-circles named?

103. 1. How is the circle written between two straight stems both of which are struck in the same direction?

    2. How between two straight stems that form an angle at their junction?

    3. How between a straight and a curved stem?

    4. How between two curved stems if both are arcs of circles that are struck in the same direction?

    5. How between two curved stems that are arcs of circles struck in opposite directions, and that do not form a distinct angle at their junction?

    6. How if they do form a distinct angle at their junction?

104. State the short rule.

VOCALIZATION OF STEMS WITH CIRCLES.

105. How are stems with circles attached vocalized?

106. Give the order of reading vocalized stems with circles attached?

108. When two stems have a circle between them, how are intermediate vowels written?

110. Where is the circle generally used?

111. When *s* or *z* is immediately preceded or immediately followed by two concurrent vowels, what sign should be used, and why?

112. When two *s* sounds are the only consonants in a word, how are they written? Give examples.

113. When *s* is the first consonant in a word that commences with a vowel, which sign is used?

114. When a *z* sound commences a word, what sign is used under all circumstances?

115. When *s* or *z* is the last consonant in a word *that ends with a vowel*, what sign is used?

THE LARGE CIRCLE.

116. When is a large circle used?

117. 1. What is the name of the large circle?

    2. What combinations is it commonly used to represent?

118. 1. How is it joined to consonant-stems?

    2. Where may it be used?

119. How are stems with the large circle attached vocalized?

120. How may a vowel that occurs between the two sounds of large circles be represented?

LOOPS FOR ST OR ZD AND STR.

122. How are the sounds *st* and *zd* generally represented?
123. How is *str* frequently represented?
124. 1. What are the names of these two loops?
2. How may stems with loops attached be named?
125. 1. How are stems with loops attached vocalized?
2. Where may the small loop be used?
3. Where the large loop?
4. Where is the large loop not used?
127. How may the small circle be added to the large circle and the loops?

RULES FOR THE USE OF ISH, SHEE, EL, LEE, ER, AND REE.

129. 1. In what cases is the stem *sh* written downward?
2. What is it then called?
130. 1. In what cases is *sh* written upward?
2. What is it then called?
132. 1. When is *l* written downward?
2. What is it then called?
133. 1. When is *l* written upward?
2. What is it then called?
134. Which is preferred in the middle of words, *el* or *lee?*
135. When is the downstroke *er* used?
136. When is the downstroke *ree* used?
137. Which is preferred in the middle of words, *er* or *ree?*

INITIAL HOOKS.

139. 1. In what relation to a preceding consonant are the liquids *l* and *r* found in a large number of words?
2. Give examples.
3. How are such compounds represented in Phonography?

THE EL AND ER HOOKS.

140. How are the *el*-hooks written on straight and curved stems?
141. How are the *er*-hooks written on straight and curved stems?
142. At which end of *el* and *sh* are these hooks joined?
144. How are the *el* and *er* hook-signs named?
145. What caution is given with regard to the *el* and *er* hook signs?
146. How may the learner be assisted in remembering the *el* and *er* hooks on straight stems?

147. How are these signs vocalized?
150. If a distinct vowel sound is heard between *l* or *r* and a preceding consonant, how must each generally be written?
151. For what are the *el* and *er* hooks principally used?
152. How may they be joined?
153. In what cases are the hooks made imperfectly?
155. Where is the sign *rel* generally preferred?

SPECIAL VOCALIZATION.

156. 1. Why is the rule at § 150 sometimes not observed?
2. When not observed, how may vowels be expressed?
158. To what hook-signs may the *ess*-circle be prefixed, and how?
159. To what hook-signs is a loop or large circle never prefixed?
160. How are the small and large circles and the *st*-loop prefixed to the straight *er*-hook signs?
161. What are these classes of signs called?
162. When signs of the *spel* and *sper* series are vocalized, what is the order of reading?
163. What is done when it is more convenient to express the hook?
164. In what cases may the consonant *r* be generally omitted?

THE WAY AND YAY HOOKS.

165. How may the consonant *w* be prefixed to certain stems, and what stems?
166. 1. How are these stems named and vocalized?
2. How is the *ess*-circle prefixed to them?
167. 1. How may *y* be prefixed to certain stems, and what stems?
2. Where is the *yay*-hook mostly used?

HOOK FOR EN, IN, OR UN.

168. 1. How may the syllables *en*, *in*, and *un* be prefixed to the signs of the *sper* series?
2. How to certain curved stems with initial hooks?
169. 1. What is this hook called?
2. Before what stems may it be used?

FINAL HOOKS.
EF OR REE HOOKS.

170. How may *ef* or *vee* be added to straight stems?
172. How is an *ef*-hook stem vocalized?
173. How is a vowel written to an *ef*-hook stem always read?
175. 1. How is an *ef*-hook written on curves?
2. What is its principal use?

EN-HOOK.

176. How may the consonant *en* be written with a hook, and on what stems?
177. How are the *en*-hook stems named?
178. How are these signs vocalized?
179. When can not the hook be used, and why?

SHUN-HOOKS.

180. How may the syllables *shun* and *zhun* be added, and by what hooks?
181. How are the *shun*-hook signs named?
182. How are they vocalized?
187. How may *shun* or *zhun* be written after a final circle?

HOOK FOR TR OR THR.

188. How may the compounds *ter* and *ther* be added to straight stems?
189. How may this hook and its signs be named?
190. How is the combination *dr* generally written?
192. May the circles and loops be added to final hooks?   How?
193. How are the circles and loops added to the straight *en*-hook signs?
194. How are final hook signs with the *ess*-circle named?
195. Where should not the *en*-hook be used?
197. How may the *ess*-circle and *ishun* be added to the *en*-hook circles and loops?
198. How may the *ess*-circle be added to *ishun?*.
199. May final hooks be used in the middle of words?

LENGTHENING.

201. What does doubling the length of a curved sign add?
202. How are these signs named?
204. What are the positions of horizontal double-length curves?
205. 1. What is the first position of downward double-length curves?
     2. What the second?
     3. What the third?
206. 1. What is the first position of upward double-length curves?
     2. What the second?
     3. What the third?
207. How is a vowel written to a lengthened curve read?
208. Where does the power of a final hook on a lengthened curve take effect?
209. What straight stems are lengthened to add *ter, der, ther?*
210. How is a final circle or loop on a lengthened stem read?

211. How may a vowel or diphthong occurring immediately before the final *r* of a lengthened stem be written?

HALVING.

212. How may *tee* or *dee* be added, and to what stems?
213. How are these stems named?
215. State the positions of half-length horizontal stems.
216. 1. What is the first position of perpendicular and inclined half-length stems?
    2. What the second?
    3. What the third?
218. In what order is a vocalized half-length stem read?
220. How may half-length stems be joined?
221. When must not a full-length and a half-length stem be joined, and why?
223. Why may not two half-lengths running in the same direction be joined?
.224. How are the syllables *ted* and *ded* generally written?
225. Give examples of *ted* and *ded* being disjoined.
226. When is the half-length stem *ess* written upward?
228. When must the stem sign for *tee* or *dee* be used, and not the halving principle?
229. When it is necessary to distinguish between *tee* and *dee*, how may it be done?
230. What is half-length *lee* when standing alone used for?
231. When a word contains only the consonants *ld*, how are they written?
232. How are *rt* and *rd* distinguished?
233. When *t* or *d* is immediately preceded by two vowels, how is it written?
235. What rules apply to the upward and downward half-length stems?

GROUP VOWELS AND THEIR SIGNS.

240. 1. How are the improper diphthongs represented?
    2. What is indicated by making the first or second stroke of a group vowel-sign heavy?
    3. Which way does the signs representing the dot vowels in combination with *i* open?
    4. Which way those representing the dash vowels so combined?
242. What may be used instead of the double vowels?
243. When *i* precedes the diphthong *i*, *oi*, and *ow*, how may it be represented?
244. How when it follows them?

245. What license is allowed in the use of these signs ?
246. What variation in the inclination of signs opening to the right and left is allowed ?

ADDITIONAL CONSONANT-SIGNS.

247. When is the dot sign for *h* used ?
248. When the tick sign for *h* ?
249. 1. When the brief sign for *w* ?
     2. When the brief sign for *y* ?
250. What is the nominal consonant, and how is it used ?

STENOTYPY.

251. How may phonographic outlines be indicated by the letters of the ordinary printing alphabet ?
252. In what are the stenotypes of up-stroke stems printed ?
253. How are the stenotypes of the stem signs distinguished from the stenotypes of circles, loops, hooks, dots, and ticks ?
256. 1. What does a hyphen between two stenographs indicate ?
     2. What an inverted semicolon ?
     3. What a colon ?
     4. What an inverted period ?
     5. What a cross ?
     6. What a simple space ?
     7. What a numeral just after the stenotype ?
     8. How are stenotypes named ?

GENERAL REMARKS ON OUTLINES OF WORDS.

265. 1. When is the final syllable *ly* expressed by the *el*-hook ?
     2. In other cases how is *ly* written ?
266. What is the rule in regard to writing the final syllable *ry* ?
267. 1. How may the final syllable *ty* sometimes be written ?
     2. For what purpose is this exceptional provision allowed ?
269. How may the final syllable *ture* sometimes be written ?

THE PAST TENSE.

270. 1. How is the past tense of regular verbs written when the present tense ends with a full-length stem ?
     2. How when it ends with a half-length stem ?
     3. How when it ends with an *ess*-circle not written inside of a final hook ?
     4. How when it ends with the *st*-loop ?

ABBREVIATION.

VOWELS OMITTED OR INSERTED.

273. What vowels may the beginner now commence to omit?
274. What vowels should he still continue to insert?

WORDS DISTINGUISHED BY DIFFERENCE OF OUTLINE, ETC.

276. How are words commencing with *il, im, in, ir, un, en* written?
277. Study the list of words distinguished by difference of outline, position, or vocalization.

OMISSION OF CONSONANTS.

278. Under what heads is the omission of consonants treated?
279. To what does the term "word-sign" apply?
281. Learn the list of word-signs.
282. How are *now* and *new* written?

PREFIXES.

284. 1. How are the syllables *com, con, cum,* and *cog* indicated?
    2. How are they written?
    3. What should be done in words commencing with *self-con?*
    4. What license is allowed in regard to these syllables in the middle of words?
    5. How is *for* sometimes written?
    6. How *magna, magne,* or *magni?*
    7. How *self?*
    8. When is the prefix for *self* joined, and when not joined?
    9. How is the prefix *with* written?

SUFFIXES.

285. 1. How are the suffixes *ble* and *bly* written?
    2. How are *bleness, fulness, iveness,* and *lessness?*
    3. *Ever?*
    4. *Form?*
    5. What is the suffix-sign for *ing?*
    6. Of *ings?*
    7. When are these signs used?
    8. How are the suffixes *mental* and *mentality* written?
    9. *Ology?*
    10. *Self?*
    11. *Selves?*
    12. *Ship?*
    13. *Soever?*
    14. *Worthy?*

OMISSION OF CERTAIN CONSONANTS.

286. 1. When may *k* or *g* be omitted from words?
     2. When a *t* sound?
     3. When *p*?
     4. When *n*?
     5. When *m*?

287. How are words ending in *ntial-ly* abbreviated?
288. When may consonants, represented by hooks, be omitted?
289 and 290. Study these lists thoroughly.
291. Read this list carefully.

PHRASEOGRAPHY.

299. What are the two modes of phrase-writing?
301. How is the small circle used in phrase-writing?
302. How the large circle?
303. What caution is there in regard to *us*?
304. How is the small loop used?
305. How is the large loop used?
306. When is the detached form of loop used?
307. For what is the *l*-hook used?
308. For what the *r*-hook?
309. For what the *way*-hook?
310. For what the *yay*-hook?
311. For what the *in*-hook?
312. For what the *ef*-hook?
313. 1. For what the *en*-hook?
     2. Within what final hooks may an *en*-hook be turned?
     3. How is *my own* written?
314. For what is the *ter*-hook and lengthening principle used?
315. When necessary, how may *other* and *their* be distinguished?
316. For what is the halving principle used?
317. For what the *ef*-hook and lengthening principle combined?
318. For what the *en*-hook and lengthening principle combined?
319. For what the halving principle and *ess*-circle combined?
320. For what the *en*-hook and halving principle combined?
321. May the foregoing principles of phrase-writing be combined with each other?
322. How may *was* and *one* be added to a preceding word?

POSITION OF PHRASE SIGNS.

323. What is the general rule as to the position of phrase signs?
324. What are the exceptions?

CERTAIN WORDS DISTINGUISHED.

325. 1. When may *can* and *can not* be written with *K* and *Knt?*
2. What restriction is there as to *could* and *could not?* and when *could, did, should,* and *that* are joined to a preceding word, how are they written?
3. How should those words generally be written?
4. How may *them* be joined?
5. How may *had* and *do* be written?
6. What words should be vocalized when joined to a preceding word?
7. How are *at least* and *at last* distinguished?
8. What three modes are there for writing *are*, and what rule governs?
9. How is *charge* written when out of position?
10. How *change?*
11. How is *part* written in phrases?
12. How should *opportunity* be written?
13. State what words are written out of position to avoid conflict, together with the conflicting words.
14. How are *society* and *system* written?
15. How are *inner* and *near* distinguished?
16. How *leave* and *live?*

326. How *ever* and *have?*

TICK SIGNS.

327. 1. How is *I* written at the commencement of phrases?
2. How before *can, can not? could, could not?*
3. How are *a, an,* or *and* written at the commencement of phrases?
4. How are *a, an,* or *and* written in the middle or at the end of phrases?

328. What tick signs with hooks are used?

329. When *I, a,* or *and* is followed by *com* or *con,* how is it written?

330. 1. What is the tick sign for *the*, and when is it used?
2. What for *he*, and when is it used?

331. May the ticks be joined with circle and loop signs and with each other?

332. What are the tick signs for *ing the* and *ing a-an*, and when are they used?

333. When may the brief signs for *w* and *y* be used for *we would* and *you?*

334. When may *of* be omitted?

335. How is *of com* or *of con* written?

336. How may *to* or *too* be indicated by the fourth position?
337. When *to* or *too* begins a sentence, how should it be written?
338. How may *from—to* be indicated?
339. May *and* be sometimes omitted?

RULES FOR PHRASE-WRITING.

340. State the general rule for joining words in a phrase.
341. 1. What may phrases be composed of?
  2. What is it not necessary for the writer to think of while making phrases?
342. What may a noun or pronoun in the objective case be joined to?
343. What may a verb be joined to?
344. What may a qualifying word be joined to?
345. What may a noun in the possessive case be joined to?
346. What may a verb in the infinitive mood be joined to?
347. What may a copulative conjunction be joined to?
348. When the idiom of the language requires one word to follow another, when may they be joined?
349. Study this list carefully.
350. 1. When may special phrases be made by the reporter?
  2. Should such special phrases be used in general reporting?

A NEW AND SIMPLIFIED CLASSIFICATION AND ARRANGEMENT OF THE

CONSONANT-SIGNS OF PHONOGRAPHY,

WITH A NEW AND COMPREHENSIVE RULE FOR VOCALIZATION, AFFORDING INCREASED FACILITY IN LEARNING THE ART.

By JAMES E. MUNSON,

Official Stenographer to the Surrogate's Court of New York, and Author of the "Complete Phonographer."

THE different kinds of consonant-signs used in Phonography may be classified under four distinct heads, and arranged in the following order:

I.—SIMPLE STEMS.

Under this head are comprised all the simple, alphabetic stems.

EXAMPLES: ＼ P, ＼ B, — K, — G, ⌞ F, ⌞ V,) S,) Z, ⌒ M, ⌣ N, etc.

II.—HOOKED STEMS.

Under this head belong all the signs that have hooks, whether the hooks be initial or final.

RULE I. ˙ The power of any hook, whether initial or final, takes effect *after* the power of the stem to which it belongs.

EXAMPLES: ＼ Pl, ＼ Pr, ⌐ Kw, ⌐ Ky, ⌐ Kf, ＼ Pn, ⌞ Fn, ⌐ Kshn, ⌞ Fshn, ⌐ Ktr, etc.

RULE II. The power of any initial hook takes effect before that of any final hook on the same stem.

EXAMPLES: ⌐ Grf, ⌞ Fln, ⌐ Kwtr, ⌐ Kltr, etc.

III.—MODIFIED STEMS.

Under this head belong the Lengthening and Halving principles.

RULE. The power of any modification takes effect after the power of the stem that is modified, or of any of its hooks.

EXAMPLES: ⌣ Ntr, ⌡ Fltr, ⌢ Mntr, _ Gt, ⌐ Klt, _ Krt, ⌐ Kwt, ⟍ Pft, ⟍ Pnt, ⟍ Pslint, ⟍ Ptrd, ⟍ Plnt, ⟍ Prnt, etc

RULE FOR VOCALIZING.

A vowel-sign placed *before* a stem is read before the stem, and consequently before any of its hooks and modifications. A vowel-sign placed *after* a stem, is read after the stem and any initial hook, and before any final hook, and consequently before any modification.

EXAMPLES: ·| *aid*, ·. *ache*, ·| *odor*, ⌡ *oval*, ⌐ *actor*, ⌣ *under*, ⌐ *ancient;* ⟍ *bay*, ⌢ *hay*, ⟍ *play*, ⟍ *pray*, |; *deaf*, ⌐ *cane*, ⌡ *vain*, ⌐ *motion*, ⌐ *cater*, ⌐ *prove*, ⌢ *letter*, ⌢ *mother*, ⌢ *mender*, |· *date*, _ *get*, ⟍ *prate*, ⟍ *blend*, ⌐ *approved*, etc.

IV.—CIRCLES AND LOOPS.

Although the Circles and Loops are generally joined to a stem, they are INDEPENDENT SIGNS, and are not to be considered as forming any part of the stems to which they are joined. Hence the following rules:

RULE I. When a circle or loop is joined *initially* to a stem, its power takes effect *before* anything else—that is, before the power of the stem, and of all its hooks and modifications, and of all its vowel-signs.

EXAMPLES: ⟍ sP, ⌐ sK, ⟍ sPl, ⌡ sFl, ⌢ sMr, ⌢ sKw, ⟍ sPr, ⟍ ssPr, ⟍ stPr, ⌡ sLtr, ⌐ sKt, _ stKt, ⟍ sPnd, ⌐ *seat*, ⟍ *sable*, ⟍ *saber*, ⌐ *session*, ⌡ *psalter*, ⌡ *slender*, ⌡ *settled*, ⟍ *sobered*, etc.

RULE II. When a circle or loop is joined *finally* to a stem, its power takes effect *after* everything else—that is, after the power of the stem, and of all its hooks and modifications, and of all its vowel-signs.

EXAMPLES: ⌐ Ks, ⌡ Vs, ⌐ Kss, ⌡ Fss, ⌐ Kst, ⌐ Kstr, ⌡ Tws, ⌐ Kfs, ⌐ Kshns, ⌡ Fslins, ⌐ Ktrs, ⌡ Vns, ⟍ Pns, ⌡ Dnss, ⌐ Gnst, ⟍ Pnstr, ⌢ Mtrs, ⌢ Mntrs, ⌐ Kts, ⌢ Mdst, ⌡ Drfts, ⌐ Knts, ⟍ Blnds, ⟍ Brnds, ·|· *teas*, ⌐ *course*, ⟍ *burst*, ⌡ *twice*, ⌐ *caves*, ⌡ *fashions*, ⌐ *matters* ⌐ *cylinders*, ⌡ *notes*, ⟍ *blends*, ⟍ *brands*, etc.

NOTE.—-The In-hook, as in ⟨symbol⟩ *unstrung*, ⟨symbol⟩ *enslave* is read *before* the circle, because it is written before it, and is an independent abbreviation or substitute for a preceding consonant-stem (N); and the Ishun-hook, as in ⟨symbol⟩ *physician*, is read *after* a circle or loop, because it is written after it, and is an independent abbreviation or substitute for succeeding consonant-stems (SH and N).

THE END.